to

Carol x

The Complete Mitsy Howard

The Enduring Curiosity of Mitsy Howard
Mitsy Howard – A Walk in the Dark
What Mitsy Did Next

Carole Susan Smith

ISBN: 978-1-916981-32-4

PublishNation
www.publishnation.co.uk

This work of fiction is dedicated to all carers,
especially those who work in residential homes,
nursing homes and retirement homes,
in recognition of their service to individuals
and the community.

About the Author

A lifelong enthusiasm for reading and writing and a well-travelled career have provided inspiration for Carole's novels and light-hearted memoirs. She has worked in Siberia, the Palestinian Occupied Territories, the Far East and across much of Europe, as well as the NHS and many different industries in the UK. Her novels, to date, are set in the UK where she lives with her husband in the Forest of Dean.

The
Enduring Curiosity
of Mitsy Howard

- A Walk in the Mill -

Part I

How Mitsy settles into her new home and has adventures

"Is it true that someone saw a ghost last week?" asked the very tall, white haired man to the people sitting at the breakfast table.

Everyone looked at everyone else and when no response was forthcoming, they all returned to their conversations as if nothing had punctured the gentle murmur of early morning voices.

Mitsy looked at the man. From his bearing and the way that he posed his question so confidently, she guessed he had been in a senior position when he was at work. She could imagine him standing at the head of a large table in a Boardroom somewhere, commanding attention. Tentatively, very tentatively, she raised her hand in line with her shoulder until she caught his eye and nodded.

The man got to his feet and walked round to the empty seat next to Mitsy, indicating with his head whether he might join her. "How exciting! Do tell me all about it!" he exclaimed, as he tucked his rather long, ungainly legs under the table.

"Well, I'm not really sure…" began Mitsy as her fellow diners left the table and slowly headed off to their rooms. "You see, I'm not a very good sleeper. Actually, I'm awake most nights until the early hours. I get bored lying in bed not sleeping, so last Wednesday I walked along the corridor to see if anyone else was awake and who was in the kitchen as I fancied a cup of tea."

The man smiled, "I think a full night's sleep eludes most of us as we get older. I'm Arthur by the way." He held out his hand in a very polite manner and Mitsy shook it gently, while continuing her story.

"I didn't switch any lights on, as the street lamps are so bright that it wasn't necessary. Just as I turned the corner there was a woman standing at the bottom of the big staircase. You know, the stairs that go up to Mr and Mrs P's apartment?" she asked.

Arthur nodded as if he knew where she was describing, so she carried on with her story.

"Well, the woman seemed to be wearing a long, white nightdress. She had dark wavy hair which hung down almost to her waist. She was quite young and pretty. I thought perhaps she was a young relative of Mr and Mrs Podsiadlo, so I called out: 'Hello! Are you after a cuppa too?'"

"The woman smiled back at me but then as I approached her, she vanished!"

Arthur's face lit up. "What do you mean - she vanished?"

"Well," said Mitsy, "she just wasn't there any more. She sort-of dissolved. I cannot describe it any better than that."

"Weren't you frightened?" he asked with concern.

"No. I really wasn't. She seemed so real and it was such a friendly smile. Anyway, Maggie was in the kitchen so she made me a cup of tea and I told her about it. Maggie said they had often wondered if there was a ghost here as there had been stories, but as no-one had seen anything for years, they assumed it was either a fanciful anecdote or the ghost had gone away. She also said I probably shouldn't talk about it to the other residents because it might frighten some of the more nervous ones."

Sally was clearing the breakfast table meanwhile, and to say she was making a bit of a clatter was an understatement. Her less than subtle behaviour suggested she really wanted Mitsy and Arthur out of the way.

Arthur appeared not to notice Sally, and continued to chat to Mitsy while the other residents left the room.

“Did you know that early in 1916, Appledore House became a Red Cross Hospital? It was used as a centre for caring for the sick and wounded British troops during the Great War. I’ve been reading up about it.”

“How interesting,” said Mitsy.

“If you’d like to know more of the history of this place, I’d be happy to share my findings with you. This is partly why I was interested in the ghost,” said Arthur. “Would you like to come out for lunch one day? We could go to the pub up the road. I haven’t been there yet and it would be pleasant to have company.”

This was not exactly what Mitsy was expecting but she found herself agreeing to meet at twelve noon the next day, for an excursion with Arthur. I hardly know the man, she said to herself but I suppose it cannot do any harm.

2

When she arrived in the hallway, Arthur was already standing by the front door. "I understand that we have to hang our room keys on the hooks here, to show that we are out," said Arthur.

"Yes. It's just a security thing. It's like they used to do in old-fashioned hotels in the days before we had key cards. Personally, I cannot quite get used to having to ring the doorbell to get back indoors but I suppose they have got to be careful if there are any residents prone to go walkabout! I've told the kitchen we shall both be out this lunchtime; I hope that was in order, Arthur?"

Arthur smiled as he took her arm and they walked across the large gravelled parking area together, turning right in the direction of the public house.

"So how long have you lived at Appledore House, Misty?"

"Oh. Actually, my name is Mitsy..."

"My mistake. I do apologise. Mitsy is rather unusual," said Arthur.

"Ha-ha! You are not the first to be confused! I grew up in the war years but my parents were a bit New Age before it was even a 'thing'; they were not exactly travellers but they did live in a caravan and had quite a bohemian lifestyle until we children came along. My elder brother was called Rock, my sister is called Sky and I was going to be called Misty. When Dad got to the Registrar's office, we think perhaps he had had too much to drink because he didn't spell my name correctly. I've been happy to keep Mitsy, although it can be a bit inconvenient sometimes."

They walked along in companionable silence for a while, until Mitsy remembered that she had been asked a question.

"I've been at Appledore House for nearly three months. I wouldn't say I'm feeling at home yet, but mostly it's OK. I think after a lifetime of being independent and largely self-sufficient it is quite difficult to live in a community with everything being done for you. Mind you, I don't miss the housework, the washing and ironing, the cleaning, the gardening, the shopping and all the work involved in preparing endless meals for one!"

Then she took a deep breath. "Arthur, I've done nothing but talk about myself. Sorry about that, please tell me how you are settling in."

At this point they approached the front door of the Standsfield Arms, an impressive-looking traditional hostelry. Arthur courteously stood to one side at the doorstep so that Mitsy could enter the lounge bar. Oak beams, a blazing fire and a cheerful welcome from the landlady set the scene for a relaxing lunch. Mitsy asked for a glass of white wine while Arthur cheerfully ordered a locally brewed beer. By the time they were settled into comfortable chairs they had both decided on a ploughman's lunch. Mitsy noticed privately that there was no attempt at political correctness here 'it's a ploughman's lunch and we'll have no truck with plough person's here!' she imagined someone saying.

"Yes, thank you," said Arthur. "I am beginning to settle in. This is only my second week. My home is in Huddersfield where I lived with my wife Ivy. Ivy passed away last Christmas after a short illness. She had pneumonia."

"I'm sorry to hear that, Arthur. You must miss her dreadfully."

"I thought I was doing alright on my own but rather clumsily I tripped on the pavement outside my house and ended up in hospital. Bruises and broken bones heal eventually but somehow, I didn't feel like going back. My daughters tried to get me to move down south to be near them. They both live in London; Jackie has a flat in North London and Marie and her husband Alan live south of the river. You can imagine that whichever one I agreed to go to, it would upset the other! I didn't really fancy living in London, it's a young person's city I think."

Mitsy smiled privately at that assumption but nodded sympathetically to Arthur.

"So, you came to Appledore House! What was London's loss was our gain!"

Oh dear, she thought. I'm in danger of appearing to flirt when all I really wanted to do was to put the man at ease. I'd better take it easy with the wine.

Fortunately, two ploughman's lunches arrived and they both exclaimed at the selection of ham, cheese – Wensleydale of course – pickles and home baked bread. There was so much on their plates that they both feared they wouldn't be able to do justice to the meal.

A large, black Labrador ambled slowly into the room. Mitsy gave him a friendly pat on the head as he stretched himself out on the rug in front of the fire. After a few minutes a member of staff came running in: "Peter, you bad boy. You mustn't come in here when people are eating."

Both Arthur and Mitsy assured her that Peter was welcome to share their fire and neither was concerned to have the pub dog for company.

"I should explain what's amusing me," said Mitsy. "My husband's name was Peter. And my son is Pete also. I'm not sure I've met a Peter dog before!"

"How long have you been on your own then?" asked Arthur.

Mitsy thought it was quite a strange way to phrase the question and to be honest, she would have preferred the conversation to concentrate on the ghost sighting rather than personal matters.

"That's difficult to answer because my Peter was a Petty Officer in the Royal Navy and he was away at sea frequently during our long and happy marriage." She didn't want to be too obvious but felt it was time to return to the ostensible reason for Arthur's lunch invitation.

"Anyway, do tell me what you have discovered about Appledore House please."

In between eating lunch and offering another small glass of wine which was declined, Arthur described some of the history of their residential home. It seemed to be his way of getting familiar with what was to be his new abode.

Mitsy was able to add an update to this, which included how Mr and Mrs Podsiadlo came to own and run Appledore House. The young couple were very fortunate to take over the care home for a modest outlay, when as a business it was not exactly thriving. They had both worked extremely hard ever since to turn it into a going concern. The residents affectionately called them Mr and Mrs P, although Mitsy had her doubts whether this was just friendly or because people couldn't pronounce their Polish surname! At the beginning Mr P did all the property maintenance and as Mrs P was a qualified nurse, she took charge of everything that was to do with the residents. These days they were semi-retired and lived 'above the shop' while a reliable team of staff basically ran everything on a day to day basis.

The warmth of the fire, the friendliness of the staff, the food and the alcohol all contributed to a relaxed atmosphere at the Standsfield Arms and the couple were happy to tell each other just a little of their lives before moving to Appledore House.

Arthur was intrigued to discover that Mitsy was an experienced heritage researcher. That was not how Mitsy explained it but rather "I dabble a bit on the internet as I'm interested in family history." It was one of the ways in which she had learned to occupy herself since her husband Peter died.

After their now empty plates had been cleared and coffee had been consumed, there seemed no reason to prolong the lunch outing. Ever the diplomat, Mitsy observed that she had probably be better getting back as she had a number of important emails to deal with.

Their stroll back took barely ten minutes, although Mitsy helpfully used the time to tell Arthur about the outings organised by the Home, as well as the weekly activities that he might wish to join in on. She was rather wary of becoming his only friend and thought it would be advisable if he widened his circle sooner rather than later.

"Thank you, Arthur. That was a lovely lunch and it made a pleasant change to go out. I shall continue to look into the history of this area and I will, of course, tell you of any further ghostly sightings!" she quipped. With that, she picked up her room key and headed off up the corridor before any further plans could be made.

3

Mitsy stood in front of the full-length mirror which was adjacent to her wardrobe. "Not bad for nearly 79," she murmured to herself. Mitsy was, indeed, still a good-looking woman and many would have thought she was at least ten or fifteen years younger. Her hair had turned to an attractive shade of steel grey, which was now its natural colour, and she was thankful to have avoided what she considered the distressful experience of her mousey-blonde locks fading to yellowish-white. She made an effort to have her hair cut regularly but this was something she had not completely resolved in her new home. There was a hairdresser's salon in the parade of shops nearby, which she tried shortly after moving in, but she really wasn't happy with the outcome. The woman was rather too used to cutting the hair of elderly ladies who wanted a shampoo and set and Mitsy preferred a more modern look. She wondered whether she could find a really good stylist in Bradford who would be willing to call at Appledore House, if she could get a few other residents to join in.

Peering more closely at her face, she noticed that a couple of so-called laughter lines were slightly more prominent. Well, I've done a lot of living and laughing so it's no surprise if my face shows it, she said to herself. She decided she should try to drink more water and get out in the fresh air more regularly.

Completing the appraisal, she ran her arthritic hands down her body. She was of slender build and apart from the gradual thickening of her waist-line, which she had failed to shift since her mid-fifties, she was really in good shape. Of course, wearing well-cut clothes certainly helped and she had always chosen classic styles and veered towards more expensive dresses, skirts and trousers in the belief that they were an investment.

Her attention was suddenly drawn towards the window. Mr P appeared to be talking to someone in the bushes. She really liked her room as it overlooked the garden on this side and there was a smaller window on the other side giving a view of the road.

She tapped on the window and Mr P stood up suddenly. He waved back and Mitsy could see he had been talking to a large ginger cat. That looks like Puss the Second, but of course it isn't, she sighed to herself.

"Well, this won't do," she said to herself, as she moved towards her writing desk, "it's time to catch up with Pete."

Mitsy had been worried at first that she would feel too cloistered by living in just one room when she moved into Appledore House. As it turned out, she was able to take over a double room that had been vacated by two people so she actually had plenty of space. There was a large bed, a chest of drawers for storage, a double wardrobe, two comfortable chairs in front of the TV, a coffee table and a work desk with chair where her laptop was always open – she really couldn't ask for more. The en suite bathroom was ideal too, with bath, a power shower, toilet and heated towel rail. She hadn't actually used the bath much although it had one of those things that help you get in and out. She thought it was actually better and easier to use than the bathroom at her old home. The room was comfortably warm and if it got too hot, she could always open a window for ventilation. It was number six at the far end of the downstairs corridor.

> Dear Pete, I did intend to email you earlier today but, in the event, I went out for lunch with a friend. All is well here and I'm keeping busy with my internet research on the family. When do you think you might get over here? Love Mum xxx

Mitsy pressed send and then noticed that she had received an email just a couple of minutes earlier.

> Dear Mum I was going to write earlier today but things are a bit busy at work. I'm coming over next Thursday so we can sort out the house. I've booked my flight, a rental car and the Travelodge so we're all set. Love Pete xxx

Mitsy laughed to think that they had probably been writing to each other at the same time. Email or Messenger worked perfectly well for them most of the time and it was cheaper and more convenient than using the phone.

She couldn't ask for a better son. He was sensible, hardworking and did everything he could to make sure she was fine after his dad had passed away. He was fifty-three so not really a lad any more but sometimes when she thought of him, she still pictured him in his school uniform and short trousers.

> Hi Pete! Message received and understood. Looking forward to seeing you! Mum xxx

Of course, she knew they had to sort out the house in Harrogate. It had been empty since she moved out nearly three months ago and it was time to tidy things up, dispose of furniture and put it on the market. She wasn't looking forward to the task, given that she would be leaving behind all those memories of her happy childhood and then making the house their own family home with husband Peter.

It had to be sold because she needed to raise the money to pay her monthly bill to Appledore House. She tried to think of it as just like paying rent but it was rather a lot of money as it covered food, laundry and personal care.

Mitsy didn’t regret the move. As Pete said at the time, it made sense to sort things out while she was still capable. He didn’t actually say ‘compos mentis’ but she was realistic enough to know that many people lose some of their mental faculties as they get older, even if it is no more than being a bit forgetful.

4

The next day, Arthur made a beeline for Mitsy at breakfast. "Any more sightings?" he asked with a glint in his eye. Mitsy smiled, "Nothing yet Arthur. Perhaps I imagined it!"

"I've found out some more about the history of Appledore House," he said. "Perhaps we could have lunch again sometime?"

"Well maybe, but that wouldn't be for a while as my son Pete is coming over for a few days. We have quite a lot of business matters to deal with."

She didn't want to crush his enthusiasm but on the other hand she really hoped Arthur would make some new friends.

Lucy, another resident, was half listening to the conversation: "Ooh, that sounds interesting Arthur."

Mitsy took her cue from Lucy and raising her voice just a little above the general murmur of conversation, "Perhaps, Arthur, you could assemble all the information you have on the history of Appledore House and give a little talk for us on your findings? I wouldn't be surprised if some of the staff would like to hear too!"

There were several nods of agreement and Lucy said, "Oh yes please!"

"Will we have a chance to meet your son?" asked Lucy, turning to address her question to Mitsy.

"Probably not; I suppose it depends on what time his flight arrives."

"Oh. Is he travelling far?"

"Not really. He lives in Dublin, so a short flight to Leeds/Bradford airport is nothing compared with his usual work travel." Mitsy was quite a private person and she didn't really want to chatter too much, but somehow, she got led by

Lucy's expression of interest into saying more than she intended.

"Pete works for the European Commission so he travels round all of the member states. Don't ask me what he does! He enjoys it anyway."

"So, you must have Irish ancestors Mitsy?" asked another person, as the breakfast table discussion developed.

"Yes. My mother was Irish. Although Pete's lived there for years. When it looked like the UK was going to leave Europe, Pete got Irish citizenship because his granny was Irish, otherwise he wouldn't have had the freedom to travel in order to carry on in the same job."

She felt that this was quite enough information for the assembled group, so she folded her serviette and rose from the table. "Excuse me, I've got lots of things to do today."

Back in room six, Mitsy looked around her room and concluded that she wasn't really sure what to do with all this spare time. She wasn't in the mood for her ancestry search so she flicked through the channels on her television without finding anything on morning TV that appealed to her. Mitsy sighed and turned off the blank screen. Her attention turned to her bookcase, where she had a few reference books, including a dictionary and a thesaurus for when she did the crosswords, as well as quite a collection of paperbacks and a Kindle loaded up with as yet unread fiction.

Her mind was already rather jumpy this morning and she knew if she didn't calm herself, by the evening she would be awake half the night and feeling exhausted the next day. She glanced at the bottom shelf of the bookcase where on moving day she had hurriedly stuffed some photo albums from the days when all family records were printed photographs, embossed on the back with the Kodak logo or similar.

First, she picked up her wedding album. It wasn't labelled as such but it did have a piece of card with *8 June 1963* sellotaped on the spine which, of course, was their special day. Mitsy sat staring at the picture of them both, just outside the church smiling happily and framed by the entrance arch. She well remembered the fuss her parents had made because Mitsy and Peter wanted to get married in a church whereas they wanted to have an informal civic ceremony followed by a party in a field of all things! Thankfully the young couple's preferences prevailed and the church wedding went ahead albeit with rather bad grace. The Big Freeze of 1963, with its long, extremely cold winter had at last come to an end. Mitsy and Peter were so relieved that the sun shone on them that day.

Next to Peter, both looking very smart in their Naval uniforms, stood Robert his Best Man. Mitsy's dress was floor-length cream voile, floaty and romantic. She loved it. She also recalled the arguments she had with her sister Sky who was to be the Matron of Honour and was determined to wear an up-to-the-minute dress with a pinched in waist and a full ballerina-style skirt. It wasn't that she thought Sky would outshine the bride, just that she wanted to co-ordinate how they all looked. Not much chance of that with her parents in any case. In the end, she gave in, as long as the dress was a plain colour and not patterned. In fact, Sky looked lovely in her trendy, pale pink creation which gave a special glow to her auburn hair.

Earlier that year, their brother Rock had died on his motorbike in a terrible road accident. Whilst it would have been easy to blame the slushy, melting snow or the wind and the lashing rain, the truth was that Rock was always reckless and it would seem that a simple error of judgement had caused him to hit the bridge head-on, causing severe injuries from which he never recovered. In the wedding photo, without it being intended, there seemed to be a gap where Rock would have stood.

Mr and Mrs Howard senior, Peter's parents, looked on proudly. They had doubts when their son wanted to join the Royal Navy and go to sea but he had certainly grown into a fine young man. They liked Mitsy and had welcomed her into their wider family.

Mitsy's parents, on the other hand, seemed determined to look out of place. Both deeply tanned, bejewelled and dressed in long kaftans recently obtained on their travels, they stuck out like a sore thumb amongst the other guests. Whilst kaftans are fashionable as holiday wear these days, at the time they did look as if they had just arrived from the Asian sub-continent. Mitsy loved her parents dearly but they could be annoying sometimes.

She smiled affectionately; what a lovely wedding day that was. Of course, she and Peter did have difficulties to deal with, as most couples do, but with the benefit of hindsight she was able to reflect on their happiness over many years of marriage and that brought a contented glow to her spirits.

'Right,' said Mitsy aloud, but to herself. 'It's time I carried on with the ancestry search.' She was really looking forward to discovering more about her father's family, although the Irish roots on her mother's side were also intriguing her. These were always known about and it did help Pete to get an Irish passport, but there was so much more to learn. She logged on to the website she generally used for this activity and sighed to find half a dozen 'hints' for her to look at. It seemed she wasted more time checking out their hints and discarding them than making good use of the access to their records.

Before she could get underway, there was a knock at the door. She smiled to herself. She wasn't really in the mood for the painstaking effort the research required, so the interruption was more than welcome.

"Hello, I'm Norma and I've just moved in next door."

"Oh, do come in Norma. Yes, sit over here where there's a view of the garden. I'm Mitsy although I expect you already know that. How are you settling in?"

"I don't know yet," said Norma. "It's all so very different."

"I found, in my first few days here, that it was strange not having things to do, so I have devised some activities to keep me out of mischief! How about you Norma, have you moved from far away?"

At this juncture in the conversation, one of the care staff appeared at the door with a tray of tea and biscuits.

"Thank you, Jo. Do you think we could have another cup and saucer as Norma and I are just getting acquainted?"

Both women were keen to get to know each other but equally nervous not to be seen as nosey. Once the tea had been poured and the biscuits offered, they both began to speak at once. After some embarrassed laughter, "Go ahead Norma, please" said Mitsy.

It transpired that Norma had indeed moved from far away. She had been taken ill while living in Port Elizabeth, South Africa. After she had recovered, her daughter insisted on her moving back to Yorkshire, to be near the family. So, not only had she a new home to settle in to, she also had to adapt to a considerable change in climate.

"Excuse me for asking but you have a really unusual name Mitsy. Does it have a special meaning?" asked Norma.

Mitsy was getting used to explaining her name to virtually everyone she met at Appledore House. She had rehearsed a simple response which she duly trotted out.

"I've no idea if it means anything! The truth is that my parents were prototype hippies before we three children put the brakes on their chilled-out existence and wanderlust. Anyway, when Dad registered my birth, we think he had had a bit too much to drink and instead of writing 'Misty' he muddled the letters up. My sister is called Sky and my brother's name was Rock – at least Dad couldn't mess those up!"

The two women laughed and it augured well for having Norma in the room next door. With Raymond, who was a quiet and courteous gentleman, living on the opposite side of the corridor, Mitsy started to feel more comfortable in her new home already. Some of the other residents had lived at Appledore for a long time and so she was pleased that she would no longer be the newcomer.

When Mitsy's son Pete had suggested that it would be sensible to move out of the large and rambling property she had shared for many years with her much-loved husband and to move into a modern and well-managed care home, she was not at all happy with the prospect. In her head she still felt like a twenty-year-old, totally free and independent. Over time though, she realised that her life consisted of cleaning rooms that she never used and trying to hold in check the endless growth of weeds and shrubs in their once-tidy garden. Appledore Residential Care Home was turning out to be a relief from all that unnecessary and soul-destroying labour and left her with time to do some fun things at last.

Norma stood up, placing her cup and saucer carefully on the coffee table. "Well Mitsy, I'm delighted to have met you and I think I should get on with some of my unpacking now."

Hmm. Not overstaying her welcome either, observed Mitsy to herself, already thinking that she and Norma would get on just fine.

Mitsy and Norma sat next to each other at dinner time and Mitsy introduced her new neighbour to everyone else sitting at their table. The meal was toad in the hole, served with fresh vegetables and steaming, flavoursome gravy. Everyone commented on the lightness of the Yorkshire pudding surrounding the locally produced sausages.

Mitsy privately thought it was all so much better than anything she could have made herself, as peeling vegetables had become impossible with her arthritic hands. In any case, eating alone had lost its appeal for her many years ago; it was good to have some company and then the freedom to go back to one's room, close the door and be private.

5

Mitsy had always been self-sufficient and it was strange for her now that her son Pete had rather taken control, once she had moved into Appledore House. All those years with Peter away at sea meant that she just got on with things until the next time he was on shore leave. Of course, sometimes she was able to accompany him on overseas postings and that had always been an adventure. She had especially enjoyed Valletta in Malta, for the hot, sunny climate and the more relaxed way of life. She missed her home and her friends though, and in some ways, she was quite lonely. The Maltese people were kind and friendly, but because their language was rather alien to her ears – it was quite like Arabic – she mainly had only Peter to talk to in those days.

Thursday morning arrived and she realised that Pete would want to take her to the old house, just to make sure there were no personal items she wanted. They had done a fairly thorough check when she moved out, but this would be the last chance to pick up any mementos. Pete had already declined to take any of the furniture himself. His three-bedroom flat in Dublin was spacious but it was modern and whilst he didn't want to hurt his mother's feelings, there was no way he wanted any of that dingy old, mahogany furniture.

It was mid-morning when Pete tapped on the door of room six. "Are you ready Mum? We've got lots to do today and tomorrow!"

In some ways Mitsy was looking forward to these outings with her son but with mixed feelings as it would be a door on her former life closed permanently, both metaphorically and in practice.

Pete explained as he settled her into the rental car that they had a busy programme of activity. First, they would go to the house and check each room carefully, collecting anything she wanted to keep. He would then take her back to Appledore House. Later, he had an appointment with a man from a house clearance company who would assess the cost of emptying the property and say what he would pay for the furniture he could sell. Pete was under no illusions that he would be offered next to nothing and he didn't want his mum to get upset over this.

On Friday, he had arranged for two estate agents to value the house and, in the afternoon, he planned to take his mother to see a solicitor. Although she was not keen to discuss it, he thought it would be sensible to update her will, and for the solicitor to set up and witness an Enduring Power of Attorney. If, although he seriously hoped not, she became unable to manage her own affairs then Pete would be able to act for her. He was hoping he could make it into an enjoyable couple of days for his mother by taking her out to lunch at some of their favourite places.

As they approached Harrogate from the Leeds Road direction, Mitsy discovered a lump in her throat. Suddenly she was worried that she would not be able to do this. She hadn't realised quite how she would feel about returning to her home town, virtually as a visitor.

Pete looked over at his mother as they passed by the Stray. Although it wasn't Harrogate's only green space it was always attractive with its avenues of trees; beautiful in springtime when the ornamental cherry trees blossomed and equally pretty through the winter months when tiny white lights festooned the same trees around the perimeter and along the pathways.

Passing by the Pump Room, Mitsy smiled to think of the one occasion that she drank the spa water. It tasted horrible! The building was now a museum, having been built in the 17th century to house the wells from which the spa waters sprung and which all the well-to-do of the time came to drink for their health. She wondered if the taste was as bad then as it was now.

In no time at all they arrived outside her house. She reminded herself that this had been Pete's home too, so he might also be feeling sad.

She loved that the house had been built from local stone and, like many properties in the area, the slate roof was surrounded by castellations. The pale blue paint on the front door was beginning to show signs of weathering but overall, it was still an attractive home. She hoped that the next owners would appreciate it as much as she and Peter had.

Walking up the front path, she noticed how quickly the weeds had taken hold. Now that was something she didn't miss, the constant worry and effort involved in keeping the garden under control. Unlocking the door, she almost tripped over a heap of post just below the letter box. "I think you can check those over later and either inform the senders of your change of address or put them in the bin!" said Pete. "I will contact the Post Office with your new address so that you will get anything important re-directed."

Mitsy sighed to think of all the extra jobs she was giving Pete, although it was a blessing that he was willing to deal with such matters.

Slowly they walked from room to room while Mitsy put anything she wanted to keep in the carrier bag Pete had thoughtfully brought with him. In fact, there was scarcely anything beyond a few ornaments and the post to take away with her.

A quick glance at the back garden told its own story. Brambles wound themselves through the fence and across what had been a tidy lawn. Opening the back door, she spotted the rose bush that Peter had bought for her one Valentine's day, flowering vigorously in spite of the overgrowth elsewhere. That reminder of her late husband and all the happy times they had spent here was the trigger for a flood of tears that she was powerless to control. Pete hugged her close until her sobs ceased, "I think we could pick ourselves a lovely bunch of red roses to go in your room at Appledore House, don't you?"

"Yes," said Mitsy, blowing her nose noisily, "especially now I've found my favourite vase."

Having assured himself there was nothing else to take with them, he guided his mother back to the car and then returned to lock up. "Mum. Shall I keep the keys now?" She nodded, still feeling rather distressed.

Driving back, they passed by Valley Gardens and Mitsy recalled the hundreds of times she had taken her sandwiches there to eat during her lunchbreak from her job at the pharmacy. "I do miss Valley Gardens," she told Pete, "but I'm already finding one or two little walks I can do from Appledore House."

Pete knew that she would feel homesick today and he wasn't really sure how to comfort her. "What would you like to do for lunch today? We could go to any of your favourite Harrogate cafés."

"I have an idea actually Pete. We could go to the Standsfield Arms which is just around the corner from Appledore House. I went there last week and the staff are friendly and the lunches are good."

This sounded like evidence that Mitsy was starting to settle in to her new surroundings. Pete was relieved that his mother was beginning to try different things so he was happy to go to the pub as she suggested, on the proviso that he would have to have a non-alcoholic drink as he was driving later.

Lunch did, indeed, turn out pleasantly and the staff recognised her from her first visit. She introduced her son to them and both chose the ploughman's lunch again. It was quite a brief lunch as Pete had to get back to Harrogate to meet the furniture clearance man.

Afterwards, he didn't say much to Mitsy about that encounter, but to be honest he was just relieved that someone would empty the house. He discovered subsequently that several charities were happy to do house clearances for a small fee but he concluded he had probably made the best arrangement because his man was willing to wait until the house was sold and had agreed to take everything, whereas some charities were known to refuse certain items of furniture that they could not recycle, which would still have left him with a problem.

That evening, relaxing in his Travelodge hotel room, he was able to catch up with a few emails for work. Over a drink in the bar, he gave some thought to how he would deal with the estate agents the next morning and, more importantly, how he would encourage his mother to sort out her will.

He needn't have worried, Mitsy had already decided that all her jewellery would go to her nieces (Sky's children) and everything else to Pete. She wished he had a partner, although he seemed to have plenty of friends in Dublin as well as Brussels and all the other places he worked. The last time she asked him if he fancied 'settling down' he laughed and laughed and then explained that he was happier living alone than with the wrong person, which of course made sense. She hadn't raised the subject since.

That night, Mitsy had her usual difficulty going to sleep. Around midnight she woke up with a start, then remembered where she was. After an hour of tossing and turning, she got up. It wasn't cold but she put her dressing gown on anyway. 'I'm not getting up properly, I'll just look out of the window for a few minutes then try to get back to sleep,' she said to herself.

The back garden looked lovely in the light of a full moon. She could see the outline of the larger bushes and the distinctive shape of the monkey puzzle tree. Mr P did keep the garden looking good and it would be a pleasant place to relax when the weather was warm enough.

'Maybe I'll get one of those bird-feeding tables to put outside the window,' she thought. It was something she missed from her old home, the chance to watch the birds throughout the year.

Wandering over to the other side of her room, she noticed how bright everything was, given that the moon amplified the street lights. Nothing was moving anywhere and the whole road was empty. She was just about to turn away to go back to bed when she noticed something strange. Across the road was an old, disused cotton mill. Normally, she gave the building little attention, but she was puzzled to see a distant glow of lights in all the windows. In fact, she thought she could see faint movement through the dusty window panes. 'Well I must be mistaken,' she thought. 'It's probably sleep deprivation!' Misty wasn't one to exaggerate usually, but she couldn't think of any other explanation.

Back in bed she pulled the duvet up round her shoulders and within seconds she fell into a deep and restful sleep.

6

At breakfast Mitsy was tempted to mention her night time observations at the old mill but then it occurred to her that, along with her sighting of the White Lady, people might think she was a bit strange. She decided to keep quiet but check the place over from time to time.

Her friends were concerned as to how she had coped with seeing her former home for the last time, so she was able to reassure them that, although she felt sad, she had valued the chance to collect a few personal items along with the post. She mentioned to the assembled breakfast group that she had brought back some beautifully scented deep red roses from her garden which inevitably led to a couple of people knocking her door later to admire them.

Pete meanwhile had been busy. Happily, the two appointments the next morning were completed highly efficiently and the estate agents had given him their valuations, so he was able to get back to Appledore House well before lunchtime. “Would you like to have lunch here, Pete? I’m sure the kitchen could squeeze an extra portion for you if I asked them now. You could then say hello to some of the other residents; I know they’re curious to meet my lovely son!”

Frankly, it was the last thing Pete wanted to do – to eat an institutional meal with a load of grumpy old ladies. To be fair, Appledore House wasn’t really like that. One of the reasons he chose it for his mother was that the residents all appeared happy from what he could see in the pictures in the brochure. What really clinched it, was that on his first visit he realised that the place didn’t smell stale like some of the other homes that he had visited. It also seemed friendly with a mix of men and women residents. Anyway, it was easiest to say yes to lunch and Mitsy duly went down to the kitchen to see if it would be possible.

I'm not sure what he had expected, but the lightly poached salmon, buttered new potatoes and mixed green vegetables were excellent. Today's cook had introduced a little samphire in with the greens and some of the older folk were quite intrigued as to what it was. Mitsy was quite used to tasting some unusual things as she had got in the habit of eating out regularly when she lived in Harrogate. In any case, she knew from her visits to the fish counter at Sainsbury's that it was samphire.

All in all, lunch was a success and the Appledore residents appreciated the chance to meet Mitsy's son. After the meal, the pair went back to Mitsy's room and Pete broached the subject of updating the will. Mitsy was no fool and she knew this had to be addressed sooner rather than later. The discussion turned out to be painless and the contents of the will were quickly agreed.

In fact, the drive over to Harrogate was in delightful sunshine and Mrs Reed, the solicitor, was so helpful. She took notes of everything Mitsy asked for and promised to send her a draft of the new will in the post as soon as possible, for her agreement. Almost as if Pete had planned it, Mrs Reed asked if she should include an Enduring Power of Attorney 'as most people do these nowadays'. They decided that the signing and witnessing of the new will could be carried out whenever Mitsy could arrange transport. She was fairly sure that Mr Podsiadlo, as the owner of Appledore House, would act as a witness to her will and would even drive her over to the solicitors to conclude the business.

As they drove back, she told Pete about Norma, her new neighbour and a little bit about how she had spent her time this week. Appledore House was well-located and Mitsy was happy to be able to take short walks on level ground directly from the front door. Turning left took her to the corner shop which was also a post office and newsagents. Everyone who served there seemed very pleasant and already they were beginning to recognise her. Turning right about ten minutes' walk away was the pub they had visited, and after quite a distance further, there was a small parade of shops. These included a fish and chip shop, the hairdressers', a chiropodist and an insurance company. She didn't think she was likely to use the latter but she planned to book an appointment with the chiropodist.

Directly opposite the Care Home was the old mill building where Mitsy had seen lights during the night. It had been disused for many years but, according to Jo – one of the care staff – it had been bought by a developer and was to be turned into apartments. She was still puzzling as to whether there were squatters or drug dealers there of an evening so she wisely didn't mention any of that to Pete. He had enough to worry about, she was sure.

Giving his mum a hug before he set off from Appledore House, Pete breathed a sigh of relief that he had managed to fit in everything without causing his mother too much distress and, equally important, he still had ample time to return the hire car and catch his flight back to Dublin. Mitsy returned to room six, feeling tired but happy that they had done everything as planned.

She still felt very sad about Puss the Third and the old house in Harrogate just didn't feel the same without her. When Pete was just a toddler, they went to the Cat's Protection League shelter in York and chose a beautiful tabby cat. Pete insisted on naming her Puss. That child doesn't have a creative bone in his body, she complained to husband Peter when he was next home. To be fair, neither did his father. Puss lived very happily with the Howard family for many years; she gave a good impression of a big, fat fluffy cushion for most of her life.

Before Pete went off to University, Puss died and Mitsy decided it would be good to get another cat for company. Puss the Second was a different character altogether and a skilled mouser. Mitsy hated having to deal with beheaded 'gifts' and worse, but over the years she became inured to this task. Puss the Second was ginger and very clever at pouncing out from behind furniture and throwing her paws around Mitsy's legs in ambush. They definitely had a love/hate relationship. Puss the Second became less nimble as she got older and one day she was knocked down by a car. Mitsy was reluctant to get another cat but Pete pre-empted this decision by arriving home one day with Puss the Third. Puss the Third was a tiny black kitten and Mitsy loved her from the first moment she saw her. She was intelligent and independent and soon learned Mitsy's ways and became the perfect feline companion.

Once Pete had mooted the idea of his mother moving to a care home, Mitsy kept presenting the counter argument that she wouldn't be able to take Puss the Third with her. Various options were reviewed but none of them seemed acceptable or viable. Mitsy was adamant that a cat cannot just be given away 'like a spare television' as she put it. Puss the Third was a living, breathing and fully functioning member of the household and as such deserved proper consideration for her future. In the end, Puss the Third provided her own, dreadfully sad, solution. She quite suddenly developed kidney failure, stopped eating and in a matter of days had to be taken to the vets for her final sleep. Mitsy always felt that Puss the Third knew what was being planned. She missed her gentle presence daily, even though there was a cat that lived nearby and regularly visited the Appledore House garden, it wasn't the same.

She had just decided that she would watch a little light-hearted nonsense on the TV before bed when there was a tap at the door. It was Joyce who was on duty that evening and calling at every resident's room with their medication. Joyce had worked at Appledore House for several years, arriving from her native Philippine island of Cebu to stay with her elder sister in the north of England. She already had good nursing qualifications and was snapped up by the care home where she had worked ever since. During a brief conversation a few days ago, she discovered that Mitsy had considerable experience of pharmacology from her time working in a pharmacy. Although not professionally qualified, Mitsy had learned a lot over time from the pharmacist himself and had enjoyed that side of the business. Obviously, Joyce had a number of people to see this evening so there wasn't time to talk but as ever she was pleasant, business-like and very careful to ensure that there was nothing that Mitsy needed.

7

Waking early the next morning, Mitsy realised that it was the day for the home's monthly outing. These were organised regularly and residents were invited to take part in what was usually a couple of hours in a minibus, visiting somewhere relatively close by. Mitsy had already been on two trips; the first was to Salts Mill in Saltaire and the second was to the Brontë House in Haworth.

The former textile mill at Saltaire had been converted into an art gallery and a shopping centre with cafés and restaurants. It had many paintings by the local – but now internationally acclaimed - artist David Hockney, some of which were for sale. Mitsy loved the bright colours used by Hockney and would have loved to own one of his swimming pool paintings. Of course, these are valuable and were out of the question for her to buy, so she satisfied herself with some postcard reproductions of his work. The next visit was to the Brontë House and Museum, which was in fact the Parsonage where Charlotte, Emily and Anne Brontë lived and wrote their books. Their brother Branwell lived there too. Again, Mitsy's lively imagination brought the visit to life.

Today's outing for the Appledore residents was to Betty's Tearooms in Harrogate. Given that she had just been to Harrogate twice this week with Pete, it hardly seemed necessary. None-the-less she had already signed up for the trip so she decided that it would do no harm.

After breakfast, Mitsy and Norma found that they were both leaving their rooms at the same time and fell into step, standing together by the front door in readiness for the outing. Norma was well wrapped up in a winter coat, hat, scarf and gloves. She was finding the change in temperature from her

South African home quite difficult to adjust to and was already contemplating buying some extra woollen jumpers to aid her transition to the Yorkshire climate.

The minibus arrived, parked in the road outside and the pair were thus able to take the two front seats next to the driver and had time to chat, while the other residents arrived in dribs and drabs.

"Mitsy," said Norma, "you know you said that your parents were travellers? Well, did you live in a horse-drawn gypsy caravan?"

"Oh, good grief no!!" replied her neighbour, laughing audibly. "We had an old white van which had a mattress and bunks in the back. It was painted on the outside with the sun, the moon and a rainbow – from what I saw in a couple of photographs, as I don't really remember it."

Norma smiled at her mistake, as she had imagined something much more picturesque.

"We were not Romany or gypsies as such. During the war, mum worked in the cigarette factory and dad was in the RAF. At the time, they lived in 'digs' which they rented. Dad never told us what he did and just used to say it was 'hush-hush' which was a term used in those days for having signed the official secrets act, I believe. After the war, it was difficult to get anywhere to live although they were on a list for a council house and neither of them wanted to live in a pre-fab. As mum and dad liked to tour round folk festivals and poetry happenings, a caravan seemed the answer. Dad was always ready to get out his guitar and accompany himself with his rich, deep voice. He was often invited to play his own compositions although I don't think he got paid much for it in the early days. Once we children grew up, it was not really a suitable way for us to live as we needed to go to school, although I suspect they would have liked to carry on in their rather bohemian lifestyle."

Misty paused for breath, having rarely shared this much information with someone who was almost a stranger. Norma nodded and smiled.

"I suppose it was hard for all of you to adjust to a more settled way of life?" asked Norma, thoughtfully.

"I don't think it made much difference to us kids but it certainly was a complete change for our parents. What happened was that someone up from London heard Dad playing and asked around what people thought of his music. Dad was popular and he received positive reports. The man asked Dad if he would like to write some music for the opening credits of a new radio programme. Dad did that, it went down well and he was asked to do some more. He didn't get paid much but he became recognised as the go-to composer for incidental music. Not long after, he was invited to go to London to discuss some music for a film. Dad quite liked the idea but he wasn't really equipped to do that sort of work from the back of our van. Anyway, they gave him the contract and enough money upfront for him to put down a small deposit on a house. I know you're going to ask me what was the film but I really cannot remember."

Norma nodded again with interest. "What an amazing start to life you had! Mine was very different but challenging in its own way. I was born in the USA then we moved to South Africa for my Dad's work while I was still tiny. I didn't really understand the political situation or apartheid and we lived a comfortable life for a few years, until the demonstrations got too violent and we moved back to the States. That was the pattern for most of my growing up years, moving back and forth, and to be honest, I didn't really know which country was my home. As you can guess, eventually South Africa 'won' when I met and married my husband."

As the minibus started up with a lurch, their conversation stopped. Ruth, one of the care staff, was accompanying them and acting as an unofficial tour guide.

"Ladies and gentlemen, today's outing is taking us to Betty's Tea Room in Harrogate. I will not be giving a running commentary but I'm happy to answer your questions and to point out anything of special interest on the way." As the minibus made its way on a circuitous route skirting the Yorkshire Moors, Mitsy and Norma continued to exchange information about their early years.

As soon as they approached Harrogate, Mitsy noticed that she was feeling much more comfortable than she expected, as well as a sense of pride in her former home town.

In no time at all the minibus was parked near Betty's Tea Room and they all spilled out onto the road in an unruly crowd. Ruth, still acting as unofficial tour guide hurriedly directed everyone to the pavement and went ahead to confirm the booking for their morning stop. As they waited for their teas, coffees and cakes to arrive, Mitsy confided a few more things to Norma.

"You see just down Parliament Street? That was where I used to work. It's not a pharmacy anymore, it's a gift shop now."

"And are we anywhere near your house, Mitsy?"

"Oh no. That's - I mean that it WAS - a large house but not here in the expensive part of town! Actually, it was my parent's house. You know I said that my Dad wrote music for films and things? When I was growing up, he had a studio for his work and we children used to run around in the woods on the edge of town. Over the years the area got built up but we've not driven anywhere near there this morning. Well, Dad was always worried that he was 'selling out to crass commercialisation', as he described it, so eventually when he and Mum were in their sixties, they chose to go back on the road. They bought a very comfortable motorhome and they decided to tour around Europe, meeting up with other musicians and generally exploring new places. They asked Peter and I to look after the house for them. By that stage Rock was no longer with us and Sky was happily settled with her family, so they signed over the house to us. It was very kind, it really helped us a lot."

Mitsy paused as everyone shuffled indoors. Once settled inside the attractive tea rooms, the conversation turned to somewhat more prosaic considerations as everyone chose from the menu and their orders were taken. Raymond had asked if he could join their table and when he went off to look for the gent's toilet Norma, keen to understand her new friend's history, took advantage of his absence to find out a little more.

"What happened when your parents came back from their travels?"

"Oh, they didn't come back to the UK. They settled in France where they both died within six weeks of each other. I believe they were truly happy there."

The friendly waitress at Betty's smiled at these two older folk reminiscing as she placed the food and drinks on the table. The Appledore guests were all enjoying the change of scenery and in fact there was quite a buzz of conversation.

Raymond returned to find his pot of tea and luxury sandwiches were already on the table.

"We didn't wait for you, Raymond, as our cheese rarebit would have got cold!"

"Of course," said Raymond, "there was such a queue I almost gave up!"

Ever the gentleman, he always showed an interest in other people, so much so that few of the other residents knew much about Raymond himself.

"Did I hear you say that you used to work near here, Mitsy?"

Mitsy smiled at the memories. "Yes, Raymond. It was a pharmacy at the bottom of Parliament Street. It was a lovely shop with perfumes, after-shave, cosmetics, lots of pretty things for hair and nails etc and of course, the pharmaceuticals. We sold lots of over-the-counter medicines as well as distributing prescription drugs. It's funny how these days there are adverts regularly on the TV telling people to ask the pharmacist for advice instead of waiting to see a GP. That used to be the norm back then. I always enjoyed helping people in that way and often we had something useful on the shelves that would sort the problem out."

"That is very much the approach we have in Port Elizabeth. Of course, we have good healthcare services in general with both state-run and private hospitals."

Norma rarely spoke about her home city and as Mitsy sensed that she was still really homesick, she didn't ask too many questions. However, she did notice that Norma tended to speak about Port Elizabeth in the present tense and she realised that in time she would need to accept that this move was permanent.

"I've never been to South Africa. Have you, Raymond?"

"Actually, I have," he responded, much to the surprise of the two women.

"When my wife and I retired, we went on a magnificent cruise that gave us the opportunity to visit KwaZulu Natal, the Drakensberg mountains, Johannesburg and the vineyards of Cape Town. It was a marvellous experience and I'm only sorry we didn't get to the 'Windy City' which I believe your home town is called, Norma."

Norma beamed with delight and the conversation continued, ranging over Raymond's observations and Norma's happy recollections. Well, I never, thought Mitsy to herself. How pleasant it is for these two to discuss their past and both clearly are enjoying it. At least they are not directing their questions at me, not that I mind, but it's good to be a listener too.

Before long, Ruth quietly called round each table where her charges were sitting, to make sure all was well and to tell them they had another ten minutes before they would need to pay their bills and head for the coach. This prompted a flurry of walking sticks as everyone headed at the same time for the toilets. Ruth, being an old hand at these things was expecting a considerable delay and had allowed for a twenty-minute hiatus.

Ruth had come to the care profession later in her life, having been a primary school teacher for many years. Frankly, there was not a lot of difference between handling a class of seven-year olds on an outing and this group, although she would never dream of telling them so!

Many of the staff at Appledore had been there for several years and Mitsy had met all of them during her first few weeks. The home was privately owned by Mr and Mrs Podsiadlo. Most people called her Mrs P although a few staff risked calling her Hannah when there was no one else around. Hannah's husband, a Polish airman, was a member of the Allied Forces during the second world war and the couple came to the UK after their home town near Poznan was occupied by German troops. Hannah was well liked by staff and residents alike. Over time, she had employed a senior nurse to take over some of her duties and Greg, the 'odd-job' man was promoted to head of maintenance. Everyone thought that was quite funny because Greg had no staff and continued to do all the odd jobs he had always done.

Having shepherded everyone back on to the minibus, Ruth felt she could relax, trusting that not much could go wrong in the next hour on the drive back to Appledore House, as was the case.

Both Norma and Mitsy were quiet on the return journey. It had been an enjoyable trip even if it had been tiring. The passing scenery was pleasant and virtually everyone was silent with their own thoughts, or nodding off in the warmth of the vehicle.

Arriving home, Mitsy was approached immediately by Mrs P who said she had some good news for her. It transpired that Mitsy's sister Sky was planning to visit and had phoned the Home to find out when would be a good time. This was not 'good news' and Mitsy was not pleased about it. For one thing, Sky could have phoned back when she was in, rather than making an arrangement behind her back as if she wasn't capable of such decision making herself. Secondly, she and Sky didn't really get on and she wasn't sure she could face several hours of Sky moaning about her husband and daughters. None-the-less, she said nothing to Mrs P as it really was a personal matter. It had been decided that Sky would visit next Tuesday for lunch, travelling by train and leaving late afternoon.

Although it really wasn't necessary, Mitsy began tidying her room, as if Sky would notice anyway. It was her way of getting her thoughts in order and she was trying hard to dispel her grumpy mood.

Try and look at it from Sky's point of view, she said to herself. She is no doubt a bit concerned that you require looking after in a care home. Rubbish, she replied. Sky doesn't care about anyone apart from herself. On the other hand, how awful can it be to listen to Sky's complaints about her lovely husband and two children, who of course are grown up and have their own lives to lead now, despite their mother's interference? The visit will soon be over and life can return to its calm and gentle pace.

In spite of speaking severely to herself and reflecting on the kindness of her own son Pete, she still felt irritated that her sister could disturb her so. Sky wasn't even here yet and she was being a nuisance!

As she paced around her room feeling annoyed, the dinner bell rang. Much as she wanted to phone her sister and question the visiting arrangements, she resisted the urge knowing that she would regret her ill-tempered reaction afterwards, so she headed off to the dining room, quietly fuming. Family! They drive you mad sometimes.

Mitsy began to relax once the meal was served. It was fish fingers, creamy mashed potato, baby carrots and broccoli spears drizzled with butter. Whilst it wasn't gourmet fare, it was hot, tasty, and easy for her to eat with her clumsy and recalcitrant hands. The day she moved in, the staff had very kindly found some lightweight cutlery which she could handle and at every meal these were laid out for her without a mention of her difficulties.

She knew she was very fortunate to have such kind people around her. However, she couldn't help - just once in a while – thinking of the superb meals she used to eat in the Harrogate restaurants with Peter. She so enjoyed all kinds of delicious seafood, such as lobster, or the locally raised beef or lamb. Even after Peter had passed away, she sometimes treated herself to a meal out in town with friends.

There was a gentle hum of conversation at the meal table, which got a little louder once the plates were cleared away and everyone waited expectantly for dessert. There were two cooks on duty at all times and today's pair were Julie and Sam. Sam had not long left school and was working towards his National Vocational Qualifications so he was always very pleased if someone praised his cooking. After the meal, he could write down the feedback in his NVQ portfolio, along with a picture of his offering. Today it was rhubarb crumble and custard, which elicited murmurs of enjoyment from around the table. It was such a pleasure to see his happy face, even though Mitsy would have preferred ice cream, finding that custard always brought back unwelcome memories of school dinners.

8

It had actually been a restful weekend and Mitsy had almost forgotten that Sky was due to visit her on Tuesday. After having spent a couple of days with Pete, she realised that sorting out the old house had been quite a relief. The red roses they brought back from her old garden still gave off a heady perfume and she could imagine that Peter was there with her. She thought that her late husband would have been happy to see her settled in this comfortable room in Appledore House, making friends and taking part in group activities. She had always been rather solitary and enjoyed her own company but since moving in she had found that someone else to talk to was pleasant occasionally.

This morning a woman was coming to run a craft group. Mitsy was uncertain whether to take part, or whether to continue her internet search. The latter had taken a back seat recently and she felt she ought to get on with it. The trouble was, it always seemed more like work, rather than pleasure.

Norma knocked on Mitsy's door. "Are you coming to the craft group? I didn't really want to go on my own," she said. Mitsy smiled, "Well I was in two minds but I'll be happy to come. Just let me get my specs and handbag." She didn't confide her trepidations that whatever it was they were going to be asked to make would be too difficult for her arthritic hands but instead headed off down the corridor towards the main lounge or sitting area with Norma hurrying behind her.

Lucy was already there, also Arthur. They were chatting quietly until Mitsy and Norma arrived. "We were just saying how surprised we were to find so many foreigners here," said Lucy, directing her gaze towards Mitsy. Initially, Mitsy was entirely puzzled by her comment.

"I'm afraid I don't really know what you mean?" she replied.

"Oh, you know. Most of the nurses are black and also the care assistants."

"To be honest, I don't notice the colour of people's skin," she responded. "I find it interesting to know what countries some people have come from and to think about how difficult it must have been to learn another language, adjust to the climate, the food and even gain additional qualifications here. I'm full of admiration for them. I imagine that many of the staff here are second generation in any case." Mitsy hoped that this conversation would end as she certainly didn't like the direction it was heading in.

Fortunately, the person who would be running the craftwork session came in the door at this moment. As luck would have it, or perhaps not, she appeared to be a woman of colour too.

"Hello, I'm Jeannie. I'm Joyce's sister. I'm here to run the craft group today. Does anyone know how many people we are expecting?"

Arthur leapt up, rising to his not inconsiderable height, to look at the list pinned on the noticeboard. "There will be about ten," he said.

"Right, we'll wait until everyone is here."

Mitsy really hoped that Jeannie did not hear the conversation that had been taking place as she arrived, so she said: "It's good to meet you Jeannie! I presume your birthplace was also Cebu, like Joyce? It must be a beautiful island."

Jeannie smiled with the warmth of the welcome and nodded. The remainder of the group appeared suddenly at the door and everyone settled down to find out what Jeannie had planned for them. It involved making greeting cards for Christmas, Easter and birthdays. They were all given card, scissors, a pot of glue and pretty things to stick on them. There were also silver and gold lettered greetings for every type of card one could think of. Mitsy sighed as she knew she would not be able to cut out anything.

"I think it might be a good idea for you to work in pairs," suggested Jeannie.

Norma moved to be nearer to Mitsy, "I'll cut, if you do the sticking," she said, thoughtfully. They worked quietly for some forty minutes, showing their creations to 'the teacher' as they jokingly referred to Jeannie. When the class came to an end, they were told they could keep any finished cards. Jeannie packed up quickly and left, after everyone thanked her for an interesting and enjoyable session.

Mitsy felt she had left some things unsaid from the conversation at the beginning of the morning, but decided not to stir things up – yet! She had little patience with narrow or bigoted views, even though she knew these could often stem from ignorance and lack of education or limited life experiences.

Later that afternoon, Mitsy decided to take a short walk. On leaving Appledore House, she turned left and headed for the corner shop. She needed to buy some shampoo although that wasn't the real reason for her walk. She wanted to have a closer look at the old mill and she intended to make it appear as if she just casually happened to be on the other side of the road.

At the corner shop she picked up a copy of the Telegraph & Argus, the local paper, and her favourite shampoo. Strolling back, she crossed over the road and ambled down the pavement on the far side, on her way back to Appledore House.

Ahead, she could see the mill. No one would say it was beautiful but it was the classic textile mill architecture from the time it was built. It was four storeys high and constructed from mellowed local stone. The slate roof was probably the only part that was in relatively good condition. The rather plain, Georgian style windows with small panes and sash cord fittings were thick with dirt and dust although the main entrance had a very grand portico and looked as if, in its heyday, this doorway was set aside for the mill owner and his wealthy gentlemen friends. The building was in such a bad state that some of the ground floor windows had been boarded up and the big mill chimney even had a tree growing out of the top.

There was a large For Sale sign at the right-hand end of the building, which she wouldn't have been able to see from her window. All in all, she concluded that no one was living or even squatting there. It was the epitome of derelict.

Crossing back across the road to her home, Mitsy noticed for the first time that the wisteria that grew across the front of Appledore House was beginning to blossom. In the past, Appledore must have been a really stylish property, she thought.

Back in room six, she kicked off her shoes, and sat down to peruse the local paper. There was not much to interest her and once she had hastily flicked past the obituaries and the job adverts, she was on the point of folding it up and putting it in the bin when she spotted a very small news item:

> Planning permission declined for old cotton mill. Developers have been turned down for the third time in their bid to convert the historic mill into twenty-three luxury apartments. Planners stated environmental concerns from increased traffic and inadequate parking for the proposed new homes as the main reason for the refusal.

Mitsy could see clearly from the picture that it was the mill opposite Appledore House. Thus, she was satisfied that her outing today had been worthwhile.

A knock at the door revealed Jo, bringing afternoon tea and biscuits. Mitsy thanked her and asked if she didn't ever have time off. "Oh, I certainly do Mitsy; it's just that Maggie is not well so I'm covering for her for a couple of days. It's only a cold but Mrs Podsiadlo prefers us not to work if we have anything that the residents could catch."

Turning to her laptop, Mitsy logged on and began to get underway with tracing her mother's family tree. Strangely enough, she had had very little to do with that side of the family, probably because her grandparents had remained in Ireland and couldn't afford to visit very often. I do wish I'd asked Mum more about our family history before she died, she thought. It wasn't that there were any secrets, probably, but it just wasn't a topic of conversation.

After more than an hour of searching, she had identified the name of her great grandmother and ascertained that she had been a seamstress. That was amusing because neither Mitsy herself nor her own mother had any interest or natural ability in sewing or making things with their hands. She concluded that that particular family trait had died out back in Ireland.

She was unable to track down her grandfather at all, which was frustrating. It occurred to her that she might ask Sky tomorrow to see if she remembered anything about him. Having reached what seemed like a brick wall, Mitsy decided that was enough for today. She already had 'screen eyes' and didn't want to look too tired for Sky's visit in the morning.

Norma had asked Mitsy to call round when she felt like it, so this was a good opportunity to do so. Norma was delighted to have a visit from her neighbour and Mitsy was fascinated to see how Norma's room differed from hers. It was considerably smaller but already Norma had made it homely with her pictures from South Africa and personal ornaments. They chatted for half an hour which was just enough for them both.

Relaxing in bed later, Mitsy reflected on the day and realised she had been rather busy. She had intended for it to be restful, so she could mentally prepare herself for Sky's visit but in spite of all that had happened she did not feel her usual foreboding before seeing her sister and for the first time in many days she slept well all night.

9

Sky arrived just before eleven o'clock. Mrs P was looking out of her bedroom window and saw her approaching Appledore House. She hurried down the grand staircase and was ready to open the door to welcome Mitsy's guest, before escorting her along the corridor to room six. Mrs P noticed, quite perceptively, that the two sisters did not hug or kiss.

Sky's appearance did not really live up to her colourful and exotic name. She was wearing a sensible, brown pleated skirt which fell to below her knees and a hand-knitted pullover in dark green, both of which were covered by a voluminous grey checked winter coat. Her wavy, auburn hair had long ago turned grey but this was barely visible. On some women, wearing a navy beret can look totally chic but on Sky, who insisted on pulling it down over her ears, she was somewhat reminiscent of the comedian Benny Hill. Her dark brown, flat lace-up shoes completed the ensemble. No one would have dreamed that these two were sisters.

Mitsy was, in fact, pleased to see Sky in her own way. She showed her round her room, pointing out the garden view and the well-appointed en suite bathroom.

"Do sit down, Sky, you must be tired after your long journey," she said with her customary kindness, ushering her sibling to the nearest armchair. This was all the invitation Sky needed to launch into her diatribe about the state of public transport, the difficulty of getting to Mitsy's new home which was 'in the back of beyond' before offering an appraisal of Appledore House.

"I don't know why you wanted to give up our family home in Harrogate. You had everything you wanted there and this – this place – is no more than a bedsit."

Before Sky could rant on any more, Mitsy interrupted to put her side of the argument: "Now you know very well why I had to move, Sky. Our old house was much too big for me to look after, given that my arthritis has got worse over the years which made everything difficult. Appledore House is lovely; it's like being in a friendly hotel with all my washing, cleaning, cooking done for me. If, later on, I'm less able to look after myself I shall be in the best place because Pete cannot keep coming over from Dublin to do things. I'm happy here."

She actually thought that it was more like a luxury hotel but she didn't want Sky to think she had that much money to spare. It hadn't really been an issue between them that their parents gave the house to her and Peter and in any case, they still had to pay the outstanding mortgage over the remaining years.

That stopped Sky for a short while, so that she could draw breath and give an update on all the supposedly dreadful things Jim, her husband, had done. Mitsy found this was one of the most distressing aspects about seeing her sister because in truth, Jim was a sweetheart who would do anything for his wife. Somehow, Sky just liked to moan about everyone and anything.

She was just gearing up for a grumble about her two daughters when the bell rang to let people know a meal was being served. Sky was in the process of suggesting this was all too regimented, commenting that 'it's like being in prison' but Mitsy just raised her voice over hers: "Ah. Lovely! Food is ready. Do you need to use the bathroom? I do hope you will join us for lunch?" and without waiting for an answer she steered her sister down the corridor to the dining room.

The other residents were all very friendly towards Sky and extremely sympathetic about the journey she had endured in order to visit Mitsy. Of course, it wasn't anything like as bad as Sky was making out but they weren't to know that this was Sky's habitual demeanour.

Mitsy was thankful that nothing too contentious came up in discussion over the dinner table. It was also an absolute blessing that the chicken casserole with new potatoes and runner beans was delicious. Sky enjoyed her meal and was very complimentary about the lemon meringue pie for afters. Sam beamed with pleasure, as it was the first time he'd attempted this dessert.

Back in room six, Mitsy asked tentatively when Sky needed to catch her train and whether she would like to have a taxi booked to take her to the station. It transpired that Sky had already booked the same taxi she had used for her outward journey and that she had less than half an hour to wait for his arrival.

"Right. That's good. Well, there's just time to ask you, what you can remember of Grandad O'Neill? I'm doing an internet search on our family and anything you can remember would be useful."

Sky did not use the internet, neither did she have a mobile phone, so Mitsy's easy facility with IT really annoyed her. On the other hand, she liked being asked her opinion so she wracked her brains to think of any useful information.

"I think grandad used to smoke a pipe," she began. Mitsy tried hard not to sigh audibly, given that this gem was hardly going to elucidate her search of the births and deaths registers. "Oh, and he played the, what was it called?"

There was a long pause and Mitsy was about to offer a list of instruments as options when there was a tap on the door. "Your taxi has arrived," said Ruth.

Sky seemed happy to be departing and as she pulled on her coat it was as if she had all but forgotten anything to do with their grandfather.

Mitsy accompanied her sister to the door, ushering her into the taxi and wishing her a safe journey home. "Give me a call when you get in, please."

Thus it was that when the phone rang much later that evening, for an instant Mitsy wondered who could be calling at this time of night.

"It's me. Terrible journey. I've only just got home. By the way, it's penny whistle." She hung up, leaving Mitsy shaking her head with disbelief.

Remarkably, Mitsy slept well. Perhaps it was relief that Sky's visit was over or maybe she was just exhausted and her body took control of her circadian rhythms and insisted she got some rest. There could have been another reason. She had agreed to another lunchtime get-together with Arthur, who was turning into a kind and thoughtful friend.

10

"Thank you, Arthur. I believe it's my turn to get lunch today."

"Certainly not, dear lady. I insist on being an old-fashioned and hopefully well-mannered gentleman. This was my invitation and I enjoy your company. Now, do tell me what your news is!"

Mitsy had been looking forward to telling Arthur what she had recently discovered. Having drawn a blank for the time being on her grandfather's background via her ancestry search and having failed to extract any useful information from her sister Sky, she had decided to look into the history of the old mill opposite. Her shopping expedition had uncovered that the property was due to be sold and converted by a property developer. Of course, it could be months or years before anything was done to the derelict building, given that planning permission had been turned down.

"Well. I think I already told you that the old mill opposite us here at Appledore House is for sale. I thought it would be interesting to know a bit of its history before it is turned into luxury apartments."

Arthur nodded silently as he tucked into his ploughman's lunch.

"It used to be called Park Mill and I think it was built in 1870. It was a steam powered textile mill and it was a very busy place for many years. There's nothing really romantic about it; for the employees it was hard, dirty work and probably only marginally better than being in the workhouse. I'm just going to eat some of this delicious ploughman's lunch and then I'll tell you more. Oh! They've given us pickled onions today. Aren't they big?! I'm not sure I can cut mine."

Mitsy chattered on, quite happy to be out and sharing her news with Arthur. He, meanwhile, leant over carefully and sliced her large pickled onion in half.

"The information about the working conditions was what really shocked me. I suppose I shouldn't be surprised but…."

They sat in companionable silence for a few minutes, taking a sip of their drinks and enjoying the lunch. Peter the pub dog was settled into his usual place stretched out on the large rug in front of the open fire.

"So, people were employed to work a thirteen- to sixteen-hour working day, even the children. The conditions were truly dreadful. Several historians commented on the nasty smelling pollution which apparently was worse in Bradford than many of the other mill towns. This was bad both inside and outside the mill. The air was hot and humid, it was full of cotton dust and the noise was atrocious. Inside, everyone managed to communicate only by lip-reading. No conversation was permitted at all unless it related to work. Many people went completely deaf after a couple of months because there was no ear protection. The workers were responsible for the machinery and if anything went wrong or if any tools were lost, they had to pay for them.

I also discovered that pauper apprentices and orphans were employed from the age of nine years. They were given lodgings, food and one hour of schooling per week. Sadly, there were lots of accidents.

Oh, I could go on Arthur, but you will get the picture. Of course, the mill owner became very wealthy on the back of this abuse. In some ways, I wish I hadn't looked into it."

They both sighed.

"That's very sad Mitsy, but it is how it was back then. Shall I tell you a bit more about the history of Appledore House? It may actually restore your faith in human nature."

Mitsy smiled, because of course she was basically a positive thinker, she was just being honest to Arthur about her emotional reaction to learning about the mill.

"Well, before Appledore House was handed over to the Red Cross in 1916, it was owned by John Doughty. The house had been in the family for several generations and handed down the male line, most of whom were merchants. At the start of the first world war in July 1914, Doughty' s only son volunteered for the armed forces and was very quickly sent overseas. Doughty, his wife and daughter remained in the area in the hope that this 'war to end all wars' would be over quickly, if not by Christmas.

When the war seemed likely to continue, the county branch of the British Red Cross sought premises to provide an Auxiliary Hospital for wounded soldiers back from the front. Appledore House seemed ideal and Violet and her mother both joined the Voluntary Aid Detachment. They were trained in first aid and home nursing, reporting first to the matron and then the commandant who was in overall control.

When they received news that John junior had died of his injuries in battle, the family were heartbroken. In some ways, it may have strengthened Violet's resolve to do whatever she could to save other young men from the same fate. She certainly would have heard from the injured soldiers some tales of the horrific conditions in the trenches and must have wondered what exactly had happened to her beloved brother."

Misty's vivid imagination could almost picture how the old house was being used at that time.

"Now, I've got quite a lot more to uncover," said Arthur, "but I have a sneaking suspicion that your ghostly White Lady could be Violet."

"Oh, how lovely! The White Lady was a young woman and she certainly had a kindly and caring expression," said Mitsy.

Lunch over, Mitsy and Arthur strolled back to Appledore House in the sunshine. It was good to have a friend to share things with, thought Mitsy.

11

Although Mitsy thought that she had probably met everyone in the home, there were several residents that she felt she hardly knew. It was interesting therefore, to have someone new knock on her door this morning shortly after breakfast.

"I hope I'm not calling round at an inconvenient time?" asked Caitlin. "We haven't really spoken since you moved in and I hoped we could be friends. My name is Caitlin although everyone calls me Kate."

"Hello Kate. Yes, I've seen you around but haven't yet managed to sit near you for a chat, at mealtimes. Do come in!"

"What a lovely room! Mine is upstairs and although it has pleasant views of the roof tops and the bottom of the garden it is not nearly as spacious."

Mitsy explained how her room seemed larger because it had accommodated a couple of people previously.

"Why don't you tell me a little about yourself and then I'll do the same," suggested Kate.

In this way, by the time Ruth was bringing round the mid-morning coffee these two had got to know each other so much better.

"Fancy us both having links to Dublin," said Kate. "I know it's a big city but it's definitely a small world! I haven't been there for years, so I suppose it has changed."

"I'm hoping to go over to Dublin for a few days, to stay with my son. He has an apartment in the city. Would you like to come too? Pete's got two spare rooms so it wouldn't be any trouble."

Kate looked surprised but very unsure of the generous offer and Mitsy thought perhaps Kate didn't have the money for a flight, or was just wary of travelling.

“Think about it. No need to decide now. I intended to go for three days midweek as soon as the weather gets warmer.”

“Thank you, Mitsy. I will think about it but now I should leave you in peace – we’ve been chatting almost all the morning!”

This morning’s conversation had reassured Mitsy that, even though she had left behind a number of friends in Harrogate, it was still possible to develop new relationships. She was especially encouraged that everyone respected her personal space, by not overstaying their welcome in room six. It was something that had worried her a great deal before she moved in to Appledore House. For most of her married life she had lived quite an independent existence and she was reluctant to give that up now.

When Peter was away at sea, although they were mostly able to communicate by phone or letter, she was responsible for the home, their son and herself. She had built up quite a supportive network of friends who were always ready to help on the rare occasions she needed to ask, and by the same token she was always happy to help them.

Being self-sufficient had its funny side too. Once Pete was at school, she looked for a part-time job, partly for the money and partly for adult conversation. In those early years before Pete got to secondary school then university, she took on all sorts of jobs. These included working as a lunchtime barmaid; waitressing; shop assistant in a dress shop; cleaner; receptionist in a hairdressing salon; school dinner lady and many other roles. Her husband used to joke that he was never sure who he was coming home to. In fact, he once opened the door and called out, “I’m home!! Who are you today my darling?” Eventually, Mitsy settled down to her job in the pharmacy and put an end to the swapping and changing. These varied jobs did, in any case, give her a chance to meet lots of people around the town and there was always something new and interesting to learn.

It occurred to her that as she had offered accommodation in Pete's apartment to her friend, it would be polite to ask Pete if he had any objection. Her quick email got a speedy response:

> Hi Pete when you were over here, we talked about me coming to Dublin to stay with you for a couple of days. I'm not planning to visit yet but I just wondered if you would mind if I brought a friend? She has family links to the city and I thought it would be nice to have a companion with me. Hope you are OK? Love Mum xxx

> Hi Mum Yes that would be fine, of course. Don't leave it too long! Love Pete xxx

That evening, Mitsy had another one of her sleepless nights. She could not think of anything that was troubling her specifically, but no matter how she tried to relax and drop off, sleep eluded her.

Eventually, she stopped battling with her insomnia and decided she would get up, get dressed and go in search of a warming mug of tea in the kitchen, where she knew someone would be sitting. So often this was the solution, a few minutes chatting to one of the staff and not worrying about her difficulty sleeping, generally calmed her enough to drop off to sleep once she got back to her room.

Glancing through the window as she pulled on some trousers and a pullover, she noticed that some lights were showing in the mill again. It is odd, she thought.

As she walked along the ground floor corridor, she wondered if she would see the White Lady again. She was still calling her this, in her head, although there was now a possibility that she was Violet, as Arthur had suggested. No White Lady was to be seen, so she headed into the kitchen and was pleased to find Julie on duty and apparently peeling potatoes for tomorrow's meal.

"I am sorry to be a nuisance, Julie, but I couldn't sleep and I wondered if I could have a cup of tea, please?"

Julie was happy to oblige as it could be a long night on duty without company. Sometimes she dozed off, but she was wide awake and only too happy to put the kettle on. She liked Mitsy, much as she did the majority of residents. One or two were a bit trying but mostly they were manageable with a smile and a kind word.

Once the tea was drunk, Mitsy was still feeling alert and restless so she mentioned to Julie the lights that she could see from her room in the old mill.

"Shall I let you into a secret?" said Julie in a conspiratorial manner. "We always sit in the kitchen when we're on night duty because it's warm. There's a room behind here, which leads directly outdoors. Shall we go and have a quick look at the old mill from here?"

And so it was that the room behind the kitchen revealed a side door to Appledore House that only the staff knew about and used. Mitsy was under the impression that it was never locked, which meant they could come and go easily without ringing the front door bell which would disturb the residents at night.

The pair walked very quietly round the side of the building and once they got to the gravelled driveway it was obvious that there were no lights on in the mill. "Oh, maybe I dreamt it. Thank you, Julie, for the tea and for putting my mind at rest."

Mitsy hurried back to her room, determined to go to sleep now. She even resisted the temptation to look out of her own window. I'm a silly woman with an overactive imagination, she said to herself. As she at last drifted off to sleep, she imagined having a conversation with Violet.

12

It was around ten o'clock after Mitsy had enjoyed some breakfast and was back in her room, putting on her coat and getting ready to head off down the road for her appointment with the chiropodist, when she could hear voices in the corridor. Raymond was obviously talking to someone. Mitsy didn't see much of him, even though he was her nearest neighbour because he usually had breakfast in his room. In fact, he would probably have asked for all his meals in his room – being quite a shy man – were it not that Mrs P encouraged him to socialise from time to time.

Mitsy thought she'd wait until the speakers moved away before she went out, then there was a tentative knock on the door.

It was Kate, looking rather sheepish. "Oh, Mitsy I'm sorry to trouble you just as you are going out."

"That's no problem Kate, what can I do for you?"

"May I come in for a moment?"

Mitsy stood to one side and gestured to her new friend to take a seat.

Kate took a deep breath before speaking. "I'm afraid I cannot come to Dublin with you; you see I'm terrified of flying. I've been worrying all night what a fool you will think I am but I just can't do it."

Mitsy smiled sympathetically. "Oh, you mustn't be concerned about that. It was only an off-the-cuff suggestion of mine. Plenty of people are unhappy about flying. I bet some of them pretend they are being 'green' when really they just don't want to fly."

"Thank you for being so understanding, Mitsy. I've only been on a plane once and I hated it. But I wondered if you would check on my family connections for me when you visit your son?"

Mitsy must have looked puzzled, almost as if she was being asked to call on a stranger's grandmother.

"If you could look up some things for me at the Dublin Registrar's Office for Births, Deaths and Marriages, I'd really appreciate it."

"Well, of course I could. But couldn't you check all that yourself on line?"

"Oh dear no. I don't know how to use the internet but I thought you could just pop in for me while you are there?"

The previous day, Mitsy had briefly explained to Kate that one of her hobbies was researching about her ancestors. She had emphasised that it was fun, interesting and all you had to do was make a note of all the known information of family names, birthdays, weddings etc and use that as a basis for building a family tree. It had never occurred to her that Kate couldn't use the internet, although it appeared that she was not alone in this and there were plenty of people at Appledore House who were unfamiliar with the use of the world wide web.

"You see, I've made a note of the limited information I've got for you to use as a starting point," she smiled, hopefully.

"Right. Well, I can make a start for you but I cannot promise to get far. It's a very time-consuming exercise and sometimes one reaches a dead end. I'm sorry Kate but I have an appointment to keep, so I have to go out. I'll put your notes safely in my folder for now and I'll look at them later."

With that she dashed off, not wishing to arrive late for her first appointment with a new chiropodist.

It was only as she walked back, with a lilt in her step now that her feet had been expertly tended to, that she began to reflect on the exchange with Kate early this morning. She could see that she might be getting more than one enquiry from her fellow residents, which would turn what she had seen as a gentle private hobby into a never-ending chore. She concluded that the best thing she could do would be to check on a couple of things for Kate and then say she couldn't find out anything else. She would also need to be alert to other people looking for help. It perhaps wasn't a kind thought but Mitsy did wonder if this was the sole reason that Kate had called round in the first instance, asking to be friends.

Back in room six, she decided to arrange her trip to see Pete as soon as possible. She hadn't actually visited him in Dublin for almost three years and it was an interesting city with lots to offer. Come to think of it, she hadn't actually been away anywhere recently as all her time had been focussed on the move to Appledore House. She decided that she deserved a little treat and it would be a good opportunity to do some clothes shopping too!

> Hi Pete. Just letting you know that it will just be me staying as it turns out that my friend doesn't like flying. Any idea when would be a good time to come over? Love Mum xx

Almost immediately a new email pinged into her inbox:

> Hi Mum. I'd love to see you any time. Next week is quiet, after that I have a string of meetings in Brussels, Helsinki and Stockholm over the next few weeks. See what you can arrange! Love Pete xxx

Mitsy immediately searched the internet for suitable flights and replied:

> Pete. I can get an evening flight this Thursday, leaves Leeds/Bradford at 19:25 arrives Dublin 20:30. There's a return flight on Sunday at 20:25 which gets me in 21:55. That should be OK,

especially if I can get a lift to the airport from Mr P. Shall I book? Love Mum xxx

Pete's instant response was for his mother to go ahead. When she closed her laptop, she felt quite excited. It was only a short trip but it would be lovely to see some familiar places in Dublin, as well as spending a little time with Pete.

13

Thursday afternoon found Mitsy packing her small overnight bag and checking and rechecking its contents. Mr Podsiadlo had agreed to take Mitsy to the airport and, even more importantly, to collect her late on Sunday evening. I must bring back some Irish whiskey for him, as a thank you, she said to herself.

Fortunately, all went well on the drive to Yeadon, which is where Leeds/Bradford airport is located. Mitsy's flight was on time and the pilot announced that they would probably arrive in well under the hour, as the wind was with them. There was hardly time to settle in her seat, read the safety instructions and drink the coffee that was provided by the friendly stewardess before the descent began. The man sitting next to her seemed impressed that an 'older lady' as he chose to call her, was confidently travelling alone and although he meant well, Mitsy had no intention of telling him her business.

As she was only carrying hand luggage, she was swiftly off the plane and first in the taxi queue. The taxi driver was courteous and given it was barely a twenty-minute drive at this time of night, she was dropped off outside Pete's apartment at Aston Quay shortly after nine o'clock.

Mitsy had only brought with her a few euros, enough to pay for the taxi but she realised she would need to change some more sterling while she was here.

After big hugs and not a little teasing of Pete's efforts to tidy his home before his mother's visit, what was left of the evening was spent in planning how to spend the next couple of days. Pete had to go to work on Friday, so Mitsy explained about Caitlin and her commitment to do a little ancestry search for her. She also was keen to do some clothes shopping for herself so that really wrapped up the whole of the next day.

"I shall cook a meal for you tomorrow evening and I've got some ideas about what we could do on Saturday," said Pete.

"In which case, I shall take you out for dinner that evening," she replied. "We can just laze around on Sunday before my return."

Whether she was feeling relaxed with Pete around, or tired after her journey, Mitsy fell asleep straight away and did not wake up once in the night. By the time she realised it was morning, Pete had gone to work, leaving her a light breakfast on the kitchen table, a spare key and a note saying when he hoped to be home.

Fortunately, the weather was looking fair and Mitsy was thankful she had not had to carry a waterproof or heavy winter coat. She set off around ten o'clock and walked along the quayside, enjoying the fresh air and the unfamiliar sights. Following instructions that Pete had given her, she turned right after City Quay down Lombard Street, easily finding numbers 12 to 14 where the Registry Office was located.

The member of staff on duty (Mitsy didn't know whether to call her the Registrar) helpfully showed her where to find the records that she was looking for. "Hmm. In some ways this is more interesting than doing an internet search," she remarked to the woman. Checking all the information that Kate had given her on the sheet of paper, it took only a short time to find some of the documents requested and she took out her notepad and pen to write down the salient points.

"Would you like a copy of those?" asked the woman. "There is a twenty-euro charge per page."

Mitsy checked her purse and found she had enough to pay for one page, so she selected the registration of the birth that Kate had asked for and made brief notes on the details from the other two.

She was pleased she had managed to get the information Kate had asked her for, but quite puzzled by what she had found. Leaving the registrar's office, she headed back towards the city centre until she came across a suitable coffee shop in which to sit down and relax.

'Well, I never,' she said to herself as she looked at the papers carefully. 'I think I shall have to be careful how to break this news to Kate when I get back to Appledore House.'

After a coffee, a pastry and a little rest in the coffee shop, she decided it was time to do some of the things for herself that she had in mind. Crossing the beautiful river Liffey at O'Connell Bridge, she made her way towards the shops in Grafton Street. By mid-afternoon she was carrying several bags with some special additions to her wardrobe including a new pair of leather boots and some luxury make-up. She had topped up her fund of euros, so she had enough to pay for the meal the next day, taxis and some to spare for another visit. Mitsy was feeling very tired now, so she decided to take a taxi back to Pete's flat.

Mitsy had always loved driving and the freedom it offered but as she got older, she realised that she was using her car less and less frequently and her driving confidence was waning. Eventually, she gave her car to one of her nieces whose need was much greater than hers. Since giving up driving, she tried to make sure that she always had enough money with her to pay for a taxi if it was necessary.

Pete had no need for a car while he lived here in Dublin. His office was a ten-minute walk away and everything else was close by. He had an account with the taxi firm that he used for his regular journeys to and from the airport, which was paid for by his employers.

When Pete got in from work, he sat with his mother for a short while so that she could recount how her day had panned out. She was so excited to show him her shopping purchases he didn't have the heart to remind her that she had to carry these all back to the UK along with her overnight bag.

“Now, Pete. Look at this with me, will you?” she said, digging out the documents relating to her friend Kate. “What do you make of this?”

Pete carefully perused all the evidence and then turned to his mother. “Well, it looks to me as if your friend’s sister was actually her mother.”

“That’s what I thought. There’s no father’s name and the people who she called Mam and Dad were actually her grandparents.”

“Good lord! Doesn’t she know?”

“I don’t think so, but on the other hand she may have had a suspicion and that may have been why she asked me to look into it. Whatever do I do?”

“Well, it’s certainly a bit of a moral dilemma. I think you do have to tell her though.”

“Yes. I’d concluded that myself. I really don’t want to do any more of these things for other people. It’s one thing to discover skeletons in your own family’s cupboard but quite another to dig them out of someone else’s.”

Pete laughed at the mixed metaphor. “Time for me to cook. We’re having seafood pasta. You can sit there with a little glass of white wine while I prepare the meal.”

After a very pleasant meal, Pete sat down next to his mother and looked her straight in the face. “Now, I hope you don’t mind but I’ve taken a chance and bought tickets for us for tomorrow, without checking with you first. I didn’t know whether I’d be able to get them until this afternoon and I didn’t want to disappoint you.”

“Whatever you’ve planned I’m sure I’ll enjoy it!” said Mitsy.

“A friend of mine has two tickets for the Dublin Racing Festival that she cannot use. She’s asked around and I’ve been waiting to hear if another friend wanted them, as she’d asked him first. I said we’d love to buy the tickets if he doesn’t want them.”

“So, what exactly is it?”

"Mum!! It's the horse racing meet of the year in Dublin. It takes place at the Leopardstown Racecourse which isn't far at all from here. My friend, Sue, who sold me the tickets, has kindly agreed to give us a lift there. It means we will have to go quite early so she can find somewhere to park. It also means there will be a bit of walking and I wanted to check that you hadn't worn yourself out doing shopping today."

"Oh, that will be lovely. I've never been to a horse race before – that will be fun. Can I bet on the horses?"

"Of course you can. We will give ourselves a budget so we're not tempted to go too mad and I'll get a copy of the Racing Post so we can pick our winners."

"You know I said I'd like to treat us to a meal out tomorrow evening? Will that still be possible?"

"Certainly will. We might be best to book straight away because the city will be busy, it being a Saturday and the Racing Festival."

"Would your friend Sue like to join us?"

"I would think so. She'll be with her friend Maura, so it would be four of us."

"I thought we could go to 'The Old Mill Restaurant' at Temple Bar," said Mitsy, "could you check with Sue and Maura and then book a table for four, please?"

With the arrangements made, there was just time for a mug of cocoa before bed. Again, Mitsy slept extremely well.

She was surprised when her son tapped gently on the bedroom door to wake her up, the next morning. He had already been out to the paper shop for the Racing Post. While Pete was getting breakfast, Mitsy had a look at the paper and remarked, "Ooooh look. There's a horse called A Walk in the Mill". Pete called out from the kitchen, "is that important?"

"Well, it might be Pete. It could be lucky!" she said to herself, under her breath.

He wandered back in with toast and coffee, glancing at the paper on the table. "No, Mum. That article you've just been reading is about a horse that was racing at Aintree recently. It won't be here in Dublin today. Let's have a proper look at today's starters."

They had breakfast together and marked their favoured horses on the paper together. Pete looked at the form, the trainer and the jockey for each horse before he made his selection. Mitsy chose hers on the basis of their names, what she called lucky numbers and the colour of the silks.

The rest of the weekend passed by in a blur of fun and laughter. Mitsy enjoyed the company of Pete's friends Sue and Maura. None of them won much money on the horses, in fact they all spent more than they won, but they didn't mind because the racing was a great spectacle and it was lovely to see other racegoers' joy when their horse came in.

As planned, Sunday was a very easy-going day. They had a short walk in the grounds of Trinity College, enjoying the green space and blue skies. Pete took his mother to one of his favourite pubs and even got her to drink a half of draught Guinness. Pete insisted it was so much better than the bottled version available in England, but Mitsy couldn't tell as she rarely drank anything other than wine and not much of that either.

By eight o'clock when the airport taxi was due, she was well and truly worn out. It had been a wonderful weekend and the memories would stay with her for a long time. Now she was ready to go home and sleep in her own bed. "See how quickly I have accepted Appledore House as my home now," she said to Pete. That, in itself, apart from the great time they had enjoyed, reassured him that he was doing everything he could for his mother.

As her plane landed at Leeds/Bradford, she could see a lone but familiar figure waiting just inside the arrivals lounge. "Good old Mr P, I couldn't ask for more," she thought.

14

Kate was looking forward to Mitsy's return and intended to meet up with her immediately after breakfast on Monday, as she was keen to know what she had discovered during her Dublin trip.

"Come in and sit down," said Mitsy, wondering just how she was going to break the news to her friend.

"First, I'm going to tell you all I've been up to, then we will get the ancestry documents out and I will talk you through my findings. I also want to know if I've missed anything exciting while I've been away."

Kate was all too happy to tell Mitsy that very little had happened at Appledore House during her short absence.

"Oh. There was one thing that was rather sad. Do you know Meg who lives a few doors from me on the first floor?"

"No. I don't think so."

"Well she was taken ill on Friday night and we had an ambulance with its sirens going and blue lights flashing. I've not heard any news, so I don't know if she is better. Or worse."

"I suppose we have to expect this sort of thing, given that we are all getting on a bit. I have to say I really don't like it when people refer to Care Homes like ours as 'God's Waiting Room'. As far as I'm concerned, I'm not waiting for anything. I'm doing my best to live my life to the full, within the constraints of my age and abilities."

After a brief summary of all she did in Dublin, Mitsy realised that she could not put off the difficult part of the conversation any longer.

"Right, Kate. You may find what I have to say rather distressing and I don't want to upset you. Would you like to have a quiet look at this birth certificate and my handwritten notes?"

Kate sat reading for a few minutes and Mitsy noticed that Kate's face slowly drained of all colour, until she was quite pale.

"You don't need to say anything Mitsy. I did have my suspicions but Mam and Dad never talked about my sister and refused to visit her when she lived on the outskirts of Dublin. Then she met an American soldier and she went with him after the war to the USA and we lost touch completely. From your other notes it looks as though she lived in St Louis for many years and only passed away twelve years ago."

They both sat quietly for a while, thinking about the implications. "I'll still think of Mam and Dad as my real parents, because they brought me up. I do wonder who my birth father was though."

Mitsy had thought about this already and decided she really did not want to pursue this line of enquiry herself. "It will probably be impossible to discover Kate. In my opinion, the knowledge could even bring more heartache. "

"Thank you so much Mitsy for your efforts on my behalf. I'm inclined to agree with you, especially as everyone is dead now and it wouldn't do much good raking over the past. Do I owe you some money for what you did?"

"Certainly not, Kate. Changing the subject, would you like to go out for a short walk with me this afternoon? I've discovered a footpath through a small wood and it would be good to have your company."

The two friends hugged each other and arranged to meet after lunch.

That afternoon, the skies cleared and the weather was ideal for a short walk, mild and a little breezy but no problem for two older ladies who were dressed for the outdoors. Mitsy's idea was to give Kate other things to think about so she didn't dwell on the news she had shared with her friend.

"Here it is!" she exclaimed at the beginning of the footpath.

“You are adventurous,” said Kate. “I’ve lived here almost three years and I haven’t discovered half the places you have.”

The wood itself barely justified the description; it was more like some scrubby bushes where children built their ‘camps’ within a perimeter of taller trees. Well, it’s got us outside anyway, thought Mitsy.

“If it’s adventure you’re after, perhaps I can tempt you to join me in my next one?”

Kate looked a bit unsure, a facial expression Mitsy was beginning to recognise.

As they walked back, Mitsy pointed out the former Park Mill and the all too obvious For Sale sign outside. She also divulged her evening sightings inside the building. Kate suggested all the explanations Mitsy herself had considered, such as squatters, homeless people, drug dealers etc and Mitsy discounted all of those for one reason or another.

“I have a feeling it’s something really exciting, to do with the history of the place,” she said. “And I have another discovery, but you mustn’t tell anyone this,” she said, very softly. “Did you know that there’s a room behind the kitchen, where the staff sit when they are on night duty?”

Kate shook her head.

“Well, there’s a door that opens to the side of the building that is never locked.”

“Is that important?” asked Kate.

“I had this idea, only last night. Suppose that the next time I saw the lights on in the old mill, and you rang your night bell so that whoever is on duty came to check on you and I used the opportunity to creep out the back and go over to the mill to look in the windows? You could just say you had a nightmare or something and keep the carer talking for a few minutes so that I had time to nip back in.”

Kate looked very dubious but giggled at the thought of such misbehaviour. Mitsy concluded that the short walk and subsequent conversation had worked its magic as Kate seemed much more relaxed as they rang the front door bell and agreed to see each other at mealtime.

After dinner, a plan was hatched. If (or in her mind, when) she saw lights on in Park Mill, Mitsy would get dressed ready to go out then she would text Kate to initiate the diversionary tactics. After a short pause, Kate would follow instructions and ring the bell for assistance from whichever carer was on duty. Mitsy would already be in place, ready for her excursion to the outdoors as soon as she saw someone heading for Kate's room. Of course, this did depend on Kate hearing her mobile buzz which might be a little unreliable if she was fast asleep. They both giggled to think what an adventure it would be. They also had a back-up plan in case Mitsy got stuck outdoors, so it was essential that she took her mobile with her. What could go wrong?

As luck would have it, that evening Mitsy tried to sleep but she was actually rather excited about their planned escapade. When she got up to check if anything was happening in the Mill, she was rewarded with flickering lights and obvious activity. She was ready and dressed in minutes, with a small torch and her mobile in her pocket. A quick check to make sure things were still happening and then she texted Kate with the pre-agreed message:

Action stations! Wish me luck 😉

She seemed to wait for ever but then Kate replied with a thumbs up. Outside her bedroom Mitsy paused, breathing heavily with excitement. In no time at all she saw Jo heading rapidly for the lift and so she hastened her steps towards the kitchen. She was a little wary in case there was more than one person on night duty but all seemed quiet when she got there.

Mitsy was surprised how easily it had all gone and as she crossed the road, she could still see people moving around in the Mill. Although she wouldn't admit it to Kate, she was really quite nervous.

By the time she reached the nearest window her breathing was close to panting. She stepped forward and looked through the dusty window. It took her several seconds to register what she was seeing and already she was afraid she had been out too long.

With a last glance at the incredible sight, she hurried back across the road, along the side of the building, in the door and closed it behind her. She had merely seconds to spare as Jo came back into the kitchen.

"Oh, hello Mitsy. Is everything OK?"

Mitsy took a deep breath and trying to make her voice sound steady and as normal as possible, she said, "I was thirsty so I thought I would see if I could have a cup of tea but now I've had a drink of water I'm fine so I'll just go back to bed and I'm sorry to trouble you." It all came out in a rush but Jo seemed distracted and didn't notice the cool air in the room from the recently opened door or Mitsy's flushed face and shaking hands.

"That's no problem Mitsy, you go back to bed then."

Back in room 6, Mitsy texted Kate a quick update:

Back safe. Real people in there! C U tomo xx

At breakfast, Kate and Mitsy gave each other a secret smile.

"Did you sleep well, Kate?"

"Oh, I had a bit of a disturbed night but nothing to worry about," she smirked.

"Will you be joining the craft group today?"

"Yes. I was planning to. How about you?"

"I've signed up, although I don't know what we will be making today. Would you call round for me before, say about two o'clock?"

Kate nodded her agreement.

15

"So… what did you see?" asked Kate that afternoon, barely before Mitsy's door was closed behind her.

"Ooooh. Sit down and I'll tell you everything! Well, the first thing I noticed as I crossed the road was that all the ground floor lights were on and I could see shadowy shapes moving inside. As I got closer, I could hear a lot of noise. When I got to a window, I looked in. The glass was really dirty but I could see lots of machines and people moving around. I believe what I saw was when the Mill was fully operational. Honestly you couldn't make it up. I wanted to stay and watch more but I was really aware that you were keeping me safe from discovery so I came straight back. It was in the nick of time because the second I got inside the kitchen door and closed it behind me, Jo came in. I had to make up some excuse about wanting a cup of tea but having a drink of water instead and dashing off to bed. She didn't seem to think it was strange. How did it go for you, Kate?"

"Although I say so myself, I think I did a rather good job of my diversionary tactics. I ruffled my hair so it looked like I had been asleep, threw the duvet around a bit and moistened my eyes to look as if I'd been crying. Then I rang the night bell and when Jo arrived, I tearfully told her I had heard a baby crying. She reassured me that it was highly unlikely but I kept saying how much it upset me. Eventually, I agreed that I may have dreamt it and I 'allowed' her to sit with me until I had settled. I was so relieved when I got your text to say you were back safely."

"Well done Kate. You are quite the little actress, aren't you?! I don't really know what to think about what I saw but it was truly an adventure wasn't it?!"

Looking at her bedside clock, Mitsy could see it was time to go to the craft class, so the pair of them left her room, both grinning like naughty schoolgirls.

Today's craft class was being run by Jeannie again. Mitsy, Kate, Norma and Arthur sat together at one of the round dining tables that Mr P and Greg had set up for the session. Jeannie introduced her topic by explaining that there were lots of sayings to explain what they were about to do. "Many hands make light work" was one of them. They were each going to knit a small square which would be a modest task for each person, then she would stitch them all together to make a blanket for a family in need. After the anticipated chorus of concerns from those who had never knitted a stitch before, Jeannie gave a simple demonstration. She also suggested that each table had at least one person who was not experienced so that the others could help.

Each table was given four pairs of knitting needles and a bag of wool in mixed colours. Mitsy's table got to work straight away. Mitsy knew she'd be slow and Arthur was spending more time dropping his needles and his ball of wool than actually managing to cast on, as Jeannie had shown them. It turned out that Norma had always enjoyed knitting and in South Africa she had been in demand to knit baby clothes for her friends' grandchildren. So Norma kindly started the knitting for Arthur and once underway he was able to finish off the square, although rather slowly. Kate was not especially enjoying the task and as far as Mitsy could see, she was still thinking about their previous night's adventure.

It surprised everyone to see how quickly the small squares grew and one or two people asked if they could knit a second square. "No. I'd prefer it if you gave a friend who's a bit slower than you a helping hand, please," she said.

In this way, the afternoon passed by in pleasant conversation and not a little industry and once again, Mitsy was happy to have found a few friends whose company she could enjoy from time to time.

16

After yet another good night's sleep 'this must be almost a record!', thought Mitsy, it seemed like a good time to get down to some serious ancestry research. Recently she had been distracted by Pete's visit, seeing her sister Sky, the trip to Dublin and a number of enjoyable activities organised by Appledore House.

This time she was planning to look into her father's family tree. Sitting comfortably at her desk, she began by writing down what she knew. Her dad, David Thompson, was born in West Yorkshire in 1913. He married her mother Iris, in 1937, which was the year of the coronation of King George VI and Queen Elizabeth. For most of his life he was a musician, playing folk music initially and later on working as a composer in various music genres. He died in France in 1989.

First, Mitsy was able to track down her dad's birth and death certificates and a couple of census references. The latter were rather random, because of the way they travelled around; they were not exactly of 'no fixed abode' but she suspected that often her parents were not registered anywhere and maybe not even paying tax anywhere! From her father's birth certificate, she could see that his parents were named Herbert and Alice. Herbert was listed as being a trader, although there was no more information than that. She didn't remember her dad ever saying much about his father, or his mother for that matter.

She was beginning to wish that she had a printer in her room, because every time she tracked something down, she had to make a handwritten note of it, in case it led her to something else of interest. It was all rather time consuming and before she knew it, the bell was ringing to signal that residents were being called to the dining room.

She did smile to herself at the relatively easy life she had, now that she didn't have to do the food shopping, meal planning and preparation, not to mention the freedom from washing up. When she lived on her own, it always seemed to Mitsy that the amount of washing up was out of proportion to the size of the actual meal as it appeared on the plate and of course, there was never any surprise regarding what she was going to eat, given that she had prepared it herself. In fact, sometimes after she had gone to a lot of trouble to make herself a meal, she couldn't be bothered to eat it. If it was suitable for freezing, she let it cool and then put it in the freezer for another day. Otherwise she put it in the bin and made herself a cheese sandwich. This didn't happen often because she was careful not to waste food when so many people around the world were starving.

Anyway, self-catering was no longer a problem and she ambled along to the dining room feeling quite cheerful.

Lucy was the only person already in the room, so Mitsy sat down next to her. She hadn't immediately warmed to Lucy so far, partly because of her narrow-minded views about people's skin colour in a previous conversation. Still, I mustn't hold that against her, perhaps she has led a sheltered life and lacks a wider view of the world, she thought. Lucy immediately started chatting and again Mitsy got the feeling that she would not be the kind of person with whom to share a secret.

"Wasn't it awful about poor Meg?" she began. Mitsy shook her head and Lucy immediately assumed that she was aware of the matter and had agreed it was awful. Before she had a chance to say anything, Lucy was already complaining, "I do think they could have done more to help. It's shocking – the state of the NHS today." At this point and before Lucy could continue, Mitsy interrupted, "I'm afraid I'm not up with this news." This was all the invitation Lucy needed and she launched into an explanation about how Meg, who lived on the first floor, was taken ill, rushed to hospital and died of pneumonia.

Mitsy didn't think it was fair to blame the NHS. In spite of all the care and attention of the healthcare team, people did die. Lucy had quite a simplistic view of hospitals where only the doctors were important and she was under no illusion that they had failed in this instance.

Lucy reminded Mitsy, in some ways, of her sister Sky who was always ready to complain about anything. By contrast, friends had often told Mitsy that they loved her sunny personality and optimistic outlook on life. She knew that she generally saw the best in people, although as she got older, she had become less likely to trust others immediately until she was sure of them. I have probably developed more grown-up defence mechanisms, she thought. Anyway, it's best to be wary of Lucy!

Fortunately, several more people arrived in the dining room and Mitsy was able to turn her attention to other topics of conversation. Delicious cooking smells emanated from the kitchen and shortly, bowls of green salad and a serving plate heaped with garlic bread arrived on the table. Finally, everyone received a portion of lasagne.

"Whatever is THIS?" asked Lucy. Mitsy sighed. If she makes one single mention of 'foreign' food I shall be tempted to tip it over her head, she thought. Of course, she didn't, but her patience was being sorely tested. Several people made comments about how lovely and cheesy it was, as well as how authentic. Others referred to wonderful holidays they had enjoyed in Italy. It was enough to deter Lucy from more negative comments so instead she turned to the forthcoming funeral for 'poor Meg'. Mitsy did her best to enjoy her meal whilst discussing across the table with other people some of the current sporting activities which were on the TV.

As soon as they had finished dessert, which was a fresh fruit salad, Mitsy got up and beat a hasty retreat to the sanctuary of room six, making a mental note to avoid sitting next to Lucy in future.

In order to clear her head, she went straight back to her ancestry research. She thought that by concentrating on this, it would stop her feeling irritated by Lucy. From Herbert Thompson, she discovered that his father (that would be Mitsy's great grandfather) was called Frederick David Thompson. He was born in 1868 and at one stage his employment was listed as 'overlooker'. Mitsy made a note of all these things on her handwritten family tree. It was more of a skeleton than a tree, but she was making progress.

Mitsy easily got side-tracked and today was no exception. She decided to search on Google what an overlooker did for a living. Much to her surprise, it seemed to be a supervisory role which was very often carried out in textile mills in the North of England. Feeling that she needed some confirmation of this, as Google isn't always correct, she thought, she phoned Arthur to get his opinion.

Arthur was delighted to be consulted and they talked for some twenty minutes on the phone. It occurred to Mitsy that she could easily have called round to his room, although she still wasn't sure of the visiting etiquette in the Care Home. I'm sure a phone call was best, she said to herself.

With a sigh of satisfaction, she felt she had made progress today and with that, she logged off.

17

Today's outing was by minibus to visit Fountains Abbey, with an optional excursion to Brimham Rocks for those who could tackle some walking. Mitsy knew Fountains Abbey really well, as it was only a short drive from her former home in Harrogate but she had decided, along with Arthur and one or two others, to miss the trip to Brimham Rocks in favour of a snack or light lunch in a café. They were all looking forward to spending time at the famous Cistercian monastery, which was established in the tenth century and set in peaceful and attractive grounds. Fortunately, the day dawned bright and clear, with no hint of rain.

As Mitsy waited for the arrival of their transport at the front of Appledore House, several others joined her. "There always seems to be a builder's skip in the car park here. I wonder why that is?" she commented.

"There's a simple, if sad reason," said Eva. "Whenever someone dies, they redecorate the room."

Mitsy looked a bit puzzled, so Eva explained further. "You know that Meg passed away last week?" Mitsy nodded. "Well, her family came in at the weekend, to take away her clothes and personal belongings. Then Mr P and Greg emptied out the furniture including the mattress. Most of that goes in the skip. The curtains and soft furnishings get washed or dry cleaned then they will redecorate the room this week. In a few days it's all as good as new for the next person to move in. There's quite a waiting list for Appledore House so we should be joined by a new resident within the week."

"Oh, I hadn't thought about that. It makes sense, I suppose," said Mitsy sadly.

By this stage it was well past ten-thirty which was the time that they were asked to assemble. Jo appeared to say that the minibus was on its way and if they were getting cold, they should wait indoors. Just at that moment, the vehicle and its smiling driver hove into view and like schoolchildren they all cheered.

Mitsy and Eva sat next to each other on the coach. This meant that Mitsy had to give her usual explanation of the origin of her name. She also discovered that Eva had signed up for the Brimham Rocks part of the trip and as Mitsy knew all too well, these pre-historic rock formations are most impressive. She was just starting to tell her companion all about them, when Eva interrupted – politely – to say that she was already familiar with the area in general and the Rocks in particular.

"I love Brimham Rocks and I have specified in my will that I would like my ashes to be scattered there."

"Oh, my goodness. I've just updated my will but I didn't think to include that sort of detail for my funeral arrangements," said Mitsy. "In fact, I try not to think much at all about dying!"

"I see what you mean but you know, when someone dies at Appledore House it just reminds you that none of us are here forever."

Mitsy was hoping to move the conversation on to a more optimistic frame of reference and fortunately they were approaching Fountains Abbey, so she recounted some of her happiest outings there with her husband Peter when he was on shore leave and also when Pete was little.

Mitsy was a friendly and thoughtful person but she preferred not to discuss really personal matters with a virtual stranger. It did set her thinking though, and later that morning while walking alone through the Chapel of the Nine Altars she began to reflect on her life and her beliefs. She did not go to church regularly, except for weddings and funerals, but she did wonder if a higher power (she wouldn't call it God) existed, even though she was quite certain that human life on earth developed through evolution. Somehow it seemed to her that all life, including animals, had a soul or spirit that was part of the essence of a being which continued after their death. This was why she wasn't afraid of the White Lady. She also suspected that the shadowy figures she saw at the old mill were like 'echoes' of people who had worked there in the past.

Her ponderings were cut short when she met up with Arthur, Norma and Kate who had been wandering together in a different part of the grounds. "Isn't it lovely," said Norma. "We've been to see the Water Garden! How about you?"

"I've had a very relaxing stroll around the Abbey and I was just wondering where you three were!" said Mitsy

"Isn't it time we got some lunch?" suggested Arthur.

Kate waved her map at the others. "Let's go to the Mill Café, it's not far."

Mitsy smiled to herself. It seemed that no matter where she went there were reminders of the mill. As well as this latest suggestion, there was "The Old Mill Restaurant" in Dublin where she had spent such a happy evening with her son Pete and his friends Sue and Maura.

Lunch here was a jolly affair, with sandwiches or wraps, cakes and chocolate biscuits and several pots of tea. Just as the four of them were beginning to think they may have outstayed their welcome in the café, the rest of their group appeared, all quite weary but glowing with warmth from their walk.

After another viewing of the main sights of Fountains Abbey and a tour of the gift shop, the four friends headed back to the coach park. Eventually, everyone was reassembled and the after the minibus driver had done a second headcount just to make sure he wasn't leaving anyone behind, they set off for home.

As they drove up the road towards Appledore House, Mitsy observed that a new sign had been erected in front of Park Mill. It said 'ACQUIRED BY' and then a company name in small letters. There were also two men with clipboards standing there. This was enough temptation for Mitsy and as soon as they had all dismounted the minibus, she walked over to where the men were standing. None of her friends noticed she was missing as they filed back into Appledore House.

"Err. Excuse me for being a teeny bit nosey, but can you tell me what is happening to the old Park Mill, please?"

The two men looked rather surprised at this intervention.

"You see, I live over the road at Appledore House and we're all interested to know if there's anything happening," said Mitsy with one of her innocent-looking, girlish smiles.

"Oh. Hello, my dear. The mill is going to be turned into twenty luxury apartments."

"But I thought the planning permission had been turned down?"

"Yes. It had been, but the plans were resubmitted with some changes and it's been accepted now. Do you want to have a look at them?"

"Yes, please. That's very kind of you."

"Well, we do want to get on with our new neighbours!" said the older man of the two.

They spread out the plans on the bonnet of their car and pointed out the changes. Apparently, the main planning reservations were about the availability of parking for future residents. This was to be resolved by clearing an area that was originally identified for two extra apartments.

"You see round the side of the building, here? Well that door, which used to be where the mill workers came in and out, will be the door to the private car park. These old outhouses and sheds will be knocked down and the area will be landscaped and parking spaces will be added. Here, you can see the artist's impression."

"Oh, that looks very nice," said Mitsy. "It will be a benefit to the area, rather than us looking at a derelict building. How soon will the work start?"

"Straight away!" said the other man.

"Thank you so much for your time and explanation. I shall tell my friends the good news." With that she headed back across the road and rang the doorbell to get back in.

Back in room six, Mitsy sat down to gather her thoughts. However, she was destined not to have much time to relax. First, Arthur phoned to tell her that his daughter Jackie was hoping to visit. He wanted the details of the Travelodge where Pete stayed, given that it was convenient for Appledore House. Mitsy was happy to help.

Barely had she put the phone down when it rang again. It was Pete. "Did you get my email, Mum?"

Whatever was Pete phoning for? "No, Pete. I've been out most of the day and only just got back to my room. Is there something wrong?"

"Far from it. We have got a buyer for the house and they want to proceed straight away. The estate agent tells me they are cash buyers, so it's all systems go. I did most of the preparatory work when I was over last but I need to go to the house as soon as possible to oversee the furniture removal. So, I'll be coming over there and calling in to see you, as soon as I get back from this meeting in Finland."

"That's great news Pete. Message me as soon as you know when you'll be here. As it happens, I've just given my friend Arthur the details of where you stay because his daughter Jackie will be visiting. I've been to Fountains Abbey today. It was a lovely outing. Anyway, I must stop nattering. Love you!"

"Love you too Mum. See you soon!"

Mitsy sighed. It was great to see more of Pete at the moment, but of course once all the house business was done, they would probably revert to seeing each other three or four times a year.

Before she had time to check the email that Pete had already told her about, there was a knock at the door. Mitsy sighed again. She actually wanted a little time to herself. It was good to go out and talk to lots of people, but sometimes one just needs a bit of headspace.

It was Kate. "I saw you chatting up those men! What was that about?"

"Come in Kate and I'll tell you," said Mitsy.

Kate sat down and Mitsy gave her a brief summary of the conversation with the developers. She didn't really want to say more until she had thought it through herself.

"Did you enjoy Fountains Abbey?"

"Oh yes. It was just what we needed; a change of scene. By the way, are you coming to the singing tomorrow?"

Mitsy had somehow failed to register that there was a singing group coming up and in fact she must have seemed to be quite confused when she told Kate that she wasn't too keen on singing as she couldn't hold a note. It transpired that it would be a visiting choir calling in to sing for them. Plenty of the residents loved singing but Mitsy found that sort of thing rather patronising so she struggled to find a polite way of declining the invitation.

"Probably not, Kate. I'll see how things are tomorrow."

With that, Kate departed, giving her friend a little hug as she went. Well, she seems to have accepted her family situation anyway, thought Mitsy.

The issues running through Mitsy's mind were quite simple really and this was what she put in her notebook:

- how soon will building works start at Park Mill?
- will the people that I've been watching disappear?
- how do I get just one more visit?
- could I use the workers' side door?
- how to get out of here and back indoors safely?

She didn't have answers to these but in any case, there was another knock at the door. Mitsy closed her notebook and heaved a really heavy sigh this time.

It was Joyce, on her evening medication round.

"Hello Mitsy. How are you doing?"

“I’m fine, thank you Joyce. I’m rather tired as it’s been a full day.”

“Are these painkillers working alright for you?”

“Oh yes. I prefer not to take them unless I need them. I think after so much walking today, I shall be glad of them.”

“I hope you sleep better tonight then Mitsy. Goodnight.”

After Joyce left, Mitsy had an idea. She knew that Joyce came to every resident in their room at around the same time every evening. She also knew that she started her room calls downstairs at the far end of the house; in other words, room six. After the ground floor, she went up in the lift and completed the process for upstairs. So…if she sneaked out via the front door or the door behind the kitchen as soon as Joyce had been to see her, she would have at least twenty minutes, maybe even half an hour, to make her exploration of the mill.

She stood for some time at the small window but there was no sign of the flickering lights across the road. Maybe it’s stopped already, she thought.

18

Mitsy loved flowers. She especially loved wild flowers. Primroses, violets, celandines and wild garlic all cheered her up, even when it was raining. The sky was grey and the heavens opened not long after breakfast so, although she hadn't intended to, she went along to the lounge where a demonstration of flower arranging was taking place. She had to give the staff of Appledore House credit for setting up so many activities to inspire the imagination of their residents. If I was still living on my own in Harrogate I would be looking out of the windows and wondering what I could do to pass the time of day once all the household chores were done, she thought.

She was also delighted to see that the flower arranger was a man. It pleased her when there were opportunities to challenge people's stereotypes. Of course, there was absolutely no reason why flower arranging should be the purview solely of women. Dave was also pleased to see that the room was filling up and he smiled at Mitsy who took a seat at the front of the room.

That's another thing, thought Mitsy. Why do people tend to head towards the back row? Are they afraid of being asked something? Or learning something? She called it 'naughty children syndrome' in her head and she couldn't resist turning around to see who was sitting in the back row. As she half expected, Lucy was there, along with a couple of other ladies and the three of them were whispering behind their hands.

Dave did ask a few questions, but these were general and not directed at anyone. He just wanted to assess their level of knowledge and experience before he launched into his demonstration.

It was all very interesting and his displays at various levels of complexity were delightful. Mitsy asked him if there was anything that she could have done to preserve the red roses picked from her garden a few weeks ago. They had been lovely at the time but began to drop their petals after a week. Dave helpfully explained about cutting the woody stems on the diagonal, removing any leaves or growth below the water line, refreshing the water, re-cutting them after six days and giving the water a boost by adding soda water or something fizzy.

At the end of the demonstration, Mrs P came into the room to say thank you and everyone applauded Dave politely. Dave had three completed floral displays that he had created as part of the presentation and he kindly handed them to the three people who, in his opinion, had contributed positively to the demonstration. Of course, he didn't say that, as he appeared to hand them out randomly but somehow the recipients, one of whom was Mitsy, knew from Dave's barely perceptible wink, that they had been appreciated. Mitsy noticed that Dave had included a red rose in her vase.

When she got back to her room, Mitsy was surprised to find a message on her phone and an email from Pete.

> Hi Mum! I'm in Bradford! Sorry I couldn't let you know before but I managed to get a late flight direct from Helsinki last night. I've already been over to the house and presided over the furniture removal. All went well. I'll phone later and drop in to see you if I can but it might have to be a quick one. Love Pete xxx

All this apparently sudden activity was disconcerting for Mitsy. She knew her former home had to be sorted out finally but she didn't feel prepared for it today. It was such a shame, as she had really enjoyed the flower arranging demonstration and had felt quite calm and collected when she left.

Thankfully, the rain had stopped so she decided to go for a quiet and solitary walk for twenty minutes in order to rebalance her equilibrium. She noticed that the 'Acquired by' sign outside the Mill had been joined by a further sign announcing the development work, some examples of the interior of the apartments and the artist's impression of the whole site once completed. By the time she had reached the post office and bought some stamps for her next letter to Sky, she had rationalised her feelings.

Just as her old home was almost a closed book to her now, a stage in her life that was over, in the same manner her fascination with Park Mill and its history was also moving into a new chapter. She walked back home, to Appledore House, in a reflective state of mind.

Indoors, a new message was waiting for her from Pete. He was hoping to call in to see his mother around four o'clock, hopefully for a couple of hours.

19

A gentle tap on the door just before four o'clock and Mitsy was amazed to see two people standing there. "Mum, this is Jackie. She's come to see her father. I believe Arthur is a friend of yours?"

Mitsy may have left her mouth open a second too long but she quickly smiled a greeting.

"I've just come up from London to see Dad and when I met Pete in the hotel earlier, he kindly offered to give me a lift. We discovered we had a connection with Appledore House just by chance! It's very good to meet you Mrs Howard. Dad has settled in very nicely, thanks to your kindness towards him."

Jackie smiled at Mitsy, nodded towards Pete then, "See you later, Pete" as if they had known each other for years.

"Come in. Come in and tell me all your news," said Mitsy, nodding towards the cardboard box that Pete was carrying. "What's that?"

Pete refused to say anything until he was actually in his mother's room and sitting down.

"Right. First of all, the house clearance went like a dream. It only took a couple of hours and the men were very careful with everything. I feel confident most of the furniture will go to good homes where the new owners will value it and will appreciate the care you have taken in looking after it over the years. The house clearance company will put some money into my account electronically and in due course I will pass it on to you."

This was more or less what Mitsy was expecting. "Pete, dear. I'd rather you keep the money; you've done all the organisation and given up your time to sort it out. I don't need it."

"Well, thank you Mum, if you say so. OK so, next bit of news, is that the house sale is going through just nicely. It will take time and at the moment the buyers are waiting for their surveyor's report. I suppose they might try to knock down the price on the basis of the findings. On the other hand, I know the couple are in rented accommodation and keen to get moved in before school term starts as the husband is starting a new job as deputy head teacher nearby."

Again, Mitsy nodded. Frankly she couldn't care less as long as the sale went through now. Everything to do with the house seemed a long way in the past.

"Right. This is the exciting bit! I did a last check round the house before the removers arrived and I found this box in the dark tucked right at the back of the cupboard under the stairs. I don't know how much you know about what grandad did when they first lived in the house?"

"He wrote music, played a bit and he used to go down to London a lot, I believe."

"What I found in this box is really interesting. At that time, probably when you were children, music used to be recorded live and captured on a wax master disk. That was then transferred to a metal electroform and to make multiple copies they stamped it with some sort of shellac material. That was in the pre-vinyl days, which started in the early 1950s. So, what I'm showing you here are some of grandad's early recordings."

They both looked through the box although nothing actually listed David Thompson on it until they got to the bottom, where there were several reel-to-reel cassettes with his name on.

"I believe when he went to London, he used to go to Alexandra Palace, playing his original score with an orchestra and that was where the recordings were made."

"Now you see, I'm not very well-informed about this sort of thing but it turns out that Jackie, Arthur's daughter, is somewhat of an expert! She works at the BFI (British Film

Institute) Archive in North London, well Berkhamsted in Hertfordshire to be precise. She thinks they will have recordings of that film music that grandad was supposed to have written."

"It wasn't 'supposed' Pete, he did write it," rejoined Mitsy, "although I just cannot remember the name of the film. He wrote the music for some radio programmes too."

"Well, I'm meeting up with Jackie later and, if you agree, she will take these precious originals back to work with her where they can properly research what they are, when and where they were produced. It might mean that we will ultimately donate them to the BFI Archive. How do you feel about that?"

Mitsy reassured Pete that she was happy for Jackie and her colleagues to take them. She was also privately rather intrigued how quickly this friendship had sprung up between her son and Arthur's daughter. She convinced herself that it was, probably, no more than a happy coincidence that they had met.

"So, is everything all right then?" said Pete. "Have you signed the new will yet?"

"No. I haven't seen it. Shall I phone Mrs Reed the solicitor?"

Pete said he would chase it up once he got back to Dublin. Mitsy thought she was perfectly capable of phoning herself but decided not to argue.

They sat comfortably together for half an hour or so. Mitsy was on the verge of telling him what she had discovered about his great-grandfather and what was happening at Park Mill, but decided in the end that it would be wisest to keep that to herself for now.

She entertained Pete by recounting the things they had made in the craft group and describing the outings. She may have exaggerated just a little bit, but only to make him laugh.

Looking at his watch, “Well, I shall pop upstairs to see if Jackie is ready, as I’m taking her back to the hotel. I thought we might have dinner together this evening. Oh, and I must take that box with me. You take care Mum. Love you!” and with that he dashed off.

It was years since she had seen Pete so animated.

20

After a remarkably good night's sleep, Mitsy was ready to face the day. She had made another appointment with the local hairdresser because she had been too busy to look into alternatives. However, she had promised herself she would try to give a more explicit description of what she wanted done to her hair this time.

Norma had asked if she could walk with her as far as the salon, so that she had a bit of exercise and the opportunity to size up the hairdresser and her clientele in order to decide whether to take the plunge herself. She was still feeling the cold, even though it was growing milder by the day.

Mitsy enjoyed chatting with Norma and so often discovered something new that she had not been aware of previously. Today was no different.

"I am really appreciating having all my clothes washed and ironed at Appledore House," said Mitsy. "Do you know, they even sewed a missing button on my blouse yesterday!"

"I can't say I noticed," said Norma. "I've been used to having the washing done for me most of my life. We always had a laundry boy."

"Oh. Isn't that unacceptable these days – I mean, using them like a slave?"

"Well. It's not quite like that Mitsy. Often, it's the only way the boys can earn some money. You have to bear in mind that with the temperatures being what they are, we need a complete change of clothes every day, if not more frequently, so there's a lot to do. I can see you might think it strange, but if you think about the British habit of paying schoolgirls to babysit their children it is not so very different."

"Yes, I see. I do love learning about these things. Are you still missing your home, Norma?"

Norma thought for a moment then said, "Not as much as I feared. I was actually quite lonely in Port Elizabeth although I didn't realise it at the time."

They approached the hair salon and Norma looked at the window displays, consulted the price list and nodded. "This will do for now. I'll come in with you and make an appointment then I will wander back at my own pace."

Mitsy had cleverly done an online search of Hair magazine and taken a screenshot of her preferred style. She showed this to the hairdresser who seemed to think she could recreate the cut on Mitsy. As it turned out, it was not too bad at all and Mitsy hurried back to Appledore House with a spring in her step. She had absolutely no reason whatsoever to hurry, but somehow it was a habit that she had not yet discarded now that so many things were being done for her.

The afternoon was spent dealing with what she called 'admin'. There was a large brown envelope in the post, which was the draft of her new will. This meant she had to email Pete to tell him he didn't need to contact the solicitors. Then she had to ascertain whether Mr P would be willing both to witness her will, as well as taking her over to Harrogate to conclude the matter. Then she had to confirm to the solicitor, Mrs Reed, that she was happy with the wording and to book an appointment for herself and Mr P at the solicitor's office. By the time she had spent twenty minutes looking for Mr P, who wasn't actually hiding down the garden, but who was difficult to track down amongst the shrubs, it was almost time for dinner.

Mitsy observed to herself that she had enjoyed every single meal since arriving at Appledore House. Today's was no exception as it was steak and kidney pie. The puff pastry was light and flaky, the meat was tender and smothered in tasty gravy. The modest portion of fresh mixed vegetables was just enough to provide contrast without her feeling too full by the end of the meal. For once she declined the dessert as she thought she had eaten enough and she was being careful not to put on weight, which she suspected would be all too easy to do here. Back in her room, Mitsy watched a natural history programme on the television. As night fell, she couldn't resist a quick peep across the road. She wasn't surprised to see the lights on inside the Mill and shadows moving past the windows.

At that moment, Joyce tapped on the door to room six. "Hello Mitsy. Excuse me being in a bit of a rush this evening as I've got an important appointment immediately after I've done the meds round!"

Mitsy raised her eyebrows in question. "It's my granddaughters' ballet show and I promised not to be late."

"Have fun then Joyce. Thank you."

Even as she was saying these words and closing the door behind Joyce, a thought entered her mind. This would be an ideal opportunity to check out the Mill. 'I can nip out of the main door while Joyce is giving out the medication to the residents upstairs and after a carefully timed visit to the mill across the road, I can creep back in via the kitchen door,' she thought.

Patting her coat pockets to check that she had a torch in one, her mobile phone in the other and a scarf wrapped across her face against the night air, Mitsy locked her room door very quietly behind her, slipping the key in her trouser pocket.

She was really excited and aware that with the developers starting work soon, it would probably be the last chance to learn more about the happenings at Park Mill.

As she tip-toed past Norma's room, she could hear Joyce's voice so she strode along with some urgency, around the corner and directly ahead to the front door of the Home. She gritted her teeth as she closed the door behind her with a click, concerned lest anyone heard her exit. Outside, she walked across the gravel, trying hard not to let her footsteps scrunch until she reached the road. There was no traffic, so she was able to cross easily, checking her watch as she went.

21

Mitsy was trying very hard to remember the layout of the building from the plans that the developers had shown her. Once she was past the street lights it was extremely dark, so her torch came in handy. She knew that there was a door at the side of the building, which was previously the main entrance and exit for the workers.

By the time she had reached this, she could see some people standing by the door. Quite afraid, she walked forward, but no one seemed to notice her. She stepped up to the door and, as a woman left the building she slipped inside. Mitsy noticed that there were lights all along this corridor but they were quite feeble. She walked further into the building and just ahead of her were two women hurrying along and talking. They appeared not to see her either and as she got closer to them, she could just make out some of their whispered words:

"What's wrong with Dottie?"

"She's in the family way. Old Thompson again, I believe."

"Oh no. Poor thing. I wonder how she'll manage?"

As they entered the main area of the mill, Mitsy was suddenly deafened by the noise and almost overcome by the smell. The women took up their stations at the looms and began to handle the cotton strands, quite expertly to Mitsy's eyes. The thread ran from floor to ceiling and someone was checking the bobbins to make sure they didn't run out, she presumed.

She could now understand why the women finished their hasty conversation because speaking was out of the question here. The smell was another matter. It was a combination of heat, oil and cotton dust. Mitsy found it hard to breathe. She stood silently by the wall, observing this hive of activity.

There was so much going on that it was hard to think clearly. All she could surmise was that somehow, much as she had suspected, she had been transported back to the time when Park Mill was operating.

She could see at least a dozen women at work, and one man. She was thankful that there were no children, although she knew from her research several weeks earlier that juveniles were employed as apprentices.

The man was striding up and down and from time to time he pointed at one of the women and gestured for her to move to another work station. I suppose he's an overlooker, thought Mitsy.

He had quite a sour-looking face, a dark moustache and a mop of unruly black hair. Mitsy thought that she wouldn't want to meet his sort in a dark alley.

Suddenly there was a bit of commotion half way down the room, but Mitsy decided she should stay where she was. Even if people couldn't see her, she might get in the way.

The overlooker strode down very close to where she stood and shouted and jabbed his finger at the worker nearby. Mitsy could see her blush and shake slightly. Although Mitsy couldn't hear what was said, she could read her lips:

"I'm very sorry Mr Thompson. It won't happen again, I promise."

Suddenly, Mitsy realised she had been gone for quite a while and in any case, she wasn't really happy watching people work under these conditions. At one level it was fascinating, like watching a history lesson using virtual reality but, being the sensitive soul that she was, it was disturbing to see how people lived and worked in these days. She left the big room and quickly headed back down the long corridor that she had followed on her way in, with the cacophonous sounds and polluted air gradually receding.

There was no one near the door, so she turned the handle and left the building almost as quickly as she had arrived. The whole experience had been quite unsettling and with hindsight she wasn't sure what she had achieved apart from satisfying her curiosity.

Outside, she realised that it was raining heavily. She put her head down but before she reached the road there was a flash and a great clap of thunder. Mitsy nearly jumped out of her skin. 'That's guilty conscience for sure,' she said to herself.

Hurling herself across the road and then the gravelled parking area in front of Appledore House, Mitsy realised she was already drenched and she almost broke into a sprint round the side of the building to the secret door behind the kitchen. Turning the door handle, she discovered that it was closed. Even worse, it seemed to be locked.

By now, Mitsy had thoroughly frightened herself. 'You foolish woman. What do you think you are doing?' she said to herself.

Trying to calm herself with deep breaths as the wind blew ferociously around the Care Home, with shaking hands she dug into her pocket for her mobile phone. Thankfully it was still there.

'Well it's a good job I'd put Kate's number on speed dial,' she thought. 'Kate. Kate. Wake up and answer the phone please!'

It seemed like an age before she heard a confused voice say, "What's happening? Who is it?"

"Kate. It's me. Mitsy. I'm locked outside!"

"Outside where?"

"Kate. I'm near the front door. Can you come down and let me in?"

There was a mumbled response which Mitsy had to hope was some form of agreement.

Meanwhile, she stood at the door getting wetter and wetter. Her hair was hanging in rats' tails and she was shivering with cold and not a little fear. Mitsy knew that her behaviour had been somewhat reckless and she was already feeling embarrassed and contrite.

22

The door opened and Kate appeared in her dressing gown with a grave expression all over her face. A few steps behind stood Mrs Podsiadlo.

"Come in Mitsy," said Kate. "Are you OK?"

"Thank you very much Caitlin," said Mrs P. "I'll take over from here. Thank you for your help. Now please go straight back to bed and don't worry, you can talk to Mitsy in the morning."

Mrs P steered Kate back towards the lift. Meanwhile, she gave a serious look to Mitsy. "You, my dear, are coming upstairs with me so that we can get you dry and warmed up."

With that, she took Mitsy's freezing cold hand and led her up the grand staircase and into the Podsiadlo's apartment.

"Right. Take that soaking wet coat off and hang it over there," she directed. As Mitsy was doing as she was told, Mrs P left the room and returned carrying a clean, fluffy and warm towel.

"You can start by drying your hair carefully. There are some tissues over there. Please dry your eyes and sit down by the fire."

Mitsy shivered with cold and fear. What had she done? Would she be asked to leave Appledore House, just as she was beginning to feel settled in? The situation reminded her of her schooldays of long ago, standing outside the headmistresses' room waiting to be told off for some misdemeanour or other. Not that it happened often, but when she did manage to get into trouble it was usually because of a spectacular mishap.

Mrs Podsiadlo, in her pink candlewick dressing gown, came back into the cosy living room with a glass of something in each hand.

"Now, have you dried your hair properly?" she asked, just like Mitsy's mother did when she was a little girl.

"Right. Sit down and have a sip of this." Mitsy gratefully took a sip of the dark liquid and discovered that it was a good quality cognac. So good, in fact, that it almost took her breath away.

"First things first. Perhaps you will explain to me why you were outside, in a thunderstorm, in the middle of the night?" she sounded really severe and Mitsy started to cry again.

After blowing her nose loudly she took a deep breath and, not quite sure where to start, she began in the middle. "I wanted to see inside Park Mill before they started the building works, Mrs Podsiadlo."

"Hmm. Please call me Hannah this evening, given that the circumstances are extraordinary. So, let's try this another way. Why did you want to go to the old mill building in the middle of the night?"

"Well. Ever since I moved to live here at Appledore House, I have been bad at sleeping. No. That's not true. I have always been bad at sleeping. It's just that I could see people in the Mill at night."

Mitsy paused, as if that was all the explanation was needed.

"I see," said Mrs P, who clearly didn't see anything at all and was hoping that the confusion would be cleared up soon. She too, was quite a light sleeper and when she heard the lift operating so late, she went to investigate. Kate was half awake and in quite a state, thinking that Mitsy was in mortal danger, so Mrs P asked her just to open the door calmly and let her take over from there.

"So, you saw people in the mill at night? Was that like the ghost you said that you saw here in the house?"

Mitsy began to feel extremely uncomfortable, as if her word was being doubted. She took another sip of her brandy and the warm fluid began to calm her.

"I am sorry Mrs P. Hannah. Yes. I did see shadows of people moving around over the road in the mill. I did an internet search and found out a bit of the history of the place. It was called Park Mill and it was built in the late 19th century. It was a highly productive textile mill which brought prosperity to the area, mainly to the mill owner's family. The workers were not treated well by today's standards, I'm sad to say."

Mitsy paused to gather her thoughts, recognising that she hadn't been exactly coherent up till now.

"Anyway, I've been seeing people moving around in the building for weeks now, but only at night. One day the developers were outside and I had a chat with them. They showed me the plans and how the new apartments were going to be designed. They said the work was starting imminently."

Mitsy wisely omitted to mention that she had already sneaked out through the door behind the kitchen and implied that this excursion was her first foray across the road.

"I thought that if I was going to see who was in the Mill, I needed to do it sooner rather than later. I am very sorry that I didn't really think about the consequences."

"Indeed, you didn't. I dread to think what would have happened if you had tripped on a loose floorboard or something. You could have been trapped there. Did Caitlin know where you were?"

Mitsy realised that she needed to be careful if she wasn't to implicate her friend.

"Oh no. Kate had no idea. I'm just thankful that I had my phone with me and I was able to wake her up."

"And now we have an explanation, of sorts, as to why you were out of doors and going for a walk in the dead of night in a thunderstorm, was the risk worth it Mitsy?"

Mitsy was in fact asking herself the same question, much as she was trying to decide how to answer. Should she tell Mrs P exactly what she saw, or would she think that she had 'lost her marbles'?

Fortunately, and very much in the nick of time, Mr Podsiadlo tapped on the door of his own living room to ask if everything was all right.

"Yes, thank you Antoni. I think we are just about finished here. Mitsy, it's time you went off to bed and I shall arrange for you to have breakfast in your room tomorrow. Well, today, as it is already tomorrow. Try to get some sleep and put this behind you."

"Thank you very much. I am sorry for the trouble I've caused and I promise never to do anything like this again," said Mitsy as she scooped up her coat which was still soaking wet.

23

Whether it was the relief of being rescued, the warmth of Mrs P's electric fire, the cognac or the comfort of her own bed, but Mitsy slept like the proverbial log and woke up feeling more refreshed than she had done for a long time.

Breakfast in her room also seemed like quite a treat and absolved her from any early morning explanations.

By ten-thirty she had just put on her purple dress, a little make-up and a spritz of her favourite perfume when there was a gentle tap on the door. It was Mrs P. "How are you feeling this morning, Mitsy?"

"Thank you, Mrs P, I am feeling just fine. Can I apologise again for my thoughtless behaviour last night? I assure you it won't happen again."

"No more apologies necessary Mitsy. I just wanted to be sure you were feeling better."

"Thank you. I don't think I have told you properly how happy I am here at Appledore House. I could never have imagined how comfortable I could be - but I am!"

"I'm pleased to hear it. Now I expect you have some explaining to do to Caitlin. I suggested she shouldn't disturb you until elevenses when Jo will be bringing two mugs of coffee to your room."

"Thank you. That will be lovely."

Mitsy had barely closed the door to Mrs P when her phone rang. It was Arthur. "Now then, Mitsy. I'm not being nosey but I just wanted to make sure that you are alright. There was a bit of chatter over the breakfast table suggesting that you had gone 'walkabout' last night and I was feeling concerned for you."

"Thank you, Arthur, you are very kind and I can assure you that I'm fine. I will tell you about it privately some time when I have made sense of everything myself. In the meantime, I would appreciate it if you said nothing to stimulate the rumour mill."

Mitsy chuckled to herself silently when she realised exactly what she had said. Why did everything keep reminding her about the mill?

"Also, I just wanted to tell you my little bit of news although I suppose it is no more than gossip and rumour just between us!" he said mysteriously.

"Ooooh. Do tell," she replied.

"You see, I was telephoning my Jackie yesterday. I usually phone her once a week, or she phones me. It turns out that your Pete has just spent the weekend at my Jackie's flat in London. Jackie was very casual about it and implied that it was a business matter. She said that he had just dropped in on his way back from a meeting somewhere. I'd have thought no more about it, except that she mentioned they had been to an art gallery together, had a meal out and a walk in the park. I have to say it sounded like a proper weekend's socialising. What pleased me so much was that Jackie sounded really happy and animated. You know that she was very downhearted when her marriage broke up and it's lovely to hear her sounding happy again. What do you think?"

Mitsy realised that Arthur was quite quick to put two and two together and she didn't want him to be disappointed.

"Well. They did have a genuine reason to meet, which I'll have to explain to you another time Arthur because there's a knock at the door which is likely to be Kate. I'm delighted that Pete and Jackie are getting on well. I'll catch up with you later and thank you for phoning."

In fact, there hadn't been a knock at the door, but Mitsy just felt she needed to think a lot of things through before she spoke to Arthur again.

Kate arrived shortly after, keen to know all about Mitsy's exploits of the previous night.

Mitsy gave her roughly the same summary as she had given to Mrs P, while they drank their coffee.

Kate wasn't going to let her off so easily though. "So…. What did you see there?"

"Well Kate, in some ways I wish I hadn't seen it. Fundamentally, I saw the mill as it was being run as a textile mill in the late 19th century. The conditions were appalling, the smells, the dust and the deafening noise. The workers were not being treated well. It was really unpleasant."

"But what did they think of you? Surely it was strange to have someone from the 21st century amongst them?"

"That was what was odd. No one seemed to see me or be aware of me. I just stood and watched."

"And why did you phone me in the middle of the night?"

"Oh Kate. I am really sorry about that. I do apologise and I will never do anything like that again. You see, I left by the front door while Joyce was doing the evening medication round. All was well at that stage and I thought I'd come back in by the 'secret' door behind the kitchen. Anyway, I probably lost track of time because I suddenly realised I'd been gone too long. I left the mill quickly, only to discover we were in the middle of a massive thunderstorm. The rain was pelting down and the thunder and lightning were quite impressive – well, it would have been impressive to anyone who was safe and dry indoors! I hurried back, only to find that the secret door was closed and locked. I got drenched trying to figure out how to get back in. Eventually I concluded that you were my only hope. Thank goodness I had my phone with me!"

"I was deep asleep so it took me a while to grasp what was happening. Was Mrs P very cross?"

"Actually, she was really kind once she had told me off good and proper. I think when you got in the lift to come down to let me in, the clanking sounds must have woken her. She made sure I didn't get chilled and of course she wanted to know what it was all about. Kate, I didn't tell her I saw any people in there – you won't tell anyone will you, please?"

Kate hugged her friend and assured her that she wouldn't say anything. "I was only concerned that you were OK, Mitsy. When Mrs P sent me back to bed last night, I couldn't sleep for worrying about you."

"I am fine, thank you. Something that has puzzled me though, is that while I was there, I overheard two women talking and they had some unpleasant things to say about the supervisor. It seems he had got a girl called Dottie pregnant and from the way it was discussed I don't think she was the first one. A bit later, the supervisor (who was called an overlooker in those days), shouted at another lady worker and she apologised to him by name."

"Well, you said it was an unpleasant environment, Mitsy, so it's not that surprising."

"Yes, but she called him Mr Thompson!!"

"So?"

"When I was searching my family tree, I discovered a Frederick Thompson. He was from this area and he was an overlooker. It's a bit of a coincidence, isn't it? He wasn't very nice. I'm not sure I want him to be my ancestor."

"Oh Mitsy. Whilst I understand that you find this ancestry search fascinating, you know from my situation that one doesn't always find good news or happy stories. I think your advice to me at the time is valid here. Probably best to leave it alone."

The two women sat watching Greg busy at work in the garden and the antics of some birds collecting twigs for their nests, then Kate said, "Right Mitsy. I've satisfied myself that you are none the worse for your escapade, so I shall leave you in peace. I hope you will give up your adventures for now! By the way, have you looked out of your window this morning?"

Mitsy was a bit puzzled as they had been looking out of the window for at least ten minutes, until it occurred to her that Kate meant the other one.

Jumping up, the pair of them dashed over to the window that looked out at the mill. There, for all to see, was a team of men erecting a high fence around Park Mill. It was solid, so that people would not be able to see inside, while the works were being carried out.

"You were right on one thing, Mitsy. If you hadn't visited the mill last night you would have missed the opportunity all together."

24

Before going to dinner that evening, Mitsy had been frightened that all the other residents would want to question her about the previous night. Whilst Kate was fully aware and would keep it secret and Arthur may have had some inkling of what it was about, everyone else would be agog with curiosity. She decided that she would pretend that it was an episode of sleepwalking and would keep her fingers crossed that no one challenged her.

As it turned out, anything to do with the night before was entirely forgotten because of the latest happenings. Antoni Podsiadlo had been taken ill that afternoon and had been rushed to the Bradford Royal Infirmary with a suspected stroke.

Mitsy was struck with remorse. Maybe if he hadn't had a disturbed night because of her antics, this wouldn't have happened.

The meal was a sober affair as all the staff had been affected; they were fond of Mr P and really upset. The dinner table conversation amongst the residents was all about how kind and helpful Mr P had been. Mitsy didn't like the way they were talking about him in the past tense; at this stage no one knew if he would recover. However, she thought it best to keep a very low profile and say nothing.

Julie and Sam had been on kitchen duty and had done their best to make a pleasant meal. The chicken curry was tasty enough and the rice had been cooked to perfection, neither hard nor too soft. Dessert was bakewell tart and again, Sam's efforts were rewarded with praise.

As soon as she had finished her dessert, Mitsy rose from the table and Arthur appeared by her side. "May I speak with you, Mitsy?" he asked.

"By all means, Arthur. Would you like to come to my room where we can talk?"

The two walked together along the corridor without speaking, until they were inside room six.

"Sorry to nab you like that Mitsy, but I really wanted to be sure for myself how you are."

Mitsy smiled at Arthur's solicitude. It's a long, long time since anyone has looked after me like that, she thought. Apart from Pete, that is.

"Let's sit down, Arthur. I don't have much to offer you to drink, but I do have a bottle of Stones ginger wine?"

"That would be lovely thank you. I haven't got around to offering hospitality in my room yet. So, what actually happened?" said Arthur, straight to the point.

They clinked glasses before Mitsy began her explanation.

"As you know, Arthur, I have been interested in the derelict mill across the road. I discovered from the internet and also the local paper that it was a busy textile mill, back in the late 19th century and has recently been sold for development into luxury apartments. I have also been puzzled by the fact that most nights, but not always, I have been able to see dim lights on inside the building and shadows which looked like people moving."

Mitsy paused to take a sip of her ginger wine and a deep breath before she continued.

"I had a sneaky look through the windows one night when Kate helped me leave the building. I came back in, after my brief peep, via a secret door at the side of Appledore House which only the staff knew about."

Arthur raised his eyebrows but decided it was best not to interrupt Mitsy's flow of conversation.

"Then I spoke to the developers who were out in the road checking arrangements for the work - it was after we got back from our outing to Fountains Abbey - and they showed me the recently agreed plans for Park Mill. They said the building work was starting imminently."

"Well, I now realise I didn't think things through properly but I went out last night and actually walked over to the mill and then I went inside the building. It was a revelation because they were operating exactly as I imagined they would have been in the past. I saw the bobbins loaded with cotton, the heavy machines and the workers. It was noisy, dirty and back-breaking work."

"Didn't they wonder who you were or what you were doing there?" asked Arthur.

"It's funny as that's exactly what Kate asked. Arthur, I've told no one except you and Kate, you won't tell anyone else, will you?"

Arthur assured Mitsy that he would keep her story confidential.

"So, anyway, no one noticed I was there. They kind of looked through me."

"I saw and heard things that I didn't expect and then I realised I had been gone a long time and came home. Except there was a massive thunderstorm, I got drenched and I was locked out!"

"Oh, Mitsy. You really should be more careful," said Arthur. "How did you get back in?"

"I had to phone Kate. She opened the door but Mrs P was there too. I got a right telling off, I must say. I'm so worried because I must have woken Mr P and now he's been taken ill. It's my fault."

Mitsy was close to tears so Arthur got up to put his arm round her in a reassuring hug. "Now, I'm sure that's just an unfortunate coincidence Mitsy and you mustn't worry about that."

"It's not the only coincidence, Arthur. In the mill, the man who was the supervisor was called Mr Thompson and he was nasty and got girls pregnant and on my internet search I found that on my dad's side of the family there was a man with the same surname and he was an overlooker in Bradford too."

Arthur smiled wryly. "Look, that's the least of your concerns. I'm sure there were many overlookers called that in the mills round here. Thompson is a local name."

Mitsy sighed. "Mrs P was very kind to me once she'd told me off. I really shouldn't have been meddling in something I don't understand."

"If you want my opinion, which you didn't ask for I know, it's time you took a break from your ancestry searching and your unaccompanied visits to old buildings!"

Mitsy looked sadly at Arthur. "But it's my hobby!"

"Couldn't you find a different one, Mitsy?"

She sighed again. "Well, I suppose so. I always planned to write a book when I retired. Maybe I could do that now…"

Part II

One Year Later

Her day had started off with a number of happy surprises, beginning with the delivery of several birthday cards from family and friends, which was followed by the arrival of a beautiful bouquet of a dozen yellow roses sent by Pete via the local florist. Mitsy did so appreciate the effort made by her son to remember her birthday and other special days. No matter where he was in the world, he didn't forget his mother.

She dressed with care, as she always did, on the basis that once an older person lets their appearance slip, it was invariably a downward slope into downright sloppiness. Today was no exception and she got pleasure from wearing the bright cerise dress that she had bought on a shopping trip to Dublin last year, a matching navy jacket with pink piping round the collar and a pretty scarf tied neatly at her neck. She even wore earrings, even though putting them on had taken ten minutes and quite a lot of cursing under her breath!

Meeting Arthur by the front door for their weekly outing to the Standsfield Arms, Mitsy was somewhat taken aback to find that she was being carefully re-directed into the lounge, where virtually everyone from Appledore House was assembled.

She looked around the room and thought how lovely it was that her friends had gone to the trouble of organising a birthday party for her. She didn't remember telling anyone other than Arthur that it would be her 80th today, so it was a genuine surprise. She smiled to think of all the friends she had made since moving in.

Dear Norma, her next-door neighbour, was there. She hadn't lost her South African accent but she had more or less adjusted to the cooler Yorkshire climate. She was great company for outings or just sitting with at mealtimes. Since the first knitting group they had attended, Norma had diligently knitted square after square for the blankets to be sewn together by Jeannie. Family members of other residents even brought in spare wool for her. Mitsy admired her dedication but still couldn't understand the appeal of the craft herself.

The twins, Mandy and Anne, were always entertaining. They had been at Appledore House for several months now and, in spite of their age, were still up to playing pranks on each other. The pair had never married, although for much of their lives they had gone their separate ways, so it was rather a bonus when Mandy decided she didn't want to live alone anymore that Anne agreed to move in too. Anne's room was on the ground floor, because she had some mobility problems and Mandy was upstairs. They were not identical twins, but they did look very alike.

Mandy had been able to take over Eva's old room, which was just what she wanted. Sadly, Eva had passed away in her sleep a few months ago. Mitsy missed her gentle presence but was pleased to discover that her ashes had been taken to Brimham Rocks by her niece, as she had requested.

As she glanced round the room, Mitsy saw that virtually all the residents and most of the staff were there. Lucy hadn't changed much and was contributing to the party atmosphere by telling jokes. As Mitsy suspected she would not be especially amused by them, she stayed the other side of the room and just smiled and nodded.

One of the significant changes during the past year was that Hannah and Antoni Podsiadlo had finally retired from the running of the Home. Antoni had recovered from his stroke, after some timely intervention by the paramedics followed by physiotherapy. Hannah was beginning to show a few signs of early stage dementia so it seemed a good time to take it easy after all those years of caring for others. Maggie had been appointed as Matron and Greg took on all the gardening and house maintenance, assisted by his son Alan. Mr and Mrs P rarely came down from their rooms, so Mitsy was especially appreciative of their appearance today.

Raymond, her neighbour, smiled across the room as he tipped an imaginary hat to her. He had at last started to come 'out of his shell' and was even to be found at breakfast most days. He remained relatively quiet and courteous and all the newcomers loved him.

Then there was Kate, smiling broadly. She was, and always would be, Mitsy's best friend. Apart from her role in Mitsy's escapades, they both knew things about each other that no one else knew, which probably had a played a part in cementing the friendship. She had fully accepted the information that Mitsy had revealed about her parentage some twelve months ago and the subject was rarely mentioned again.

Arthur had become a reliable and special friend too. Every Wednesday lunchtime, Mitsy and Arthur made the short walk up the road to the Standsfield Arms for something to eat and a drink. They had become more adventurous over time because, although the ploughman's lunch was delicious 'well, we don't want to get stuck in a rut, do we?' said Mitsy. Peter the dog was usually in front of the fire before they arrived these days, except in the warmer weather when they sometimes sat in the beer garden.

This was how Arthur was able to set up the birthday get together because Mitsy just thought they were going out for their usual Wednesday lunch. Everyone was invited and only a few residents were unable to be there for one reason or other.

Among the staff who were there, some of whom were not on duty but had called in anyway, were Maggie, Sally, Julie, Jo, Joyce, Ruth, and young Sam. Greg could not be persuaded to come in from the garden as he was not comfortable with anything remotely formal, much as he was fond of Mitsy.

Arthur tapped a spoon on the side of a glass to get everyone's attention. "Hello, everybody. I'm sure you don't need me to remind you that it is Mitsy's birthday today. She won't tell me how old she is and I'm too much of a gent to ask, so we won't be giving her the bumps!" Mitsy smiled because of course Arthur knew exactly how old she was. "In a few minutes we will ask her to cut the birthday cake, but in the meantime please raise your glasses to wish Mitsy many happy returns along with health, wealth and everything she might wish for!"

Everyone clinked glasses and chorused their good wishes. There was a lull in the conversation and although she hadn't had a chance to think it through at all, Mitsy found herself making an impromptu speech.

"Thank you, Arthur and all my dear friends. What a lovely surprise. Little did I think, some eighteen months ago, how happy and contented I would be living here at Appledore House. To be honest, I was really quite nervous to make such a big change in my life, having lived in my home in Harrogate for more than seventy years! This place, and all the people here - that's staff and residents – have been a joy to know and I do hope we all have many more happy years together."

She sat down to lots of applause and Arthur appeared with a large knife with which to cut the cake. Of course, he knew she wouldn't be able to cut it herself, given what she liked to call 'my badly behaved hands', so as soon as everyone turned back to their conversations, Arthur discretely attempted the task himself.

After the party, Mitsy spent almost an hour in the garden, peacefully watching the birds and talking to Greg. She may well have delayed his gardening plans, but like most of the other staff members he believed that conversation with the residents was almost as important as getting jobs done. The pruning would wait for another day.

26

Thursday dawned bright and clear, so Mitsy decided she would get what she called her ‘admin’ done in the morning and perhaps go for a short walk in the afternoon.

First, she wrote a short note to thank Pete for the beautiful flowers and to tell him about her surprise birthday party. She actually wasn’t sure which country he was in, but he always managed to pick up his emails.

Then she accessed her online bank account. After the house was sold last year, and all the solicitor’s fees and taxes paid, Pete had deposited a considerable sum of money in savings for Mitsy. They had worked out how much was needed for her monthly payment to Appledore House over the year, and how much she would need for spending money for twelve months. Pete had also added a little more for any contingency such as his mother’s laptop expiring. That sum was then transferred to Mitsy’s account so that she could manage her finances herself.

Once a month, Mitsy checked that the Appledore House payment had gone through. Of course, it always did but she preferred to check herself. Then she calculated how many things she had bought online and deducted the total from her monthly spending budget.

It wasn’t exactly a time-consuming task but it was good practice, she thought, to keep her mind active. She scanned back over the past twelve months, almost as part of her 80th birthday reflections. She could see when she’d had that rather expensive shopping trip to Dublin; it was lovely to see Pete, although they didn’t have the Dublin Racing Festival to go to that time. She could also see when she had cancelled her subscription to that ancestry website, not long after her Park Mill adventure.

She closed the banking page down, but the task had given her pause for thought. It still troubled her that her forebears could have been associated with the mill opposite. Mitsy tried to put it to the back of her mind, as the lunch bell rang.

Sitting next to Anne during lunch, Mitsy asked her what she enjoyed doing in her leisure time. "Now that's a sore topic!" she said and for an instant Misty wished she hadn't asked the question. "You see, I used to spend almost all of my spare time exercising. I ran a ballet class and I attended a friend's yoga sessions, as well as going swimming once a week. Then, really quite suddenly, I realised that my hips and knees didn't want to do those things anymore."

"I'm sorry," said Mitsy, "that must be both disappointing and frustrating?"

"Well, I carried on for a while but everything got too painful."

They sat in silence pondering the unkindness of ageing.

"I do have a new hobby though!" exclaimed Anne, as if she had just thought of it. "I'm into photography now. I can see so many interesting things from my ground floor room so I'm teaching myself to capture shots of birds, when they don't fly off, and flowers when they do."

"Oh," said Mitsy. "You could come to my room if you like, as it looks out directly into the garden. You could watch the birds on the feeder I've put outside my window."

Anne smiled her thanks and said she would enjoy that, maybe some time next week.

Lunch was macaroni cheese and as soon as she had finished hers, Mitsy left the dining room with a new resolve to revitalise her family tree.

Back in room six, in front of her laptop, she did a quick search to see if there were any other websites offering similar access to the ancestry one that she had used before. She was delighted to find several and picked one that offered the first month free of charge. She signed up, which involved agreeing to pay a modest amount each month. She could see that it was possible to cancel the arrangement before the end of the first four weeks, which appealed to her just in case she decided not to do much more searching into the family tree.

Next, she looked for the notebook she had been using which was tucked away on a bookshelf. She wasn't terribly impressed by the notes she had made previously. Hmmm. I didn't really get far last time, she said to herself. I shall try to be more focussed today. She began with checking her father's details and not surprisingly, given that she already knew them, was able to confirm quite quickly when David Thompson, musician, was born and when he died. She was also happy to find the date when David and Iris were married, although she didn't really remember her parents celebrating their anniversaries the way she and Peter did.

Then she went back to her dad's birth certificate and found that his father was called Herbert and his mother Alice. Herbert was shown as a toolmaker although Mitsy was unable to find out what industry he worked in.

Mitsy was quite weary by this stage, so she decided that some fresh air would help her to concentrate. The walk to the woods that she and Kate first took, so many months ago, immediately came to mind.

Out in the main road, she was able to see that the development work at Park Mill, was almost finished. A large sign heralded the opening of the show home next week, along with claims that several apartments had already been sold. I shall be pleased when they take that ugly fencing down so we can see the façade again, she thought to herself.

The short walk did indeed revive her spirits. She had picked some wild garlic which she hoped might be useful for the kitchen staff. The pretty white flowers were attractive, even if they only used them for garnish. Back home, when she rang the doorbell, Maggie opened the door and smiled to see that some colour had returned to Mitsy's cheeks.

Back at her desk, Mitsy addressed herself to the task with renewed vigour. Her grandfather's name was Herbert Thompson and she wanted to find out more about his father. While she had been out, the website had obligingly identified some possible leads and she worked her way slowly and carefully through the options. She found the Frederick David Thompson that she had spotted some months ago but she also found a plain Frederick Thompson. She realised that she had made an assumption that the former was accurate on the basis that the middle name of David had been handed down the male line. Checking more carefully, the dates of death did not quite tie up. Frederick Thompson, moreover, had lived and worked in Leeds. In the census data, there was no employment information at all, although Mitsy thought that he would have been middle aged at that date.

She went back again to the records for Frederick David Thompson, the overlooker who she had previously guessed was the man in charge at the mill. Again, the website came up trumps by finding some church records which could well have been his burial. Suddenly Mitsy saw what had been staring her in the face right from the outset – that this Frederick David Thompson died at the age of 24 and could not be her great grandfather, and it seemed rather unlikely that he was the overlooker at the mill either.

I suppose it was quite a popular name and I do blame myself for so quickly jumping to a conclusion, she thought.

Rather chastened by the experience, she proceeded to check out the details of the Frederick Thompson from Leeds. He appeared to have a great number of siblings, many of whom did not survive into adulthood. At this point she absolutely drew a blank and was unable to find out anything else, which was disappointing as she had hoped to discover something exciting or interesting.

Mitsy was just wondering whether to persevere when her phone rang. It was Arthur. "'Just wanted to see how you are," he said.

“I’m fine thank you Arthur. I’ve had a rather trying day working again at my family tree. I suppose one bit of good news is that the man who I thought was my great grandfather isn’t and anyway he wasn’t an overlooker at the mill.”

Arthur was not really sure what Mitsy was talking about but he did have a hazy memory that it was all rather important to his friend at the time of her escapade in the old mill.

“Oh, well I’m glad that it’s good news Mitsy. I also wondered if you have heard anything recently from your son Pete?”

“No, I haven’t. Oh! There’s an email from him. I didn’t see it earlier because I was so busy looking at the ancestry stuff. Mmm. He says he is popping over to see me on Saturday, just a quick visit en route to somewhere.”

“I just wondered because by some coincidence I had a phone call from Jackie, saying something similar, that she would be calling in on Saturday about midday on her way back from a meeting in Edinburgh.”

Mitsy smiled. “Well, I never. That is a coincidence!”

“And the other reason I was phoning you Mitsy, is that I was going to suggest that next Wednesday, we call in to look at the new apartments across the road before we have our lunchtime session at the Standsfield?”

“Would we be allowed? I mean, if we have no intention of buying one?” she giggled.

“I won’t tell them if you don’t! It’s a date then! See you soon. And don’t be spending too long working at that computer of yours while the weather is lovely.” With that he rang off, leaving Mitsy to ponder all manner of things.

27

Today's outing for the Appledore House residents was billed as a 'magical mystery tour', although Mitsy privately suspected that the minibus driver would just meander around wherever he pleased. Yes, that probably was a little unkind but as it turned out, not far off the mark.

First, they headed straight into the city centre, which was rather busy as it was full of Friday morning shoppers. Sally was with them as the responsible member of staff. She was relatively new to Bradford so the assembled group were only too happy to point out landmarks.

They bombarded her with information:

"See, that's the Alhambra! It's a beautiful building. It's a theatre and they have all sorts of plays on there. And the Christmas panto – don't forget the panto!"

Mitsy mentioned to Raymond, who was sitting next to her, that the National Museum of Photography, Film and Television was supposed to be worth a visit. She pointed it out as they drove past. "Oh look. That couple holding hands going into the museum, don't they look ever so much like my son Pete and Arthur's daughter Jackie?" She said it out loud and wondered afterwards whether people would always think of her as the woman who saw imaginary things.

As they drove round the busy streets, there was much discussion by the passengers as to which curry house was the best. Mitsy favoured the Kashmir, which is one of the oldest in the city. She and Peter used to go there quite often. The restaurant doesn't have a license to sell alcohol but you were allowed to take your own bottle in and just pay corkage.

Soon, the minibus was heading away from the city and passing through Shipley, Keighley and Ilkley. En route, the passengers were still pointing out the sights to Sally. The driver parked at the Cow and Calf Rocks viewpoint up on Ilkley Moor and everyone got out for a breath of fresh air and for some of them to take photos.

Finally, to complete their outing, the minibus took them to the market town of Otley and then back to Appledore House. All in all, it was a pleasant tour and everyone thanked the driver as they descended the vehicle.

Mitsy generally opted for these trips even though she knew the places well, because it made a change from sitting in her room. She also appreciated the fact that someone else was doing the driving.

28

Mitsy woke early on Saturday, partly because she was looking forward to seeing her son Pete, and partly because the sun was shining straight into her face. Every day, someone came to clean and dust her room in the morning and as she was right at the far end of the corridor, they usually began with room six. It helped that everyone knew she was an early riser. Today it was Sally, who had accompanied them on their outing the day before.

Sally vacuumed very efficiently and then cleaned and disinfected the bathroom before finishing off with polish on the furniture in the living area. When Mitsy first moved into Appledore House she was quite embarrassed to have someone clean for her but over time she had got used to it. Sally also changed the towels today and on Monday the bed linen would be changed too. It all went off in a big van to a laundry in the centre of Bradford and was returned three days later fresh, clean, aired and ironed.

Mitsy and Sally talked about the previous day's drive and the surprise birthday party on Wednesday. Mitsy also mentioned that her son was calling in to see her later today. These little conversations were of no real importance but, as Mitsy was astute enough to recognise, they were important in terms of a person's mental wellbeing. Had she still been living on her own, she may not have had an opportunity to talk to another person for several days on end.

As it turned out, she didn't have to wait long, as Pete arrived just in time for coffee.

They sat and chatted about all sorts of things and Pete mentioned that he would like to take Mitsy out for lunch to the Stansfield Arms. She noticed that he kept looking at his watch, which was unusual as he didn't generally worry about time. In fact, he had a tendency to be late, even when it was important. At twenty to twelve he suggested his mother should get ready to go out, so they could have a leisurely walk to the pub.

Mitsy was already wearing a smart trouser suit so she didn't see the need to change. To please Pete, she brushed her hair, put on just a little make-up and finished off with perfume.

"Will I do?" she asked, twirling in front of him.

"Yes, mother. You look lovely!"

Mitsy noticed that Pete was wearing aftershave and in fact had made quite an effort with his appearance himself.

They walked past the rental car Pete had hired and strolled comfortably together along the level path to the pub.

At the door, Patsy the landlady came out: "Ah Mr Howard, your table is in the dining room and your guests have arrived already."

Mitsy looked at Pete whose expression was annoyingly blank so she couldn't figure out what was happening.

"I know you usually eat in the bar, but I thought it would be nice to sit in the restaurant today, especially as we have guests," he said to his mum.

As they crossed the threshold of the restaurant, Mitsy was delighted to see Arthur waving to her and Jackie sitting next to her father.

"Well, fancy seeing you here!" she exclaimed, somewhat unoriginally.

Pete moved back a chair for his mother to sit down while commenting, "We have some news to share with you."

Jackie smiled at Mitsy. "Good morning, Mrs Howard. How are you today?"

Mitsy smiled and nodded, waiting for some announcement.

"We wanted to tell you both together," said Pete.

"We're getting engaged!" the happy pair chorused.

Amid the cacophony of congratulations and laughter, Patsy walked in carrying a bottle and an ice bucket. "This is on the house. When your son and your daughter booked the table, someone let slip that it was a happy occasion. We do enjoy seeing Arthur and Mitsy on Wednesdays here and the Standsfield Arms wishes everyone all the very best."

After she had left the room, with their thanks ringing in her ears, Mitsy exclaimed, "My goodness, bubbly twice in one week! I could get used to this!"

Pete opened the bottle and proposed a toast to his wife-to-be and then to their parents, thanking them for unwittingly bringing them together.

Conversation paused while they chose from the menu, with three of them choosing roast beef and Jackie going for the vegetarian option.

Once selected, Mitsy decided to cut to the chase. "So…. how did all this happen and what are your plans?"

Jackie explained that they met by chance at the Travelodge when both were visiting their parent. Of course, Mitsy and Arthur were well aware of this, but let the couple continue.

"By good chance," said Pete, "I mentioned to Jackie about grandad's recordings and it turned out that she is a specialist in this field."

"Yes," said Jackie. "It's been so interesting! Your father, Mrs Howard, was well-known in his time. He wrote the incidental music for quite a number of radio shows, although he was often not credited. One of the recordings that Pete showed me was for a comedy programme called, "You Don't Say…" and it is the only copy in existence. Of course, his music for the film "Fire Over England" was really important and was the backdrop to the action which showcased the early work of Laurence Olivier, Flora Robson, Vivien Leigh and Raymond Massey."

Pete carried on, "Anyway, I needed to see Jackie with some more of the tapes and recordings – well, actually it was a good excuse for me to see her again – and we realised how much we enjoyed each other's company."

"And how is this going to work, with one of you in London and the other in Dublin? Not wishing to pour cold water on your happiness," said Arthur, ever the practical one.

"Actually, it has worked out better than we could have hoped," said Jackie. "We have had several months of commuting back and forth to see each other, so there's been time to think it through carefully. Where I work has been having a reorganisation and I volunteered to be one of the people who works from home in future. I shall be living with Pete in Dublin for three weeks each month and I will be in my London flat for three or four days of the remaining week. This means I can meet with colleagues, collect materials and then head back to my main home with Pete the rest of the time. It also means that if Pete needs a London stop-over at any time, he can use my place."

Privately, Mitsy thought that this arrangement would prove rather expensive over time because running two homes in two busy, and expensive, cities seemed an extravagance. However, she held her tongue because they seemed so delighted to have found a solution to a long-distance relationship for now. In the future, she hoped to tactfully share some of her own experience with them both. After all, maintaining a long and happy relationship with one's partner away at sea had taken some doing as she knew all too well.

By this stage of the explanations, the meals had arrived so everyone concentrated on eating while making comments on the happy news.

The remainder of the champagne was finished off by the older couple, as Pete and Jackie had a short drive and a flight before getting home.

"Thank you both for your consideration in telling us together," said Arthur. "I don't think either of us would have been able to keep it a secret from the other."

Jackie looked at her watch, and nodded to Pete who excused himself as if he was heading to the gents. As it happened, he went to pay the bill, as discretely as possible. On his return, he smiled and said, "I suggest you two sit and have a coffee to finish off your meal, while we head for the airport. I'm sorry it's a flying visit but we both have quite a busy schedule next week."

"Oh," said Jackie. "I know what else I meant to say. First, I hope that when you next come over for a shopping trip Mrs Howard that I can join you. You can bring Dad if you like, although I'm not sure it's his scene! Also, we haven't made any wedding plans yet. Pete's proposal was all quite sudden and we wanted to tell you first."

"That sounds good to me," said Mitsy, "with one proviso. Please call me Mitsy! I shall enjoy shopping with you too."

Mitsy and Arthur kissed and hugged their offspring as the pair dashed off for the journey home.

"Well," said Mitsy to Arthur, after they had left. "I think we both had a suspicion about their developing friendship but I had no idea it had progressed this far. I'm so happy for them. I thought my Pete would remain a bachelor for the rest of his life and I do know he's quite choosy, so this is great news. I hope it works out for them."

"I'm fairly confident it will," said Arthur, "and Jackie may not have chosen so well for her first marriage but she's older and wiser now. It's great news!"

"As ever, the Standsfield has done us proud. Now let's have some coffee."

29

The early part of the week flew by, with Mitsy only going out to the post office to buy a congratulations card for Pete and Jackie. She thought it would be something for them to keep as a memento of this happy time. She asked Arthur to sign it too as she assumed, correctly, that it wouldn't have occurred to him to get a card.

Mitsy was noticing that she had far fewer sleepless nights the longer she lived at Appledore House. It may have been something to do with having fully settled in to the Care Home or just that she had fewer things to worry about now. Of course, with that very ugly high fence around the housing development, there wasn't much for her to see at night.

On Tuesday, the hated fence was taken down and a couple of trucks took the sections away. Mitsy was a little surprised that the building looked much the same as it did before the works started. Obviously, one or two important changes were in evidence, such as the sapling that had been growing out of the mill chimney had been removed and she was guessing that the structure had been capped so it didn't happen again.

She was looking forward to seeing round the interior of Park Mill with Arthur the next day. She remembered very clearly what she saw on her nocturnal visit that night a year ago and she was keen to see if she could recognise anything.

When the day arrived, she made sure to dress smartly, although she was well aware that people lived in jeans or track suits these days and no one thought any the less of them. Still, I prefer to keep up my standards, she said to herself.

Meeting up with Arthur by the front door of Appledore House, Mitsy's excitement was obvious. She was hopping from foot to foot and an enormous grin adorned her happy face. "Now then, my dear Mitsy, I don't want to raise your expectations because the new apartments may be quite a disappointment you know."

They walked across the road, with Arthur trying to keep Mitsy in check. "Stop rushing!" he admonished.

An estate agency had set up the Open House event and quite a few people were lurking outside the impressive portico for the temporary office to open.

Finally, two very smart young women in corporate navy suits appeared, unlocked the door and gestured for people to go in. One of the apartments had been fully furnished, in order to give an impression of what it would be like to live there. A corner of the spacious living room had a desk in the corner with leaflets and information sheets.

It was clear that one of the women would be taking on greeting duties and the other was there to show people round.

Arthur and Mitsy followed the crowd, looking in every room and making quiet comments to each other. What was immediately obvious was that each apartment was very modern and did not in any way reflect the age of the original building.

They exchanged glances as the guide extolled the virtues of all the integrated kitchen appliances. It was difficult to feign much interest because living at Appledore House meant that those things were someone else's worry!

The bathroom was well equipped, much like Mitsy's bathroom at Appledore House, although here it was attractively decorated with mirror glass tiles. Mitsy couldn't help wondering how that worked out when one wandered in, all bleary-eyed of a morning. Imagine seeing multiple versions of oneself undressed and half-awake!

The bedrooms were fine, all attractively colour co-ordinated. The lounge had an enormous television, again they presumed to show potential buyers what a luxury apartment could offer.

Mitsy found it difficult to see where the main room of the former mill had been, as she remembered it. There was no sign of the high ceiling or, of course, the looms, the machines or where the cotton bales stood. She concluded that much of the interior of each apartment had been pre-fabricated and installed inside the outer shell of the building.

"Excuse me," asked Mitsy, bravely, "these apartments do have parking, don't they?"

"Oh yes. Every property has a numbered space and there are parking lots for guests. The concierge will ensure that only residents park here."

Of course, that wasn't quite what Mitsy wanted to know, but she persevered: "and how do we access them?"

The young woman was all too happy to show Mitsy and Arthur the way to the corridor that led outside. "Please come back this way so that we can answer any questions that you or your husband still have."

Mitsy and Arthur grinned at each other being described as husband and wife and headed off down the corridor.

"Oh yes, this is how I remember it. All those rooms in there were the recent additions but this is the way I came in."

Soon, they were at the back door which led them out to the parking area as described. As well as the parking bays, all numbered they presumed to tie up with the apartment numbers, there was a small sitting area with an ornamental tree. "I suppose they've made the best of a small space," said Arthur.

"Do we go back in?"

"I don't think so, Mitsy. If we're not careful they will be signing us up to buy one! That is, of course, if you've seen enough?"

As they walked steadily towards the Standsfield Arms, laughing and making general observations about the modern layout of the properties, Mitsy became thoughtful.

"You know, Arthur, I could see how the building had been the mill I saw, and I recognised the shared areas like the portico entrance hall and the corridor going out to the car park, but actually I couldn't "feel" the presence of the people I saw. I cannot explain it better than that, other than to say it all felt blank and empty."

"Do you think perhaps that this visit to Park Mill has given you, what they call in modern parlance "closure"?

Misty nodded thoughtfully and recognised what a good and kind friend Arthur was.

"I've also been thinking…"

"Whoa, don't overdo the thinking Mitsy!" said Arthur playfully.

"Yes, I've been thinking that seeing the White Lady and the people working in the mill was all part of my adjustment to a major life change. I was very stressed and quite afraid of making the move to a Care Home. I think that made me hypersensitive to the emotions of others, even those who only remained in spirit form. Does that sound silly?"

"Not at all. It's only natural that we feel uncomfortable with life changes like that. I think perhaps you were seeking to find associations within your new home area. I mean, look at me, I spent hours looking into the history of Appledore House, for much the same reasons."

They arrived at the pub and Mitsy gave Arthur a hug. "Thank you for being such an understanding friend."

"My pleasure, madam," said Arthur, as he made a bow as if to an imaginary royal personage.

A small portion of fish and chips was ordered for each of them as they sat in their usual corner of the bar. Peter the dog ambled in, accepted a pat and curled himself up on the rug even thought the fire was not lit.

"So, just to conclude Arthur, I have decided not to do anymore ancestor hunting. It was a good idea after my husband died as it gave me something to focus on. It was useful for the family at the outset as it gave us evidence of our Irish heritage for Pete to settle in Dublin. I'm not sure it serves a purpose now."

"You know what I think? That programme on the telly has a lot to answer for!"

"What programme?"

"I think it's called 'Who Do You Think You Are?' They have a celebrity who is taken all over the place for example, to the USA, Ireland, Australia or Germany and they show them things about their forebears. It's quite thought-provoking and entertaining but it does give the impression that anyone can do this. In reality the BBC has a team of researchers working for months before they film the episode and only then when they have a good tale to tell!"

"Well, you could be right Arthur. Anyway, I'm leaving it alone for good!"

After they had enjoyed their fish and chips, Mitsy looked at her watch.

"It's been a lovely morning Arthur, and now I must dash because I have someone phoning me this afternoon after two-thirty. Can we head back now, if that's OK?"

Arthur was intrigued but did not like to ask about the phone call as it was probably something private like a solicitor. From what he knew of Mitsy's sister Sky, it wasn't likely to be her, he thought!

Grabbing her door key inside Appledore House, Mitsy hurried off with a friendly farewell and "See you tomorrow."

30

The next morning, three people received somewhat mysterious text messages from their friend Mitsy. All it said was:

> Please meet me in the garden at 15:00. Tea and chocolate biscuits provided! ☺

At ten to three - which was early because none of them could wait - Arthur, Norma and Kate assembled in the garden. There was a small table with a flowery table cloth and four chairs set out as if it was waiting for them. Having questioned each other on the purpose of their meeting and with no-one any the wiser, they sat down to wait.

Jo appeared with a tray of cups, saucers, a milk jug and a full teapot but she had no idea what it was all about either.

Mitsy could see her friends arrive from her bedroom window which was overlooking the garden but she wanted to wait until the moment was right. Eventually, she emerged herself, carrying a plate of biscuits.

"Well this is lovely; we should do this more often!" said Kate.

Mitsy smiled. "I'm happy with that, especially if we have tea in the garden every occasion I have a book published!!"

The group exploded with comments until Mitsy patted the air to ask them to stop.

"I'm sure you are all aware that I have been writing a book for some months. Yesterday I had a phone call from someone who I can now call 'my publisher'!"

Mitsy poured out the tea and handed round the biscuits while everyone congratulated her and exclaimed how lovely it was to have a real author in their midst.

"What is it about?" asked Norma.

"What's it called?" asked Kate.

"How soon will it go into print?" asked Arthur

"Ha-ha, only one question at a time," said Mitsy. "It won't be published for a while, as I still have to do the final editing. Then I'll be choosing the cover and writing all the bits and pieces such as crediting those who helped and the dedication.

"It's called ***Violet's Story*** and I have Arthur to thank for that. It's a novel based on some of the history of this house and what happened when it was a Red Cross Hospital. Most of it is entirely fictitious."

The little group carried on chatting for a while and Mitsy thought how wonderful it was, to achieve something new at her age. She also realised that she was very happy here, amongst friends. Life was good.

Mitsy Howard

- In The Dark -

1

Mitsy fastened her seat belt and smiled at Elaine as they set off down the road towards Baildon. At one level she was excited to be going out for a change of scenery and on the other hand she was rather wary of the visit they were about to undertake. It had all started last week when Mitsy called round to Elaine's for a coffee. Elaine lived in the end of terrace house next to Appledore Residential Care Home, where Mitsy lived.

In her first couple of years at Appledore House, Mitsy had developed plenty of good friendships including Caitlin (who was mainly known as Kate), Norma, Arthur and Raymond, but it was also good to have a friend in the 'outside world', as she liked to think of it.

Elaine was one of those people for whom life is never straightforward. Not for her the cosy simplicity of meeting a partner, getting married and settling down together. Oh no. She had had more partners than even Mitsy could envisage and then children with several more. Her latest crisis involved discovering that her current husband had been living with another woman during the week while giving Elaine the story that he was working away from home. The girlfriend was under the impression that he spent his weekends with an elderly and needy mother. When this girlfriend turned up on Elaine's doorstep there were fireworks, a lot of shouting and the said husband's belongings thrown out on the street.

While Mitsy was listening sympathetically to this shocking tale of woe, Elaine mentioned that she was seeing a clairvoyant the following week. Mitsy had a feeling that even a clairvoyant could not have predicted Elaine's current situation. Before she had time to comment or agree to the proposal, Elaine had decided that Mitsy would find this interesting and had committed her to the trip.

The journey from their part of the outlying area of Bradford would take less than half an hour, depending on the chilly winter road conditions and the traffic density. This was the first time Mitsy had experienced Elaine's flamboyant style of driving and apart from her tendency to comment on the contents of shop windows as they passed, as well as offering 'advice' to other drivers, Mitsy felt that perhaps if her friend paid a little more attention to what was actually happening around her, other people would feel much safer.

Eventually the traffic thinned out as they crossed the moors and headed towards the farm where the clairvoyant was to be found. Mitsy ventured to say that she was rather unsure about meeting this man.

She explained that she was feeling rather sceptical that someone could communicate with the dead and she thought that there must be some trickery afoot that would enable anyone to see into the future. This belief was no doubt due to her previous experience when attending a spiritualist demonstration a few years earlier. On that occasion, she had gone with another friend whose husband had recently died. The meeting was held in the local town hall and the place was packed. Milly had been so excited to think she might hear something from her husband and had made sure that they arrived early, in order to get seats near the front. In fact, they were so early that they arrived while the chairs were being set out and so they ended up having a friendly conversation with the woman who claimed to be able to access those who had recently departed this life.

It was all very interesting and several people heard messages from family members. Then Madam Vericello, as she was called, focussed her attention on the front row. "I am hearing from a gentleman who wants to speak to his wife. Her name is M." Milly jumped up with excitement. "It's me!" The messages conveyed to her were "Be careful in the garden" and

"Look after the dog." As Mitsy and Milly drove home, they had to sadly conclude that there was no evidence that these messages were genuinely from Tom. For a start, Milly did not have a garden worth a mention and even less likely, she did not have, and had never had a dog. Mitsy then pointed out that Milly was wearing a silver necklace with a pearl pendant in the shape of the letter M. "Sorry Milly, but it's more than likely Madam Vericello saw that, while we were helping with the chairs."

Aside from the disappointing incident with Madam Vericello, Mitsy herself had experienced some remarkable contacts with the spirit world only last year. At frequent intervals a young woman in white clothes appeared to her at night. Mitsy named her the 'White Lady' privately. After she had perhaps unwisely mentioned this at the breakfast table, she became known amongst some of the residents at the Care Home as 'the woman who sees ghosts'.

Then, Mitsy's legendary curiosity got the better of her when she saw people moving around in the derelict building across the road in the night time. She spent several weeks trying to figure out who they were and what they were doing. Eventually, she could not resist the temptation to have a closer look. This necessitated a couple of clandestine visits to the old disused mill which was opposite Appledore House. While she was there, she saw a number of people who she guessed must be ghosts from the past. Mitsy discovered that they were not aware of her presence at all and she was able to watch them as they continued with their back-breaking work weaving cloth and managing heavy machinery. It was distressing to observe their situation and the working conditions that they had to endure, as well as seeing the way they were treated by the supervisory staff.

Of course, it was all rather risky so she had enlisted the assistance of her friend Kate, to help her get out of the house surreptitiously at night. The whole escapade came to a sorry, and soggy, end by Mitsy being locked out of doors in the pitch dark in a thunderstorm. She had not told Elaine about this episode and now that the mill had been converted to modern apartments, there seemed little need to say anything. However, she did think that meeting this clairvoyant was likely to turn into a waste of time, just like her outing with Milly.

Elaine listened to Mitsy's explanation of why she wasn't keen to meet a clairvoyant. "I think you might find this an altogether different experience, compared with the spiritualist meeting that you went to with your friend Milly. But don't let me force you into it, I can just as easily go in for the session on my own."

Mitsy, never being one to miss out on an adventure and always keen to try new things, decided to take Elaine up on the offer. Besides, this trip out in the car in January at least offered something to divert her, as she was beginning to feel a bit bored by being stuck indoors.

As they headed in the direction of Baildon Moor, Elaine chatted as she drove. She was an attractive woman, slim-figured and blonde. Mitsy was fairly sure that her hair colour wasn't natural but she liked the idea that her friend looked after herself and her appearance. Mitsy knew very little about Elaine although she rather hoped she would pay a bit more attention to the road in case it was icy.

"You haven't met my eldest daughter June yet, have you?" Before waiting for an answer, Elaine began to fill in the gaps in her life story for Mitsy. "June was born when I was still a rather naïve teenager. In fact, I've never been sure exactly who *was* her father," said Elaine. Mitsy had to think about this for a minute or two and concluded that a silent response to that revelation was for the best.

"Then I met Joe and almost as soon as we were married, I fell pregnant with Alan. Joe adopted June formally so that we all had the same surname. He was lovely at the beginning, but it just didn't work out in the long run and we divorced when both the kids were still little. Alan and June still keep in touch with their father but it's years since I've seen him."

Mitsy was beginning to feel rather old-fashioned having only had one lover who was her husband, Peter. They were together for many years before his death, although for the majority of their married life Peter was in the Royal Navy and so they had many periods apart.

"Of course, when I met Reg, I thought I'd fallen on my feet. He was – well he still is – a good looking fella. Our son Grant takes after him in appearance, I think. It's hard to believe Reg and I had nearly twenty years together before I discovered his fancy woman. Our youngest daughter Ellie, won't speak to him now."

At this point in the story, they were approaching some buildings and a rather rundown smallholding. Elaine turned off the single-track road and brought the car to a rapid halt on the gravel outside a farmhouse.

Before they had time to knock on the door, it was opened by a friendly-looking woman who introduced herself as Mrs Hardcastle. They went inside and were directed to a couple of seats by a blazing open fire, heaped up with logs.

A middle-aged man appeared at her side and immediately smiled as he greeted them: "Hello Elaine, do come through. How nice to meet you Misty. You can chat with my mother today while Elaine has her reading."

Mitsy didn't like to correct him immediately regarding her name and she had already decided beforehand to approach the whole thing with a completely open mind, but not to give the man any clues about herself. She turned to where the man had pointed and saw that Mrs Hardcastle, who had opened the door to them, was now sitting knitting. She quietly gestured to Mitsy to join her at the dining table, while she stood up and took the kettle to the big white Belfast sink. "Tea or coffee?"

By the time Mitsy had answered, Elaine and the clairvoyant had disappeared. Mitsy was quite happy to talk to the older woman. She smiled to herself. She wasn't sure how she had expected a clairvoyant to look, but Ian Hardcastle looked like anyone you might see in the post office queue.

Mrs Hardcastle also seemed to be both pleasant and very ordinary. "I'm knitting Ian a thick winter pullover but I have a feeling it will be summer before I'm finished!" she laughed.

Handing Mitsy a steaming mug of tea, she sat down at the table again, put her knitting to one side and removed from a pile of magazines and newspapers a catalogue of some sort.

"My other task today is to choose from this seed catalogue. We need some maincrop potatoes to go in next month, as long as the ground isn't too hard."

"I expect it gets pretty cold up here on the moors during the winter months?" asked Mitsy.

"Oh yes, it blows a hooley across the tops sometimes."

Mrs Hardcastle perused her catalogue silently then continued by listing out loud all the other vegetables that they would be growing over the coming season, as Mitsy sipped her tea and looked out of the window across the recently turned soil, to the dry-stone wall and the bleak moorland beyond.

Elaine's half an hour seemed to pass quickly and when she came out of the adjacent room, her face was flushed but smiling. "Your turn, Mitsy!" she said.

Ian Hardcastle clearly didn't miss much, as the first thing he said when Mitsy took her seat in the next room was: "Oh I am sorry I got your name wrong Mitsy," as he handed her an A4 pad of lined paper and a ballpoint pen. "This is for you to make any notes you want. Some people like to make a recording on their phones which you are certainly welcome to do. Now, can you let me hold something of yours that you have worn for a long time, such as a ring or piece of jewellery?"

Mitsy's hand went immediately to her wedding ring but she wasn't keen to remove it and, in any case, it wouldn't come off easily. She handed her wrist watch to the man, he closed his eyes and held it for a few moments as if savouring its essence.

"It helps if you believe in this," he said, "but it's not essential."

He then began to speak while his eyes stared straight ahead, almost as if he was watching a video screen, Mitsy thought later.

"This watch was given to you with love, by Peter." Mitsy was amazed at first, and then she thought how easy it would have been for the man to ask Elaine one or two basic questions about her, or even to go on the internet and get some basic facts about the Howard family. What he said next though, seemed different.

"You've had a very interesting life, full of adventures many of which have been all on your own. That escapade in the Mill across the road from where you live now, showed you that you are able to get in touch with people who are long gone."

For a start, Mitsy had never told Elaine about her night-time visit to Park Mill and that certainly wasn't recorded anywhere. Although she had seen, at very close quarters, the workers in the mill it had not exactly occurred to her that she was able to conjure up ghosts. Of course, her nightly visitations by the White Lady would probably be considered as seeing a ghost too.

Ian Hardcastle continued to describe things about Mitsy's father, his career in music, her son Pete in Dublin and even facts about previous generations of their family. He knew about Mitsy's brother Rock dying in a road accident, as well as the fact that she had miscarried a baby girl not long after she and Peter were married. These were things that no one but herself would know about. She wrote as fast as she could, jotting down the basic information she was being given. His words flowed fast and even included idiosyncratic things that she was aware of, such as the hidden cellar in the house in Harrogate, that no one else would know about.

"You loved your home and garden but it was all too much for you to look after on your own."

He ranged from one topic to another, as if the words were spilling out faster than he could manage to say them.

"Your night time visitor is Violet. She wants you to know that she means you no harm, she is just interested. She will be leaving you soon."

"You will find yourself in a dark place but not for too long." Mitsy wasn't sure if this was a real situation or her likely psychological state.

She noticed that the man did not really differentiate between things that had already happened and things that might happen in the future. It was just as if he was seeing a film with her in the starring role.

"You have a good life with your husband; when he is home, he can hardly keep his hands off you!"

Misty had a feeling she could detect the man blushing slightly and she wondered fleetingly just what Ian Hardcastle could see. She tried very hard to write everything down and cursed the fact that she could not do shorthand. Perhaps it would have been better to have recorded the session on her phone after all.

"I'm happy to see you today but you won't need to see me again as you will have all the answers to your questions."

"I'm getting messages from John, Robert, Ivy and Harold. They are sending encouragement."

These names were not especially meaningful to Mitsy but they could easily have been distant family members.

"You are going to take a special trip to London, there's another to Nottingham and a return visit to Dublin."

"Your friend Elaine will be with you sometimes, but not when you go to the United States of America."

Mitsy was rather amazed that at the age of eighty she would still have the time and energy to fit in all this travelling.

Despite her intention not to say anything, she could not resist a brief interruption: "oh my goodness, when will I go to the United States?"

A frown crossed Ian Hardcastle's face and he looked a little annoyed as he appeared to come out of his trance-like state to answer her question, "I don't know when things will happen, or even if they will, I only get information about possibilities."

Soon after, almost as if the thread was broken, he stopped. Mitsy felt a bit embarrassed as he had shared some quite intimate information with her. He smiled in a kindly way, "I'm afraid there's no point in you asking me anything now, as I have no knowledge of what I have been saying."

As they returned to the kitchen where Elaine was waiting, they handed over £40 each. Before the session Mitsy had thought it was quite a lot of money but afterwards she was comfortable with the outlay. Mrs Hardcastle had also mentioned that they did not receive any 'money from the government' as she put it, but lived on Mr Hardcastle's earnings from sessions such as this.

Back in the car, the pair were quiet for a while as they set off for the return journey.

Eventually, Elaine said, "Well. What did you think?"

"It was very interesting and he told me things that no one else but me would know. There was a lot of information and I shall want to read and re-read my notes to make sense of it all."

"Good. I shall have to think about mine too. He told me that I wouldn't be going to Torremolinos this Easter. I'm a bit disappointed as we've booked and I've paid the deposit."

This was all news to Mitsy but she was wary of asking questions and distracting Elaine's rather erratic driving. After a pause while they negotiated a tricky junction, she said, "Oh I didn't know you had a holiday planned?"

"Yes. We usually go a couple of times a year, in the school holidays."

That left Mitsy all the more confused because as far as she knew, Elaine was living alone after her very recent separation from Reg.

"Are you going with the children?" she asked eventually, not wishing to be nosey but aware that Elaine was really trying to get her to ask.

"Good Lord, no. I'm going with Martin. He's the head chef at the school where I used to work as dinner lady. As I said, we usually have a couple of trips away during the school holidays. His wife thinks he's on a management course!" she laughed.

Mitsy was, by this stage, thankful that no response was required as they were just about to pull up at Appledore House. It seemed that her morning out with Elaine had given her more than enough to think about.

2

Back at Appledore House, Mitsy sat quietly in her room waiting for the dinner bell to ring. She carefully folded up her scribbled notes from the session with Ian Hardcastle and concealed them inside the top drawer of her desk, planning to re-read them later. After lunch, which was a warming steak and kidney pie as befitted the season, Misty returned to her room.

She sat in her rocking chair, idly contemplating all the information she had received from the clairvoyant, as well as her friendship with Elaine and the many strange things that had happened since she moved into Appledore Care Home a couple of years earlier.

She had settled happily into her new home, after some initial apprehension. It was so good not to have to worry about carrying heavy shopping, preparing and cooking meals for herself as well as trying to keep the garden under control since Peter passed away. All those chores had become increasingly challenging as her arthritis worsened. She still found it a little uncomfortable having her clothes washed and ironed, her room cleaned and her bed made without lifting a finger herself, but every month when she checked her bank account and saw the fees that she was paying to Appledore Residential Care Home she consoled herself that Peter would have wanted her to be comfortable. Their son Pete lived in Dublin and worked all over Europe, so he was keen to sell the family home to fund his mother's on-going care, especially as he wasn't in a position to keep flying over to help out. She didn't want to give him any extra worry and indeed it was a relief to both of them when the house in Harrogate was no longer hers.

All her life, Mitsy had some difficulty sleeping and she often spent long hours during the night, standing at the bedroom window reflecting on life. To entertain herself she often used the time while she was awake to privately make up stories about those who lived around her. Not long after moving to her new home she had seen ghostly shapes in the disused mill opposite. Perhaps if she hadn't been so curious and naturally adventurous, she could have gone back to bed. As it was, she had taken a couple of night-time walks over to the mill and caused quite a stir amongst her fellow residents on one occasion by getting locked outside in a thunderstorm. Thankfully, most people had forgotten about Mitsy's escapade and Mrs Podsiadlo, the owner of the home, had kept a close eye on her ever since. The old mill had subsequently been converted into modern loft apartments, so there was no danger of that kind of adventure happening again.

All this worrying, however, seemed to have stirred up some ghostly activity. Only last night, just as she was dropping off to sleep, a slight sound disturbed her and when she opened her eyes there was a young woman standing at the bottom of the bed. Anyone else might have screamed out loud in fear, but Mitsy suspected this was just another visitation from the kindly young lady that she now knew to be Violet. She was the daughter of the Doughty family who had cared for wounded soldiers sent home from the battlefield during the First World War. Mitsy was not at all concerned, given that she had written a novel about how Appledore House had been converted from a family home to a Red Cross Hospital at that time, before becoming the twenty-first century Residential Care Home where she now lived.

Violet did not seem to want anything, she merely stood quietly as if watching something or someone. Mitsy was tempted to speak to her, but the last time she did that, the gentle apparition promptly disappeared. Slowly, very slowly, Mitsy raised herself up on one arm so that she could see her more easily. Violet was wearing a long white gown again, but this time her naturally curly brunette hair was braided and tied back under a mob cap. She was very pretty and Mitsy wished she knew more about what had happened to her. She knew that Violet's brother John had been killed in battle but she had very little idea what had happened to the rest of the family after the war.

Just as Mitsy's arm was beginning to get pins and needles from being in the same position for too long, Violet seemed to leave the room. She didn't go out by the door, like you would expect, but faded through the wall next to Mitsy's bed.

Well, thought Mitsy, I suppose I'm quite fortunate that she only seems to visit me, as I imagine some of the other residents would be terribly disturbed if they knew that a ghost still lived here.

Fortunately, Mitsy felt sure that Violet meant her no harm and within minutes she had dropped off to sleep. She had almost forgotten the encounter by the morning, and it wasn't until Ian Hardcastle had mentioned her name that she was convinced that the clairvoyant had some very interesting powers!

As she sat in her chair gazing out at the garden that afternoon, she reflected on her friendly ghost. It's strange that Violet only seems to appear when the room is in total darkness, thought Mitsy. It's as if I can only see her when there's nothing else distracting me. I do wish she would speak. Appearing and disappearing is all very well but I'd love to know if she approves of the book and the story I wrote last year. After all, as the main love interest in the book, she might be amused to know what my imagination cooked up for her, she thought.

Mitsy rocked back and forth, wondering why Violet generally only appeared when she was troubled. It was almost as if she gained a higher level of consciousness at such times, which enabled her to sense things which others might describe as supernatural. She sighed gently to herself at these unanswered questions.

The rocking chair was a Christmas present from son Pete and his fiancée Jackie, and it was ideal for watching the birds in the garden, reading a book, or just chilling out which was what she was intending to do for the rest of today. She was delighted that her son had, at last, found a partner to share his life with. I suppose, she thought, that not so many people fall in love later in life and maybe that makes it all the more special. The fact that he and Arthur's daughter met while both were visiting their parents at Appledore House was such a happy coincidence.

A gentle tap at the door of room six broke into her train of thought. Outside, Kate stood expectantly. "Are you coming to 'dancercise' in the garden?" she asked Mitsy.

"No, not today Kate. I've already been out for a drive with Elaine this morning and I think I overdid the exercise on our walk yesterday. I'm absolutely fine but I'd prefer to take it easy today. Why don't you call in for a chat and a cuppa tomorrow morning?"

Kate nodded, smiled and headed off down the corridor as Mitsy closed the door softly behind her.

3

As Mitsy looked out at the garden, watching several of her friends gather for the music and movement exercise being held on the lawn, there was a knock at the door. Mitsy sighed. It seemed that there was little chance of a relaxing afternoon, or time for a nap to catch up with lost sleep. She went to the door and discovered a rather apologetic Raymond standing outside, clutching a carrier bag.

"Hello, Raymond. What can I do for you?" Raymond was Mitsy's neighbour who had the room directly opposite hers, across the hallway.

Raymond began to look even more awkward so Mitsy, being sensitive to his discomfort, waved him in. "Come on. Come in and sit down so we can talk rather than standing on the doorstep."

Raymond sat down on the chair she was pointing at and placed his bag carefully on the floor beside him. He didn't seem keen to speak so Mitsy smiled and gestured towards his bag. "What have you got there then, Raymond?"

Over the couple of years that she had known him, this was the first time he had approached her for anything. In fact, for several months he stayed in his room and would not come out at all. Eventually Maggie had convinced him to have some of his meals with the other residents. Much of that original shyness had gone, but he was always polite and very much the listener in any conversations. This meant that few people at Appledore House really knew much about him.

"Well, you see. I like to spend my spare time sketching, Mitsy."

Mitsy withheld any comments she could have made about the fact that virtually all their time was 'spare' these days.

"Oh. I didn't know that, Raymond. How lovely! What sort of things do you sketch?"

Raymond looked a bit coy again, before he answered. "People, mainly. Generally, it's from memory."

"How interesting. Have you been a closet artist for years?" she grinned.

Raymond looked puzzled for a minute, before he grasped what she was saying.

"Oh, yes. I never tell anyone what I do. For a start they might want to see what I have drawn and then they might not like it." He paused, as if wondering whether he dare continue. Mitsy, sensing this was difficult for him, nodded and smiled. It was one of those situations where silence was the most helpful response.

"Well, you see. I wondered whether you would be willing to sit for me. As a model?"

Mitsy, more worldly-wise than some might give her credit for, nodded again as if to encourage more conversation from Raymond.

"Oh. And you can just sit in your chair comfortably."

He added as an afterthought, "with clothes on."

Mitsy breathed a quiet sigh of relief. She didn't think Raymond was the type to draw nudes, but then again, one cannot jump to conclusions.

"I would be honoured to model for your drawing Raymond. Thank you. Would you like to do it now?"

"Yes, please. I usually do a first sketch and then work on it a bit more the next day."

"This is ideal for me because it was what I wanted to do this afternoon, just sit and think. Now, tell me what sort of pose you are looking for, please."

"Just sitting relaxed and your head raised a little and turned slightly to the right looking out at the garden."

Mitsy complied with the instruction and began to let her mind wander. Raymond drew from his carrier bag a sketch pad and a selection of pencils. Before long, the only sounds were of Mitsy's steady breathing and the slight scratch of Raymond's pencil on paper.

Probably some forty minutes passed like this. Mitsy smiled to herself inwardly because she was the most fidgety person she knew, yet she had managed to sit still in order to help Raymond and of course, it was actually very restful for her. Almost like meditation or mindfulness, she thought.

Eventually, Raymond put down his pencils and let out a long and voluminous sigh. "Thank you very much Mitsy. Would you mind if I came round tomorrow afternoon at the same time, to work on it some more?"

"Please do. I found it very relaxing in fact and it will do me good to sit still."

Mitsy was very careful not to ask to see what he had made of her, in the light of his earlier comment. She did wonder if she would ever be allowed to see the sketch but thought that, even if he didn't want to share it, she had helped him in his work.

Raymond closed the door behind himself and Mitsy could hear the key turning in the lock in the room opposite.

She wandered over to her mirror and tut-tutted to herself. She really should have worn something smarter than these old stretchy trousers and long, droopy cardigan. Of course, she didn't know when she got up this morning that she would be invited to be an artist's model, but she did have pride in her appearance.

Mitsy stood in front of the mirror and ran her fingers through her hair. It was short and straight, edged with curly wisps that framed her small round face. She wore very little make-up other than her 'secret' lotion which was in fact self-tanning cream which she used to good effect, giving her face a healthy glow all year round. It wasn't really secret as she had told all the women at Appledore House at one time or another when they had complimented her on her healthy complexion.

She found the interlude with Raymond strangely relaxing and she was already looking forward to her modelling session with him the following day. He was an interesting but enigmatic man. Once, when a group of residents were visiting Betty's Tea Rooms in Harrogate, Raymond opened up a little about travels with his wife after they retired. She had no idea what he had done for a living but she decided that he was one of those people who did not like to be asked questions. Maybe he will mention it when he comes round to do the sketching tomorrow, she thought. Then she realised that it wouldn't be helpful to talk when he was concentrating on his drawing.

I wonder if his work had some connection with the art world, she asked herself. He looks a bit 'arty' with his long grey hair curling up over his neck.

The next day, Raymond actually looked even more the part because he was wearing an artist's-type smock. Mitsy still felt that he would prefer if she didn't ask questions so she welcomed him in to her room and took up her seat in much the same position as the previous day.

Raymond was as taciturn as ever, so Mitsy sat quietly again. This time it was more difficult to keep still, perhaps because she knew what to expect.

After it seemed as though she had been sitting still for an hour (although it was actually nearer twenty-five minutes), she wriggled a bit. "Excuse me Raymond but I seem to have cramp in my leg."

"Oh, yes that can happen," he responded. "Would you like to see what I've done?"

Mitsy was amazed at this but pleasantly surprised. "Yes, please. May I?"

Raymond nodded and she stood up carefully, walking over to where he was resting his sketch pad on the edge of her desk.

"Oh. That's lovely, Raymond. You've made me look so calm!" she said. In fact, what Mitsy noticed as much as anything was the care and attention to detail that Raymond had taken to display the folds in her clothes, the shadows across her body from the sunlight streaming in the window and her hair style which faithfully copied the view much as she would see it in her mirror. Like anyone who doesn't really like having their photo taken, Mitsy was not so keen to see the careworn lines in her face but overall, it was a good likeness and she realised that Raymond was really talented.

"I'm really impressed Raymond. You've been hiding your light under a bushel, or whatever the saying is!"

"Thank you Mitsy. I've realised that when one lives in a community of people like this, it's best not to divulge too much otherwise everyone takes advantage of you without realising it's not really fair."

Mitsy nodded, observing that was probably the longest speech Raymond had given in the past two years.

"I have probably done enough for now. I'd prefer it if you don't mention my sketching to anyone else."

"Of course, Raymond. Thank you very much."

With that he let himself out of Mitsy's room, while she rubbed her calf absentmindedly given that the cramp had already gone.

It's fascinating how little we really know about each other, she thought.

4

Life may have settled into a gentle pattern as far as the residents were concerned, but for the staff it was just beginning to get disrupted. In the forefront of their minds was Hannah Podsiadlo's worsening condition and her husband's inability to deal with her dementia. The couple had done a wonderful job owning and running the residential care home for so many years but it now needed a new team at the helm. It had already been decided that Mrs P would need to go to a care home that could better meet her special needs, when Antoni had another massive stroke from which he didn't recover. Maggie and the team were doing a wonderful job holding the fort but virtually all the residents were fearful of the future, long before the word coronavirus was part of everyday conversation.

If one believed in miracles, which Mitsy as a lifelong optimist did, then the arrival on the scene of YourCare Ltd in the guise of Gerald Longhope was more than timely. Mr Longhope owned three care homes in the Bradford area (he liked to call his modest business empire 'a small chain') all of which had quite a good reputation. Mrs P, in one of her more lucid moments, explained to him that she owned a lovely private care home which she would have to sell in order to fund her own care. A deal was done which ensured that Appledore House could continue in the manner it was accustomed, Mr Longhope added to his business portfolio and Mrs P did not need to worry about the future any more. Of course, there was a lot of activity with surveyors and solicitors which Maggie handled efficiently.

Coincidentally, it was 14th February, Valentine's Day, when Maggie held a meeting in the resident's lounge, firstly with all the staff and barely half an hour later with the residents, to let them know that the home would have a new owner. She reassured everyone that in practice there would be very little change. All the staff were able to keep their jobs and initially the resident's fees would remain exactly the same for at least six months, while Gerald Longhope took stock of the business. Even if Gerald wasn't Saint Valentine and love wasn't actually in the air, it was very good news.

Hannah Podsiadlo's departure was a sad affair as virtually all the residents had cause to thank her for what she had done to make their lives in retirement more comfortable. Mitsy in particular remembered her kindness over the incident in the old mill opposite, when she had unwisely made that night-time visit to the disused cotton mill in pursuit of ghosts.

As Mrs P needed specialised dementia care, it was decided that she would move to one of Gerald Longhope's properties which was dedicated to this. It was also felt that she would be less likely to still consider herself the boss of Appledore House, which had already proved to be a bit of a problem.

On moving day, Hannah was having one of her confused periods and it was thought kindest not to prolong the farewells. Everyone stood in the car park in front of the building to wave goodbye to her, although the poor woman was dreadfully distressed because she did not know where she was being taken. There were many tears shed by staff and residents alike and still some scepticism about the new arrangements.

It was around this time that a reporter from the Telegraph and Argus, the local newspaper, got wind of Mitsy's recently published book. This was entitled Violet's Story and told a fictitious version of events about the time when the care home was a Red Cross Hospital during the First World War. Mitsy believed she had seen the young woman's ghost several times since moving into Appledore House and had built her story around that and the true history that her friend and fellow resident Arthur had uncovered. The journalist had telephoned the home and asked if he could meet Mitsy, so that he could write an article about the author.

It was also around this time that the news was full of reports of a terrible virus which was causing an untold number of deaths in China and which was threatening to gradually creep across the globe. At first, it all seemed rather sad but distant and the conversation around the place generally seemed to think it would not affect the UK or European countries and, in any case, it would probably just stop after a while, like the Asian flu that was around in the 1950s.

In some ways it didn't matter that the residents hadn't grasped the true severity of the coronavirus epidemic but it was extremely fortunate that the care staff made sure that they were as well informed as they could be, so that careful plans could be made.

Maggie, who had always been highly responsible in relation to her staff and her wider family as she considered all the residents, spent quite a lot of time on the telephone to Gerald, planning how they should keep everyone safe. The decision was taken first of all to ask all friends and family members of residents not to visit in person for the time being so that the risk of bringing infection into the home was minimised.

Mitsy was not expecting to see her son Pete for a while as he was really busy at work in Brussels and travelling to meetings from his home in Dublin, so she happily continued to send and receive short emails with an occasional phone call when possible. The new arrangements were less well received by some of the other residents but maybe at this stage they were less aware of the risks than Maggie and her team.

The reporter from the local paper was advised that he could not visit in person but he could interview Mitsy by telephone. Mitsy also offered to send him a recent photograph of herself which could be used by the paper.

The man turned out to be charming and their pleasant conversation did not cause Mitsy any concern, at the time.

After the reporter decided that his newspaper would not use the photo she had supplied and when she saw what he had written, Mitsy was much less happy:

Octogenarian has her first novel published

> The history of Appledore Care Home fascinated the eighty-year-old Mrs Howard and as she looked into how the family home of the Doughtys was turned into a Red Cross Hospital for wounded soldiers back from the front during the First World War, she was inspired to write about it. The former shop assistant who had worked in a local pharmacy is one of the elderly residents and it would seem that during her first year living in the home, with time on her hands, she decided to put pen to paper. Not all of the book is based strictly on fact and she claims even to have seen the ghost of one of the characters. Well done Mrs Howard for bringing history to life!

Mitsy read and re-read the piece and, apart from being furious that so much was being made of her age, as if that was relevant, it came across to her as rude and patronising. She was also disappointed that no mention was made of her friend Arthur, as she had explained carefully to the journalist that it was he who had done all the research and should have been credited. She wondered if she should write to the paper to complain.

She decided that she would confide her disappointment to Arthur before he got to read the paper himself.

"Good morning Arthur, I hope I'm not disturbing you?" asked Mitsy as she telephoned her friend who lived upstairs on the first floor.

"Certainly not, Mitsy. I always enjoy a chat with you," he replied.

"I'm not at all happy with the short article that flipping journalist has published in the Telegraph and Argus. It's rude, ageist, patronising and incomplete!" she confided with a level of gusto Arthur was not used to from his gentle friend.

"Now then Mitsy, why don't you read it to me and I'll tell you what I think."

Poor Mitsy was barely able to get the words out because she was so angry but, as ever, Arthur had a more measured way with him and invariably managed to soothe Mitsy's ire.

"Well, I don't mind in the slightest that my small contribution was not mentioned. It delighted me that I set you off on the writing path with my little bit of research. Let's face it Mitsy, it's been a lot safer than your exploits in abandoned buildings during thunderstorms in the dead of night!" he teased.

Mitsy knew he was right but she wasn't easily distracted from her angry reaction to the article. Arthur also knew that she would calm down shortly, so he added: "and given it's a local weekly newspaper it will be forgotten in days and wrapping someone's fish and chips by the weekend! By the way, we're still on for lunch today at the Standsfield?"

"Yes, of course Arthur. I'll see you at noon. Thank you for being so understanding."

Arthur really was a lovely friend and he had appreciated Mitsy's kindness and welcome ever since his first few weeks at Appledore House. Their Wednesday lunch outing to the local pub had become a bit of a ritual and it did them good to get out of the confines of the Care Home. Their friendship became even closer when Mitsy's son Pete and Arthur's daughter Jackie had met and fallen in love. Serendipity is wonderful, thought Mitsy, as she put the phone down thoughtfully.

5

Not long after the episode with the local journalist, Appledore House (along with every household in the country) was faced with the knowledge that the UK had not escaped the coronavirus.

Maggie and the care team had already taken the sensible step of preventing visitors coming into the home. They had also switched to having all of their provisions delivered regularly to the kitchen door by someone from the nearby supermarket. Their previous arrangement had been to have a monthly delivery from a big superstore in Bradford for all the standard items, and this was augmented by one or more of the staff calling in to several of the local shops, including the butchers and a fishmonger every week, to buy all the fresh produce. The local pharmacy was already well equipped to deliver medication to Appledore House, and happy to continue.

As far as Mitsy could understand, Maggie was planning to introduce further protection for the residents. This was explained at another set of meetings for the staff, then separately for the residents.

Firstly, residents would not be permitted to go out of doors at all, for the time being. Mitsy and Arthur exchanged glances, knowing that would bring to a halt their Wednesday lunchtime trips to the pub. It also meant that none of the outings in the minibus would be happening. This was quite a considerable constraint for them all. Mitsy was pleased that her room overlooked the garden because that meant she could still watch the birds and wave to Greg as he worked on keeping the grounds attractive and in order.

The more surprising innovation was that some of the staff would be moving in to live on the premises "for as long as it takes", as Maggie explained. Some staff had volunteered to spend the time in lockdown away from their own families and to live alongside the residents. Maggie explained what symptoms everyone should look out for and then if anyone had already caught the virus, they would need to stay in their room and would be cared for by one of the team wearing protective clothing which she called PPE. Suddenly, this all seemed rather frightening and serious.

The practical implications soon became evident when a large motorhome was carefully manoeuvred and parked on the front driveway. The staff who would be moving in, were to be accommodated in Mr and Mrs Podsiadlo's former apartment, as well as two of the resident's rooms that were currently unoccupied and the newly located motorhome. Under the circumstances, it seemed to be organised with the minimum of fuss.

Maggie was careful not to be too alarmist but she also impressed on everyone that leaving the care home was strictly forbidden.

The pattern of each day took on a new momentum, with people staying in their rooms much of the time, unless they were going for a walk in the garden. They could meet up with other residents outdoors but had to keep a 'social distance' apart. Breakfast and lunch were served in their own rooms but it was decided that one cooked meal each day would be served communally in the dining room. Tables were spread out so that diners maintained a distance from each other and it was agreed this arrangement would continue unless any cases of Covid19 occurred. Everyone was given a new bar of soap as well as hand sanitiser and they practiced singing "happy birthday" twice through, to make sure that they were washing their hands thoroughly.

Mr Longhope did his best to obtain gloves, aprons and face coverings for all of the staff but he didn't have total success.

It seemed every other care home had the same idea and stocks ran low quickly. He was also concerned that seeing the care staff dressed in PPE would be disconcerting for the residents, although they were already getting used to seeing hospital staff on the TV news programmes fully kitted out.

The skeleton staff (Maggie had suggested this was not the best way to describe them, but the habit persisted!) did their best to provide interesting activities for the residents but to be fair, they had very little spare time.

The daily TV presentation on the pandemic given by the government was, initially, watched avidly by everyone. Over time, the number of deaths began to depress people and so it was agreed that in the main TV lounge, only the news headlines would be watched. Those who wanted to see the whole transmission were, of course, still able to watch in their own rooms.

During March, Clap for our Carers started and having watched the response on the television, several of the residents wanted to stand out in the street at eight o'clock to applaud the NHS and all the key workers. Maggie put her foot down and explained that after being so careful not to have contact with people outside Appledore House, it didn't make much sense. The following Thursday it was agreed that they could applaud indoors after dinner, which seemed much more meaningful to Mitsy as it was a way of saying thank you to all the staff at Appledore House.

If she had been able to leave the home, she would have noticed large thank you signs in many windows, along with rainbows painted by children and adults alike.

Mitsy did notice that the pandemic had introduced a whole new lexicon. Terms like "social distancing", "PPE", "coronavirus", "Covid19", "key workers" were used all the time and handwashing, wearing a face mask and using sanitiser became normal. Even the phrase "the new normal" crept into conversations.

The knowledge that shops and schools were closed and parents were being urged to work from home as well as supporting their families with lessons, brought it all into sharp focus too. There was an episode of panic buying toilet rolls and pasta in the supermarkets, which didn't affect Mitsy directly but it was indicative of the reaction across the country. Maggie had explained that any staff or residents believing that they had symptoms would have to be tested from April.

The new arrangements with a rigid lockdown continued for several weeks before any sign of trouble. Then word went round that one of the residents, Lucy, had been feeling ill for several days and in fact may have caught the virus. She had been isolated and cared for by one member of staff in full PPE. In a matter of hours of the rumour circulating, an ambulance arrived and transported the afflicted Lucy to hospital. Maggie immediately introduced a more severe form of lockdown, with everyone being confined to their own room day and night. Meals were delivered by staff and left outside the door, dirty plates were left for an hour or so before being collected. Apart from the evening medication round, delivered by the ever-reliable Joyce wearing a face mask, full PPE and carrying hand sanitiser from one room to the next, no one set eyes on another human being.

Finally, Mitsy learned from a phone call with her friend Kate that Lucy had barely survived the night, and had passed away in the early hours of the next morning. Kate had more information to share also. It would seem that Lucy had "just popped out to the post office" one day during the previous week, after Maggie had already told everyone that they must not go outdoors. Mitsy and Kate had mixed feelings about Lucy's death. While neither of them would have had any ill wishes towards her, they were not at all surprised that if anyone was going to flout the rules it would have been Lucy. Mitsy herself had had one or two run-ins with Lucy in the past and felt that she was not the easiest of people to get on with.

Maggie ensured that everyone had the same information about Lucy's demise and asked that they all tried to be patient with the situation, until they were sure that the virus had not been passed on by Lucy. Lucy's room was stripped and deep cleaned and of course, no one could attend her funeral. In truth, no one really wanted to leave Appledore House at all at this time.

During the lockdown, Mitsy had started to have more frequent phone calls with Pete. He was happy to reassure his mother that he and his girlfriend Jackie were both fit and well. The extra time together in Pete's Dublin apartment seemed merely to cement the strength of the relationship and whenever he passed the phone to Jackie, she was full of information about their deferred wedding plans. Pete was concerned that Mitsy was not getting out at all, but under the circumstances he couldn't fault the way Appledore House was handling the situation. He noticed his mother didn't seem to be fully aware of the dreadful death toll specifically in care homes around the country and he wasn't sure whether she was just blanking out the bad news or whether he was getting a different news feed in Dublin.

A couple of weeks after Lucy's death, Maggie asked everyone to meet in the garden, where it was possible to keep apart from each other. The early May sun was bright but weak, although the air was fresh and the smell of newly blossoming spring flowers added to the air of hopefulness. She said it would only be a quick meeting because everyone was standing up. She confirmed that it was considered to be safe for residents and staff to see each other once more, as there didn't seem to be any further evidence of infection. She thanked everyone for sticking to the rules. She didn't say 'except Lucy' but Mitsy thought it was glaringly obvious that Lucy had brought it on herself. Maggie reminded people that they could not leave the building but that they could sit in small groups in the garden. For this purpose, Greg and his son would be bringing some additional seating for them to use.

Looking back at this time subsequently, Mitsy felt that in many ways they had been sheltered from the worst of the danger by the kindness of the staff, many of whom would have dearly liked some time off and to see their families. Although it was beginning to be obvious that many care homes had suffered a dreadful loss of life, it seemed that Appledore House had been in a relatively safe bubble. There was also the news that vaccines were being developed, although there was a long way to go with testing to make sure these would be safe.

Some of the residents moaned about being bored but the majority managed to use the time to read, write letters, knit or take up some other fairly solitary hobby or interest.

Virtually everyone (including the staff) had read Mitsy's book and said that they had enjoyed her telling of Violet's story. She had ordered a number of copies and even autographed them for her friends.

Mitsy had also become quite popular as the resident who could order things on-line for others. It still surprised her how few of her fellow residents were confident with using a computer. They would happily spend hours on Mitsy's laptop perusing the shops, as much as anything else for their personal entertainment, until she reminded them that she needed to contact her son or write a letter to her sister Sky.

From time to time, she got a little fed up with this but on the whole, she was happy to help. Mostly, they wanted her to order small items for them such as hand cream, underwear from Marks and Spencer or toys for the grandchildren. She was aware that she was racking up considerable bills on her credit card on behalf of others who always promised to pay her "when everything goes back to normal." Eventually, Maggie got wind of this and suggested gently that Appledore House needed to make some alternative arrangements during the pandemic, given that no one could go out to the shops or the bank. Mitsy was actually rather grateful for the intervention although she would never have complained.

The matter was relatively easily resolved by each resident agreeing how much spending money they wanted every month and this was added to their invoice from the home. Maggie then discretely called in on each person with an envelope containing their cash, which they signed for. Frankly, Maggie could have done without the extra work but she knew that these things needed to be managed and all above board.

When it turned out one morning that all of Mitsy's debtors had arrived at her door at much the same time with the money they owed her, it meant that she had a significant amount of cash loose on her table. Arthur had called round to room six and discovered Mitsy surrounded by heaps of ten- and twenty-pound notes. He wisely suggested that Mitsy should ask if this could be put in the safe.

Everyone was beginning to feel a bit happier, given that by late July, there were plans afoot to ease lockdown and to find ways to permit visitors, even if this involved temperature taking, testing, PPE and distance keeping.

6

Ruth tapped on Mitsy's door quite early after breakfast. She knew that Mitsy would be fairly bright and chirpy, unlike some of the residents who seemed to wake up rather grumpy and take an age to get going each day.

"Good morning, Mitsy. May I change your bed linen?"

"Oh, of course Ruth. Do come in. You know I still haven't got used to you doing things for me, even after all this time. But I do appreciate it. When I lived on my own, even when Peter was alive but away at sea, it was jolly difficult for one person to change a duvet cover. I don't know how you do it so efficiently!"

Ruth smiled, as this was the usual conversation that they had every Monday morning. "Ah, there's a knack to it. I get plenty of practice!"

Ruth deftly removed and replaced both of the pillow cases on Mitsy's double bed. Mitsy found her bed comfortable and it had not seemed necessary to change it for a single bed when she moved in, although she had been assured that the mattress had been replaced since the previous occupants of the room had left. She wisely did not ask what had happened to them as she had guessed that residents rarely moved away.

"Oh, by the way, there's a letter for you on the hall table, Mitsy. Would you like me to fetch it for you?"

"Oh, no that's alright Ruth, I'll pop along and get it now."

Back in room six, Ruth continued to change the sheets, the duvet cover and the bathroom towels, as well as restocking the toilet rolls and generally making sure everything was clean and comfortable. She liked Mitsy and was always happy to service her room first, as it got the day off to a good start. By lunchtime she was heartily sick of the task, even though she knew it was an important part of caring for residents.

"Guess what Ruth," said Mitsy as she came back in her room. "I've got one of those silly scam letters telling me I've won a trip abroad. I suppose they'll be asking for fifty pounds deposit and my bank account details now!" She slung the letter in the waste paper bin, which Ruth had just that minute emptied.

Ruth sighed gently and retrieved the letter and the envelope which Misty had screwed up into a ball.

As she walked outside to drop it into her black bin bag, she glanced at the letter heading. "Hmmm Mitsy, I'm trying not to be nosey but I'm not so sure it's a scam. Look, it says you have won the caption competition. Do you remember doing a competition?"

"No Ruth, I don't think so. I often get these dreadful begging letters asking for money for someone's sick sister."

Mitsy took the letter from Ruth and perused it again.

"Oh. I do remember now. It was in the back of a magazine someone gave me. I wrote a rhyme about peanut butter, sunrise, surprise and the Big Apple. Surely they don't want to use it?"

Ruth took the letter back and read out loud: "Many congratulations Mrs Mitsy Howard! We are pleased to offer you our first prize, which is a long weekend trip to New York for two people. Please contact us on the number or email address below to arrange receipt of your tickets."

"Wow! That's exciting. I've never been to New York. Do you think it's genuine?"

"Well, it does look like it," replied Ruth.

"Yes, but we're not even allowed to leave the house at the moment let alone travel abroad," said Mitsy, suddenly remembering that they were in the middle of a worldwide pandemic.

"I think you should contact them anyway and just find out what the situation is."

With that, Ruth closed Mitsy's door and picked up everything she needed for servicing Norma's room next door.

Before Mitsy took any precipitate action, she sat in her rocking chair to re-read the letter and think things through:

Two people. Well, who would I like to take with me? I wouldn't go with Elaine because she would probably spend the whole trip trying to get off with the waiters. Norma is nice but I don't think I would want to spend more than a day with her; we don't actually have much in common apart from us both living at Appledore House. I would happily spend the time with Kate, but she is terrified of flying as I discovered when I invited her to stay with me at Pete's apartment in Dublin. Arthur would be a good companion and I know he would look after us both. On the other hand, people might assume we are married, just like they did when we went to the Open Day for the new apartments across the road in Park Mill. Oh, it's so difficult. I wonder if Pete would like to come with me? He travels all the time for work so it might be a busman's holiday for him. In any case, he and Jackie will be getting married soon. Hmm. Now I've just had a really good idea, she concluded.

Mitsy decided to immediately test out her idea by writing to the company.

Dear Sirs
I am delighted to have won your competition and would like to accept the first prize trip of a long weekend for two in New York.

As I am sure you are facing a similar situation in the USA, we are not permitted to leave the country while the Covid infection rates are high.

Could you kindly confirm if there are any time limits on your prize (within reason) and whether I would be able to transfer the tickets to my son and his fiancée? Much as I would like to visit the Big Apple, it would be a wonderful honeymoon for the couple.

Yours sincerely
Mitsy Howard (Mrs)

7

Not long after lockdown had eased a little, Maggie received a phone call from the BBC. It appeared that someone had read the article about Appledore House which was printed in the local paper some time earlier and they now wanted to film a piece about Mitsy and her book. Maggie was under no illusion that this was partly intended to cast a more positive light on what had been happening in care homes across the country but she agreed to talk to Mitsy about it and on the proviso that she was willing, they would make arrangements for an interviewer and camera crew to talk to Mitsy in the garden of Appledore House, as long as everyone maintained the appropriate social distance.

Mitsy was initially totally against this development but after some quiet reflection, she could see some benefits. For a start, she could correct some of the erroneous impressions about 'the elderly' that the newspaper journalist had propagated. Secondly, she could explain how very fortunate they were in Appledore House with the care and kindness shown by the staff in doing their best to protect the residents against Covid19. She now knew from the TV and radio that many care homes had been left to cope without PPE and had, in fact, had residents returned to care homes from hospital or elsewhere while they were still able to pass on the virus. While Mitsy wasn't especially political, she did think she could make some valid points. And lastly, if a few more people read and enjoyed her book that would be no bad thing. Accordingly, she told Maggie that she was willing to do the interview if it could be arranged without inconvenience.

Well, a date was set and it seemed that everyone wanted a piece of the action. Greg was understandably concerned that his garden would look perfect for the cameras. He could be found outside every day, from dawn to dusk, assisted by his son, pruning, trimming and generally titivating his domain.

Greg had been exceptionally busy recently because he had also been asked to order and construct a specially modified summer house in the garden. The idea was that, in due course, residents would be able to see family members in an outdoor and Covid-secure environment.

When Mitsy discovered that Tracey, one of the care home's staff and a former ladies' hairdresser, had been asked to trim or set their hair by almost all the women residents, she realised that her friends had intended to be in the garden during the interview and hoped to 'just happen' to pass by while she was talking to the interviewer. A discreet word with Maggie soon put a stop to that. Whilst she wasn't especially nervous, she didn't think she could deal with the whole thing properly if everyone else tried to photobomb the filming.

She discussed the potential interview with her son Pete, who had some very helpful ideas based on his own experience with the media.

He suggested that she should decide on the three most important points that she wanted to make and that she jotted them down on a postcard which she could keep in her hand or in front of her which could be used to jog her memory, if required.

He also said that if she was asked something that she didn't want to answer, all she needed to do was to look directly at the interviewer, nod, smile and carry on with one of her three main points! Mitsy thought that was very funny but she realised that it was what politicians did a lot of the time.

She asked Kate and Norma for their advice about what she should wear and both picked out the same dress, which was in many ways a relief as it saved further indecision.

Arthur, dear Arthur, was happy for her to have the limelight for a few minutes and insisted that she said nothing about the book being his idea in the first place.

Finally, the day arrived and Mitsy was pleased that the interviewer was a woman. Her name was Joanna and she skilfully put Mitsy at ease as they walked to the garden seats. Joanna had to sit two metres away and the cameraman (there was only one, which was less intimidating than the 'crew' she had envisaged) stood a considerable distance away but obviously with a powerful lens. There was a fluffy-looking microphone projecting towards her on a long arm but Mitsy did her best to ignore that.

Thankfully it was quite mild and sunny but Mitsy wore a jacket as she was a bit chilly – or maybe just a bit nervous.

Mitsy explained to Joanna before the interview that she was really very angry at the way the local newspaper journalist had made an issue about her age, rather than concentrating on the book itself.

Joanna was careful therefore not to make the same mistake and she began by asking some general questions about how long Mitsy had lived at Appledore House and where she had lived previously. Then she directed her careful questions to find out how the book came about, what Mitsy enjoyed about writing and how much was based on fact.

Mitsy, for her part, cleverly wove her in opinion about the excellent way that Appledore House had responded to the pandemic, in spite of the "delays in decision making and limited support from government."

Joanna ignored this last observation and moved swiftly on to ask more about the history of the house and then to close the discussion down by congratulating Mitsy on her first book, asking if she would be writing another.

Unfortunately, Mitsy had not prepared for this final question and actually hadn't a clue whether she would write again. Completely off-the-cuff she responded, "Well, Joanna. Maybe you could call in to see me in a year's time and I can update you on progress?!" delivered with a smile and the slightest hint of a wink.

Joanna nodded to the camera man and Mitsy concluded that she was conveying ‘it’s a wrap’. She had probably been watching too many American movies but the principle was about right.

Joanna and the cameraman thanked her very much for her time and explained that the segment would be shown on Look North which came on at six-thirty after the national news at six o’clock but they couldn’t say exactly when. “I could get one of the team to phone you in advance on the day, if you like?”

“Oh yes please, that would be really good,” said Mitsy.

As it turned out, several days later when Mitsy got the phone call, it appeared that she was going to be seen not only on Look North but also at the very end of the main national news, just before the weather forecast.

She told Maggie, as well as messaging her son Pete in Dublin. Soon, the whole of Appledore House was buzzing with excitement. Sadly, because they all had to keep two metres apart, only a few could sit in the resident’s lounge and everyone else had to watch in their rooms.

All in all, Mitsy was quite pleased how it turned out. The whole piece lasted barely three minutes and it was exactly the same segment on the national news as on Yorkshire television. She was happy with the questions and her answers and Appledore House had done itself proud if you were looking at the view of the front of the property and the back garden, as well as being an example of how a good care home was coping with the pandemic. It was a relief to find that her age was not mentioned at all and they even included her opinion about insufficient government help for care homes.

Of course, by the next day it was already yesterday’s news (literally) and sadly the news highlights were reporting on the tragic number of deaths. They had, though, started to add in deaths from Covid19 in hospitals and in the community, which included Care Homes.

Mitsy was also pleased to receive a phone call from Gerald Longhope, congratulating her on her appearance on national TV and joking that he would soon be appointing a head of PR if she would like the job. They laughed, but Mitsy knew that his thanks were genuine and she was also aware that her words had gone some little way towards thanking the staff for their dedication. Life, of course, didn't go back to normal but the BBC's presence had at least offered an entertaining interlude to break up the monotony of everyday life under lockdown.

8

Mitsy had plenty of friends to talk to, even during lockdown. There was Norma who lived in room five next door, Kate who was upstairs and Arthur who also lived on the first floor. She sometimes sat with them at a social distance or in the garden as well as enjoying a chat on the phone but she knew that it would be really lovely to see her son Pete and her friend Elaine in person.

Although Elaine lived next door to Appledore House and they spoke on the phone from time to time, she too missed their mid-morning coffee and chat as well as Mitsy's company.

Pete's first visit to Appledore House during the pandemic was a brief affair, as it had to be highly managed to fit in with his time off work, his flight times and the practical arrangements agreed with Appledore House. Maggie and the team were careful to limit each resident to only one visitor and these had to be spaced out so that they did not accidentally meet with other residents' visitors. Everyone had their temperature taken and had to answer a formal set of questions including their health status, their contact details and if they had recently been tested. Pete arrived on the dot of two o'clock, having landed at Leeds/Bradford airport shortly after midday. He rang the doorbell and was greeted by Shirley, who he hadn't met before.

"I'm Mitsy Howard's son," he said, "the two-p.m. appointment."

"Let me just check," said Shirley, as she consulted a printed list on a clipboard just inside the door. "Mitsy has been doing very well, especially with all the excitement of the television filming. I know she's looking forward to seeing you. You realise that you can only meet in the summer house in the garden and that you cannot touch each other. Do you know the way to the garden?"

Pete indicated that he did, although his voice was a bit muffled through his face covering. He walked round the exterior of the building, tapped on the door of the summer house and was delighted to see his mother's cheerful face through the Perspex screen. It was a real tonic for him. Even though she was wearing a mask, he could see that her eyes were bright and she was beaming with happiness.

Of course, they were both delighted to see each other to catch up with news. Emails and messaging are fine up to a point, but there's nothing like a proper two-way conversation.

Mitsy updated Pete in some detail as to how Appledore House had been handling the pandemic, including the sad death of one of their number. Pete had heard his mother mention Lucy previously and his eyes betrayed a slight twinkle as she raised her eyes heavenwards as she described Lucy's behaviour. Thankfully, no one else had taken stupid risks and by isolating themselves with the very kind support of the staff, there didn't seem to be too much danger now. Pete was reassured by the care that Maggie and her team were taking to keep everyone safe.

Of course, she explained, with the embargo on visitors partially lifted, there was still a chance that someone who had no symptoms would unwittingly bring the virus into their midst. Then the conversation turned to happier things.

Mitsy was delighted to know that Pete and Jackie were still enjoying each other's company. Pete looked really well; in fact, he may even have put on a little weight. He had worked right through the lockdown periods mostly from home with lots of Zoom meetings with his colleagues across Europe.

For her part, Mitsy was looking quite relaxed and rested and she was happy to tell Pete that she had enjoyed giving the television interview and although she had been nervous, she confided that she wouldn't mind doing it again.

"So, will you be writing another book, mother?" asked Pete.

"No. I don't think so dear. It was actually a lot of work and there are other things I want to do with my time."

Pete nodded, thinking that was probably wise. He did hear, third hand, about his mother's escapade in the disused mill across the road and although he would never tell her that he knew, he concluded privately that writing a book was probably much safer but maybe not as much fun.

The time for Pete's visit flew by and both were taken aback when Shirley tapped on the door of the summerhouse to say that their time was nearly up.

It had been quite an effort and expense to get up early, take a taxi to Dublin airport, then the 'red-eye shuttle' flight to Leeds/Bradford, a taxi to Appledore House and then repeat the whole journey in reverse, just for an hour's visit. On the other hand, to see his mum through the Perspex screen and know that she was doing alright under these difficult circumstances was absolutely worth it.

As he was getting himself ready to depart, he tapped his pocket and remembered he had something to give his mother.

"By the way mum, I've got a letter which was addressed to Dad. It was forwarded to me from the people who moved into our old house in Harrogate. They didn't know your address and I suppose they were a bit confused as it was addressed to Mr Peter Howard and they just assumed it was me. I don't think it is though, as it has a Portsmouth postmark."

They weren't quite sure whether it was safe to pass the letter from one to the other but in the end, Pete proffered it round the end of the screen to his mother and Mitsy picked it up, looking slightly concerned in case it was infected.

She opened the letter and as she read it aloud to herself and Pete, she had a feeling this was not something her son needed or wanted to hear:

Dear Peter
It seems so long since I saw you. I hope you are well. I had the baby it was a little girl she is called Chelsea. I have moved to Nottingham but mum is still in Portsmouth. Would you come to see me sometime?
With love from your little Esmeralda

"Oh dear. Oh dear me. I'm not sure what to make of this Pete. I'm completely in the dark as regards anyone called Esmeralda."

Pete was at a loss too. As far as he was aware, his father had always been totally trustworthy and faithful to his mother so this development was a dreadful shock. "I'm not sure what to suggest, Mum. I'm really sorry. I had no idea…" he trailed off, sounding concerned and puzzled.

"Leave it with me, Pete. I shall have to think about how to deal with this Esmeralda. Don't worry about it. I expect there's some perfectly simple explanation."

Mitsy wasn't anything like as relaxed as the impression she gave to her son. It was not in her nature to jump to conclusions but at this stage, it was hard not to imagine something really distressing.

However, it was time for Pete's short visit to end. They had talked about things they would like to do once the threat from the coronavirus was over. Mitsy said that she would love to visit him again in Dublin and she would take up Jackie's offer of a girls' shopping session. Of course, there was some conversation about the forthcoming nuptials, although neither knew whether this could take place as planned. Pete reassured his mother that he and Jackie would happily postpone their wedding until she and Jackie's father Arthur could be present.

Mitsy did so want to give her son a good hug and a kiss but as that wasn't permitted, they spent several minutes at the door, saying goodbye and feeling the strangeness of the circumstances.

9

Somehow, the mystery of the letter from Esmeralda didn't seem the thing to confide to her friends at Appledore House. People didn't really talk about their spouses there. The truth of the matter was that for many of them it was too distressing to recall a happy marriage and the person they had lost. Conversations therefore tended to deal mainly with the here and now.

She had given the letter much thought all the rest of the day and much of the night. She looked again at the rather childish handwriting, as if that would give some clues to the young woman who wrote it, but nothing helped to assuage her worries. Mitsy was really rather cross about this worrying distraction because she had hoped that she had seen the last of her insomnia.

Eventually she decided that she would seek the advice of her friend Elaine about the letter. They hadn't seen each other since the trip to the clairvoyant and although Elaine only lived next door to Appledore House they hadn't been able to see each other since lockdown.

Originally, they met last year when Mitsy was walking to the corner shop. Elaine was busy, in what passes for her front garden. It was actually a small paved area with a few plants in pots. She liked to sit there in her deckchair while the weather was good but on this particular day, she was out sweeping up the leaves which had blown in from the beech tree across the road. After several conversations across the fence over a few weeks, Elaine invited Mitsy indoors for a coffee and this turned into a weekly get together every Friday morning. Of course, some months had passed since their outing together in January.

It was quite strange to see why the two would be friends, as they had very little apparently in common. Elaine had been married for a number of years when she discovered that her husband had, in fact, been living a double life. He was what they used to call a 'commercial traveller', selling specialised equipment to doctor's surgeries and dental practices. This meant he was away from home Monday to Friday most weeks. He had been very careful to cover his tracks so Elaine had no idea that he had a girlfriend with whom he lived during the week. The girlfriend, called Alison, eventually got a little curious about the 'elderly mother' who held such a sway over her lad that he had to be home with her every Saturday and Sunday regardless of the importance of alternative uses of his time.

There was a very shocking confrontation on Elaine's doorstep and a subsequent dumping of her husband's clothes in the front garden, followed by immediate initiation of divorce proceedings. Elaine had decided that all men were bastards and, not surprisingly, she was not inclined to trust people easily.

She did, however, think the world of Mitsy who had listened to her story sympathetically and did her best to help Elaine to rebuild her self-confidence somewhat.

Mitsy had been very careful not to sing the praises of her late husband to Elaine and their conversations usually centred around clothes, hairstyles, television and music. Elaine had spent most of her life working as a hospital cleaner with a few periods as school dinner lady. Mitsy had such a wide range of part-time jobs under her belt she was able to identify with some of the tales that Elaine told. When the latter finished her work at the local school last year, she was grateful for a friendly ear on a Friday morning which helped pass the time.

For her part, Mitsy told Elaine about her time working in the pharmacy in Harrogate. It was a job she loved and it made a pleasant change after all the term time only jobs that she had worked her way through while Pete was still at school.

At the outset, that pharmacy job had seemed doomed to failure. Not long after she started there, the owner, who was a fully qualified pharmacist, retired and the shop was sold to a new gentleman who employed a friend to manage the prescription side of things. Mitsy was asked to stay on to sell the make-up and perfumes etc. The new pharmacist, called Clive, was very friendly and Mitsy thought it would all work out well. Eventually, she realised that Clive was more than just friendly and he had erroneously thought that because her husband was away at sea, she would welcome his advances.

There followed several weeks of uncomfortable cat and mouse chases around the shop, even though Mitsy told him in no uncertain terms that she was happily married and not interested in him. He seemed to think that she enjoyed these skirmishes and would not take no for an answer. In a small business like this, there were no Human Resource policies and no recourse to anti-harassment legislation at the time.

Finally, Mitsy approached the owner and asked to speak to him privately when he called into the shop to check on stock levels. Clive grinned at this, thinking she would not risk losing her job by complaining. Mitsy had anticipated this and carefully explained her dilemma to the owner. Much as she enjoyed her job and the work involved, including encouraging quite a few regular customers to call in to buy expensive perfumes and make-up, his pharmacist's behaviour was causing problems in terms of Health & Safety. Twice recently, he had made mistakes with medication strengths. Fortunately, she had been able to spot them before the tablets were distributed to patients. She wondered whether Clive had some problems in his private life that were leading to him being distracted and making mistakes? She explained that she was not complaining, rather she was concerned for the reputation of the pharmacy and the safety risk to patients. She asked if the boss could ascertain privately if there was any reason why Clive could not keep his mind on the work. Of course, although the prescribing mistakes that she described were genuine, this was a risky strategy because Clive could have made any sort of counter claim against Mitsy.

As it turned out, his behaviour settled down and his antics stopped. Eventually, Mitsy discovered that Clive had been going through a rather acrimonious divorce and his attentions towards her were probably in order to salve his self-esteem, not that that made his behaviour any more acceptable.

A fly on the wall would have heard a very serious and grown-up conversation between the two male friends with Clive's welfare being considered, along with great praise for the shop assistant who the boss recognised was worth every penny he paid her. "She's ideal for this job Clive, and I want you to do everything you can to make sure we don't lose her. Your own job hinges on it. Customers see Mitsy first and they trust her. As do I. Please sort out your personal life and make a success of Tindall's the Chemist."

In time, Clive's divorce went through and he found a new girlfriend. He was always grateful privately to Mitsy for handling his bad behaviour the way she did, even if he didn't know exactly what had been said. Nothing was ever discussed but he began to treat her with respect, as one would have hoped and expected. The remaining years of Mitsy's service at Tindall's were extremely happy.

Of course, this didn't change Elaine's view of men but she appreciated Mitsy sharing the story with her.

So, when she received a phone call from Mitsy during the period that Appledore House was in partial lockdown, she listened carefully as Mitsy read out the letter from Esmeralda to her.

"Hmm. That's tricky Mitsy. You don't remember your Peter ever mentioning a girl called Esmeralda? Or anyone he knew in Portsmouth?"

"Elaine! He knew dozens of people in Portsmouth! I'm completely in the dark over this. I think I'd remember Esmeralda, it's an unusual name."

"It's Spanish, I think," said Elaine.

"Well it might be. It's also the name of the prostitute in the story of the Hunchback of Notre Dame."

"I don't think you should read too much into the girl's name. Read it to me again, please."

So Mitsy read Esmeralda's letter to Elaine again, over the phone. Elaine thought long and hard and Mitsy was actually wondering if the phone had got cut off when she finally gave her opinion.

"I think you should write to the girl, tell her that you are Peter's wife and that Peter has passed away. Say that as soon as lockdown is eased, you had planned to visit the Nottingham area with a friend and if you have time, you will both call in to say hello."

"Oh, I'm not sure about that Elaine."

"Well, I am. It's about an hour and a half drive from here to Nottingham; we will make a little outing of it and if you change your mind, we can always give it a miss. I think you should stop worrying about it for now. Can I also suggest that you give her my address, rather than Appledore House? I will, of course, pass any reply directly to you but it does give you the option of keeping this private between us and it means she couldn't trace you if you want to be anonymous." Elaine was probably being extra cautious but she did have the experience of her husband's girlfriend appearing on the doorstep unannounced.

"Thank you, Elaine. I'll try not to worry. You are very kind."

And so, the response was pondered over and eventually written, much on the lines that Elaine had suggested. She left the letter in the hall for posting by anyone who was able to drop it in a post box, given that the residents were still asked to remain solely in the building.

This didn't mean that the issue was closed, oh no. Mitsy went over and over in her head whether it would have been possible, let alone likely, that her husband had had an affair.

When she and Peter met, although it wasn't exactly love at first sight, it was very close to that. Misty was immediately attracted to this dashing young sailor and found him both kind and good company. Over time, they found they had a similar outlook on life and a shared sense of the ridiculous – some might call it a rather wacky sense of humour. Once married, their relationship developed and blossomed into mutual trust and respect. Mitsy believed that physical attraction was essential in a good partnership but trusting and respecting your spouse was paramount.

When Peter went away on naval deployment, she knew that he was just doing his job and his loyal duty. Her part in this was to look after herself and the home and subsequently to raise their son, and not to give Peter cause for concern while he was away. She was always absolutely delighted when he sent word that he would be docking shortly and when he expected to be home.

Once Peter was on home leave, it was almost like a honeymoon each time as they used the opportunity to catch up with all the things that couldn't be put into a letter, email or conveyed in a short phone call. They enjoyed being with each other so much and made the most of these relatively short patches by going out walking, enjoying the local pubs and restaurants and of course, taking young Pete with them to various activities befitting his age.

Mitsy adored her husband and it would never have crossed her mind to be unfaithful to him. She had always assumed the same was true for Peter. The old adage 'a girl in every port' seemed ridiculous and had never for a minute seemed likely.

What she couldn't understand was that she had never heard mention of Esmeralda. Peter did not talk about his work, hardly at all, and she knew that some activities were private and subject to legislation, such as the Official Secrets Act. For this reason, she rarely asked him anything about his work, assuming that he would tell her of any amusing incidents and for the rest, it was not for discussion. If Peter had a longer posting to somewhere pleasant, she was often asked if she wanted to go with him. This was the case when they stayed in Valletta in Malta for a couple of years, before Pete was born. She knew from this experience that it was easy to make friends with local people for a while and thus she could only assume that Esmeralda fell into this category. That would have been fine were it not that Esmeralda said in her letter that her mother still lived in Portsmouth. Portsmouth being where Peter's base was. She sighed. Maybe she would not get a reply to her letter and she would remain totally in the dark about this part of Peter's life.

10

Not long after breakfast one morning, Mitsy knocked on the door of her next-door neighbour Norma.

"Good morning Mitsy. Do come in. I've got my chairs at a suitable social distance," she laughed.

"How are you?" asked Mitsy, thinking that she hadn't seen Norma look so well ever since she moved in, not long after Mitsy herself did.

"I'm great thanks. I was going to ask for your advice today."

"Oh yes? Ask away!"

"Well, it's my daughter's birthday coming up soon and as you know, I haven't been able to see her because she's a key worker at Bradford Royal Infirmary. I'd like to send her something really nice for her birthday but I don't know what."

"I've only met your daughter Sandy a couple of times so I don't really feel able to make a suggestion," said Mitsy. "Tell me a bit about her interests and anything you have thought of for the present."

The pair chatted for ages but apart from Norma's idea of a "nice scarf" not much else presented itself. They sighed and smiled at each other.

"I can see it could be quite difficult what with ordering a scarf, buying birthday wrapping paper and brown paper, buying a card and then getting it all to the post office on the right day, especially during lockdown. But I do have an idea! Have you heard of Moonpig?"

Norma looked confused and shook her head.

"Well, maybe you didn't have it in South Africa? It's an on-line shop where you can design your own special birthday card with Sandy's name on it and even a photo if you wish.

They print it and post it for you. They also do presents including beautiful bouquets of flowers or potted plants, which would be delivered to Sandy's door. What do you think of that for an idea?"

"That's perfect! Can we do it now?"

They returned to Mitsy's room where her laptop was always ready for such things and within half an hour the job was done. Norma was thrilled at the simplicity of the solution and Mitsy was pleased to help.

"I'll just pop back next door and get the money I owe you," said Norma.

She was missing for quite a while and eventually Mitsy tapped gently on the door to make sure that her neighbour was alright.

"I can't believe this," said Norma. "I'm certain I had £45 in my purse yesterday, in fact I thought I had checked it not long after breakfast this morning before we went to your room to choose the Moonpig card and flowers. But there's only £5 left. I know there were two twenties and five pounds in coins. I really don't think I put them anywhere else. I'm not usually so forgetful."

As with many older people, Norma always had a slight fear that something like this was an early sign of dementia.

"Look don't worry Norma; you can owe it to me and pay me back when you get this month's 'pocket money'!"

Mitsy closed Norma's door quietly behind her, noticing as she did so that the door to Raymond's room opposite was wide open.

" 'Morning Raymond!" she called out, cheerfully.

"Oh. Raymond isn't here," said Shirley. She was a relatively new member of staff who had been transferred from one of Gerald Longhope's other care homes. "He's having his hair cut!"

There was something puzzling Mitsy but she couldn't quite make it out. She shrugged and went back into her own room. Somehow her visit to see Norma had unsettled her, so she sat down in her rocking chair and opened the book she was reading.

By lunchtime Mitsy was feeling much more relaxed and looking forward to her portion of quiche lorraine, new potatoes and crisp green salad. She loved the food at Appledore House and especially appreciated that she no longer had to worry about shopping, preparing, cooking, serving and washing up any more.

She took her seat, opposite Arthur and smiled as it was clear that he had had his hair cut too. "Oh Mitsy. I never thought I would yearn for a haircut but to be honest the length of my hair has been driving me mad during lockdown. We have just discovered that the lovely Joyce, she of the evening medication round, was also a trained hairdresser and she has trimmed the hair of all the men in the building. It's so much more comfortable now."

Mitsy nodded as she understood perfectly what a relief it could be.

"I do like Joyce and you know, she wouldn't take a penny in payment. In the end we had a whip round just to say thank you."

At this point Raymond, who was sitting nearby, called out, "I shan't forget that I owe you some money Arthur."

Arthur gestured as if to say it didn't matter but Raymond was having none of it. "No. I wouldn't dream of it. I just feel rather embarrassed Arthur, as I was sure I had some change in the top drawer of my bedside cabinet."

Misty's ears pricked up at this and even though it was none of her business, she couldn't help but wonder just what that young woman Shirley was doing earlier on that day. An image flickered into Mitsy's mind of Shirley standing by Raymond's bedside cabinet and, if she was not mistaken, closing a drawer rather suddenly.

Lunch over, Mitsy went back to her room and prepared for her afternoon walk. As she combed her hair and selected a pretty pashmina to cover her shoulders, a plan was forming in her mind.

"Arthur. Sorry to phone you immediately after lunch but I wonder if you would be able to help me out this afternoon?"

Mitsy explained to Arthur what was on her mind and he readily agreed to join in. "What fun! You do have some crazy ideas, Mitsy"

The stage was set and Mitsy left room six with perhaps a little more clatter than usual, calling out loudly to Raymond as she went: "Just going out for my afternoon stroll in the garden."

Meanwhile, Arthur very quietly tapped on the door of Raymond's room, entered and explained the plan.

Mitsy did a circuit of the lawn and inspected the flower beds before settling down on one of the garden seats which just happened to give a quite good, if distant, view into her own room. After about ten minutes she was able to discern a shady figure just inside her room. She raised both of her arms, as if stretching after a nap and received a thumbs up signal from Raymond's window. Slowly, very slowly she got up and walked as casually as she could, back inside the house.

Mitsy's calm demeanour belied the turmoil inside her stomach as a flock of butterflies took flight. As she closed the door behind her, she could hear a whistle and raised voices. Oh dear, I do hope I haven't got this all wrong she said to herself.

Back inside room six, with mixed feelings, she saw that her plan had worked. A few minutes later Arthur and Raymond arrived at her door, on the verge of giggling like schoolboys. "Maggie would like to see you, Mitsy. Come back and tell us what happens, please."

Arriving in Maggie's small office, she saw Shirley with a very flushed face and possibly a hint of tears.

"Mitsy," said Maggie "could you please describe what you have just seen?"

"Well," said Mitsy. "I was aware that both Norma and Raymond had some money missing but it wasn't until I saw Shirley in Raymond's room, closing the drawer of his bedside cabinet, that it crossed my mind that Shirley might have something to do with it. Then I was out in the garden having my afternoon walk when I saw someone in my room. I believe that a twenty-pound note that I left on my table has gone missing."

"That is a very serious allegation you are making," said Maggie, looking with a steely gaze directly at Mitsy.

"Yes. I am well aware of that. Perhaps I should mention that the money I left on my table is easily identified by the small letter M that I have written on the corner."

Maggie leaned forward, held out her hand and Shirley very reluctantly drew some money out of her overall pocket. Maggie checked the notes over very carefully. She held one of the £20 notes towards Mitsy, "Is this yours?"

"Yes. Yes, it is."

"Thank you Mitsy. I would like you to go back to your room now and I will come to speak to you later."

As she left, she heard Shirley mutter under her breath, "interfering old busybody."

That quite shook Mitsy. As a child she was always praised for having an enquiring mind. As an adult there had been times when her curiosity got the better of her, but she had never before been accused of being a busybody!

Of course, as soon as Mitsy approached room six, two eager faces appeared round the door of Raymond's room.

"I cannot tell you much yet boys," said Mitsy, "but I have identified one of the missing notes. I suggest we reconvene a bit later when Maggie has updated me. I will phone you both."

After a comforting cup of tea, Mitsy had started to feel better. She was a kind woman and did not like to cause trouble, but on the other hand, so-called petty pilfering had to be stopped.

A gentle tap on the door, suggested that Maggie was coming to tell Mitsy what had happened. In fact, it was Norma, wanting to know what was going on since she heard the kerfuffle in the hallway. Mitsy quickly gave her a brief summary and promised to say more later.

Just before six o'clock, the dinner gong sounded. Everyone left their rooms to see what was happening. Assembling all the residents in the lounge and dining room, as well spaced out as possible, Maggie very carefully informed them all that Shirley had left Appledore House and would not be coming back.

"This is sad news for us all, but as I'm sure you are aware, our staff are expected to be totally trustworthy and in this instance one member of staff was suspected of stealing. I'd like to thank Mitsy for her keen observation and her ingenious way of ensuring that we had proof before making allegations. Also, thanks to Arthur and Raymond who apprehended Shirley 'in the act'. This will now be an end to the matter and in due course we will be recruiting for Shirley's replacement."

As Maggie was coming to the end of her announcement there were a few murmurs around the room. "Any questions?"

Kate found herself speaking for those sitting near her: "We wondered if the police had been called?"

Maggie smiled. "I have informed Mr Longhope and he will decide what further action will be taken, beyond the instant dismissal. I should perhaps mention that I have spoken to everyone whose money was taken and have returned it to them immediately. May I remind you all that we are living in difficult times and dealing with the pandemic is challenging enough without these additional difficulties. Now, if you are planning to eat this evening, please take your seats!"

Mitsy was pleased that Maggie had informed everyone, but of course they all wanted to know what she had done to trap the thief. Her little ruse of writing a letter M on her money was admired by all and the general opinion was that she had done them all a service by spotting what was going on.

Raymond added: “I’m really grateful you had your eyes peeled Mitsy and I’m happy to help you in your sleuthing any time.”

By the time Mitsy had finished eating, she was feeling much better about the whole exploit.

Later that evening she received a phone call from Gerald Longhope: “I hear we have our very own Miss Marple!” he joked, referring to the Agatha Christie crime stories which showcased the detective skills of Jane Marple.

“Oh, I don’t know about that, Mr Longhope”

“Well, I do and thank you very much. A small token of my appreciation will be delivered to your door tomorrow.”

Just as Gerald Longhope had said, a beautiful bouquet of mixed flowers arrived for her, rounding off the whole adventure very nicely.

11

Gradually, lockdown was eased across the country and this permitted some minor changes at Appledore House, although Maggie and Mr Longhope insisted that the wearing of face coverings, use of hand sanitiser and social distancing had to continue. The shielding programme was paused also and in the wider world people were encouraged to go back to work if the arrangements were Covid-secure. A brief heatwave saw a mass exodus of people who had been tired of being cooped up, all heading for the seaside.

The national news offered little reassurance that life was going back to anything like normal and it was evident that many companies had gone into administration or had closed their doors permanently, causing job losses and widespread unemployment. Students of all ages had adapted to on-line learning but were missing out on the essential socialisation they could have expected at university or school.

Among the many slogans proposed by the government was the "rule of six". Officially, care homes were expected to remain totally isolated but it was decided that the use of the summerhouse in the garden could be extended to slightly larger family groups in the same household "bubble" as long as everyone was tested. Maggie also found some sensible ways to give residents secure outings, as she was concerned that the impact of endless isolation on their mental health would create more problems in the coming winter.

No one knew if the easing of regulations would last or whether it was merely a brief chance to see loved ones before the next spike in Covid infections and deaths. Pete and Jackie had set up a monthly zoom meeting with Mitsy and Arthur and they were all happy to have that level of contact, given that travel was complicated by different regulations across the English regions and in Ireland. Pete was still in Dublin much of the time but whenever he was travelling for work, he was able to arrange it so that he could stay over with Jackie in London when she needed to be there too. The couple had already decided that they would have a very quiet wedding and that it could wait until it was safe for people to travel again. Mitsy had wisely not mentioned any of this to her sister Sky, as she was bound to make a fuss if she wasn't invited.

Thankfully, Appledore House had no further Covid-related illness or deaths but they remained very cautious about mixing with anyone from outside. Residents were allowed to have one person in their 'bubble' and so Mitsy took the opportunity to visit her friend Elaine next door, although they just sat outdoors in the garden and talked.

Elaine enjoyed hearing all about Mitsy's sleuthing and how Shirley was caught in the act. "You are brave Mitsy. I wouldn't have dared."

"Oh, I don't know about that. I think you were very brave Elaine, when you confronted that woman who came to your house. "

Mitsy was very careful not to refer directly to when Elaine's husband cheated on her. "By the way, did you receive anything from that Esmeralda woman?"

"Not a peep, Mitsy. I would certainly have phoned you if I had."

"In some ways that makes me all the more curious," said Mitsy. "I think I might take up that offer of yours to visit the woman when we can. I don't like living with mysteries."

After coffee and a chat, the pair agreed to return to their usual Friday morning coffee arrangement in Elaine's front garden: "after all, we're in the same bubble now," said Mitsy.

As the weather was so mild, many of the residents of Appledore House spent their time sitting in the garden. They continued to keep a two-metre distance and Greg and his son had helpfully located the garden seats so that everyone could talk without shouting.

Mitsy thought it quite funny that some of the older folk at the care home were still not quite sure how far two metres was, so they talked instead of two yards' social distance. She was less amused by those that didn't seem to have the knack of using their face coverings to cover both the mouth and nose. She decided that it was such an important part of them all surviving the virus that being polite just would not help; she was often to be seen pointing at a fellow resident and calling out "manners"!! Eventually, most people realised that it was only courtesy to get it right and to demonstrate that they were trying hard to protect others.

Some of the staff had been able to go home to see their families although they still wore full PPE at work. The hand washing, sanitising and wearing of face coverings became second nature. Everyone knew that the pandemic was not over, but a modified return to normality helped the care home to feel a more relaxed and happier place. Regular testing became the norm and any hint of symptoms or a positive test meant that staff would self-isolate for two weeks until they had a clean bill of health. This, of course, presented endless problems for Maggie in sorting out who was available for which shift and she largely gave up on the normal rota system.

It seemed, from international news, that every country's virologists were engaged in developing a vaccine with trials underway in the race to find one - or more - that were safe and effective. The daily news was still focussed on the distressing death toll and the numbers of people tested and infected.

Slowly, very slowly, Appledore House began to provide suitably distanced outings for those who wanted to take part.

One of the many advantages of Appledore House being part of Gerald Longhope's set-up was that YourCare Ltd had a minibus complete with its own driver. Everyone called the driver Osbourne but Mitsy was never quite sure if that was his first name or a rather old-fashioned way of addressing him by surname!

Mitsy had avoided all such trips in the minibus until now, as she wasn't sure about being closeted with other people, even though they were only her fellow residents. The outings didn't actually go to anywhere specific, as most venues such as stately homes, art galleries and museums were still closed and so the trips usually only involved a drive around the area to see places that she was already familiar with.

Eventually, she realised that it would be sensible to venture out again, before she became too afraid to do so. Even walking next door to Elaine's to sit in her front garden made her feel vulnerable and it seemed uncomfortable and slightly frightening to both of them. So, when Norma asked if she fancied signing up for a cruise in a narrowboat on the local canal, Mitsy reckoned that it would be well ventilated and as safe as everyone could make it.

The trip involved a short ride in the minibus to nearby Skipton where they would embark on a two-hour afternoon cruise complete with a cream tea. At £20 per head, it seemed good value and a lovely way to see the countryside from a different vantage point.

In fact, there were only twenty places because the cruise company was sticking strictly to social distance requirements. Just for a change, Maggie decided she would join the residents for this trip, along with Ruth who often accompanied them on their outings.

It was a fine Wednesday afternoon and the minibus collected them promptly at two o'clock and drove directly to the canal side car park. Osborne, Maggie and Ruth made sure that the short walk to the waterfront was safe for everyone, and well away from any members of the general public. The narrowboat was called 'Lady Luck' and everyone remarked how colourful it was, decorated with traditionally painted castles and roses as well as a collection of potted plants adorning the deck. The staff providing the cruise were wearing gloves and face coverings and were at pains to explain they had all been tested. They also took the temperature of every passenger, even though Maggie was sure it wasn't necessary.

Eventually, everyone got settled in their seats with Mitsy and Norma sitting together across a large table. "This is lovely! We all get a window seat," said Norma.

The skipper introduced himself and explained that they would be cruising along the Leeds and Liverpool canal in the direction of Keighley. He also said that passengers were advised to stay in their seats, unless they needed to use either of the two toilets, which were pointed out. He commented how happy he and the crew were, having been unable to take Lady Luck out for such a long time.

Not long after they set off, the two hostesses began to bring round the cream tea. It comprised dainty sandwiches and pretty cup-cakes, along with a pot of tea for two. They could ask for extras if they wanted.

Mitsy was too happy to eat, at the beginning. The gentle thrum of the engine was very relaxing and she and Norma were so excited to see a heron fishing, some mallards both male and female, as well as a swan with a clutch of cygnets in tow and several moorhens and coots. Mitsy thought she caught a glimpse of a kingfisher but it was gone in a flash of colour so she couldn't be sure.

The view from the narrow boat was ideal for bird watching but it wasn't so easy to pick out landmarks. Mitsy thought she spotted Airedale General Hospital but to be honest, it could have been any large modern building. Almost without anyone noticing, the vessel turned round and retraced the route back to Skipton from where they had embarked. The two-hour trip passed so quickly and everyone said that they had really enjoyed themselves. The on-board staff were ready to help anyone with mobility needs but as Mitsy and Norma were feeling independent, they strolled along at their own pace, making their way back to the minibus where Osbourne was waiting.

It was strange to be out of doors in a bustling and cheerful town environment amongst people they didn't know, but not unpleasant.

Mitsy thought, as she dropped off to sleep that night, that it had been a delightful trip and an ideal way to go back out into the big wide world after being closeted for so long.

12

One morning, Mitsy received a phone call from Robert, an old friend of her husband Peter. In actual fact the two men had both joined up at the same time and in their early days in the Royal Navy, they were assigned to the same vessel. Robert was also the Best Man at their wedding.

She was surprised to hear that Rob – which was what he now called himself – currently lived not far away in Wakefield. He asked if he could call in that afternoon to say hello. Of course, Mitsy said she would be happy to see him and would inform the staff at Appledore House, as he would need to be logged in the visitor book and could only see her in the garden summerhouse. She also reminded him about wearing a face covering, social distancing and hand cleansing.

It was strange really, because Peter and Robert had very little contact after those early years in training together. He had called at their house in Harrogate a couple of times, staying overnight on his way to somewhere else, not long after they were first married. Then they had largely lost touch.

When Peter died, Mitsy's son Pete contacted Robert to invite him to the funeral but it transpired that he was not able to attend. Mitsy could only conclude from today's phone call that he had got her current address and contact details from her son. She was rather puzzled because she had been under the impression that Robert (oops, must remember to call him Rob, she thought) still lived in Portsmouth.

After lunch Mitsy changed into a smarter dress, deciding that the jeans or leggings that she wore most days were a bit scruffy to receive a visitor. She brushed her hair, applied just a little make-up and finally wafted some of her favourite perfume around herself. The scent always made her feel a bit sad as it was one of the last gifts Peter gave her.

When it was time, she made her way out to the summerhouse and waited. On the dot of two o'clock there was a knock on the summerhouse door and Jill, one of the Appledore House staff, was there with Mitsy's visitor. Mitsy confirmed that they would appreciate some tea in a little while and Rob entered the divided room, making a move to give Mitsy a hug before it was obvious that there was a screen between them.

Mitsy was immediately surprised to see a small, plump and quite elderly man. His face was shiny and quite pink and his grey hair was cut quite severely, as if he wanted to look like he was still on active service in the navy. Of course, over the intervening years Rob had aged as much as she had and she realised with a shock that she barely recognised him. Strangely, she had expected to see the man who was standing at Peter's side on their wedding photos.

"Hello, Rob. This is a pleasant surprise! Do sit down and tell me how you have been all these years," she said, gesturing to one of the chairs located on the other side of the screen.

Behind the face mask she presumed Rob was smiling but it was hard to tell. He settled down and prepared to launch into what seemed like a well-prepared speech. Well, thought Mitsy, I suppose I have always done the same in explaining to people the genesis of my own unusual name.

"First, I must say how well you look Mitsy. The years have been kind to you and I always did envy Peter nabbing the most beautiful girl in the room."

Mitsy flushed a little pink and smiled. She wasn't used to receiving such compliments.

He took off his jacket, sat back in the chair, crossed his legs and appeared to be making himself comfortable. He took a deep breath and continued his speech.

"Where do I begin? I've had a good life, you know. I enjoyed my naval service and travelled all over the world.

When it was time to retire, I was settled in Portsmouth, as you will remember. The first few years were happy and I had plenty of friends to spend time with. I had dabbled a little in investments and at one stage everything I owned was tied up in interesting projects."

He paused for breath and Mitsy got the impression that a difficult part of the story came next.

"Unfortunately, my business dealings went badly wrong and I lost everything. Everything. Lock, stock and barrel. Some of it was my own fault for being too trusting and some of it was plainly fraudulent behaviour on the part of someone I had considered to be a friend."

Mitsy was unsure quite how to respond to this, so she shook her head in sadness and disbelief.

"I lost my home and every penny I owned. It was a total disaster. I honestly didn't know where to turn for help. Thankfully, a lady I used to meet at bingo offered me a roof over my head, otherwise I would have been living on the streets. I had to rent it from her, of course. I also had to find some funds in order to pay off several loans. It was a very worrying time. Then my sister died and I received a small amount from her estate, which enabled me to clear most of my debts."

He paused and Mitsy assumed that he was either taking a breath or smiling, while he prepared for the next part of his tale.

"Another lady I had been friendly with for some time, who lives in Wakefield, invited me to visit her for a break from my troubles. I stayed with her for eighteen months but the relationship didn't last. I'm now renting a one room flat nearby."

"Oh, my goodness Rob. You have had a difficult time. I'm pleased to hear you are more settled now though," said Mitsy.

At this point there was a tap on the door and Jill appeared with tea and biscuits. She had to take a mug of tea and a plate of biscuits to the visitor, before entering by the other door to deliver similar to Mitsy.

"Thank you very much, Jill," said Mitsy.

"So, tell me all about you Mitsy! This seems a very nice place," said Rob, glancing round the room in the summerhouse and then the garden beyond.

"There's not much to tell really, Rob. I moved in a couple of years ago, and everyone is very kind and helpful."

"So, what happened to that lovely big house you lived in, in Harrogate?"

"After Peter died, it really became too much for me. I couldn't manage the garden and just cooking for myself was a challenge as any chopping, peeling and preparing was too painful. Pete – you will remember we had just the one son – found Appledore House for me. I moved in straight away and we sold the house. There's no more to tell, really."

Mitsy took a sip of her tea, while Rob looked again around the summerhouse and the visible parts of the rear garden.

"And where do you stay?" he asked.

"Oh, I have room six on the ground floor. It's very pleasant with an en suite bathroom, large bed, plenty of cupboards and storage space and a desk where I do my writing. You can just see it there, the room with the double windows," she pointed.

Rob nodded. "Oh, that will do nicely. What a lovely room. Two big windows looking out across the garden. I didn't expect there would be so much space."

Mitsy was a little puzzled by Rob's comment, but assumed she had misheard.

"Yes, it's a double room. It's much bigger than all the rest, I think."

"I imagine that Peter left you comfortably off?" asked Rob.

At this, Mitsy shook her head as she was really not happy to talk about her financial situation which she had always considered to be a private matter.

"I suppose you have money to spare, now the Council pays for your home?" he continued.

Deciding it was time to curtail this line of enquiry, Mitsy raised her voice, just a little.

"Oh, no Rob. I think there's some misunderstanding here. The Council do not pay for anything."

"Right. So, I could just move in, like a lodger?" he winked at her.

In her head, Mitsy said WHAT! The very CHEEK of it! How DARE he!

She took a deep breath. "I don't believe there are any vacant rooms in the house at present, but anyone wishing to come to Appledore House has to show the company that owns the property some evidence of being able to pay the fees, which are considerable," she responded, as coldly as possible.

"Oh, well. It was worth a try. We could be really comfortable together Mitsy, you and me."

Mitsy was shocked and distressed at Rob's brazen approach to her. It's no wonder his relationships don't last, she thought to herself. I bet he goes after any woman who has a little money put by.

Very quickly, she decided it was time to put a stop to this conversation once and for all.

"No, Rob. That will NOT be happening. I was extremely happily married to Peter and there is no way I would contemplate another relationship. I think it's probably time you headed back to Wakefield."

Rob, realising that he had drawn a blank and his plan had failed, stood up, buttoned up his jacket and stepped towards the door. "No hard feelings then. Look after yourself darling," he smiled as he turned the handle.

Mitsy, usually so courteous to everyone, could not bring herself to reply.

After Rob left, she returned to the safety of room six and turned the key in her door. She needed some time to herself.

13

As time went on, Mitsy had decided that she needed to know what her dear departed husband and Esmeralda had been up to. With her recent experience of Robert still fresh in her mind, she had reminded herself that people are not always what you might expect. She had remembered Robert as a quiet, courteous man but clearly, he had developed his chat-up lines over the years and while away at sea. She shivered to think of his horrible approach to her. By comparison, the men who lived at Appledore House, such as Arthur and Raymond were so kind and respectful of everyone – both men and women.

She genuinely thought that it was most likely that Peter and Esmeralda had some kind of relatively innocent friendship, but with Elaine's negative experiences in mind she wanted to clear up the mystery.

There had been no response to her letter and so finally she agreed that she and Elaine would take the trip to Nottingham. She thought that they could stand on the doorstep of the address she had for Esmeralda and meet her at a distance, just to put her own mind at rest, if indeed that was how it turned out.

According to the regulations, if she wanted to go out, she was permitted to make the trip but she would have to spend two weeks in isolation when she returned. Frankly, that was no great hardship given that she wasn't able to see Pete yet and if she had already spent time in the car with Elaine then it wouldn't be a problem to stay in her room for a couple of weeks. She asked Maggie if the visit would be OK as she urgently needed to see a relative. Of course, she was desperately hoping that Esmeralda's child was not in any way related!

Although it hadn't influenced her decision, she did remember that the clairvoyant had told her at the start of the year that she would go to Nottingham. She found that interesting at the time, as she didn't know anyone who lived there. Mind you, Ian Hardcastle hadn't predicted the pandemic, had he?

Elaine and Mitsy set off early for their trip to Nottingham, hoping to arrive at their destination by mid-morning. Mitsy had been really quite nervous about going out and it wasn't helped by the thought of meeting Esmeralda and her child. She had rehearsed in her mind, overnight, various scenarios and how she might deal with them. She tried to make it an enjoyable outing because, after all, Elaine was kindly taking her out and so Mitsy had insisted that she paid for a tankful of petrol. In spite of the modest pleasure derived from seeing the outside world after so many months in lockdown and shielding, she was terrified that they would discover something dreadful on this visit. All this was well concealed from Elaine, as Mitsy was a proud woman as well as being naturally optimistic and she dreaded the thought that her husband had been unfaithful.

On the way, the pair had a lot of laughs because Mitsy insisted on using the Satnav in Elaine's car to find the house they were heading towards while Elaine thought they could just drive near to the address and ask someone. It turned out that Elaine had never used the device and was rather wary of all the stories of people getting directed to the middle of a field. Of course, no such thing happened and so they followed directions suggested by the well-modulated voice all the way.

Arriving at "Sunnybank" as Esmeralda's house was called, they were surprised to find that it appeared to be a multi-occupancy property, providing sheltered accommodation. Mitsy rang the doorbell, then stood back a couple of paces as a young woman came to the door.

"Good morning. We've come to see Esmeralda," she said.

"Oh, we don't have anyone of that name. Are you sure that you have the correct address?"

Mitsy and Elaine looked at each other nonplussed. Mitsy held out the letter from Esmeralda with the address which was plain to see. She shook her head. "There must be some mistake. I'm sorry."

Just as the friends turned to leave, feeling deflated and rather disappointed, Elaine thought of something. "Do you have a young woman here with a daughter called Chelsea?" she asked.

"Oh. You mean Emma. Yes of course." She called along the corridor "Emma sweetheart, you have two visitors."

Almost instantly a young woman appeared with a small child at her side. Both Mitsy and Elaine noticed immediately that she had a lovely smile, which lit up her face. She also had Downs Syndrome.

After introductions, Emma invited Elaine and Mitsy to sit in the garden while someone made them a pot of tea. The toddler took a fancy to Elaine and clambered onto her lap.

Gradually, the mystery unfolded. Years earlier, while Emma was a still a child herself, Peter Howard had arrived on Emma's parents' doorstep asking for a bed for the night. When his ship had docked that afternoon, he had intended to head straight home for Harrogate but a rail strike had left him stranded. Seeing the B&B sign, he hoped he could stay over. That one evening cemented a friendship with Emma's family that lasted many years. He especially loved their little daughter and very quickly introduced a nickname for her; this was how Esmeralda came about. Peter, entirely unknown to Mitsy, got into the habit of staying with them for his first night on land, so that he could make the journey by train directly to his home in the North of England the following day with the minimum of changes and delays. This became his routine, it seemed, even when he had a car to drive home in.

Mitsy breathed a silent sigh of relief that the letter which had caused her such distress, could so easily be explained. She was thankful that Elaine had encouraged - almost forced - her to check the whole thing out. If they hadn't, she could have taken that secret worry to her grave. The learning from this morning's outing was interpreted in her mind as 'in future I shouldn't put off exploring something I don't understand as it could easily have a simple and happy explanation.'

Emma did not divulge anything about her child's father, it was none of their business in any case, but she spoke fondly of Peter and how he was like an uncle to her. She had been saddened to hear that he had passed away but didn't know how to respond to Peter's wife under the circumstances.

All too soon the friends realised that they should leave Emma and her daughter so that they could make the journey back to Bradford in good time. They thanked Emma for explaining and wished her all the best.

As soon as they were out in the street, Elaine observed "Fancy that. A young mongol girl."

"No, Elaine that's not a nice way to talk about her. Emma has Downs Syndrome and as far as I can see, she is doing a great job bringing up her daughter single-handedly," said Mitsy. "Mind you, I am amazed that Peter never mentioned Esmeralda to me or talked about her family and the bed and breakfast. I suppose he thought I would complain that he didn't come home as soon as they docked."

Later that evening she gave the whole episode more thought. It was such a relief that Esmeralda was in fact a sweet young lady who had considered Mitsy's husband as an honorary uncle. It did make her wonder if there were many other things that Peter had just never shared with her.

The outing to Nottingham was to be the last for everyone for some time. Not long after, the Covid infections rose again and the death rate soared. So, the country went back into lockdown. Whilst that was for the best, it was disappointing for many people, especially those who had anticipated meeting up with others, especially those having planned family gatherings. Pete and Jackie were sanguine about the situation; given that it had taken so many years for them to find each other, a little longer waiting to marry would not be a problem.

By November, Appledore House was promised their first vaccinations for residents and although December 8th was mooted, Dr Andrews the local GP thought it could be a little later.

When that day came and arrived, those avidly watching the TV news for information were deeply disappointed.

In fact, December 12th was vaccination day and the whole process was managed highly efficiently by Dr Andrews and her colleagues. What no one really anticipated was that virtually every resident had one or two minor side effects and the mood in the place was really low for a few days. Although it was largely sore arms and headaches, the level of confidence fell for a while.

Maggie had taken good note of all this and did her best to ensure that the staff vaccinations were staggered, so that if anyone did need time off at least they would not all be away at the same time.

As Mitsy sat watching the government presentations on the TV in her room giving cheerful updates on the number of vaccinations given, she could not help shouting out: "tell the truth!" although even she accepted that a couple of days feeling under the weather was worth it, compared with the alternative. It became obvious to her too, that many care homes had lost so many of their residents to Covid, including those who had no other underlying health issues apart from being older.

Mitsy and Arthur had their regular zoom session with their offspring and agreed that Christmas this year would be at a distance, regardless of what the government might decide at the last minute. They promised to have a virtual present opening on Christmas Eve, which was something to look forward to even though it would be different.

14

It was a strange Christmas for Mitsy, as it was for people the world over. The staff of Appledore House, as before, put the residents first – often ahead of their own family members. There was a Christmas tree, the singing of carols and exchange of presents. Even those of other (or no) faith joined in with the festivities. Christmas lunch was deemed "one of the best" and yet, most people would have preferred the dreadful threat of the coronavirus gone and a quiet Christmas with a family visit allowed.

Every week the local GP called in, checking on anyone of concern. She was also very pleased to support the regular virus checks that the staff undertook before starting duty, as well as bringing news when the promised second dose of the vaccine would arrive.

The "skeleton staff" had gone back to live with their families and the staff who had been on furlough were slowly reintroduced. The big motorhome was moved and the Podsiadlo's apartment was redecorated and turned into a double room in the event that Appledore House had a couple wishing to move in.

The news of Hannah Podsiadlo herself was not so good; it seemed she no longer recognised anyone and spent most of the day sleeping. Several of the staff had been visiting her and they all found it extremely upsetting, given that they had known her as such a vibrant, active woman when they worked for her. It was almost as if she had lost heart when Antoni died and there seemed nothing to live for now. Eventually, Maggie suggested that the visits should tail off, although she promised to go herself from time to time to update Hannah on happenings at Appledore House. This did seem a rather pointless exercise but it saved the staff from getting so distressed.

One of the first changes which seemed to signal that life might be returning to something like normal, was the arrival of two new residents. The first was Ted Bickerstaff. Not long after his wife died, Ted moved in to Appledore House. This was a long way from his home in Cornwall but his children had found it all too difficult to support him at such a long distance, especially as they were not permitted to travel under the coronavirus restrictions. He was born in the Bradford area and in fact had spent most of his working life here, so it was perhaps not surprising that his three children were still living nearby. Ted and his wife moved to St. Austell for their retirement, having spent many happy summer holidays in their caravan there. The grandchildren loved to visit during the long summer holidays so the arrangement had worked well for a number of years. They were disappointed not to be able to stay with their grandparents in Cornwall in the future but excited that they would be able to see grandad more often, in due course.

Mitsy, always kind and friendly to newcomers and knowing how distressing a bereavement can be, along with the accompanying life changes including a house move, made a point of sitting next to Ted in the dining room and engaged him in conversation.

"You will find everyone is friendly here Ted," said Mitsy, at the first opportunity for a chat.

"I'm not bothered. I keep myself to myself," retorted Ted.

"That's good. Will you be interested in coming to the activities once a week, or joining the outings once they start again in the Spring?" she ventured.

"No. I didn't want to move and I'm not interested in anything organised."

Mitsy sighed. Clearly Ted was not open to friendly overtures and Mitsy wisely decided not to push the point.

Maybe he would be more pleasant to talk to once he had got used to everything.

The other newcomer was Dawn. Although Ted was having difficulty settling in, Dawn Jones was a different matter altogether. She wasn't happy about moving to Appledore House either, which she immediately confided to Norma, but she couldn't see any alternative because her daughter had put her foot down and made it plain that she couldn't have her mother moving in with them. Norma needed all her diplomacy to deal with that tactfully!

Before long, Dawn was sharing her troubles with Mitsy and Arthur and in fact, anyone who was willing to listen. Mitsy concluded privately that it was no surprise that her daughter didn't want her mother to move in with them if she was always complaining about everything. Of course, some of this behaviour echoed that of her own sister Sky. Sky visited once, not long after Mitsy moved to Appledore House and it had been such a stressful day that she had managed to find excuses not to invite her again. There were scarcely any positives regarding the pandemic, but not seeing Sky was definitely one of them.

Ted steadfastly refused to speak to anyone and stayed in his room, whereas Dawn was invariably to be found in any of the shared areas just waiting to pounce on a resident or member of staff to vent her grumpiness on anyone willing to listen. Although everyone was kind and did understand what a difficult transition moving to a residential care home could be, they were all getting a bit tired of her irritability and complaints.

In spite of some of the restrictions being lifted briefly for Christmas this didn't apply to care homes and in any case Mitsy and Arthur were not able to resume their weekly pub lunchtimes. This was because the pub was still closed and had been closed throughout the pandemic and partly because, as Mitsy said, her heart just wasn't in it. It had been such a sad time and although Appledore House had only lost Lucy, it was obvious that many other places had not fared so well. They had no news of the Standsfield Arms but they both feared that the pub had not managed to keep going during the lockdowns and would have to close permanently.

By the new year, the government was keen to encourage people back to work but according to the television news the world seemed such a different place with endless hand washing, sanitiser, the wearing of face coverings and everywhere marked out with social distancing lines.

There was one thing that brightened Mitsy's day. She received a letter from a Beth Mackenzie. Apparently, Beth was a distant relative of the Doughty family. Following some long-winded communications that she had received via text message from a friend who lived in England, Beth had concluded that she could be related to the Doughtys. Her friend had seen the news item when Mitsy had been interviewed about her book and so she contacted Beth. Beth was twelve years old and quite excited to think she had "famous" ancestors. She mentioned this to her mum who kindly did a little research and confirmed that the Doughtys were indeed related to them. Then Beth's mum got in touch with the BBC to ask if they could have some contact details for the author of ***Violet's Story***. All this took some months and, quite frankly, it wasn't a priority for anyone. However, Mitsy was delighted to communicate with the twelve-year-old and enjoyed hearing from her and learning about life in the Highlands of Scotland.

One morning, shortly after breakfast, Mitsy was in her room listening to the radio and pondering how to fill her day. In fact, she was in the bathroom cleaning her teeth when she heard something that stopped her in the middle of her ablutions.

"Good morning. This is Saturday Live on BBC Radio 4. This week on our 'Thank you' slot, we have a heartfelt thank you from Irene Stott in Yorkshire. This is where one of our listeners has an opportunity to thank someone for their help when they had not been able to do so at the time."

The familiar theme music for this section of the programme, 'I Wanna Thank You' by the Enchanters blasted out of her radio as Mitsy squeezed some toothpaste on to her brush.

"My name is Irene Stott and I was a young student when this happened. I was hitch-hiking and you gave me a lift all the way from London to York as you were on your way home to Harrogate."

Mitsy wandered back into her room, interested because the woman who was speaking had just referred to her home town.

"You were very kind and patient as you talked me through a very difficult and upsetting situation. You saved me from making a grave error of judgement for which I will always be grateful. Thanks to you, I now have a beautiful teenage daughter who means the world to me. I was terribly afraid that I would be forced to give up my baby for adoption, which was not uncommon at the time. You also helped me think through the implications of having a child with no means of support."

"You even took me to the railway station and paid for my ticket for the onward train journey. When I asked if I could repay the money that you gave me, you said no, just look after yourself and your little baby. I only know that you were a sailor and that your name was Peter. When she was born, I called my daughter Petra and I want you to know that I really, really appreciated the hours you spent listening to me during that car journey and your efforts to guide me on a more sensible path than the one I was contemplating. Thank you, Peter from Harrogate."

By the end of this speech, Mitsy found herself in floods of tears as it seemed likely that the girl was thinking of an abortion, or even harming herself and the baby she carried. Then she wept some more, as she was almost certain that the Peter she referred to was her Peter.

"I love you, Peter Howard. Even though you are not with me any more, I shall always love you," she said out loud to herself, wiping her eyes and heading back into the bathroom to finish cleaning her teeth.

"Well," said the announcer, "thank you Irene Stott for sharing that with our listeners and of course, if Peter the sailor from Harrogate is listening, do contact us so that we can put you and Irene in touch with each other."

Mitsy sighed. What a lovely man her husband had been. It was just like him to be the voice of reason and common-sense while the poor girl was no doubt beside herself with worry.

A little later in the day, Mitsy wondered whether to get in touch with Irene. As she had been quite distracted for the rest of the programme, she hadn't really paid attention about how to get in touch. It took, in any case, only a couple of minutes to search for the details on the BBC website.

Saturdaylive@bbc.c.uk

Dear Saturday Live
I was listening to your programme this morning and a Thank You was broadcast from Irene Stott. I believe that the person who helped her was my late husband, Peter Howard. He was in the Royal Navy and we lived in Harrogate. It was just the sort of thing he would have done. I would be happy to communicate with Irene by email and you are welcome to pass on this email and my contact details to her. I would prefer, at this stage, for this to remain confidential.
Yours sincerely,
Mitsy Howard

Mitsy received a standard acknowledgement from the BBC and after a week or two, thought no more of the matter. Then, well into the third lockdown, she received a letter which pleased her very much.

Dear Mrs Howard
I am so happy that you heard my 'Thank you' on the radio. I had wondered for years how to express my gratitude to the very kind man who listened to me, calmed my fears, made some gentle suggestions and fundamentally put me on the path that I knew in my heart was right.

As your husband had suggested, my mother was much more understanding than I expected (once she had got over the shock) and she supported me then and ever since. At the time, she was also a single mum so you may imagine how difficult it all was. Mum has since married and I could not ask for a better step-dad and grandad to my girl.

I'm sorry I did not reply immediately to your email, which was passed to me via the BBC. I realised that if we were to get in touch, I needed to tell my daughter Petra what had happened. I did not want her to get the wrong impression and I certainly did not want her to think that she was not wanted.

Petra knows now and she would like to meet you too.

I am sorry that your husband passed away and I hope this is not all too upsetting for you. Do you still live near Harrogate? When lockdown ends, we would like to visit. Would that be possible?
Yours sincerely
Irene Stott

This contact made Mitsy happy and she emailed a reply to Irene, explaining her current situation and suggesting that they meet up in a socially distanced way, once that was possible.

Overall, the atmosphere at Appledore House was quite positive as the residents had been given a date for their second vaccination. Gerald Longhope had been very active too, making sure that all the staff had their vaccinations around the same time. One or two employees in his other homes, so they heard, were doubtful about being vaccinated. Accordingly, all staff had received a friendly but firm letter from him, explaining that a vaccination was advisable and would be considered as a 'genuine occupational qualification'; in other words, in order for them to be considered suitable for a job in his care homes, they needed to show that they had been fully vaccinated.

The only blight on the general good mood was the newcomer Dawn, who continued to complain about everything. The word went round, privately between the more established residents, that Dawn had lodged several complaints with Maggie about various staff members. When she did not get the satisfaction she sought, she sent a formal letter of complaint to YourCare Limited, threatening to go to the newspapers.

One afternoon, Kate was idly looking out of her bedroom window when she saw a taxi draw up and she heard the driver knock on the front door. This was especially puzzling as it was still forbidden for anyone to leave the building, unless it was an emergency and they were willing to go into two weeks' isolation on their return. A few minutes later, Kate observed Dawn carrying a small overnight bag followed by the taxi driver, who was wearing a face covering and carrying two very large suitcases.

Of course, Kate wasted no time phoning Mitsy but both were quite puzzled as to what exactly was happening.

That evening, when Joyce delivered the evening medication, Mitsy asked if she knew where Dawn had moved to. Joyce looked at her watch, deemed there was enough time for a quick chat and sat down next to Mitsy.

"Well, you see, Dawn made several complaints about the staff and the arrangements in general here at Appledore House. Each complaint was investigated, both by Maggie and by one of the matrons at another of Mr Longhope's care homes. It was concluded that they were not genuine or valid but Dawn demanded that her daughter acted upon these complaints. So, Dawn's daughter had a meeting with Maggie and Mr Longhope and it was decided that it would be helpful to check on Dawn's mental health."

Joyce paused for breath and realised that this tale might be a bit vague and distressing for Mitsy, so she explained: "when the doctor came round, she asked Dawn some simple questions like what is today's date and who is the Prime Minister. It was a full mental health assessment and she concluded that there were no new health concerns. It was agreed that Dawn's daughter would have to find another home that had a vacancy and that she would move her there as soon as possible because it was clear that no matter what the Appledore House staff did, we could not meet her needs."

"Oh my goodness," said Mitsy. "So, she was moving to her new care home this afternoon?"

"Not exactly Mitsy. You see, the whole episode was a ruse to move into her daughter's house, we think. While Dawn's daughter was making arrangements for her mother to stay in another care home, Dawn took things into her own hands, booked a taxi and moved out, going directly to her daughter's house. Maggie received a phone call this afternoon to say that Dawn had arrived at her daughter's house and was safe and well."

"That's really sad when someone doesn't settle in well," observed Mitsy.

"Yes, it is. But I have to say – don't tell anyone else I said this – that it's really not fair on hardworking staff to be deliberately difficult and make such a worry for us all."

"Thank you for explaining it to me. Can I tell anyone else?"

Joyce thought for a minute, knowing that Mitsy could be discreet if she asked her.

"It might be best to keep it to yourself for now. I think Maggie will inform you all that Dawn has moved, when she speaks to you at lunchtime tomorrow."

"Thank you, Joyce. I'll keep mum!!"

That night, shortly after Mitsy settled herself down for sleep, the White Lady, otherwise known as Violet appeared at her bedside. It seemed that she sensed there had been a bit of an emotional upset and stood quietly watching nearby. Mitsy gradually relaxed and by the time she was dropping off to sleep, the kindly ghost just disappeared through the wall.

Some while later Mitsy, being a light sleeper, woke to hear a lot of shouting and doors banging. This was very unusual. In fact, having experienced some noisy neighbours during a hotel stay once, she had been wary of moving into communal living in a residential care home for fear of regular disturbances like this.

Under normal circumstances nothing could be further from the truth and Appledore House had always been very calm and quiet at night since she had moved in, which made the current fracas all the more troublesome. Eventually, all was quiet again but by that stage Mitsy was too stressed to sleep so she put on her dressing gown and sat reading a book for half an hour or more. When she realised that she had read the same sentence several times over, she concluded it was time to go back to bed, now that the household was also settled.

At breakfast the next morning, there was an explanation of sorts. Apparently, Ted – one of the recent arrivals at Appledore House – had seen a ghost.

He did not come to breakfast but his neighbours were full of the news. He claimed to have seen the White Lady and had been heard shouting, "That bloody woman! She needs to be locked up for making that ghost appear like that out of the blue! I'll give her ***Violet's Story***! As if I don't have enough to worry about!"

Mitsy was quite upset to hear herself described like that but her friends told her not to take it to heart. In fact, they all thought it was quite funny now it was broad daylight.

According to the gossip that was being shared freely at breakfast, the previous evening Val had been on night duty. Val was new and had been recruited to replace the disgraced Shirley. Until now, all her night shifts had been completely without incident. As this was her first job in a care home, she was not really sure what to expect. Consequently, she was having a nap in the back room behind the kitchen and did not hear anything to begin with.

Ted, it has to be told, had been reading Mitsy's book about the time when Appledore House had been used as a Red Cross Hospital station for receiving injured men returning from the Front during the First World War. After a couple of hours of light sleep, he got up to use the toilet. This was when Violet appeared in his room. The poor man was so frightened he wet himself and this made him angrier. He flung open the door to his room and shouted for help. When no one came, he slammed the door and rang the emergency night bell with some vigour.

Val came quickly to see what was the problem and, because she knew nothing of Mitsy's book or indeed the White Lady, she was under the impression that Ted had been dreaming or maybe was exhibiting some form of dementia. Ted shouted so loudly that the residents in the two neighbouring rooms both came out to see what had happened, but only after they had heard Val's calming voice.

After considerable discussion, it was agreed that maybe reading Mitsy's book just before bed had caused the ghostly visitation. Val sent Ted's neighbours back to their respective rooms and then did a thorough search of Ted's bedroom, confirming that it was completely free of visitors either worldly or spiritual. Eventually everyone calmed down.

At hand over the next morning, Val reported the incident and this left Maggie with a dilemma. They certainly did not want Appledore House to get the reputation of being haunted as that would worry everyone living there and that could also impact on the business generally and its good name. She was aware that Mitsy's book had brought some positive publicity to the care home too. She had a discussion about the episode on the phone with Gerald Longhope and he suggested a way forward.

Mid-morning, Maggie tapped on the door of room six, bringing Mitsy a pot of coffee, two cups and a plate of chocolate biscuits. When Mitsy saw this offering, she felt sure she was in trouble and would be asked to leave the home that she was now happily settled in. Thankfully, this was not the case and Maggie gave Mitsy a quick summary of the events of the previous night. Being a discreet woman, Mitsy did not divulge that she had already heard the gossip over the breakfast table.

"I'm not sure quite what we can do, Mitsy," she said. "It may be that we will have to live with this ghost making infrequent appearances although I'm not too happy about that."

“Well, Maggie. Violet has been dropping in on me quite a lot recently but I have a very strong feeling that we are coming to the end of her visits,” said Mitsy. She did not want to explain that she had been to a clairvoyant earlier in the year or that he, from what she could recall, had indicated that the White Lady would be leaving soon.

“I wondered whether we could get the local newspaper in and perhaps tell a little white lie, getting them to report that the ghost is no longer here?”

Mitsy was not at all happy with this suggestion. She was extremely uncomfortable about telling lies, whether they were white ones or whoppers, and she had no confidence in the journalist she had spoken to before, who she thought had made her sound elderly and somewhat deranged.

“I’m not sure about that, Maggie. For one thing, Ted would immediately be in a position to contradict this and that could do more harm than good. May I make a suggestion?”

“Of course, Mitsy.”

Mitsy sat quietly for a moment, sipping her coffee before she replied:

“I think we should let the whole thing go totally quiet for as long as possible. As I said, I’m pretty sure that we have seen the last of Violet although I cannot say why. We would need all the staff to be aware that the less discussion of the subject the better. Then, when nothing has happened for two or three months, I would be willing to give another interview to the Telegraph and Argus. I’d prefer it not to be that man who wrote the article last time but I’m sure that you or Mr Longhope could arrange for someone different. I would talk about a young lady who lives in Scotland who is related to the Doughtys and how she is studying the history of Appledore House at school. Her name is Beth and I think they would like to write about her, rather than me. As part of the interview, I would casually throw in the fact that there is no ghost now, implying that it was something that happened a good while ago. Again, the less said the better.”

Maggie agreed that it would be a better approach and with that, she left Mitsy to finish her coffee and biscuits.

Mitsy sat reflecting quietly on everything that had happened. I'm sure we've seen the last of Violet, it's such a strong feeling, almost as if she said goodbye to me last night, she thought to herself. As Ian Hardcastle had suggested, Violet was just interested. Given that Ted had been reading ***Violet's Story*** just before he went to bed, maybe she was just checking to see what he thought of the book!

She did appreciate Maggie and Mr Longhope treating her as a fully functioning adult, by asking her opinion. She consoled herself that with a bit of luck the whole thing would die down and she wouldn't even have to speak to a reporter either.

15

One of the great consolations during the pandemic which counteracted Mitsy feeling too imprisoned, was the possibility of spending time in the garden of Appledore House whenever she wanted. Not only could she watch the birds feeding just beyond the windows of her room but she could venture out of doors in order to sit and listen to the birdsong or take a walk round the lawn, inspecting the shrubs and flowers that were planted in the beds. Before the pandemic, she had been accustomed to going for walks in the surrounding area of the care home once or twice a week either alone or with a friend, so it was a relief currently to be able to get some fresh air in the garden even if it was just for twenty minutes or so.

She was concerned not to be out of doors when others were, because of the difficulty in keeping one's distance. She had tried it a few times but, because some of her best friends were a little hard of hearing, they tended to gradually move closer than social distancing advised. The alternative was to raise one's voice but this, of course, increased the likelihood of spreading germs anyway. Only a few of the other residents enjoyed walking round the garden but that was usually in the morning. After breakfast and before lunch was the norm and hardly anyone had a late afternoon stroll. In this way Mitsy was able to get some fresh air and enjoy the outdoors on her own most afternoons, even though it was relatively limited exercise.

As she sat on her favourite seat – the one she had used to spot Shirley getting up to no good in her room that afternoon – she saw Arthur through the glass of the back door. He came out and wandered over to Mitsy asking, "may I join you?"

He sat down carefully, assessing if he was sufficiently distant and shuffled a little to the left.

"Of course, Arthur. How are you?"

"I'm fine thank you. I've got some news!"

"Ooooh. Do tell."

"Jackie has been in touch to say that they have decided to get married in London after all. I'm not sure why, but I have a feeling that they thought we could both more easily get a train down to London from here. As it happens, I didn't mind getting a flight to Dublin."

"Honestly Arthur, I'm quite happy wherever it is. Have they sorted a date yet?"

"No. They didn't want to put us at any risk, so they were waiting until everyone has had their two jabs plus two or three weeks. I told them we had ours last Wednesday, so we're nearly ready."

The pair sat comfortably together as the last rays of the sun dipped down below the hedge behind them.

"I didn't think that organising a registry office wedding would be too complicated given that there are so few guests but it seems that they have had a lot to think about in terms of witnesses, flowers, music etc."

"Did you ask what would be the colour theme, Arthur?"

"No. Should I? I don't know anything about these things."

"Well. Look at it like this. If we know what Jackie is planning to wear, I can decide what would be best for the 'mother-in-law of the bride' to wear. I don't want to upstage or clash colours with her."

"Hmm. I hadn't thought of that sort of thing. To be honest, when I was in business, I always had someone to organise things and I just turned up, not really being aware of the advance planning involved."

Mitsy smiled. "I don't really know anything about your business Arthur. What exactly did you do, apart from leaving it to someone else to organise?" she teased.

“Haven’t I told you the story? Well, at University I had no idea what I wanted to do so I was, I suppose, waiting for something to present itself. I did a business studies course but I didn’t really imagine there was any sort of business I would like to go in to. Then Ivy and I met, got married and decided we would like to have our honeymoon in Istanbul; it had not long before, in 1930 I think, changed its name from Constantinople. Ivy thought it would be a fascinating place to visit and sort of amusing given that she was changing her name to mine.

Anyway, while we were there, we discovered many beautiful carpets and rugs in the Souk, you know – the covered market place, and I bought a few with our wedding gift money. Yes, I know!” At this point in the story Arthur raised his hands in submission, although Mitsy hadn’t said a word and hadn’t even raised her eyebrows. Arthur continued, “I know other people would have bought china or cutlery to start our new home with, but I had these beautiful floor coverings shipped back to England and I subsequently sold them at a decent profit in the local market. As soon as we finished Uni, I made some slightly more formal arrangements and it expanded into a proper business fairly quickly after that.

I used to go over to Turkey and after a few years to India so I could order a good stock of rugs to import. At the outset, I stored them in a friend’s garage. Then I made a few contacts in some upmarket department stores in London and Manchester, you know like Selfridges and Heal’s, and they started to sell them for me. Eventually, I was able to employ a few people and I became the Managing Director. The team did all the footwork and I did the negotiations. Ivy did the bookkeeping in the early years, until Jackie was born then we recruited a finance director. When Ivy and I decided it was time to retire I sold the business. That’s all to tell really.”

Mitsy nodded. “That’s a really impressive CV Arthur, you should be proud of your business acumen.”

“Thank you Mitsy. I really enjoyed what I did, so it was quite a lot of fun and often it didn’t seem like work.”

“I now know why you look underneath rugs when we are out visiting. I presume you are assessing the quality?”

“Ha-ha that’s true. I’m looking at the way a rug has been woven, but I didn’t realise anyone had noticed me!”

Mitsy shivered slightly as the temperature outside was dropping. “I think I’ll go in now,” she said.

“Yes. Me too. I’ll see you at dinner.”

16

One afternoon Mitsy was outside, sitting on one of the garden seats that was located at the edge of the lawn. She was idly watching Greg, who was pruning the berberis bush. Greg's son Alan helped him out some days although he had not been around so much over the past year as he had been busy delivering food parcels for the local council. Today they were chatting companionably while Greg pruned and Alan collected the clippings.

"You two *are* busy!" she called.

"Well, there's always a lot to do, Mitsy," replied Greg.

"Hmm. It's a big garden, isn't it? It's about the same size as my garden was when I lived in Harrogate."

"Really? That must have been an awful lot for you to do on your own. I wouldn't manage the grass, the shrubbery, the orchard and the apple trees, the soft fruit and the vegetable plot as well as the greenhouse without Alan's help when he's free!"

"Oh. I thought the end of the garden was at the laurel hedge?" said Mitsy, feeling quite confused as she wasn't aware of fruit trees, vegetables or a greenhouse here at Appledore House.

"Oh no my dear. It goes on and on, beyond the monkey puzzle tree and the summerhouse where you meet your families, all the way to the old shelter built into the hillside behind. Those soft fruits and apple trees help to keep the kitchen well stocked in the summer and autumn; that's how you have such lovely pies and crumbles. We grow tomatoes and other salad stuff in the greenhouse. Fancy you not being aware of that!"

Mitsy smiled and then realised that she was distracting them from their work. Greg had always been happy to talk to her but under the circumstances she didn't want to hinder their work and as she was trying to avoid close contact with them both too, she wandered further down the garden than usual.

As she ambled past the monkey puzzle tree, she saw that to the left of the laurel hedge there was a small gap. This pathway led into the orchard where there were half a dozen apple trees that Greg had mentioned. She also saw some of the soft fruit bushes and was able to identify raspberries, rhubarb and blackcurrant. Beyond that there was a green house. This was full of plants in trays as well as other things sitting on the ground in pots.

How silly of me not to realise that the garden went on so much further beyond the laurel hedge! I should have realised that our rhubarb crumbles and apple pies were part of Greg and Alan's contribution to our wellbeing in Appledore House, she thought.

"Ha-ha! If I had known this before, I could have been out for much longer walks to this area, as it's very private," she said out loud, but to herself.

Mitsy had noticed that during lockdown she often spoke out loud, even though there was no one listening. I hope I'm not going batty, she thought.

Right at the very bottom, she discovered a building covered by a mound of grass and weeds which was virtually buried. She thought it was rather charming with a curved roof and a small wooden door at the front. To the left of the doorway was a millstone and there was a watering can on the right. The whole structure looked quite picturesque. The door was hanging ajar as if one of its hinges had broken and she could see that it had been propped open with a log. It reminded Mitsy of Bilbo Baggins' house in The Hobbit.

Greg appeared nearby with a wheel barrowful of clippings to put on the compost heap. He approached Mitsy with his usual gruff greeting. "I see you've discovered the rest of the garden Mitsy!"

"Oh, thank you Greg. I was just wondering what that shed is used for?"

"That's no shed my lovely, it's an old shelter from the second world war I believe."

Mitsy turned her face towards Greg and nodded. "Oh yes, I was only a baby when those were being built. They were for people to stay in safely when the air raids were expected."

"That's right. This one is made from galvanised corrugated iron panels. It's an Anderson shelter."

"What's inside this one, Greg?"

"Dunno. I've never been in it."

Mitsy nodded, smiled and continued her walk around the garden. But, being Mitsy, she couldn't resist pondering what could be inside the old building. Later that evening, after doing a Google search on Anderson shelters, she discovered that these temporary structures could be quite cosy during the frightening air raids and people often slept down there. They named them after John Anderson, the Home Secretary at the time. The one in the grounds of Appledore House seemed to be quite well made and was partially buried in the ground to offer extra protection. I wonder who used it? Maybe I'll explore it some time, she said to herself.

17

During the evening meal at Appledore House, there was a lively discussion about what was on the television later. Mitsy did not contribute to the debate because she rarely enjoyed any of the soaps or comedy programmes that the others seemed to prefer. It's not that she didn't appreciate the occasional light-hearted series, just that she was rather choosy over which to watch.

Back in her room after dinner, she picked up a book, flicked through a few pages and decided she wasn't in the mood for reading. She sighed. There was nothing really to enjoy or to entertain her. When she lived in Harrogate there were always plenty of things to do. There were friends and neighbours to chat to, restaurants, pubs and wine bars to meet up in, the theatre and cinema and of course her darling Peter to talk to. After he passed away, she still had all the same facilities available, but no husband to share them with. Over time, Mitsy managed to make a life for herself as a young widow. She joined a local walking group and started evening classes to learn Italian. The evening classes were in the afternoon and the young woman who was leading them was very pleasant; at least, all the younger men in the group thought so! Mitsy didn't really think she would go to Italy; it was just interesting to learn another language.

Then when she moved to Appledore House, at the beginning it was such a relief not to have the chores and the garden to worry about that she was content to relax in the privacy of her room. Of course, it was different before Covid, when she could go for walks and outings, have a weekly pub lunch with Arthur and enjoy trips such as travelling independently to Dublin to spend a weekend with Pete.

She had previously spent a while doing her ancestry search, some of which was fruitful but, in the end, she gave up because it was frustrating when she kept coming to a dead end.

Writing ***Violet's Story*** had entertained her for several months, but again, she got to the point during the editing stage when she was thoroughly bored with Violet and all the characters she had made up. It was fun to get her book published and she appreciated some of the subsequent publicity but she had already decided that she didn't want to write another book, not for a while anyway.

There was a time when she enjoyed clothes shopping on line and she derived much pleasure from this, making sure that she always looked smart and attractive. Once her fellow residents started getting her to order things for them, shopping for herself took a back seat.

She glanced out at the garden and spotted an unusual bird on her bird feeder. Fetching her Pocket Guide to British Birds she concluded that it was a lone greenfinch, enjoying the seeds she had put out.

Mitsy looked at the clock and realised that it was only ten minutes since she had returned to her room after dinner. She was tempted to shout out loud "I'm bored!!" but she didn't. She smiled to think of Pete when he was a child, as it was one of his frequent complaints. Then, during his teenage years, "I'm bored" was accompanied by sulkiness, as anything she suggested was spurned with total disdain. Of course, he grew out of it but Mitsy wondered if she was actually approaching a second adolescence herself.

Suddenly it occurred to her that she needed a hobby of some sort. Almost as quickly she decided that she would learn to paint. She had been intrigued by her neighbour Raymond, who was clearly skilled at producing good, true-to-life sketches but she immediately had in mind something more colourful.

Her first port of call, of course, was the computer where she quickly ordered a sketch pad, some HB and 2B pencils, some paint brushes of various sizes, a full set of watercolour paints and a beginner's guide to painting and drawing. She smiled with the satisfaction of having given herself a goal and, with that achieved, she turned on the TV to watch something that required very little concentration.

Later, when Joyce tapped on her door for the evening medication round, she found Mitsy gently dozing in front of a blank screen.

The new project gained momentum as soon as her painting equipment arrived. At the beginning, she took her sketch pad out of doors and, sitting on one of the vacant garden seats she drew 'still life' such as leaves and flowers. She did attempt a couple of bird pictures but she soon realised that her early efforts resembled some as yet undiscovered form of dinosaur! Coupled with the fact that these were unrecognisable, the birds themselves failed to co-operate by sitting still so that she could observe them and all she could capture was a ball of feathers flying away.

Part of the reason that Mitsy's drawings were not entirely successful, was the way that arthritis affected her hands (she often referred to them as "my badly behaved hands") as they were quite swollen and deformed and it made them ache dreadfully if she was holding anything in the same position for long. It was for this reason that Pete had arranged the phone in her room to be routed through Alexa, so that she didn't have to hold the handset. Perhaps if she had given this some thought before enthusiastically launching herself into her new hobby, she could have saved herself some discomfort.

The addition of watercolour paint did improve some of the early plant and leaf sketches and although the finished articles were truly dreadful, Mitsy found that the intense concentration required was quite relaxing and prevented her from mulling over the many insignificant things that she was worrying about.

She took the whole process seriously, reading her beginner's guide and learning from a couple of TV programmes. One of the latter was where inexperienced people competed by being given different painting challenges each week but this tended to trouble her because those who were voted out of the series were often upset and disheartened. Another programme showcased different artists and their lives. This was fascinating and highly informative about the way of life in different times and in many countries around the world. It also led her to think that perhaps she would get more pleasure from working with oil or acrylic paints and by concentrating on abstract works. The large brushes would also be so much easier to hold and would not require the same level of accuracy that her experimental watercolour work did.

Accordingly, the computer was drawn into service again and she ordered an easel, some acrylic paints and brushes, a palette and some canvas boards. It was a good thing that she had enough spending money to spare this month as her new hobby required quite a considerable outlay.

Mitsy found that when the weather was fine, she could spend an hour or so in the garden with her easel and paints, just enjoying the freedom to express whatever was going through her mind. The other residents persisted in passing by and asking what it was she was painting but after a while they tired of getting the same answer, which was "I don't know yet".

When it was cold or wet, she was happy to paint in her room.

Gradually, she began to feel quite pleased with her efforts and her smaller paintings and modest canvases began to turn into quite impressive pieces. Maggie kindly gave her an old curtain which she could use to cover up any work in progress, which put a halt to most of Mitsy's friends asking about her painting.

One day she stood back, looked at her canvas and said to herself, "That's it. That's what I've been trying to convey."

Eventually, she hoped it could be hung prominently on her bedroom wall. It was called 'My People' and she signed it discreetly at the bottom right-hand corner 'M Howard March 2021'. It didn't really bother her that no one else understood what it was about. Arthur asked her to explain it to him and as he was such a kind and thoughtful person, she did her best. Sadly, Kate was less sensitive and blurted out, "oh Mitsy, that looks like an explosion in a paint factory" before realising this wasn't the kindest of observations. Really what she was trying to express was how, amongst her friends and family, everyone was very different in personality and yet they impinged on each other to make a glorious whole that she was very grateful for.

Once 'My People' was dry and was ready to be hung on the wall, Mitsy began to tire of her new hobby and began casting around for something else with which to occupy herself. She and Arthur often spoke about how much they missed their weekly lunchtime visits to the Stansfield Arms but, of course, there was no telling when that could resume.

Apart from Arthur, Kate too was a good friend and they often sat together in her room or Mitsy's, talking about all sorts of things.

"I shall be eighty-four next week," she told Mitsy one afternoon.

"Oh, I nearly forgot. I've got your birthday present here," said Mitsy.

"Can I open it now?"

"Certainly not! It's bad luck," she replied.

"Well, I've never heard that before," said Kate.

"My mum said so, so it must be right," laughed Mitsy.

"I can't believe it really," commented Kate.

"What do you mean? That it's unlucky to open a gift before the correct day?"

"No, Mitsy. I mean I cannot believe how old I am. I never expected to reach this age. My parents, as well as my birth mother – you know, my sister – they all died in their late sixties. I'm pleased that I'm still going strong but I do think about death a lot. Do you?"

"No, not really. In my head I still feel twenty or thirty, but sometimes my body insists on reminding me otherwise," she said. "For example, a twenty-minute walk is as much as I want to do these days. And if I've been doing lots of things in the morning, like emails and online shopping, my brain is too tired to do anything else in the afternoon."

"People say that if you live in a care home like this, it's God's Waiting Room. I think that's horrible. Don't you?"

"Yes. I do Kate. I believe that we all have much to discover in life and lots to offer other people, no matter what age we are. In fact, we are fortunate because we have so much life experience – even if it's only 'well, I wouldn't do that again!'"

The pair smiled at each other, both recalling deeds past and present. Kate went back to her room, birthday present intact, for now.

Eventually Mitsy developed a new hobby. She began to take photos of plants in the garden on dry days, and then she entertained herself turning these pictures into cards that could be used for letters or birthday greetings. She didn't admit to anyone else that she was bored because they were, after all, in the same situation.

Everyone was hoping that life would go back to normal now that they had all had their booster vaccination and the third lockdown was due to end shortly. The residents had received their second vaccinations in March and subsequently all of the Appledore House staff had theirs too. Mitsy heard that in some places people were refusing to have theirs, which she thought was unhelpful and selfish. She couldn't understand people who would not wear their face coverings either. Yes, masks were a bit awkward but after all this time you got used to it. Thankfully, no-one was at all sceptical at the home. They had seen how poorly Lucy was and had no doubt whatsoever that lockdowns and individuals taking careful precautions would be the only way to manage Covid. Mitsy herself was less clear as to whether or when life would return to normal. As she got older, she was determined to make the most of every day.

18

One afternoon, after Mitsy had sent emails to her son Pete and to her sister Sky, she closed the laptop and stared out of the window. She liked to receive letters and cards but no one seemed to write them much these days.

She decided that as it was dry and quite mild, she would take her regular walk in the modest grounds of Appledore House. Now I know that there's more to the garden than just up to the laurel hedge, maybe I could walk a bit further and explore that old building, she said to herself. All was quiet in the garden and no one was around. Greg and his son were attending to the wisteria, which grew resplendently over the front of the building, rewarding them with a glorious display of blue hanging flowers in May and June.

In the back garden, Mitsy wandered past the flower beds, the monkey puzzle tree and what people were calling 'the bird sanctuary'. It was a rather grand name for the bird bath, a couple of feeders and a bird box intended to appeal to the blue tits. Mitsy already had a feeding station directly outside one of her bedroom windows, which she had put in place not long after moving in. It attracted a mixture of the smaller garden birds. That laurel hedge needs a trim, she thought, although she was aware that a flock of hedge sparrows roosted there and sometimes established their nests there too. I suppose Greg is leaving the growth for now and trying not to disturb them, she thought.

She wandered past the apple trees and then the greenhouse, which currently nurtured baby tomato plants, some mixed lettuce leaf and a selection of herbs which would all be used by the kitchen.

Further down the garden, right at the bottom, she noticed that the door of the old Anderson shelter was now swinging open. She walked up tentatively and called through the open doorway, "Hello. Is anyone in there?"

Receiving no response, Mitsy boldly entered the building. It was very dark, I suppose because there are no windows, and it seems to be larger inside than out, just like a Tardis! she mused. Several steps inside and once her eyes had grown accustomed to the dark, she saw a table. In fact, it was one of those school desks that she remembered from the 1950's with a round hole at the top right-hand corner where a white ceramic inkwell used to sit. On the desk was a small torch, which she picked up switched on and gave it a shake. Although the torch wasn't powerful, it did at least illuminate much of the main room.

Mitsy could see that there were six bunk beds. These had been made from big, strong metal poles with sailcloth or some sort of sturdy canvas slung across them and fixed in a V shape so that one person's feet would be over another person's head. I expect during the war, smelly feet would be the last thing on someone's mind, she commented to herself.

In another corner there was a tall metal cupboard, a bit like the sort they used in school or gym changing rooms. Next to that was another small square desk and a tiny chair and Mitsy concluded that the last two items had probably come from a primary school.

She sat down on the little chair to try to imagine what it must have been like during the war, as she didn't really remember anything from that time. She wondered if this shelter was possibly used by the descendants of the Doughty family. Mitsy's book ***Violet's Story*** had charted the time when the family handed over their home to the Red Cross, during the First World War, so this shelter would have been built over twenty years' later.

Inside the cupboard there was a pile of magazines. Of course, they would need something to do to pass the time during air raids, she realised. Picking one off the top of the stack, she held her torch over it to see what kind of magazine it was and the date it was printed.

"Oh. Oh, dear me. I think this is what is known as porn. And not just gentlemen's top shelf magazines," she said to herself. Not that Mitsy was terribly familiar with this genre of journalism. She could, however, ascertain that anything that closely allied men and farm animals in this manner was not necessarily agricultural.

She hastily put it back on the pile and was just pondering who on earth would look at this kind of stuff, when she heard a scraping sound, a thud and a muffled voice. All she heard was "… don't want any of the residents going in…"

Mitsy leapt up from the seat and realised in an instant that someone had closed the door. Making her way over to the door carefully in the pitch dark, she turned the door knob and pushed, but nothing moved.

"Oh. Oh. Oh, dear me," she said again. "I think I'm shut in."

Her embarrassment at discovering the salacious magazines and a dawning awareness that she shouldn't really have been in the air raid shelter had stopped her from calling out loud, which would have been sensible. By the time her predicament had become obvious to her, the disembodied voices (which were probably those of Greg and Alan) had disappeared.

"Well, Mitsy. Your curiosity has really done it this time. Whatever shall I do?" Mitsy often talked softly to herself, usually it wasn't audible but at the moment she was quite scared and spoke out loud as if someone else was there to help sort out this situation.

After a few minutes of feeling helpless, she concluded that there was nothing she could do except wait until she was missed and hope that the staff had enough imagination to envisage that she was locked in an unused building at the far end of the garden. Put like that, it didn't seem very likely.

She tried the door once more, her hands shaking as she directed the torch to the door knob. No, it wouldn't budge and what was worse, she noticed that her torch was fading slightly to a warm gold rather than the clear blue light she started off with.

I should have brought my own torch, she thought. Of course, the last time she had used that, was during her somewhat disastrous night-time exploration of the derelict mill opposite. That was a couple of years ago and the building had since been turned into a block of luxury apartments.

"Right Mitsy. This is no time to panic," she said firmly to herself. "You must accept that you could be spending the night here, in total darkness, and make the best use of what light is left in the torch." She sounded braver than she felt.

Scanning round the room once more she noticed a small cushion, covered in red and white gingham. In broad daylight it would probably have revealed itself to be rather dirty and no doubt mouldy. She guessed it was smelly too but it would at least provide some sort of pillow for her head. Mitsy checked each of the bunk beds and concluded wisely that she would be best to use a lower level one, as she was not as nimble at the age of eighty as she used to be.

Hmm. I'm not sure, but I think tramps and rough sleepers use newspapers to provide some insulation from the ground where they are sleeping, she wondered to herself. Mitsy picked up several magazines and began to open them up from the middle and lay them on her chosen – but make-do – bed. She began to giggle at the thought of sleeping on top of those pictures and their decidedly lurid content.

By this stage her torch was fading badly and she needed to give it a good shake every so often to revive it.

She sat down again to consider what to do. She noticed that the room was very, very dark as there were no windows and not even a chink of light leaked in from the door surround. Of course, during the war everyone had to have blackout curtains so that enemy planes did not have any buildings with lights on for them to aim at. Even an air raid shelter would need to be as well concealed as possible.

There was also quite a strange smell. She sniffed the air and concluded that it smelled of earth – not surprising as the floor was compacted soil - and stale air because there was no natural ventilation.

She walked over to the door again and gave it a kick and a good shake but nothing would budge.

“Right. Well, I suppose everyone will be going in to dinner now. I’ve no idea of the time because since lockdown I haven’t needed a watch and I’ve stopped carrying my phone with me given that I’m in my room most of the day.”

Mitsy was aware that she had made a serious error of judgement by going into the old shelter and that she had landed herself in quite a predicament. Tears began to roll down her cheeks as she silently cursed her foolishness. She could not think of any way to alert people to the situation nor any way to make things more comfortable while she sat out the night. She did realise that a night in the outdoors, even in April when temperatures could drop below zero, could bring on hypothermia in people of any age.

Mitsy was already feeling hungry. She tried hard not to think of food but she was aware that today’s menu included roast beef and Yorkshire pudding, which she loved.

What shall I do if I need to go to the toilet? No, not if but when? She waved the torch around and was sad to find there was no clue as to what the previous occupants did. Maybe they had a bucket? Well, there’s no sign of one now so I shall just have to go on the floor in a corner, she sighed; how embarrassing.

After all this preparation, Mitsy realised that she would just have to sit it out, even if it took all night before she was rescued. She shivered and pulled her light cardigan around her shoulders. Finally, she sat down on the little wooden chair, turned off her torch to save it for when it was essential and began to practice her deep breathing.

19

While Mitsy was preparing to sit the night out, she couldn't know that it was actually only four-thirty. In the total darkness of the shelter, she had lost track of time and it seemed much later.

Meanwhile, Kate was wondering why Mitsy hadn't called her on the phone as she had promised. With nothing else to do, she eventually took the lift downstairs and tapped on Mitsy's door. There was no answer so she assumed that, untypically, Mitsy had forgotten. Raymond, who had the room opposite, came out when he heard her knocking. "Hello there Kate. Were you looking for Mitsy?" he said.

"Well, yes I was Raymond. I expected her to give me a call this afternoon and she didn't."

"I saw her heading off for her afternoon walk in the garden a couple of hours ago but I don't know where she is now," he said, closing his door slowly.

Kate went back to her room and watched some detective story on the TV. It was pretty dire but it passed the time until the dinner bell rang.

Virtually all the residents at Appledore House enjoyed the meals that were prepared for them, especially all the warming casseroles during the winter months. Roast beef and Yorkshire pudding was also a favourite. The cooks tried hard to give them nutritious and tasty food, so the beef was sliced thinly and the Yorkshire pudding was very light with a few green vegetables for balance. Since the start of lockdown, the staff had found it really difficult to buy everything they wanted, especially in the early weeks when there were many shortages. Today's meal would be a special pleasure for all of the residents were it not for a small but determined lady who was at this moment shivering in a disused air raid shelter.

Kate was quite concerned to find Mitsy had not turned up for the meal. She leaned across the table to ask advice from Arthur, who was virtually Mitsy's best friend. "Arthur. Have you any idea where Mitsy might be? I knocked on her door this afternoon and she didn't answer. Raymond said he saw her go out for her walk in the garden ages ago."

Arthur had no idea either but he was rather concerned. "Did you open the door of her room to see if she was inside, maybe she had a fall?"

"Oh no. I didn't think of that."

"You stay where you are and make sure I get plenty of gravy while I just pop along the corridor to check."

Arthur was back in no time at all, before any of the staff even noticed he was missing. He leant across the table and in a low voice said, "No Kate. No sign of her. I know she wouldn't be silly enough to go beyond the building given the coronavirus restrictions. I suggest we finish our meal and discreetly have a look for her in the garden without causing alarm for the time being."

Kate nodded and they both ate their meals rather hurriedly and without the usual relish.

"No that was lovely thank you but I don't want a dessert today," said Kate to Michael, one of the relatively new staff members who had moved over from one of Mr Longhope' s other residential care homes.

As soon as possible, Kate and Arthur left the building by the main door, skirted round the side and into the rear garden. Kate had sensibly fetched a coat as she was feeling the early evening chill. They walked past the lawn with its multiple seats, looking carefully everywhere and calling softly "Mitsy, where are you?"

Beyond the monkey puzzle tree, Arthur remarked that he hadn't actually been this far down the garden before, assuming it was all deep undergrowth.

"No. Neither have I, Arthur. Actually, I feel a little bit afraid. Did you hear that owl hoot? It's lovely in some ways but a bit spooky."

Kate's nerves were getting the better of her and she was chattering away so much that Arthur was starting to feel concerned for her. Very gently, he took Kate's hand and said, "Let's walk slowly down to the very bottom of the garden and if there's no sign of Mitsy then we will need to go back and tell one of the staff." Before long, they came to the front of the Anderson shelter. It was barely visible with the grass and weeds covering its roof.

"Oh. I don't think I knew this was here," he said.

"Mitsy. Where are you?" they called.

Mitsy was in fact sitting bolt upright in the small school chair and had dozed off. Whatever it was that attracted her attention, she thought she heard voices so she reacted quickly. "Help. Please help me".

Kate nearly jumped out of her skin and grasped Arthur's hand even more tightly.

"Mitsy. Where are you? It's Arthur and Kate here."

"Oh, thank goodness. I got locked in this air raid shelter," Mitsy breathed a sigh of utter relief. "Can you get me out?"

Arthur bent down towards the door and realised that it was not going to be easy.

"Mitsy. Are you safe inside, for the time being? It seems that there is a very large and heavy mill stone that has been rolled in front of this door. We will have to get help to move it."

Now that she was almost safe, Mitsy gave in to all her fears and started crying.

"Please don't upset yourself Mitsy. We will get it sorted and have you out of there straight away," said Kate, expressing more confidence than she actually felt. Perhaps it was holding Arthur's hand that helped.

Arthur suggested that Kate stayed outside the door and talked to Mitsy while he fetched help. That was easier said than done and Kate was none too keen to stand in the pitch dark all on her own. However, she thought how much more frightening it must be for Mitsy trapped inside this old metal building. Mitsy had been so kind to Kate in the past, so it was the least she could do.

"I'm standing guard here Mitsy. Arthur will get someone to help in moving the big millstone. Do tell me how this happened Mitsy," she said, once Arthur had headed back up the garden.

Mitsy gave Kate a brief summary of her exploits, missing out any reference to the dodgy reading matter. They agreed that entering the place probably wasn't the most sensible thing to have done, rather on a par with Mitsy's visit to the derelict mill.

"I wonder how the millstone got in front of the door?" asked Kate.

"Oh, I imagine that it was Greg and Alan tidying up before finishing the day's work in the garden," replied Mitsy. "It was nobody else's fault except mine. I'm so grateful that the two of you came to look for me."

More voices could be heard across the grass and within a couple of minutes Mitsy could just discern Ruth's voice.

"Hello Mitsy. It's Ruth here. How ever did this happen?"

"I was just interested to know more about the Anderson shelter and I peeped inside and sort of sat down to check it out and suddenly the door was locked."

"I see. Well, we all know how your curiosity sometimes gets the better of you! I'm afraid this isn't going to be quite so easy to sort out though because the door isn't locked. It is blocked by a very large millstone which is too heavy for us to move. I'm going to phone Greg now and see if he can come over or suggest what we could use as a lever to move it. In the meantime, please stay calm and we will get it sorted."

Mitsy did try to stay calm, but she was very uncomfortable to think that Greg would know that she knew about his magazine stash. Of course, it may not have been his, but it was hardly likely to be a topic of conversation between them in the future.

As time went on, she began to get rather distressed because she was cold, her muscles were aching and she needed a toilet. She felt she couldn't grumble as she had brought the whole episode on herself.

Eventually, she could hear Greg's voice. "Hello there Mitsy. I hear you've been exploring again!" he said.

"Hello Greg. I'm ever so sorry you've been called back to work because of my foolishness." There was a wobble in Mitsy's voice that revealed how frightened she really was.

"Now then. There's no need to get upset. We'll have this big millstone rolled out of the way in no time."

There was a lot of pushing, shouting, heavy breathing and calling to one another but eventually Mitsy could hear the stone move.

"Right my dearie-oh. I think the door should open now," said Greg's reassuring voice.

Mitsy stood up and the door was opened. All she could see was a crowd of friendly faces. In some ways, if someone had been very cross with her it would have been better. As it was, everyone's kindness in the face of her misdemeanour was all the more upsetting and she burst into tears as she breathed the fresh, rather cool evening air.

Apart from the fact that there was quite a crowd, they all appeared to be holding torches which they shone into her face. For a moment she felt as if she was being attacked by the paparazzi. Then everyone burst into a spontaneous round of applause. It was all quite bizarre.

Ruth stepped forward and gently clasped Mitsy's hand. "Right. That's enough excitement for one evening. Come with me Mitsy and after you've freshened yourself up you can have some of the dinner that we've saved for you."

Mitsy breathed a very, very deep sigh of relief and, for once, did exactly as she was told.

20

Friday morning turned out to be a bumper day for letters in the post. Having collected them from the sideboard inside the front door where the postman had left them, Mitsy wandered back to her room hardly believing that she had five letters! I bet they are all just advertising rubbish of one sort or another, she said to herself. Although she loved to receive letters in the post, she had become rather wary, not to say cynical, in recent times.

The post arriving this morning was a helpful distraction from being trapped in the dark yesterday. She had come to no real harm and, as much as anything else, she had frightened only herself. She couldn't help thinking what might have been the outcome if her lovely friends Kate and Arthur had not thought to look for her.

The Big Apple Awaits You!
The Big Apple Awaits You!
The Big Apple Awaits You!

Dear Mrs Howard
Thank you for your letter. We were pleased to hear that you will be accepting your prize of a long weekend in New York. Given the current circumstances with the global pandemic, we are happy to extend the date for taking this special prize until the end of this year. We would normally not transfer this to anyone other than the prize-winner

prize him or herself but our Managing Director has given permission on this occasion for your son and his fiancée to accept the trip on your behalf.

A condition of the prize is that the happy couple would need to be available for a small part of the trip, no more than an hour, for publicity photographs.

Please let me have contact details for your son so that I can make the necessary travel arrangements.

Yours sincerely
N. Trowell
Natalie Trowell

Following yesterday's escapade, Mitsy had been questioned rather closely over breakfast by all who were sitting on the same table and frankly, she could not explain her actions entirely. She needed something to take her mind off the whole affair.

Mitsy smiled to herself. Well, at least that envelope is good news. I must write to Pete and tell him. It will be a lovely surprise, she thought.

The second letter was a white envelope with a Portsmouth postmark. Oh, I'm not happy about opening this but I'll have to see what it is, mused Mitsy.

43 Lansdowne Way,
Portsmouth PO1 6SD

Dear Mrs Howard
Please accept our condolences on the loss of your husband, Peter.

My husband and I were very pleased to hear from our daughter Emma that you and a friend had kindly visited her in Nottingham. She's a good girl and is doing well bringing up Chelsea on her own, although it helps that her residential care home is very supportive.

We had no idea that Mr Howard had passed away. We just assumed that he had retired from the Royal Navy and that we would not hear from him again.

Emma probably told you how fond we were of him and throughout his many stays over the years we grew to know all about you and your young son. He was devoted to you and was always impatient to get home.

If you are ever in the area, you would be most welcome to stay with us. We don't run the B&B any more but you would be considered as a friend.

Yours sincerely
Maybelle Armitage

Well, that's very kind, thought Mitsy. I doubt that I would ever go to Portsmouth, though. If Peter was here, I would certainly give him a piece of my mind. Fancy never mentioning these kind people or the little girl he used to tease and call Esmeralda. If only he had told me that he stayed over so that his journey was more manageable the next day, I would have understood. I've never been the jealous sort so it would never have occurred to me that he had a 'fancy woman' as Elaine would put it.

Mitsy recognised the handwriting on the third envelope and took a deep breath before opening it.

My Dear Sister
Isn't this lockdown just dreadful? I haven't been able to go to the shops for three weeks!!! Of course, Jim has been no use at all. He just hides in his garden shed and pretends he has lots to do. The girls are not allowed to visit either and I really could do with Avril to cut and set my hair and Mel to help me with the chores. Jim makes such a lot of work I could do without him being under my feet all the time.

I suppose it's all very nice for you in that Appledore House being waited on hand and foot. No wonder you had time to write a book. We did not manage to see you on the television although my next-door neighbour said it was very short but that you seemed alright.

Lord knows when we will be able to visit again. Jim said he wants to come next time so at least I won't have to suffer that dreadful train journey on my own.

Love
Sky xx

Mitsy sighed and raised her eyes heavenwards. It was just typical of Sky to focus totally on herself. She was almost tempted to write back straight away, observing that she and all her fellow care home residents were a bit tired of being locked up for many months, let alone the three weeks that Sky was complaining about. At Appledore House everyone was thankful they had not suffered the same fate as Lucy and the thousands of people who had died of Covid19 not to mention all those who had lost their loved ones and others who were still suffering from long Covid.

But she realised that even slightly sarcastic comments from herself would only make Sky's temper all the more irritable. So, she put the letter to one side, intending to reply when she felt more kindly disposed to her sibling.

The next envelope contained a rather sad letter and a potent reminder of the times:

Longstaff, Wentworth and Reed LLP
Castle Parade,
Harrogate
N. Yorkshire

Dear Mrs Howard
Re: Your Will and Power of Attorney

I am sorry to have to inform you that Mrs Wendy Reed, Solicitor, who handled all your legal requirements and services as above, sadly passed away recently. She was a much-valued partner in our business and will be sorely missed. She was taken ill quite unexpectedly with Covid19 and in spite of excellent care in the local hospital, did not survive.

As you can imagine, we are extremely busy dealing with all of Mrs Reed's clients and I would ask you not to contact us unless the matter is urgent. In due course we will let you know who will be taking over her caseload.

Yours sincerely
Mary Hobbs
pp Longstaff, Wentworth and Reed Solicitors

Oh, that's so sad, thought Mitsy. Mrs Reed was lovely and so helpful when Pete and I went over to sort out my will and the power of attorney documents. I suppose I'd better let Pete know too. It certainly puts into perspective Sky's moans about not being able to go out for three weeks.

Finally, Mitsy opened the fifth envelope addressed to her in very neat handwriting.

Dear Mrs Howard
Thank you very much for writing to me to tell me a little more about my ancestors, the Doughtys. My teacher was very interested and we had a lesson about the First World War.

Now I am going to do a project for my school about the house you live in and the way it has changed over the years. I found a picture on the internet of Appledore House as it is now, but I wondered if you had any earlier photos of it?

I hope you don't mind me asking. Thank you.

With best wishes
Beth Mackenzie

Mitsy sat for a few minutes thinking about Beth's request and concluded that she would need to ask her friend Arthur if he could assist. After all, he did the original research on Appledore House that led to her writing the book.

For now, she was happy that none of today's letters were going to cause a problem of any sort. So, she tucked them all under a paperweight on her writing desk, intending to deal with them later.

21

For once, the sun was shining, the temperature was mild and no one else was sitting on the bench seat in the garden. Misty strolled out and sat down gently with a small smile of satisfaction.

Then the back door opened and her heart sank. Damn! Now I shall have to sit and talk to someone without a functioning brain cell, she grumbled to herself. It wasn't really like her to be so nasty about her fellow residents. It was more than likely that the extended period of lockdown had had an impact on them all. Some people missed the daily chit-chat and were delighted to gossip about anything, while others had accommodated to the imposed isolation and had started to prefer their own company. Mitsy was in the latter category.

Fortunately, the person emerging from the back door was Arthur, and Mitsy was really quite fond of him. They had both missed their weekly lunches in the Standsfield Arms where they had been able to relax together and talk about anything.

"Hello, Arthur. How nice to see you! I hope that lovely daughter of yours is well?"

"Yes, thank you Mitsy. Jackie is fine. Soon you will be able to call her your daughter-in-law, you know."

"Oh. Have the wedding plans advanced at all?"

"I'm not aware if they have, but surely they will be able to organise it soon."

"That reminds me, Arthur. I have a surprise for them. Do you remember me telling you that it looked as if I had won a prize in a competition?

"Er, vaguely," said Arthur. To be honest he had no recollection of the conversation at all but thought it was safest to give an indeterminate response.

"Well. It turns out it wasn't a scam and they are giving me a weekend in New York."

Arthur smiled weakly, feeling rather concerned that he might be teetering on the edge of accompanying Mitsy across the Atlantic. He wouldn't really mind as he genuinely enjoyed spending time with her; it was just that he didn't fancy spending half the weekend on a plane.

"The company have been very kind and because of Covid they have allowed the prize to be taken later this year. Even better, they are allowing me to give the tickets to Pete and Jackie. I've written to Pete but he hasn't replied yet. Do you think they will accept?"

"Oh, that's so kind of you Mitsy. I should think it will be ideal if they can fit it in along with their busy work schedules."

Arthur smiled. "Did you hear the news this morning? Apparently, the government is allowing people in residential homes to go out once more. I know we've been able to sit out in our garden here ….and some especially curious people have been even more adventurous!! But it seems we are being let out of our building as long as we stay outdoors and everyone can meet another person as long as they do all the usual hands-face-space stuff."

Mitsy grinned at Arthur's teasing reference to her nearly calamitous visit to the air raid shelter and nodded to indicate that she too had heard the news.

"I'm not sure it will make much difference really, Arthur. I don't actually want to go to the shops and we have everything we need here."

"That's true. But it is all part of everything easing, which means Jackie and Pete will be able to book the registry office soon."

He paused and they exchanged a smile. Mitsy thought how fortunate she was to have met Arthur here. He was, in many ways, her best friend.

"Oh. Before I forget, Mitsy, I did ask Jackie if she had any preferences for what you could wear to the wedding or what she was having as her colour scheme for the big day. You were right, she had that all planned. She said that her dress is cream with large pink and blue flowers. To be honest I couldn't really imagine it but as it's supposed to be a secret as far as the groom is concerned, I didn't like to ask more as Jackie hinted that Pete had just come into the room while we were talking on the phone."

"Oh, that's fine Arthur. I will probably wear my cerise dress and jacket then. I'll have to get a hat. That will be fun trying to order one on line, I don't think. You, of course, will be able to choose a tie and a pocket handkerchief in either pink or blue. You have got a smart suit, haven't you?"

Arthur grinned as he realised that Mitsy was getting really excited. It would do them both good to have something to look forward to.

"Yes. I've got a smart suit. I last wore it to Ivy's funeral so it will be a chance to give it an airing for something happy. Perhaps you could help me find a suitable tie etc? In cerise, so we are co-ordinated?"

Mitsy was never sure whether Arthur was teasing her or not, so she erred on the side of caution, "Happy to help!" she said.

Arthur stood up. "Well, I'll love you and leave you," he said, heading back to the door.

She knew it was only a turn of phrase, but she rather liked it. Of course, no one could ever replace her dearest husband of over forty years. With Peter she had lived a very independent and self-sufficient life, especially when he was away at sea for weeks or months at a time. Although she was making no comparisons, she did like the way Arthur 'looked after' her. She had not really experienced that level of care from Peter because she had to make her own decisions most of the time. Those ranged from when to buy a new, second-hand car to whether to get a plumber in to fix a leak. If she had an accident, which she did once when she sprained her ankle, she had to ask her neighbour to collect young Pete from school and get some shopping in for her.

Arthur had proved himself to be thoughtful, caring and reliable. He had kept an eye out for her when she went missing yesterday, organised a search party of himself and Kate, and fetched help when it was needed to move the big millstone from the doorway.

Mitsy recognised that he understood her ways well. She was cross about the newspaper reporter making her feel old, earlier in the year but Arthur soothed her irritation and put the whole thing into perspective.

In modern day parlance, Mitsy realised that Arthur was always 'there for her'. It was a good feeling.

22

Mitsy was definitely rather unsettled and bored. The business with the Anderson shelter had left her rather wary of embarking on any more adventures or exploration for the time being.

Her experiments with painting had come to an end and her big, colourful artwork now adorned the bedroom wall. Jason, who was Maggie's grandson, had kindly organised the fixing of it and so it seemed that she had nothing with which to occupy herself.

Ruth had been in to change the bed linen this morning and while she was dusting the furniture, they had a little chat about nothing in particular, the weather and whether Mitsy's shoes needed cleaning.

She sat in her rocking chair and sighed. She was as happy as she could be at Appledore House, given the restrictions of the global pandemic. But she was still a bit bored.

She decided to tidy her desk drawer. On the top was a notebook that she had used to record all the on-line purchases that she had organised for the other residents. In the right-hand column, there was a large tick against each person's name when the outstanding money had been settled. Thankfully, Maggie and her team had realised it had all become a stressful and tedious chore for Mitsy, even after they had restricted the activity to Fridays. Eventually they had enlisted the support of a student who was training to be a carer and he carried out a similar task for the residents two evenings a week, as part of his coursework.

Another notebook, which was only partly used, had recorded some dates and names which were findings that Mitsy had made in her earlier phase of ancestry research. That exercise had led her to jump to some conclusions as well as misunderstandings when she made her night time visits to the disused mill. Ultimately, she had hit a brick wall with all of that, even though there was plenty of scope for discovering more about the Irish side of the family if she decided to look into it some more, in the future. The ancestry searches were another example of how her fellow residents took advantage of her kind and generous nature by asking her to find out things for them too. After the rather distressing discovery that Caitlin's birth mother was actually her sister, Mitsy decided not to be available for those kinds of things anymore.

A large A4 notepad showed lots of jottings from a conversation she and Arthur had, relating to the history of Appledore House. This had been used as the basis for her first, and only, novel ***Violet's Story***. When it came to writing the book, Mitsy typed straight on to her desk top computer and edited it mostly herself. Now, as she read through the historical facts that Arthur had shared with her, she was surprised to see how closely she had woven them into her book. She had enjoyed the process of writing a novel, but as she hinted to the BBC presenter, she really didn't have any plans to write another. She did enjoy sharing her ideas with young Beth, so the fact that she and her classmates could learn about the past was pleasing.

Tucked at the bottom of the drawer were a few handwritten letters from her husband Peter that she had somehow managed to save when the Harrogate house was sold. Peter rarely wrote when he was away at sea. It was more practical to phone or send an email. Mostly, he wanted news of how she was and what their young son Pete had been doing, but there were just a few occasions when he was feeling especially romantic and he would write or send flowers. She took his letters out of the drawer, reread them – even though she knew them almost word for word – and found herself crying all over again. She still missed his presence daily and sometimes the smallest thing would trigger her distress and the familiar ache of loss would return. He was a good and loving husband as so many recent events had confirmed. In truth, she never doubted his fidelity for a minute and she suspected that spending too much time with Elaine had led her to question his motives.

Just as Mitsy was straightening the contents in order to put them back in the drawer, she noticed that a few loose sheets of paper had been crushed into a concertina shape behind everything else. Taking them out she discovered they were the notes she had written when she and Elaine saw the clairvoyant. "Now what was his name?" she asked herself out loud and immediately saw that she had written on the back 'Ian Hardcastle' and the date of the visit.

She closed her eyes and imagined she was back in the farmhouse up on the moor. She could almost hear the wind howling round the building.

She remembered how Mr Hardcastle had taken her watch, rubbed it gently in his hands before saying that the watch was given to her by Peter, with love. At the time she had thought the man had quizzed Elaine for a few facts in advance but it soon became obvious he was getting his information from elsewhere, wherever that was. He knew all about her 'escapade in the Mill' as he described it and even more remarkably, he was able to tell her what films Mitsy's father had written the sound track for. Given that her sister Sky had no recollection of this and even Jackie with all the resources available to her at the British Film Institute had difficulty unearthing, it was impressive.

Mitsy was reassured that the ghost that so frequently visited her at night (the White Lady) was Violet and, re-reading her notes "she wants you to know that she means you no harm, she is just interested. She will leave soon."

Mitsy paused as she read the next bit, "you will find yourself in a dark place, but not for long". Hmm, you can say that again Mr Hardcastle! All those things that happened relating to my darling Peter which left me so much 'in the dark' about his life and then, the ghastly experience of being locked in the air raid shelter in the pitch dark.

There were several other things that amused her. "There's a special trip to London, another to Nottingham and a return visit to Dublin. Your friend Elaine will be with you sometimes but not when you go to the United States of America."

Well, all in all, he got at least half of the future travel correct and identified so many other things that no one else would know about. She realised that she had stopped being quite so sceptical of the paranormal since visiting Ian Hardcastle.

Mitsy smiled. Clearing out the desk drawer had restored her equilibrium. Life was still good, regardless of the occasional bump in the road.

What Mitsy Did Next

1

"I'm going to have my colours done tomorrow," said Mitsy to Eva as she ran her fingers through her hair. "How about you?"

Eva looked a little puzzled. "I just had my hair done last week. I think it's OK for now."

Eva was new to Appledore House and so she was unsure how things were organised here but she appreciated Mitsy's kindness in helping her settle in.

"Oh no," said Mitsy. "I meant I'm going to that session that's being held here in the dining room tomorrow afternoon. You know how as you get older your hair changes colour; your skin tone alters and all the clothes you bought when you were younger look wrong and don't fit nicely? Well, there's a 'colour consultant' coming to advise us on our colours. My friend went to a session once and she told her she was autumn colours. That meant that gold, orange and brown shades looked best on her. It was funny really because she ended up sending most of her clothes to the charity shop and buying new. And new make-up. I seem to remember her husband was not best amused!"

Eva smiled, "oh, that sounds like a good idea. I've never had my colours done! Where do we pay?"

"No need. It's all part of the events and entertainment that Appledore House organises for residents. There's a notice on the sideboard in the dining room. You just sign up to say you will go. I think sometimes if they choose something no one signs up for, they cancel it. Of course, there are probably maximum numbers but I've always been able to go to everything I've signed up for."

Eva nodded. She had not really expected anything so pleasant. Before she moved into Appledore House she was rather worried that everyone would sit around dozing all day with a nurse calling in occasionally to make them do exercises. It was turning out much better than she had feared.

"In the summer we have outings too. A minibus takes us to National Trust properties and we even had a riverboat trip on the canal once. Of course, the pandemic put a stop to the outings but things are starting to get better now."

Mitsy had gently steered Eva to the dining room where they found a clipboard leaning up against a china dog. Eva was happy to sign up and to take part. There was a maximum of ten people for tomorrow and only five names listed so far. Mitsy wondered out loud whether it was open to men but they concluded that the men probably didn't need make-up advice!

Currently, Appledore House had seven men and twelve women residents so anything Maggie organised needed to be suitable for the majority as well as not excluding the rest.

Mitsy left Eva at the door to her room, as she was meeting her friend Arthur for lunch today.

During the coronavirus pandemic, Appledore House had been very careful to follow all the guidance set out by the government during its televised announcements. Residents were required to stay in their rooms alone, where meals and medication were delivered by staff wearing personal protective equipment.

One day, one of the residents who was always known to be a bit perverse and difficult, flouted the rules by going out to the post office. Sadly, she caught the virus, rapidly succumbed to covid19 and died soon after. Lucy's death was a shock to many of the residents and brought into sharp focus the real dangers of the virus. Everyone began to accept that the rules were there to protect them.

It was a difficult time for all, not least the staff. A small group of them generously agreed to move in to the care home for the duration (not that anyone knew how long that would be), living in a motorhome and a couple of the unoccupied rooms. Of course, this meant that they were not able to be with their own families for which Mitsy and her fellow residents were much indebted. Eventually, once testing for coronavirus became available and more reliable, the 'skeleton staff' as they were known, were given time off so that other members of staff could take their places and relieve them.

Later, special arrangements were made for friends and family members to see their loved ones but this was only possible by booking in advance and visiting one at a time in a temporary building in the garden. By this means they were totally segregated from residents and had to communicate by gesture and through a glass partition.

Gradually the restrictions were partially lifted but still the residents spent a lot of time alone and the staff continued to wear PPE. Thankfully, when the weather was good, the garden became a favourite place for people to meet, enabling everyone to have some face to face conversation while keeping a social distance.

It will never be known how much the enforced solitude affected people. Many of the residents had been used to living alone before they moved into Appledore House but even they found the lack of human contact difficult to bear.

Before the pandemic, good friends Mitsy and Arthur were in the habit of spending one lunchtime each week in each other's company. They usually went to the nearby Standsfield Arms where they invariably had a ploughman's lunch; Mitsy had a glass of dry white wine and Arthur had a half pint of the local bitter ale. They were well known to the owners and had even held a celebratory meal when their offspring Pete and Jackie got engaged.

Eventually all the residents of Appledore House were told they could go out again, if they wore a face mask when indoors. Mitsy and Arthur were quite amused as they realised that would make having a meal and drink impossible. However, Arthur suggested that they could have a walk along the road to the pub which they considered to be their local, so they could check whether eating and drinking in the pub garden would be possible, avoiding the need for a face covering.

The whole experience felt strange, to be 'out in the world' again. They agreed that the short walk would be good for them but neither felt sufficiently confident to do more than walk there and back the first day. Discussing this with their fellow residents, it seemed that several of the others had felt uncomfortable on their first outing too.

Gradually life returned to what was often called 'the new normal.' "Shall we venture out for a bite to eat on Wednesday?" Arthur asked Mitsy one morning. Mitsy considered this briefly and then nodded.

The meals at Appledore House were good, so that wasn't really the reason the pair went to the pub. It was just that they both felt it stopped them from getting too insular. After a lifetime of self-reliance, moving into a care home could feel quite restrictive for many people.

Mitsy had settled in to Appledore House quite well, relinquishing housework, shopping, cooking, and gardening with pleasure. She soon made friends with the staff and other residents as well as enjoying the occasional visit from her son Pete when he was able to get time out from his work. When Arthur moved in, Mitsy was one of the first to offer the hand of friendship to him. So it was that a weekly pub lunch became their custom.

Going out had become such a strange occurrence that on Wednesday morning Mitsy stood in front of her wardrobe wondering what to wear. It amused her to think that the whole business of lockdowns had meant that many of the residents had started to wear pyjamas, track suits or other casual clothes most days.

She opened the wardrobe and scanned the row of hangers. She had a very smart suit which had not been worn, that she was saving for when Pete and Jackie got married. Next to that was a long-sleeved black and white houndstooth dress that looked quite smart under her black leather jacket. She glanced at the window and concluded that this would probably be safe enough unless the weather changed dramatically.

Not that she would admit it to anyone else, but it seemed she had gained some weight during the pandemic. 'That's not surprising, as I've had no exercise,' she muttered to herself. Mitsy could often be found having silent conversations with herself – it was obvious because her lips were moving - and if anyone ever mentioned it, she would smile and explain that at least she got sensible answers that way.

Meanwhile, upstairs in his own room Arthur was having a similar clothing dilemma. He was always a smartly dressed man and he felt that it was a matter of courtesy to look presentable when he went out. His wife had always chosen his clothes and when she passed away, it took him quite a while to refresh and replace his older clothes without her guidance. As much as anything else, every item he took from his drawers or wardrobe had a story attached. 'Ivy bought this shirt for me before we went on that first holiday to Scotland. It was so cold, that I nearly didn't wear it at all!' he remembered.

He was fond of Mitsy and she had become a good friend since he moved in to Appledore House but he was very aware that no one could replace his Ivy.

As the hall clock chimed twelve, Arthur was pleased to see Mitsy walking down the corridor towards him.

"Ready?" he asked, as if they were setting off on an adventure, which perhaps they were.

They hung up their room keys on the board by the door, showing that rooms six and fourteen were unoccupied. This was mainly for the benefit of the staff who would then be able to clean the vacated rooms. Later in the day, the key board was useful to show if anyone had failed to return after going out. This rarely happened and anyone showing the slightest sign of forgetfulness of this nature was carefully looked after until it became necessary to move them to one of the other homes that specialised in dementia care. Mrs Podsiadlo, the previous matron and owner of Appledore House, was accommodated in a special care home of this type.

"I've told Vicky in the kitchen that we didn't want lunch today," said Arthur.

With that, they closed the heavy door quietly behind them, crossed the large, gravelled, parking area and turned down the road towards the pub.

Since the pandemic, Arthur had become a little less stable on his feet and had taken to using a walking stick. Mitsy had not realised that this modification would change their walking pace and it took her a little while to adjust. Being a thoughtful and considerate person, she managed to appear to amble slowly alongside Arthur without drawing attention to this.

The Standsfield was barely a ten minute walk away and when they arrived Arthur put his head round the door to ask if they could eat in the pub garden. It seemed that was no problem at all and they walked round the side of the building to where some tables were set out.

One of the young women servers appeared immediately to ask what they would like to eat and drink.

"Oh, I think we will have a glass of dry white wine and half of bitter, for old times' sake," said Arthur, glancing at Mitsy to check that she agreed.

"Have you been here before, then?" asked the young woman. Mitsy was all too happy to recount the many times she and Arthur had enjoyed their Wednesday lunches.

"That's nice. I'm quite new here. I lost my last job because of covid but I was lucky to get this job straight away when they had a vacancy here," she chatted. Within minutes the owner of the pub came out to greet them, carrying their drinks. She was keen to find out how they had been, as well as sharing news of how the pub had fared during the pandemic. Apparently, the Standsfield Arms had struggled quite badly during the lockdowns and they had to make virtually all the staff redundant. She intimated that they were only just getting things back to normal.

“Now, we have a new menu. Did Louise tell you?”

Arthur and Mitsy shook their heads in unison. “I’ll get her to bring you one.”

“We haven’t said hello to Peter yet,” said Mitsy.

Peter was the friendly black Labrador that used to sit at their feet every time they visited.

“Oh dear. I’m afraid that’s another piece of sad news you have missed. Peter was taken ill right at the beginning of the pandemic. We couldn’t take him to the vet as they hadn’t sorted out their covid arrangements and by the time we did take him he was too poorly to be helped. I’m sorry but we had to have him put to sleep.”

Mitsy blinked and blew her nose loudly and Arthur shook his head. They had both become fond of the dog.

“We do have a new puppy though and I will bring him to see you later.”

Smiling, she went back into the bar and they could hear some orders being taken before Louise came out with the new menu.

“Hmm. I’m not sure what to have,” said Arthur.

Mitsy perused the new menu too. “I wish things didn’t change. We used to like our ploughman’s lunches but now I’m not sure what to choose either.”

Eventually they both plumped for toasted cheese sandwiches with a shared side salad. It was tasty and they agreed that the new menu was probably an improvement.

Just as they were getting ready to leave, a small bundle of black fur came rushing into the garden, rapidly followed by Louise. “Mickey, you naughty boy, come here at once!”

This was indeed the new puppy. Inevitably he brought a smile to Mitsy and Arthur’s faces and they both concluded that Mickey would be a happy addition to the Standsfield Arms.

Strolling back to Appledore House, they agreed that it had been pleasant to go back to the Standsfield, even though so much had changed.

"I can't believe almost three years have passed. I suppose we are fortunate that although so many people were very ill with covid, not to mention those who died, we two have escaped relatively unscathed," said Arthur.

"I imagine it will be many years before we know the impact of the pandemic on the economy, on missed education, how to deal with long covid and mental health problems," replied Mitsy.

Arthur nodded and smiled. "See you later, Mitsy. Thank you for coming out today."

2

Colours

Julie, the colour consultant, introduced herself as she glanced around the room at the residents who had arrived for the style and colour consultation.

Mitsy was sitting in the front row, looking smartly dressed, with Eva, the new resident next to her.

The other four people sitting behind looked much the same age and so Julie was not surprised to see a mix of white and grey hair, along with one younger woman with long dark hair tied up in a modern bun. The latter was Maggie who ran the care home. She had decided to give herself the afternoon off in order to take part in the session.

Julie began by asking some questions, such as "what are your favourite colours?" and "who can guess what are the current on-trend colours?" She then explained how choice of colour can affect mood, self-confidence, and perception.

The talk moved on to explain that skin tone can alter from one season to the next, as well as when we grow older. This means that make-up we loved when we were in our twenties and thirties may no longer suit our colour palette.

Julie asked for a volunteer and Eva raised her hand to do so. The next part of the session involved materials of various colours being held up to Eva's face while other members of the group voted for their preference. Eventually, Julie revealed which colours had been popular (she said "worked for you") and indicated that the gentle pinks, blues, and lilac colours were summer colours that could be worn as pale and delicate or bold and bright, as long as they remained within the same colour range.

There was some discussion about neutrals and again Julie gave the group guidance on wearing black, navy, brown, burgundy, or grey as well as whites, creams, and pastels. The colours chosen for Eva were divided into her key colours and support colours.

It was all getting very interesting when the tea trolley arrived and they stopped for tea and cake, as well as informal chatter about what they had learned so far.

After the tea break, Julie began by showing – using herself as a model – how clothes in different shapes and styles could enhance or ruin one's appearance. She suggested that she could come back for a further session on shape and style, referencing the TV programme that most of the group had seen with Gok Wan, the image consultant. She did promise not to make them expose themselves to family and friends while naked!

Then, everyone in the group was asked to find a partner so that they could help each other select the most suitable colours while Julie walked round offering suggestions and advice. Mitsy and Maggie worked together and found the whole exercise fun as well as instructive.

The last part of the session was much as Mitsy had expected. They were advised to go through their wardrobe selecting things that were in the wrong colour or those that had not been worn for a year. The latter raised some murmurs of dissent, given that everyone had been in lockdown and unable to wear many of their favourite or 'best' clothes. Julie accepted this and said perhaps it would be best to discard things that had not been worn for four or more years.

To finish, everyone was given a little chart with their own selected season's colours and advice about matching hair colour, make up, jewellery and glasses.

Mitsy was intrigued to find that she was summer too, although her range of colours was more extensive than Eva's.

Eva, no doubt prompted privately by Maggie, gave a little speech to thank Julie for her time, patience, and helpful insights. Everyone applauded and Julie collected her materials and props for the session before leaving with the promise to come back soon.

Back in room six, Mitsy opened her wardrobe and sighed. It looked as though the charity shop would be the recipient of a considerable bundle of lightly worn clothes. On the positive side, her new outfit which had been bought for the impending family wedding, whenever it happened, turned out to reflect her newly established colour palette. “Well, that’s a relief,” she said to herself.

3

Norma

One morning, after Mitsy had been to the local post office to restock her collection of birthday, condolence, and congratulations cards, she was intrigued to find a young man standing just inside the front door of the house. He was peering closely at one of the oil paintings in the hallway and appeared to be making notes on a clipboard.

Mitsy, ever curious – some might even say nosey – paused to ascertain what was going on. "Hello," she said, "you seem to be looking for something. Can I help?"

The young man straightened up quickly. "Er. No. No thank you," he replied. Bending down he handed Mitsy an envelope. She realised immediately that she had dropped one of her recently purchased greeting cards as she balanced her handbag on the hall table while reaching for her door key.

"Oh, thank you so much. I've only just bought these at the Post Office as I like to have spare cards in just in case there's an unexpected birthday, or death…."

Realising that she was chattering to this stranger unnecessarily, she turned swiftly towards the main corridor and headed towards her room. Room six was warm and comfortable and she sat down immediately, loosening her shoes that were beginning to pinch a bit. She thought no more of her encounter with the young man as she checked her phone for messages. Just as Mitsy was wondering what to do next, there was a gentle knock at her door. It was Kate who lived upstairs.

Kate was a good friend and they had already had shared some adventures.

"Are you OK?" she asked solicitously

"Yes. I'm fine. Shouldn't I be?" she quipped

Kate looked carefully at Mitsy as she sat down on the comfortable old armchair that Mitsy had pointed to.

"Where have you been, Mitsy?" said Kate, with just a trace of concern or possibly irritation.

"Nowhere," replied Mitsy rapidly, almost as if she was guilty of something.

Kate sighed and looked as if she was going to cry, so Mitsy changed her demeanour immediately.

"Why? What's wrong?"

"Well, you know Norma next door has not been very well?"

Mitsy nodded.

"Er. Um. She was much worse this morning. They called an ambulance but sadly she passed away before they could take her to hospital"

Mitsy's eyes filled with tears and the two women hugged each other. They were, sadly, used to fellow residents being taken ill and from time to time this did not end well. Norma was well liked by them both. She had been happy to make her home at Appledore House, having moved from South Africa to be nearer her daughter.

"Oh. I'm so sorry. It's been nice having Norma in number five and she had settled in so well. Does Raymond know?" Raymond, who lived in the room opposite Mitsy, was a quiet and thoughtful man who was fond of all his nearby neighbours.

"I'm afraid it was Raymond who heard Norma calling out and he alerted the staff that they were needed," said Kate.

"Oh dear. I know it comes to all of us sooner or later but this is really quite a shock. I've just been down to the post office to buy some stamps and cards so I wasn't aware that Norma was taken ill."

The two friends sat quietly contemplating the sad news.

"I popped round just to make sure you were OK," said Kate. "I'll leave you in peace for now. Shall I knock for you when it's lunchtime?"

Mitsy nodded as she opened the door for her friend.

After Kate had gone, Mitsy felt at a loss to know what to do. She wasn't in the mood for anything cheerful now. Eventually she checked her emails again and then her bank account, neither of which raised her spirits. Glancing at the clock, she realised that she had roughly an hour before lunch, so she pulled on a jacket in order to go for a quiet walk around the garden.

She was really pleased to see Puss. This was Mitsy's name for a beautiful, shiny black cat that frequented the garden. She called the cat Puss as that was the name of all the cats Mitsy had previously owned. 'Not that anyone owns a cat,' she said to herself. People thought that Puss lived nearby, maybe in one of the new flats and came over the road to enjoy the garden and the attention the residents gave her. Of course, they did worry about Puss crossing the road but no one really knew what to do as the collar she wore did not have any form of identification.

Much later, after a couple of slow circuits of the garden, Mitsy felt a bit better after some deep breathing and quiet contemplation on the loss of Norma her neighbour. Back in her room, the phone rang and it was Kate. "Sorry Mitsy, I washed my hair and it isn't dry yet so I shall be a bit late for lunch. Would you go ahead without me and save me a seat please?"

Mitsy reassured her friend that she would make sure she didn't miss anything tasty. Meals at Appledore House had always been enjoyable and quite a source of daily pleasure for the residents. However, Mitsy was not alone in noticing that the quality and possibly even the quantity of their food had gradually deteriorated and reduced over the last couple of years. Mitsy's son Pete had explained that certain food shortages had occurred for several reasons. The war in

Ukraine had led directly to oil and grain no longer being available for export. For the UK, leaving the European Union had also meant that trade with many of the 27 member states had stopped or had become more expensive. Other reasons had been suggested by the government or the news media but as Pete worked for the European Commission, Mitsy was inclined to believe his version of events.

To be honest, they had not really noticed the lack of tomatoes, salad leaf and cucumber during the winter months and although the catering team at the care home had done their best, the more observant amongst the residents had realised that the quality of meat, fruit and vegetables had continued to deteriorate for some time. Unlike many of those people who now needed to use food banks, the residents were somewhat cushioned from the harsher realities of life.

Mitsy walked slowly along the corridor to the dining room. As she turned the corner, she saw a young woman that she did not recognise who was looking at a vase. She turned it upside down, squinted at the manufacturers mark and made a hasty note on her clip board. Turning to another item on the sideboard, she picked it up and proceeded to scrutinise that in much the same way.

Misty couldn't help noticing the blonde hair (probably out of a bottle she said to herself), the copious make up, the plumped-up lips and a tiny butterfly tattoo on the neck.

"Oh, hello," said Mitsy. "Have you lost something?" she realised as soon as she said it that her question sounded a bit foolish.

"Ha-ha, no thank you," she said, "I was just admiring this Clarice Cliff vase, it's lovely, isn't it?" with that, she smiled and headed straight for the door, brooking no further discussion.

'How strange' said Mitsy to herself. 'I wonder what that is all about? Maybe she's a rather nosey relative of one of our residents. Or maybe she's connected with the young man who was looking at the painting in the hall.'

The sound of lively chatter preceded the arrival of three residents and within minutes they were quizzing Mitsy about the demise of her neighbour Norma.

Mitsy was still feeling too upset to talk about it and sensibly, once the little group realised this, the conversation turned to the pleasantly mild weather and what they were likely to be served for lunch.

Kate appeared only a few minutes later and Mitsy was pleased that they could both sit down as the staff came in to set the table.

One of the things that Mitsy had appreciated from the outset at Appledore House was the way all the staff took care to support those with mobility or other problems. It was no surprise that several people had difficulty hearing and others needed a walking stick or a rollator walking aid. Very discreetly, once Mitsy had chosen her place at the table, Tracey – a new member of staff – placed a small set of cutlery beside her. Smaller knives and forks made it much easier for Mitsy to control what she liked to call 'my badly behaved hands.' She was not alone in suffering from rheumatic joints but this modest concession was especially helpful for her.

"So, what can we expect for lunch today, Tracey?" asked one of the older gentlemen.

"Oh. I don't know, Sadiq. I have only just come in. I'm sure the others will have made something tasty," she replied.

At that moment Mitsy's friend Arthur arrived and sat down next to Kate. "How are you both?" he asked quietly, realising that they would both be all too aware of the sad news.

Mitsy nodded and smiled gratefully, knowing that Arthur was sensitive enough not to ask further questions.

As the tables began to fill up with hungry residents, Tracey returned with a tray laden with soup bowls, spoons and – from the delicious smell preceding her – freshly baked bread rolls. "Hooray!" exclaimed one lady when she subsequently carried in a large soup tureen and smilingly served everyone with home made vegetable soup. Suddenly the gentle murmur of conversation was replaced by the sound of crunching bread rolls, the spreading of butter and the clink of spoons against china.

Once everyone had finished, there was a short discussion about which vegetables had been used and a few conversations about plans for the afternoon, then everyone dispersed to their own rooms.

It was only as Mitsy got back to her room that she realised she had not seen Raymond at lunch. She tapped gently at his door and when Raymond opened it, she could see he had been crying.

"Raymond. You missed soup for lunch. Is there anything I can get you?" she asked.

"No. I'm fine thank you Mitsy. I didn't feel like eating so Maggie brought me a sandwich to have when I was peckish."

Mitsy nodded and smiled. "I'll leave you in peace then. Let me know if you want company," she said.

4

Wedding Plans

Pete and Jackie's wedding had been deferred because of the restrictions that everyone had been living under during the covid pandemic. It was disappointing, but both believed that as it had taken them so long to find each other, a few more months would not matter.

As it had turned out, serendipity had played a part in the couple meeting each other in the first place. Pete's mother Mitsy had suggested to Jackie's father Arthur that the hotel Pete used for a good local stop-over when he was visiting her at Appledore House might be useful for Jackie. This was how the two met by chance over a hotel breakfast before visiting their elderly parents. Subsequently Jackie had helped Pete by researching Mitsy's father's music career, which was the sort of thing she did for a living. It was a rather long distance romance, with Jackie living in London and Pete in Dublin but as Pete's work required him to travel extensively, he managed a London stop-over at regular intervals.

More recently, the couple had started to phone Appledore House on a Sunday afternoon. First, they called Mitsy and then phoned Arthur. Often Pete and Jackie were together in either Pete's flat in Dublin or at Jackie's in London. Once Appledore House residents were permitted to mix again, Arthur started to call in to see Mitsy and then it became a four-way video call.

Eventually, it seemed that it might be safe to proceed with the nuptials and on one of their Sunday calls Pete was delighted to announce the date and the venue. The couple had decided to marry at Camden Registry Office as it was close to

Jackie's flat in London. This would be convenient for them and was also helpfully located near Kings Cross Station so that their parents could travel down for the wedding by train.

Mitsy was immediately delegated the task of finding out how she and Arthur would travel. Before long she had booked their train tickets on line and asked if Greg, the gardener, would be able to take them to the station and collect them much later the same day. Given Mitsy's unfortunate experience when she was locked in the disused Anderson shelter at the bottom of the garden, which was partly caused by Greg and his son unwittingly sealing off the doorway with a large mill stone, she felt that anything he could do to atone for his error of judgment would be helpful!

Misty had planned for them to travel from nearby Bradford Interchange but this involved one change later in the journey, so she opted for the Leeds to London train instead. This would take them directly to King's Cross station without the need for any delay from changing trains en route. It turned out that if they set off early enough, they could arrive before midday so they would be in good time for the afternoon ceremony.

Jackie had invited a school friend Jess and her husband to act as witnesses. Pete did not invite anyone as he was happy to have just his mother and future father-in-law there, so the whole event would be quite a modest affair. It was agreed that no one else in the family would be involved as they preferred to focus on 'tying the knot.' Both Pete and Jackie had attended weddings of friends that had turned into a major worry and diplomatic planning exercise, not to mention considerable expense. Mitsy had agreed whole-heartedly as she knew that her sister Sky would find some way to steal the limelight and make a scene if they did invite her. It would be safer to tell her after the event!

To begin with, Jackie was rather concerned to find that her husband-to-be had booked Camden Registry Office which was situated in the local Town Hall. She was aware that the Town Hall had recently been renovated at great expense and was reputed to offer a lavish main venue hall seating over fifty people. This had been described in the local paper as the Heath Suite. On further investigation, they found that a smaller, more intimate room was also on offer.

The four of them discussed the plan for the day and they agreed that no one really wanted a formal event. Finally, it was agreed that they would all have a light lunch after the ceremony at Jackie's before Mitsy and Arthur caught the 16:33 train back. The following weekend it was proposed that the newlyweds would visit Mitsy and Arthur and take them out for a meal to complete the celebration.

Mitsy had already discussed with Arthur what they should wear and what would be appropriate as a wedding gift. All they needed was good weather, no risk of covid spoiling the event and the day would be perfect!

Over the time that Mitsy and Arthur had both lived at Appledore House, they had grown to like and respect each other. Mitsy was prone to having mishaps and adventures and Arthur was often called upon to keep an eye on his friend.

Opposite the care home there had been an old mill building which Mitsy had unwisely decided to visit during the night. She had not been able to resist her curiosity once she had seen shadowy figures in what was thought to be an empty building. While there, she had been amazed to see ghostly mill-workers. They did not appear to see her but she was able to see for herself what dreadful working conditions they experienced in the nineteenth century. Unfortunately, she was unable to get back inside Appledore House without getting soaking wet in a thunderstorm and attracting the wrath of Mrs P, the co-owner of Appledore House. If the truth were told, you could not have a more kind and considerate care home owner but of course Mrs Podsiadlo was concerned that Mitsy could have come to real harm that night over in the disused mill building.

It was Arthur who initiated the search party the next time Mitsy went missing and although she was only locked in the gardeners' refuge everyone was all too aware that an unintended night out of doors for an older person could lead to hypothermia.

Mitsy was well-liked by most of the other residents at Appledore House. She was respected for her 'joie de vivre' and insatiable curiosity, and she had at various times made use of her lively imagination by writing a book, completing a vibrant oil painting, and initiating research into family ancestry. She was prone to getting bored and this was not helped by the stringent lock down regulations during the early days of the covid pandemic.

Having a wedding for her and Arthur to prepare for, was a least a short term distraction of which she took full advantage.

A chance comment on last Sunday's family phone call revealed that Jackie intended to keep her own name and just add Pete's surname to it when they were married. So, she would become Mrs Benson-Howard. She thought it would be easier for people who knew her only through her work at the British Film Institute. Mitsy was not so sure about this. 'I was happy to take Peter's name when we married,' she mumbled. As Pete did not seem concerned, she kept her thoughts to herself.

5

The Mystery Unfolds

That afternoon, Mitsy began to think about what she had noticed earlier in the day. First, a man peering at the signature on an oil painting in the hall and then a woman studying the pottery vases in the dining room.

As she thought about it, she berated herself for being so uncharacteristically unobservant. 'How is it that I've lived at Appledore House for all this time and I hadn't noticed the paintings or the china ornaments?' She sighed to herself. 'I suppose when I moved in, I was far too preoccupied with moving from my family home to a strange place. At the time, I was concerned about losing my independence and worrying so much about how Pete would have to sell the house in order to pay for me moving in here.'

Mitsy's room was at the back of the building and overlooked the attractive garden. It had been her priority in terms of settling in. She made sure that she had a desk for her laptop and that there was a wardrobe and a chest of drawers for her clothes and a bookcase. Having a few of her own things around her helped her to feel more at home.

The more Mitsy reflected, the more she was puzzled by the strange man and woman looking at paintings and ornaments. 'I wonder what is so special about them?' she asked herself.

She concluded that this mystery needed some discreet investigation. Picking up a pad of yellow post-it notes and a pen, she left her room and walked nonchalantly along the corridor. Apart from carrying the wherewithal to make notes, she had also mentally prepared herself with an alibi. If she saw any of the residents or staff members and they asked where she was going, she would say she was popping in to see Maggie to check if her monthly payments to Appledore House were up-to-date.

Maggie had done a sterling job as matron and boss of Appledore House since Mrs Podsiadlo had moved to Gerald Longhope's care home for those with dementia. Mitsy had always got on well with her, especially since she had detected a member of staff stealing money from the residents. Maggie found Mitsy quite an enigma; her insistence that she regularly saw a ghost in the building seemed so fanciful but in many other ways she seemed to have her feet on the ground.

Approaching the painting in the hallway, just inside the front door, Mitsy glanced up and down and decided that the coast was clear. The painting, now she looked more closely, seemed to be a quality oil painting which featured an attractive seascape with coastline and beach. A small signature was just about visible in the bottom right hand corner which credited the work to Helena Krajewska. Quickly, Mitsy jotted down the name and tucked the note into her pocket.

Next, she headed towards the dining room. There, she was surprised to see Billy, one of the part-time kitchen staff. He was slowly wiping the cutlery with a tea-towel. Mitsy, skilled at diverting attention when this was needed, walked straight in, and asked "Billy, have you seen Raymond this morning?"

Billy smiled. "I think he came in for an early breakfast, Mitsy," he said. Of course, Mitsy knew this but at least it appeared to explain her presence in the dining room mid-morning.

"That's good. Thank you, Billy. You look busy!" At the same time as these pronouncements, Mitsy casually picked up the vase that she had seen the unknown young woman handling. "This is pretty. I don't think I have seen it before."

Turning it up to look underneath, she commented, "Oh it's Clarice Cliff. There's a signature here" and placing it back on the sideboard, she turned to Billy again "well, thank you very much. I'll leave you to your spoon polishing!"

Back in her room, Mitsy carefully noted her findings in a new note book. After a coffee and a biscuit, she turned to her computer to make good use of the search engine or 'Mr Google' as she liked to call it.

Half an hour later, Mitsy had carried out her research and made some notes.

> *Helena Krajewska born 1910 died 1998 Warsaw. Mid-20th century Polish realist/impressionist artist, worked in oils. A similar painting like this seascape is currently worth £1,400*
>
> *Clarice Cliff born 1899 died 1972 English ceramic artist based in Tunstall, Stoke on Trent. A vase in the 'Bizarre' range worth £70+*

'Well,' said Mitsy to herself. 'There's more to this than meets the eye.' She decided that she should carefully identify the paintings and decorative china spread all around the house in the public areas. Apart from relying on 'Mr Google' she would need to learn more about these items and this could involve watching 'Antiques Roadshow' and several other relevant television programmes. Mitsy was easily bored and was always on the look-out for a new project, especially if it gave her a chance to learn new things.

She thought fleetingly about her own painting project, when she had dabbled in oil painting a year or so ago. She glanced up to her wall where the sole evidence of those endeavours was hanging. She still liked it and thought maybe she would start a new painting some time. Of course, Raymond who lived opposite was a much more skilled artist but he preferred to keep his talent to himself.

Never one to delay getting started on a new project, she turned on the television and immersed herself in learning about the various items on offer in 'The Bidding Room'. By the end of the programme, she had a new page full of neatly written notes about all manner of objects and furniture, as well as estimated values and the price eventually agreed by the experts.

Satisfied with her work, she decided to wash and change ready for dinner. This was one of Mitsy's habits that had continued even after she had retired from work. Given that she had worked mainly in the retail sector including a pharmacy, all of which were clean places, it wasn't really necessary to change her clothes after work but for her this neatly punctuated daytime and evening.

When the dinner bell rang, she was ready to meet up with the other residents to chat about the day. She decided that she would keep to herself the puzzle of the unknown couple who had been scrutinising things around the home, until she had some answers.

6

The New Normal

Mitsy was wary of everyone who tried to insist that the pandemic was over when clearly there were many people who were still affected by the virus. Although most news reports appeared to be playing it down, the data on the number of people ill or dying was still available on the government website if, like Mitsy, you knew where to look.

An email from her sister Sky highlighted the point. It seemed that Sky's husband Jim had caught covid and had been seriously unwell for three weeks. True to Sky's nature, her comments concentrated on how this was his own fault – for going in to work – and how much his illness had affected her. Sky had called upon her two daughters to help look after him as it was 'all too much' for her. In the last sentence of the email, she mentioned as an apparent afterthought, that Jim's elderly aunt had died after catching the virus in her care home in Kent and her neighbour was suffering from long covid. 'Hmm. This is very far from over,' said Mitsy to herself.

She was sad to know that Jim had been ill. He was a kind and thoughtful man who was a reliable mainstay of the household; she often wondered how he managed to cope with Sky and her constant complaining.

She wrote a reply immediately to her sister, reassuring her that she was well, not that Sky had enquired, and hoping that Jim would be feeling much better soon.

Just as she was contemplating whether to describe how Appledore House had taken precautions or to mention Lucy's death from covid, the phone rang. It was Elaine, Mitsy's friend who lived nearby.

"Now we are all back to normal I thought you might like to come round for coffee on Friday," she said. "I've got loads to tell you and it would be good to see you, at last."

Mitsy explained that she had only just started going out again and all the residents had been advised to wear a mask indoors. Her recent lunch in the pub garden had worked well, so she suggested they had an outdoor coffee. Elaine sounded a bit deflated but agreed that they would have an al fresco coffee if it did not rain.

Checking her diary, which had hardly any entries this year, Mitsy realised that next week would be one year since Jackie and Pete got engaged. 'Oh, I do like anniversaries,' she said to herself, as she checked her collection of spare cards for all such situations. She did not have anything absolutely right for the occasion so she picked a blank card showing two affectionate rabbits, hoping that would suffice.

As there was nothing else to do, she decided to walk across the road to take the card to the post box. Affixing a postage stamp to the envelope, she wondered if the stamps would soon have an image of King Charles III on them. Not that she was a royalist particularly, although everyone at Appledore House had watched the coronation on the television. To be truthful, Mitsy didn't watch much at all, just the bits shown on the news while they were all having a celebration tea and cakes in the residents' lounge.

Back indoors, as she headed towards her room, Mitsy noticed three small vases on a shelf over the radiator. 'I'm sure I've not seen those before either,' she observed, as she picked up each of them and made a mental note to investigate Moorcroft pottery later.

As she opened the door to her own room, a middle-aged couple came out of room five next door. Mitsy recognised Norma's daughter and her husband. She immediately offered her condolences.

"Oh, hello Mitsy. We have the rather sad task of clearing Norma's belongings today," she said. "Maggie said that we needed to take away anything personal and the things we don't want will go in a skip so they can redecorate the room."

Mitsy was all too aware of the process after someone dies at Appledore House but as she didn't want to add to the couple's distress, she just kept her silence.

Back in her room, she remembered to investigate the Moorcroft pottery that she had spotted in the hallway. It seemed that William Moorcroft was born in 1872 into a family of potters. He pursued some serious art studies before deciding he would prefer a practical career rather than an academic one.

His pieces were recognisable by the attractive colours he used along with a technique he introduced which is known as tube-lining. Mitsy realised that there were too many different designs for her to remember although she had a feeling the vases in the hall could include Poppy, Crocus and Hibiscus patterns. This was when she realised that all she needed to do was to take a surreptitious photo of the items with her phone so that she could compare them against the pictures on the internet later.

There was a knock on the door. Norma's daughter stood there with a glass vase in her hand. "We just wondered if you would like this to put your flowers in, Mitsy, and as a keepsake from Norma. She was fond of you and I'm sure she would wish you to have something. "

"Oh. How kind. Yes, I would love to have something to remember Norma by."

She took the attractive frosted glass vase and placed it on the top of her bookcase. Later, she consulted Mr Google and much to her surprise it appeared that the vase came from the workshop of Rene Lalique. Mitsy was not sure if it was genuine, but the mark on the bottom suggested that it was.

She smiled to think that barely a week ago she had a limited knowledge of antiques but since she had started to learn what she could from on-line antique experts as well as those on several TV programmes, she was beginning to recognise famous names.

That evening, when Joyce came round with the evening medication, she admired the new vase. Mitsy explained where it had come from. "It will be nice to have something to remind me of Norma. You know, I hadn't really noticed before, Joyce, but we have some pretty pieces of pottery around the house as well as some interesting oil paintings."

"Oh yes," said Joyce, "Mr P was quite the collector."

Mitsy was not sure how this related to the former owner of Appledore House and looked rather puzzled.

"When Mr and Mrs Podsiadlo took on the care home, it was empty and all the rooms were bare. Mr P started to go to local auctions to buy furniture as it was cheaper than going to a furniture shop and in any case post-war there wasn't much around. I think he also picked up job lots of china and cutlery and once they had got the place the way they wanted it, he just kept on going to the auctions. It was quite a hobby for him."

Joyce liked Mitsy and although she didn't often have time to chat with all the residents during the medication round, she did sometimes make an exception.

Mitsy spent the rest of the evening trying to find out more about her Lalique vase. She concluded that it was really valuable and thus too good to fill with water and cut flowers so she found a permanent spot for it on a high shelf where it would not get knocked over.

Her notes on antiques were turning into quite a document and now Joyce's information about how most of them came into the house had added to the interest.

7

Elaine

The sun was shining mid-morning on Friday, so Mitsy was happy that her invitation to have coffee with Elaine would take place in her garden.

Tapping gently on the front door, she was surprised to find that it was opened by a man. In some ways, it was not a surprise because nothing Elaine did could surprise or shock Mitsy any more after some of their shared adventures.

"Hello," said the man. "You must be mum's friend Mitsy? Do come in." Mitsy shook her head as Elaine appeared behind him.

"No that's OK Grant, we're having coffee in the garden."

With that, she waved her hands to indicate the side path round to the back of the house. As Mitsy wandered round slowly, she wracked her brains to remember if she had ever heard Elaine talk about a son called Grant. She had heard about Elaine's other children but she was almost certain that Elaine had never mentioned a son.

Settling down in one of the deck chairs already set out, she waited until Elaine emerged from the back door.

"Oh, its lovely to see you Mitsy. It hasn't been the same having chats on messenger or the occasional phone call, has it? How have you been?"

Mitsy gave a brief summary of how the residents of Appledore House had fared, much of which Elaine already knew. Frankly, not much had happened during the lockdowns that was worth sharing. She mentioned briefly the deaths and illnesses but she preferred to keep the tone of their conversation as light as possible.

"I was pleased to say hello to your son. I'm not sure I know much about him?" said Mitsy, thinking that this would give Elaine an opportunity to tell her all sorts of things.

"Aaaaah. Grant. Yes, well he's been a naughty boy so he's been inside for a while."

Mitsy was rather confused by this, especially as the information had been delivered with a phoney cockney accent. He was already inside the house and as a grown man it wasn't likely that he was being kept prisoner by his mother. She kept quiet, knowing that Elaine couldn't resist telling a story.

Eventually it transpired that 'inside' meant in prison, where Grant had been for several years. Mitsy felt he must have done something very wrong to be incarcerated for such a long time. She felt it was rather rude and intrusive to ask what his crime was, so she asked the next thing that came into her head: "Oh dear. Which prison was he in?"

"Wandsworth nick. I couldn't visit during Covid so we haven't seen each other for ages. But let me tell you my important news!" said Elaine with some enthusiasm as she poured out the coffee from a mid-sixties' coffee pot. Mitsy was privately amused that she was beginning to observe such things with ease. She nodded.

"Well. You remember Martin who is the head chef at the school where I used to work as a dinner lady?"

Mitsy smiled as she recalled how this man regularly pretended to his wife that he was attending a management course, so that he and Elaine could have a sunshine holiday together. She wondered why the abandoned wife never queried how he came home from this work commitment with a suntan.

"Martin has left his wife! I think he wants to move in with me. Well, to be honest I think she might have guessed he was playing around and she has kicked him out."

Mitsy raised her eyebrows but didn't respond. Serial boyfriends, often married to someone else, seemed to be a pattern in Elaine's life.

"Of course, he's got no chance. I'm waiting until he asks and then I'll explain it's not possible as I've got my son here."

Finally, Mitsy managed to get a word in edgeways: "So has your son Grant moved in with you permanently?" she asked.

"Good lord, no. It's only until he gets himself sorted but Martin won't know that."

"You're fond of Martin, though?"

"He's nice enough but I couldn't live with a man that has dirty fingernails."

Somehow that comment put a stop to anything Mitsy could think to say. She could not contemplate how a head chef feeding hundreds of school children daily could have dirty fingernails.

They both stared into their coffee cups imagining Martin and his alleged dirty fingernails. Mitsy really couldn't think of anything helpful to say. Fortunately, Elaine launched into the silence to ask after Pete and Jackie. Mitsy described the forthcoming wedding arrangements.

"Well, that sounds like you have it all fully organised. It's a shame it's so soon, otherwise I would have willingly given you a lift. I shall be taking Grant back to London in a while, once he's got a few things organised."

Mitsy turned her attention to Elaine's garden, which was brimming with attractive flowers, despite appearing rather untidy. Elaine enjoyed gardening but she had some unusual perspectives on gardening activity. She always left weeds until they had flowered and turned to seed, for the benefit of the bees so that they had a regular source of pollen. Seed heads were then supposedly left for the seed-eating birds. She resolutely refused to water any plant, even if it had turned yellow with thirst. This was because if it could not survive the climate in her garden then 'it doesn't deserve to live here' she suggested. Mitsy felt that any mention of climate change would not affect Elaine's thinking on the matter.

"Your garden is looking good, Elaine," said Mitsy.

Elaine cast her eyes over her small patch. "Oh, look. The wind has blown over the roses. Would you like some to put in a vase to cheer up your room?"

For some strange reason, Elaine had very little insight to Appledore House, given that Mitsy did not find her room depressing in any way. She acknowledged the offer and within minutes she was presented with a generous bunch of pale pink roses. It seemed an appropriate time to make her goodbyes and she guessed that Elaine had things to do with Grant as she made no complaint as she walked with her from the back garden to the front gate.

"Let me know how the wedding goes! Take pictures!"

"I will try Elaine. Thank you for the coffee and say goodbye to Grant for me."

Mitsy smiled to herself. Any time she spent with Elaine always left her feeling amused. Whilst she would never dream of sharing the matter of Martin's dirty fingernails with anyone else, it would continue to entertain her.

8

The Wedding Day

Mitsy straightened her hat and smiled at her reflection in the full length mirror. She was genuinely quite excited to be going to her son's wedding. Of course, it would have been so much better if her husband Peter had been alive to see his son get married after all Pete's years of bachelordom but under the circumstances it was rather fitting to be heading off to London shortly with Arthur, father of the bride.

There was a gentle tap at the door and Greg was there, ready to take her and Arthur to the train station. Mitsy checked her handbag, gloves, and the meagre contents of the shopping bag that she was taking for sustenance during the journey. Meanwhile, Arthur appeared, looking very smart in his dark suit. Arthur had mixed feelings about wearing the suit he had bought for Ivy's funeral but it did not really make sense to buy a new suit just for one day. Of course, Arthur had given his daughter Jackie away before, but sadly that marriage had not lasted. He was feeling very hopeful that marriage to Mitsy's son Pete was a much better prospect.

Greg headed out to his car, keen to ensure that his two passengers would be comfortable for the short journey to the station. He was not quite sure how to converse with Mitsy, given that she had recently got trapped inside the old air-raid shelter that he used as a garden shed at the bottom of the garden. It was, of course, a simple error not to have checked there was no one inside before he and his son rolled the large millstone in front of the door. After all, what sensible person would go into a pitch-dark building for no reason? Greg had worked for many years at Appledore House, and when he was not keeping the garden under control or harvesting the fruit and vegetables he raised for the care home, he was happy to do any odd jobs. He was often to be seen chatting to the residents but he was a little uncertain as to how Mitsy would see him now that she had discovered his collection of rather dubious and exotic gentlemen's magazines. He concluded that the less said about that the better.

The roads were quiet at this time of the morning and it did not take as long as he had expected to get to Leeds station. Greg pulled up at the taxi rank at the front, as that seemed a good place to stop in order to give Mitsy and Arthur easy access to their train. After checking with Mitsy the expected time of the train they would return on, and promising to be there to pick them up, Greg jumped out to open the doors of his car with a flourish, just like he had seen hotel commissaires do on the television.

Mitsy and Arthur thanked Greg and headed across the concourse to find out which platform their train would be standing at. Mitsy was giggling. "I was wondering if Greg was going to salute us," she said. They walked slowly as Arthur had decided it was best to take his walking stick to steady his steps because it was likely to be a long and tiring day.

Thankfully, all of Mitsy's careful planning including the on-line ticket purchase came to fruition without a hitch and they were speedily directed to their platform. When the train arrived a few minutes later, they were delighted to find that they were in a quiet carriage with only a few other passengers. Although Mitsy did not say it, she did hope that they would not be subjected to screaming children or teenagers listening to noisy music. As it turned out, because it was an early train, the passengers all seemed quite serious and bound for work so they too were hoping for a peaceful journey.

Not long after the train set off, Arthur and Mitsy started to quietly point out to each other some places that they knew or had heard of. The train's first stop was Halifax and as they approached, it was easy to spot Wainhouse Tower and many of the old mill properties.

As they began to relax, Mitsy brought out from her shopping bag a bottle of water. "Would you like a drink, Arthur?"

"Not at the moment, thank you Mitsy. I might wander along to the restaurant car for a coffee perhaps. I'll get one for you too, of course."

They had eaten breakfast earlier than usual because of the time they had to leave and Mitsy was already feeling peckish. She brought out a packet of crisps from her bag which she shared with Arthur.

Just as the train left Halifax, a ticket collector walked through, checking tickets as she went. She enquired in a friendly manner if they were having a special day out and Arthur was pleased to tell her that they were going to London for his daughter's wedding.

Next, they passed through Wakefield and again the historic buildings stood out against the skyline.

"Wakefield has been designated City of Culture in 2025," said Mitsy.

"How do you know these things?" asked Arthur, although he realised that Mitsy always watched the Look North news on the television and read the local paper. He realised, almost too late, that Mitsy was still harbouring a grudge against the local journalist who insisted on emphasising Mitsy's age when reporting on the author of ***Violet's Story***, the novel she had written which was set in Appledore House. Quickly, before she could say anything about local papers or journalists, Arthur decided to fetch coffees for them both and headed off in the direction that the ticket collector had indicated.

Arthur was missing for a long time and Mitsy was just beginning to wonder what had happened to him when he appeared, smiling, with two steaming coffees and a couple of packets of ginger biscuits.

Before long the train passed through Pontefract and by that stage Mitsy and Arthur were chatting away and not really following the route any more.

Arthur was keen to tell Mitsy how happy he was that Jackie would be marrying Pete. They agreed that the couple seemed to have hit it off from the day they met. Given that they had managed to maintain a long distance relationship with one of them in Dublin and the other in London, not to mention the difficulties and loneliness of surviving lockdown alone in different countries, it augured well for the future.

Mitsy responded by saying that her son Pete was obviously 'choosy' having not found a suitable candidate to be his wife before now.

The conversation drifted off onto other subjects, mainly around events at Appledore House and so neither of them noticed how quickly the journey was passing until the train stopped at Doncaster station.

Mitsy consulted her notebook and announced they had better start getting ready for arrival in London. Both decided to make use of the toilet, which was a shaky experience as the train was hurtling along at high speed. They took it in turns to use the toilet in order to keep their seats and belongings safe. Mitsy returned after she had checked her makeup and Arthur said that he needed to comb his hair, not that Mitsy thought it was necessary!

As the train pulled into Kings Cross station, Mitsy noted that it was eleven o'clock and thus the train was precisely on time. Even better, she could see Pete at the end of the platform, waiting for them.

Within minutes all three had negotiated the short walk to Jackie's flat. After hugs and kisses all round, they were treated to another coffee. Then Jess and her husband Olaf arrived and they were left to talk to Mitsy and Arthur while Jackie and Pete went to get changed into their wedding clothes.

As it was the first time that Mitsy had been to Jackie's flat, she was content to look around discretely and she recognised various items that had come from Pete's home in Dublin.

Pete looked very smart in his navy suit, complete with matching waistcoat and crisp white shirt. Mitsy was always proud of her son, especially today. Jackie appeared soon after, wearing a pale pink and blue dress with matching jacket and fascinator. She also carried a box that had just been delivered by the florist with a delicate posy of mixed pink and blue flowers that echoed the colours of her dress. There were matching corsages for Pete and all the guests.

"I think we are almost ready," said Jackie.

"Just a moment," said Mitsy. "I wondered if you would like to wear this necklace?" She carefully lifted a dainty heart-shaped enamelled locket which sat on a velvet choker and held it out to Jackie.

"Oh. That is beautiful!" she said. "How did you manage to find something the same pink as my dress? With pale blue velvet?"

"Ha!" said Mitsy, "you know the saying 'something old, something new, something borrowed, something blue'? Well, I hope this will meet those requirements. Part of it is old and borrowed but I wanted to give it to you, if you like it."

Jackie gave Mitsy a kiss and smiled at Pete. "I couldn't have picked a better mother-in-law," she said.

Then she smiled, "I was thinking we could go across the road now but we're a bit early."

Pete suggested that they could probably walk slowly to the Town Hall, then take some photos outside and that was what they did.

Camden Register Office has an imposing exterior in Judd Street and thus it was an ideal setting to mark the occasion with some photos. By the time everyone had taken a photo for everyone else ("can you do one on my phone now" etc.) it was time to go inside, meet the registrar and proceed with the ceremony.

The room was small but pleasantly decorated. The registrar shook hands with Jackie and Pete and made some comment about music. Pete delved into his smart suit pocket and produced a DVD. Jess, Olaf, Mitsy and Arthur took their seats and within a couple of minutes some charming and restful music began to play. Pete smiled, winked at his mother but Mitsy had no idea what that was about.

Arthur stepped forward to be next to his daughter, Mitsy stood next to Pete and the two witnesses stood to one side.

The music stopped and the familiar words were spoken by the registrar. In a matter of minutes Pete and Jackie were husband and wife, the register was signed and witnessed and several more photos were taken.

Once outside, Jess and Mitsy insisted on throwing confetti and the men were tasked with recording that too. Pete and Jackie held hands, gazed into each other's eyes and everyone applauded.

Back at the house, Jess and Jackie proceeded to organise where everyone would sit, at the same time as bringing out plates and plates of food. Pete fetched some glasses and opened a bottle of champagne noisily. Arthur proposed a toast to the happy couple and to everyone in the room. Jackie thanked everyone for coming and there was a quiet hum of conversation between eating the sandwiches and snacks.

"Did you like the music, Mum?" asked Pete.

Mitsy looked slightly puzzled. "It was nice, and just right for the occasion, but I didn't recognise it."

"Well, it was written by David Thompson," said Pete, grinning.

"Oh! Really!"

Mitsy turned to explain to the others, "That was my father, Pete's grandfather. He was a composer and in fact he was partly responsible for Jackie and Pete meeting."

Jackie joined in, explaining how she had been able to research through her work some of the music that had been recorded for TV and radio. "What was funny was that the piece we played at our wedding came from a radio programme. It was a sort of forerunner to the Archers and the episode was about a family wedding. We thought it quite appropriate!"

Finally, Pete looked at his watch and reminded Arthur and Mitsy that their train home would be leaving in half an hour.

With many hugs and kisses, the parents left, reminding the newly-weds that they planned to visit them 'up North' next weekend. Saying goodbye to Jackie's friends, they hastily made their way to the station.

Both Mitsy and Arthur spent much of the homeward journey asleep; the excitement and champagne affecting them both.

At Leeds station, good as his word, Greg was waiting for them. "How was it?" he asked. "Perfect. Just perfect," said Mitsy and Arthur in unison.

9

Secrets

The day after the wedding, Mitsy learned something about Arthur that she would never have expected. They were both sitting in the garden watching Greg prune the laurel bushes. They were still rather tired from the wedding trip so they didn't have much to talk about.

"You did have a long and interesting career in the carpet trade, didn't you Arthur? You told me all about it some time ago. Did you never wonder what it would be like to do something else?" asked Mitsy.

Arthur smiled. "That's an interesting question Mitsy. Why do you ask?"

"Well, I've done all sorts of things myself, mainly to fit in with Pete's schooling and of course my Peter was away at sea a lot so I was always on the lookout for something new to amuse myself with. I cannot imagine what it would be like to work in the same business for the whole of one's life."

Arthur smiled again and looked over to where Greg was working, almost as if he was trying to decide how to answer Mitsy. They sat quietly for a few minutes, then Arthur looked directly at Mitsy with a cheeky grin.

"If you are very good Mitsy, I will tell you a secret."

Mitsy's eyes lit up. She was always ready for a story and, as Arthur knew all too well, she was the soul of discretion.

"OK. I did have another career but no one, not even Ivy knew about it."

Mitsy's face took on a serious expression as she realised that this was something important to Arthur.

"In my last year at University, I was approached by a man who asked if I would be interested in some business trips to other countries, with all expenses paid. At the time, I was intrigued but rather naïve. I agreed to give the job a try and to let him know if I liked it. I wasn't told what the job involved and, with hindsight, he could have been getting me involved in drug-running or something illegal."

"Oh Arthur, how exciting!"

"Well. First of all I had to sign some official papers to say that I would not divulge to anyone, ever, what I did. It seemed that I would be working for a secret branch of the government, I think. Then I was given a new passport. It was my photo (I've no idea how they got that) but a different name and details. The man, whose name I never found out, handed me an envelope with a train ticket, a cross-channel ferry ticket, more train tickets, and typed details of two hotels I had to stay in. The instructions were to travel to the indicated destination and wait for someone to contact me. He was to give me a very small packet which I was to guard with my life and bring it back."

"Oh wow!" said Mitsy, under her breath, "what happened?"

"The trip turned out much as I expected. I saw a couple of capital cities and had some pleasant meals in top hotels. That was all. When I got back, the man who invited me to carry out this assignment met me in the local park and I gave him the tiny packet without the faintest idea what was in it."

"And then what happened?"

"Oh, a month or so later he got in touch with me again. He asked if I enjoyed the trip, which I did. He then said he had another assignment for me if I wanted to do it. I wasn't really sure because I did not know what I was getting into. I said that I did not want to do it if it was bringing something illegal into the country. The man said that it was quite the opposite and that I was helping the country by bringing information that would be helpful to the government in the event of a war."

Arthur smiled. "I decided I would do it again, at least one more time, as it was quite an adventure for a young lad like myself."

"And did you?"

"Well, Mitsy as it turned out, I did several trips to different places. Each time I was to bring a very small package home with me. I have a feeling it was a roll of film but I don't know. Anyway, a few months after this I met Ivy but of course I did not tell her about these business trips. I was having too much fun taking her out so when the man approached me again, I told him I didn't want to do it anymore. He asked for the spare passport back, which I gave him. I never saw him again."

"Wow. That's amazing. I would never have imagined that you were a spy!" said Mitsy with a grin.

Arthur looked round the garden again. "Please don't ever tell anyone this Mitsy. I honestly don't know what I was getting involved with. But, since you asked if I'd ever had any other job, that's the truth."

"Of course not. I won't even mention it again, but thank you for sharing your secret life with me."

"You can see now, why I got the travel bug and how the carpet business came about?"

"Indeed I can. What an amazing experience you had."

Arthur looked at his watch. "Well, I am expecting Jackie to call this afternoon and I'd like to be in my room so I don't miss her."

"Of course. Please give her my love."

"See you later, Mitsy," he said over his shoulder, as he strolled across the grass back into the house.

10

London-bound Again

For the next few days, every time either Mitsy or Arthur went into the lounge or the dining room, at least one of the residents asked to see the wedding photos. Most of the staff had already admired the pictures of the happy couple as well as commenting how smart Mitsy and Arthur looked. Mitsy was pleased she had worn that navy suit with the cerise piping; it was attractive as well as being comfortable. Added to which, she now knew that the colours were right for her!

She found the whole experience of travelling to London and back in a day somewhat exhausting, as had Arthur. They agreed it would be preferable in future for Pete and Jackie to visit them at Appledore House when the couple were free to do so. The plan to come up to see them the following weekend had to be deferred because Pete had business to attend to in The Hague and would not be back until very late on Friday. Another date was agreed and Arthur re-arranged the lunch for the four of them which he had previously booked at The Standsfield Arms.

Mitsy phoned her friend Elaine to give her an update on the wedding. Elaine was pleased to know that it all went well and she was keen to share her news. It seemed that she had not heard any more from Martin the school chef, once she had told him that her son had moved in with her. "Of course, he hasn't really moved in, he's just staying here until he can sort out a flat in London now that he's out of prison."

For a week or two, life settled back into the old routine. Arthur visited a friend who lived in Wakefield, Mitsy had her coffee mornings with Elaine and they resumed their weekly lunch at the pub. They rarely saw people wearing face masks and it did feel more like it used to be before the pandemic.

One day, Mitsy was waiting to watch a TV programme that was likely to show their part of Bradford, and possibly Appledore House. Several of the residents were meeting in the TV lounge and Maggie had promised to join them. Invariably the first to arrive, Mitsy was looking around the room when she noticed the china dog. For once she had her phone with her, so she hastily took a photo of it before anyone else arrived.

The half-hour programme was not especially inspiring. The camera rapidly panned past the frontage of the care home before anyone had time to see it properly and then focussed on the apartments across the road. These had been recently renovated and adapted from an old cotton mill. A few people were aware that Mitsy had ventured into the old mill one night, but they were all too polite to mention her escapade. The remainder of the programme showed the Alhambra Theatre and other well-known sights from the city.

Back in her room, Mitsy remembered that she had taken a photo of the ornament that was in the resident's lounge. A few minutes' search on the laptop and Mitsy had a new entry for her antiques notebook.

> *Porcelain Staffordshire dog in copper lustre made in 1860 matching pair valued at £195; single? £*

She thought it might be worth looking around the house in case there was a second dog as she guessed that one from a pair would not be worth as much two.

Suddenly, the phone rang. "Mitsy, it's Elaine here. I was just wondering if you would come to London with me next week?"

After Mitsy's recent tiring day trip to London by train she was on the verge of declining the invitation when Elaine interrupted her: "I'll be driving down to drop off Grant, as he's found a flat. It's between Streatham and Brixton. It has been nice having him stay but I shall be glad to have my home to myself again. Anyway, I'm happy to do the driving but it would be so much nicer to have your company, especially for the return journey."

Mitsy felt she could not refuse, as Elaine had been a good friend to her since she moved in to Appledore House and she had never once asked a favour of Mitsy.

They discussed when this journey would be and Elaine said she would prepare a flask of coffee and sandwiches. All that was needed was for Mitsy to inform a member of staff that she planned to be out for the day.

Thus it was that Mitsy slipped out of the house at eight-thirty in the morning as they had agreed. Elaine was all ready to go and Grant was not far behind. It seemed that Grant would sit in front as he had long legs. Mitsy was not too happy about this as she tended to feel travel sick in the back seat of cars if she could not see directly ahead. None-the-less, the three of them set off for their 'road trip' with the minimum of delay. Mitsy had already noticed that since Grant had moved in with his mother, Elaine was beginning to use various Americanisms or words that more properly would be found in rap music. It made her smile.

There was not much to see once they were on the M1 motorway; only the back of Grant's head and a never-ending line of traffic. Grant and Elaine chatted away, while Mitsy felt somewhat excluded from the conversation. She could barely hear what they were talking about and when she did catch a phrase or two, she had no idea of the context.

From time to time, Mitsy nodded off to sleep. Each time she woke up she felt nauseous until she sat up straight, breathed deeply, focussed her line of sight between the two front seats and waited until her balance returned to normal. The drive seemed interminable.

After what seemed like several hours, although it was barely two, Elaine appeared to be turning off the motorway. Mitsy could see that they were heading for the services at Watford Gap. In fact, they pulled into the petrol station and alongside the pumps. Elaine at last appeared to acknowledge Mitsy's presence and asked if she wanted to use the toilets. This was truly a relief for her, in both senses, and she extracted herself from the back of the car, breathed in deeply and promptly fell over.

"Good grief, Mitsy. What ever happened?" asked Elaine.

Mitsy brushed away her concerns and suggested maybe her legs had got a bit numb sitting in the same position for so long.

"Right. Well, I'll fill up with diesel, use the loo and then we will be on our way. It's not far now."

Mitsy thought this last pronouncement was rather optimistic but said nothing.

In fact, it was not long before they turned off the M1 and the satnav started to give directions towards their destination. Elaine was rather pleased with herself as she had not made a good job of route finding when using this technology previously. She also began to include Mitsy in the conversation, which made the journey pass more quickly, it seemed.

Eventually, they arrived in a wide tree-lined road with large Victorian brick-built houses. Grant peered closely at every house until he spotted number 158. "Here. Here it is!"

Elaine realised that all the parking spaces were for residents only, but she reverse-parked into a small space and said, "We're not stopping, you know. We've got a long way to go back."

Mitsy moved into the front seat and after Elaine had just "popped up" to see Grant's flat they set off again barely ten minutes after they had arrived.

The first part of the return journey was conducted in silence as Elaine needed to concentrate on the traffic, getting into the correct lane and following the dulcet tones of the satnav woman.

Once they were back on the M1 again, Elaine began to relax. "I must say Grant's flat doesn't look too bad. I was worried he was going to end up in a squat again but he said he must have a proper address for the probation officer to check."

Mitsy felt at a bit of a loss, not knowing anything about the crime, the penalty, or the aftermath.

Mitsy ventured, "Do you think he will be able to keep out of trouble now?" It was a bit risky but she wanted to find some way to get Elaine to talk. This did the trick and suddenly the floodgates opened.

"Yes, I feel better about things this time."

Mitsy wondered privately how many times Grant had been in prison.

"Last time he got in with a bad lot and they all ended up in a squat and growing cannabis."

"It must be worrying for you," said Mitsy. She reflected privately how fortunate she was that her Pete had gone from university, to the Civil Service, to working for the European Commission. He had never once asked for money, support or somewhere to live. Of course, Pete may have done some bad things she was not aware of, but somehow, she doubted it. In fact, Pete had been a tower of strength after his father, Peter had died and he dealt with selling the family home and arranging for his mother to move into Appledore House.

As they headed further north Elaine seemed to relax and chat more naturally.

"You know, Mitsy, when Grant first got into trouble, I thought it was teenage misbehaviour but I'm inclined to think it's in his genes. Not that his dad Reg was a bad man, but he wasn't totally trustworthy."

Mitsy felt she could not comment, knowing what she did about Elaine's numerous men friends including the illicit holidays with Martin over the years.

As it was, Elaine seemed more comfortable sharing information about Grant as the journey continued.

"This latest stretch ('she really does know the lingo,' thought Mitsy) he was done for GBH and handling stolen goods. The silly fella left his finger prints on some jewellery that came from a big house on Wimbledon Common and in the same week he got a bit handy with a man in the pawn shop. He never used to have a temper but fortunately he didn't do too much damage and the man was only in hospital overnight."

Mitsy was at a loss to know how to react to these revelations but as she looked across at Elaine's dashboard, she noticed a red light was showing.

"Elaine, did you know your oil warning light is on?"

"Oh yeah, it's been on for ages. I think it will go off by the time we get home."

"But Elaine, you're not supposed to drive with it on. I think you are supposed to pull over and call the AA or the RAC or something."

While Elaine was shaking her head casually at what she deemed an unnecessary fuss, they both realised that smoke was starting to come out from under the car bonnet.

"Pull over, Elaine. Pull over onto the hard shoulder!"

Elaine appeared to take no notice but by this stage, Mitsy was shouting at the top of her voice: "STOP!! For God's sake stop! Pull over!"

As they slowly rolled to a halt, Mitsy flung open the passenger door, grabbed hold of Elaine's arm and pulled her roughly towards the outside. As this involved Elaine scrambling over the gear lever, it turned into an ungainly mix of legs and arms.

"RIGHT!" shouted Mitsy. "We have to go up that bank and stand out of the way of the car or any other vehicles."

Clinging on to Elaine's arm and dragging her somewhat unwillingly up the grassy bank, they were both horrified to hear a WHOOMPH behind them as Elaine's car burst into flames.

They sat down shakily on the bank, both too shocked to speak. It had all happened so quickly that there had been little time to think. The car burned ferociously, sending thick smoke billowing across the motorway. The traffic started to slow down and they could see people craning their necks to see what had happened.

After a few minutes a car with a flashing blue light appeared and as it approached, they could hear it was also sounding its siren. The police car drove on the hard shoulder, carefully avoiding the traffic that had now backed up on all three lanes of the motorway.

"Right, ladies. Is anyone hurt? Is there anyone else in the vehicle?"

Elaine shook her head.

"And which of you is the owner of the vehicle?"

Elaine wordlessly indicated it was herself.

Before any more questions could be asked, a fire engine hurtled up, also using the hard shoulder. Nothing was said, two uniformed men just stepped down from their fire engine and carefully unreeled a hose. A third fireman checked with the policeman that Elaine's car was empty, before they proceeded to douse it with water.

Mitsy noticed that hazard warning lights were flashing on many of the cars held up by their conflagration.

It seemed to take only a few minutes to put out the fire, during which time the policeman had radioed for incident signs to be switched on and had reassured Elaine and Mitsy that cars catch on fire all the time and can be caused by a fuel leak, electrical fault, or a damaged rubber hose.

Elaine started to cry when she realised that her car would never be driveable again. Mitsy suggested that she would probably be covered by insurance, although that did not seem to be much compensation for the shock and distress caused.

The policeman asked how far it was to their home and explained that he would not be able to offer a taxi service.

"That's alright," said Mitsy, taking control of the situation. "If you could take us to somewhere safe to stop, such as a service station, we will phone Appledore House where I live and I'm sure someone would come to collect us."

Neither of them had been paying much attention to the road or where they were, because they had been chatting so much, but the policeman said that there was a service station only a couple of miles away.

And so it was that within twenty minutes Elaine and Mitsy were sitting at Woolley Edge services, drinking coffee, and waiting for the ever helpful Greg who had been pressed into service again by Maggie, to collect the stranded women. The fire brigade was making sure that the fire was fully extinguished and the policeman had arranged for a pickup truck to remove the blackened shell of what had been Elaine's car.

"Well," said Mitsy. "That was an experience I wouldn't want to repeat, but at least we are both safe and sound."

11

Any Port in a Storm

After their ill-fated road trip, Mitsy phoned Elaine the next morning to check that she had recovered from the shock of her car catching fire. It seemed that she had already been in touch with her insurance company who said they would send an assessor out to look at her car, or what remained of it. Elaine was certain that it would be considered a write-off and had enquired how she was to manage in the meantime. Accordingly, the company were arranging for a hire car for Elaine to use until she received the compensation. "It won't cover the cost of another car," she confided to Mitsy. "Maybe I'll have to put up with Martin after all."

Mitsy believed that if Elaine invited Martin to move in with her just because he had a car, this episode would not end well, but she had learned over the years not to offer advice, especially when it was not asked for. Instead, she agreed to go round for a coffee later, even though it wasn't their usual day.

Her next task – why was it that life seemed to comprise one job after another? - was to write to Sky to tell her that Pete and Jackie had got married in London. She felt sure that Sky would be offended not to have been invited but Mitsy thought it was best to let her know shortly after the event, ascribing the reason for such a small gathering to covid. In any case, she was not sure if her brother-in-law had recovered from his bout of the virus so she assumed he could still be contagious.

Looking out of her window for inspiration while attempting to compose this letter, she realised that a pair of golden eyes were staring at her. Mitsy blinked and then smiled. "Hello, Puss," she said to the open window. The visiting black cat had found a way of sitting just outside Mitsy's window, on some recently discarded seed boxes. Mitsy assumed these had been placed there temporarily by Greg or his son.

She could hear the cat was purring quietly so she got up to give her a stroke. Mitsy herself had shared her home with several cats in the past; all were called Puss, some even had regnal numbers. She enjoyed it when cats from nearby houses visited Appledore House – it made the place feel more homely. Her own cat had crossed over the rainbow bridge not long before she moved to Appledore House.

Once she had finished her letter to Sky, she changed her slippers for shoes and took her coat out of the wardrobe so that she could walk to the letter box. Although she could quite easily have sent Sky an email, she thought that a pretty notelet with a carefully thought through explanation would be more acceptable. She realised that emails can easily be deleted unintentionally, whereas a letter can be read and reread over several days. She sometimes wondered why she had to tip-toe around her sister's sensitivity but she knew the reason really was because Sky could be quite nasty if she did not agree with you.

Walking down the corridor, she could hear a bit of a commotion in the hallway. She could see that there were three women, standing in a huddle, around a large set of suitcases. Their noisy chatter suggested that there was something wrong.

Mitsy, always helpful and just a little curious as to what this was all about, said: "Hello! Does anyone need any help?"

They explained that they were moving in to Appledore House temporarily until the flood waters around their care home receded. Of course, Mitsy was aware of the torrential rain that different parts of the country had experienced recently. In fact, she had considered that it might have been a blessing if the heavy rains had come a week later and maybe doused the horrible fire that engulfed Elaine's car. But she really had not anticipated flooding on the scale that would drive people from their homes.

Just as Mitsy was responding to this information, Maggie came hurrying along the corridor and proceeded to speak to them all.

"Ah, Mitsy. You can help here. Would you be kind enough to show Meena to her room? She will be staying in room five." Maggie directed the other two ladies towards the lift where, Mitsy presumed, they would be taken to two empty rooms.

"Meena, I'll take one of your bags and you can come with me. It's not far," said Mitsy. "I live next door, so if there's anything you want just knock."

She opened the door to room five and was briefly taken aback. Of course, it wasn't Norma's room any more but Mitsy didn't expect it to have changed so much. The room had been completely emptied, repainted in a soft cream colour while the walls were covered by an innocuous patterned wallpaper. The curtains were the same as when Norma had lived there but Mitsy could tell by the smell that they had been laundered to within an inch of their life and pressed with a steam iron so that they hung stiffly at the window.

"Here we are. I hope you will be comfortable. A bell sounds when it is mealtimes. I can knock for you today, if you like?"

Meena smiled her thanks and turned towards her wheelie suitcase, ready to make the room more personal.

Mitsy went straight into her room, closed the door and sat down on the bed. She realised that she had not posted Sky's letter but conceded that as it was the weekend it would not make much difference if she took it to the letter box tomorrow.

She could not resist sharing the news of this morning's happenings, so she wrote a message to Arthur:

Would you believe it, Arthur? All that dreadful rain has flooded the care home of some people living the other side of the city, so three of them have come to stay at Appledore House temporarily. One of them has moved into Norma's old room. Her name is Meena. She seems a bit shocked. I'm so glad we live on the top of a hill here. How are you? Anything exciting happening in your world? Mitsy x

Mitsy always signed off all her emails with an X but she did worry sometimes if Arthur might misinterpret this. She knew he was fond of her, as she was of him, but she was one hundred per cent certain that it could only be as friends so far as she was concerned.

She had an unpleasant experience a while ago, when one of her husband's friends from long ago visited and made it clear that he was interested in a relationship with her. He had been the best man at their wedding but Peter had largely lost touch with him over the years. Mitsy concluded that the man was mainly after her money, which made her feel ghastly and let down. It also meant that she was wary of any male advances, however friendly.

Within minutes a reply came from Arthur:

Yes. What a shock it must have been. Two of them have moved in up here on the first floor. They do seem rather distressed because they had to leave in a hurry as the water was rising.

Not much happening here. Jackie is working from home today and she phoned just for a chat. I'll see you at lunchtime Mitsy.

Mitsy was amused that their days were so punctuated by mealtimes and in the absence of anything else to do she called the cat over to her window, to give her a stroke.

In due course, as promised, she tapped on the door to room five so that she could show Meena where to go for lunch but after waiting a few minutes with no response she set off alone.

Mitsy was rather distracted as she approached the dining room, but she noticed out of the corner of her eye that the oil painting in the hallway was missing. This was the one that had been created by the Polish artist.

In the dining room, Maggie was waiting to address everyone who was there:

"Hello everyone. I just wanted to let you know that we have three guests staying with us at Appledore House for a short while. As you no doubt know, the torrential rain we have experienced locally and across the country has caused some serious flooding. Meena, Judy and Charlotte were unfortunately affected and along with several of their friends they have had to leave Grove Park Care Home while the waters recede and their rooms are dried out and redecorated. So, where is Meena?"

Meena waved her hand and everyone called out hello.

"And Judy?" again a friendly chorus of hellos.

"And Charlotte, who prefers to be called Charley."

The assembled group said their hellos to Charley then Maggie signalled to the staff that they could begin to serve the lunch.

Mitsy had noticed several weeks earlier that their meals were becoming less imaginative and the ingredients seemed to be of poorer quality than before. Today's lunch was no exception. A serving plate with small slices of quiche was placed in the middle of the table, along with a salad as accompaniment.

Billy turned to head back to the kitchen but Mitsy was too quick for him. "I say Billy, where are the tomatoes and cucumber to go in this salad?" she asked.

Billy looked a bit uncomfortable, as if he was not sure if he was supposed to answer. He always found Mitsy a little intimidating but he did not dare ignore her. "Oh, I think the order was a bit short this week. We didn't get much lettuce either," he said, wondering if this was too much information.

Mitsy turned to Arthur who was already tucking into his food, so she decided it wasn't worth making a fuss.

She noticed that the three new people (it's probably best not to refer to them as 'refugees' she said to herself) were sitting together, which was understandable after their frightening experience escaping from the flood waters.

Much later, after lunch was finished and the tea and coffee cups had been cleared away, Mitsy asked Arthur if he had any plans for the afternoon.

"No. Well, maybe I will settle down with a book. I feel like a lazy read this afternoon. How about you?"

"That's a good idea Arthur. It's probably for the best in this ghastly weather," she said, glancing at the window where it was evident that the heavy rain and blustery winds had not eased up yet.

Mitsy could not remember if she had anything worth reading but she thought if the rain held off for a while, she could go to the post office where a good selection of newspapers would be available.

The rain did not abate. If anything, it seemed to be getting worse. Puss was still sitting outside of Mitsy's window.

"Shhh," said Mitsy to the cat, "if you want to come in you will have to be very quiet."

Of course, Puss was quiet in any case but she seemed to understand what Mitsy was saying and when the window was opened just enough for her to creep indoors, she did so with alacrity.

Mitsy sat in her comfortable chair, Puss purring gently in her lap, for a long while. It was perhaps one of the most relaxing afternoons that Mitsy had spent in recent times. It gave her a chance to reflect on life and all that had happened this year.

12

Troubled Times

It was always a bonus when the weather cleared up on a Wednesday so that Mitsy and Arthur could resume their weekly trip to the Stansfield Arms. Walking over together gave them a breath of fresh air, some modest exercise, and on this occasion, an opportunity to talk about Pete and Jackie's wedding. Arthur had brought with him a small photograph album which the newly-weds had sent him. Apart from showing the pictures to Mitsy, he knew that the pub staff would be pleased to see them too.

"We will be toasting their health and future happiness here, soon," said Arthur to the pub landlady as she took their order, "as soon as that son of Mitsy's can get a space in his busy work diary!"

Sitting in their usual corner, Mickey the new puppy dashed over to see them and nearly caused an accident with the drinks. Once the wedding photos had been admired and Mickey was removed to a safe place, they were able to relax.

"Arthur, can I ask you something?"

"Of course, my dear friend."

"Have you noticed how the meals at Appledore House have deteriorated recently?"

Arthur paused, reflected for a moment, then replied, "Well, yes, now you mention it I have. There isn't as much food on each plate and the quality is not what it was. I presume that the staff are having more difficulty sourcing ingredients than they used to. It's no secret from what I see on the news that there are shortages of fruit and vegetables. They were also saying that olive oil and toilet rolls were in short supply too."

"That's what I thought. The trouble is, they've also increased our monthly payments."

"I know. That's because electricity has gone up in price a great deal everywhere. The government was supposed to be helping people out over that but the letter we got from Mr Longhope said that it didn't apply to care homes so they had to increase our payments. I'm not sure we can do anything about it, as everyone is suffering at the moment.

"Yes, that's what I thought Arthur. The thing is, most of us who live at Appledore House are relatively protected from these troubles, but I think there must be lots of people who don't know how they are going to cope."

"Well, I think that's right. It must be very worrying if you have a family to feed or if you live in rented accommodation that the landlord plans to sell."

Mitsy and Arthur sat pondering these troublesome times before Mitsy changed the subject. Somehow Arthur felt he had not heard the last of this topic. Maybe Mitsy had an idea to help people?

"I must tell you something naughty," she giggled. "You know that beautiful black cat that wanders round the garden?"

"Mmm."

"Well, she keeps coming to see me."

"What's wrong with that?"

"Well, she comes in the window of my room, sits on my chair or even on my lap. She's really lovely, but I don't think I should be allowing her in, she must belong to someone."

"Oh, I don't think that would matter. Her owners probably think she's out hunting or something."

Mitsy was going to confess that Puss stayed overnight with her most nights but decided she had said enough, so she stopped. In any case, their lunch had arrived so they concentrated on enjoying that.

"Do you have any idea when Pete and Jackie might be able to visit us?" asked Arthur. "It's just a bit embarrassing as I've cancelled our dinner for four here twice!"

"No. I'm afraid not, Arthur. He seems to be very busy with something important at the moment. I will send him an email this afternoon."

It was Arthur's turn to pay (they took it in turns so that their lunch outings were fair) and he had thought he could re-arrange the family get-together while he was paying at the bar.

"Right then, Mitsy. I think we had better be heading back before the next downpour. I don't like this summer weather, do you?"

They managed to dodge the showers and within twenty minutes were ringing the door bell at Appledore House. Jo opened the door for them as there seemed to be a bit of a commotion going on, with Tracey appearing to direct some people up the stairs. Tracey had been one of the staff who had kindly stayed at Appledore House during the first lockdown and she was well-liked by all the residents.

Arthur nodded to Mitsy, "Well, thank you for your company this lunchtime Mitsy and I'll see you later."

Mitsy headed along the ground floor corridor towards her room, noticing as she went that the impressionist painting by the Polish artist was still missing.

By the time she opened the door to her room, she could hear her phone ringing.

It was Kate. "Oh Mitsy, I'm so glad I've got hold of you. One of those new people has just been diagnosed with covid. No one has told us anything yet but I thought it might be best if you don't have any contact with that Meena next door to you."

Mitsy thanked Kate for the alert and, realising that the unfortunate person was living upstairs, she immediately phoned Arthur to pass on the news to him.

By mid-afternoon the word had gone round to virtually everyone. Just to be careful, Maggie had decided that they would re-instate an in-house lockdown and she had personally called into every room, wearing a face mask, plastic apron and disinfecting every door knob. All the residents were told that dinner would be eaten alone in their rooms.

Anyone looking at Mitsy could see she was crestfallen. They had barely got used to the new normal. She concluded that there was no way that Pete and Jackie should plan to visit for the time being, so her email to Pete was clear on that point. She didn't know if Jackie was in London or Dublin so she cc'd Jackie and Arthur, just so everyone got the same information.

While she waited for dinner to be delivered, she poured herself a glass of ginger wine to cheer herself up.

'Would you believe it?! We've had floods, fire, famine and now pestilence!!' she grumbled to herself. Of course, the flooded care home did not directly affect her, although Elaine's car fire was frightening enough. Food shortages did not yet constitute a famine and a recurrence of covid was a nuisance but she hoped it would not spread around the home.

13

The White Lady

Mitsy was disappointed that it had been necessary to lockdown again.

Back when Pete suggested that she might be happier living in residential care rather than staying in the family home in Harrogate, she thought it might be preferable to feeling lonely on her own and with nothing to do except housework and gardening. Overall, she was in quite good health for her age but shopping, lifting, cleaning, weeding, ironing etc all took their toll and it was a great relief when so many of the daily chores were taken away from her.

Of course, it was not cheap to live at Appledore House but she and Pete had done their sums and calculated that the money raised from selling the family home would provide for a good number of years in residential care. They did joke that Pete would have to chip in, if she lived beyond her 100th birthday. Much as she looked forward to receiving a telegram from the Queen, Mitsy was sure that King Charles would continue the custom, if he was still around to do so!

Looking back over the time that Mitsy had lived at Appledore House, she was amazed at how easily she had kept herself fit, active and happy. She had flown, on her own, to Dublin to stay with Pete and that trip had included some ancestry research, some clothes shopping, and an outing to the races.

She often went for a short walk locally on her own to enjoy the fresh air, the green grass, some wild flowers and the trees. Occasionally she had the company of a friend. These outings were much more pleasurable than going to the paper shop or post office. She enjoyed the garden of Appledore House to walk around too, except for the time she accidentally got locked into the air-raid shelter.

The staff of Appledore House, before the pandemic, organised regular day trips and Mitsy had taken full advantage of these. There were also courses to attend, such as flower arranging and craft workshops.

Mitsy's own attempts at oil painting would probably be described as chaotic by those who preferred representational art. She did, however, recognise that some people such as her neighbour Raymond, had a real talent for drawing from life. She even sat for him once and was impressed by his skills.

And so, being locked down again presented Mitsy with the challenge to amuse her self as well as possible. Of course, she had already written her book entitled ***Violet's Story*** but she was not in the mood for repeating that experience as it requires detailed research and the effort of writing every day is laborious. She enjoyed reading but realised that she had read everything on her bookshelf as well as several eBooks that she had previously downloaded.

Mitsy was not enjoying being shut down again. She picked up the phone to talk to Arthur, since they could not go out for their weekly pub lunch outing. Then she thought better of it. Arthur probably would not appreciate an interruption to whatever he was doing, she thought.

She had been spending an increasing amount of time watching various antiques programmes on the television. The Antiques Roadshow, Bargain Hunt, Salvage Hunters, The Repair Shop, Flog It! The Bidding Room and Antiques Road Trip were firm favourites. She realised that not all the items they showcased were antiques, some were reproductions and others were curios. It was interesting though and she was amused to notice that some of the china she had taken to the charity shop before she moved to Appledore House had probably been of some significant value. Each time something like the items at Appledore House came up on a TV programme, she got out her notebook and jotted down dates, makers, and value. This kept her entertained for hours. Probably because the weather had been so dreadful, she had been forced to stay indoors and so was able to indulge this latest project.

Under different circumstances, she was not much of a television watcher, preferring to spend her time out of doors or browsing the local shops. During the earlier lockdown Mitsy and her friends had all got used to ordering things online. In fact, at one stage because Mitsy was good at such things on the internet, she was besieged by fellow residents asking her to order things for them. Once Maggie realised that this was becoming a burden to Mitsy, she set up some alternative arrangements by offering a part-time job to a school leaver.

Now that they were confined to their rooms, the television was appreciated again.

The residents were told that Judy, who was one of the three women staying at Appledore House temporarily because their care home had been flooded, was the unfortunate soul to have caught covid. The word went round that she was not dreadfully ill, but was being kept isolated so that the virus would not spread. It was hoped that Judy, along with all the other residents, would be less seriously affected because they had all had a full set of vaccinations as well as boosters.

Much of this information was conveyed by Joyce when she came round with the evening medication. All the staff were wearing PPE again and had quickly adjusted to their revised routine of delivering meals outside people's doors, waiting for a couple of hours, and then collecting the dirty plates to be washed up.

"Joyce, do you know why that oil painting that was hanging just inside the front door has been moved?" asked Mitsy. Joyce was not aware of this painting and to be honest it did not really feature in her list of daily priorities but she promised to find out for Mitsy. Mitsy realised that this could take several days.

Meanwhile, Puss had decided that she would be comfortable staying with Mitsy every night. She often appeared outside the bedroom window just when Mitsy finished her dinner and was taking her tray to be collected later from outside her door.

'I know it's silly of me, but I do enjoy your company Puss. If we don't tell anyone, I'm happy for you to sleep at the end of my bed every night. I love to hear your purr when I'm not asleep.'

Mitsy had a lifelong difficulty in sleeping. She did not like to describe herself as an insomniac because that sounded like there was something wrong with her. It was merely that she did not sleep the whole night through. She was quite excited to discover recently that in medieval times it was natural for everyone to have two sleeps. Recent research showed that this habit of biphasic sleep was found in many cultures around the world. It was speculated that the custom disappeared with the advent of electric lighting. Whatever the case, Mitsy usually went to bed around nine or ten at night, slept until one o'clock, spent a couple of hours reading or just awake, before returning to the land of nod.

Before the pandemic, Mitsy sometimes visited the small room behind the kitchen, to see whichever member of staff was on night duty, where she cadged a cup of tea. No one really minded as Mitsy was pleasant company.

These night-time awakenings were often the time when Mitsy saw the person she called the White Lady. After a while, she reached the conclusion that she was a young woman called Violet who became a nurse when Appledore House became a hospital for wounded soldiers during the First World War. Arthur had carried out research on the former use of Appledore House and Mitsy had, with some imaginative embellishments, turned this information into a novel called ***Violet's Story.*** At the time that Mitsy's book was published everyone was quite proud of their fledgling author, although a few people were not so impressed to think that a ghost inhabited the care home.

The next evening, Joyce tapped on Mitsy's door to distribute her medication. There was little improvement in Judy's health so the lockdown continued.

"Good evening Mitsy. Here's your evening tablets. How are you feeling?"

Mitsy confirmed that she was quite well.

"I remembered to ask about that oil painting. Maggie said that it had gone away to be cleaned. I think she said that the valuers advised that it would be worth more like that."

Mitsy thanked Joyce but still felt rather confused. Who were the valuers? Why were things being valued? Why were they sneaking around the house – rather than being open about their purpose - looking at paintings and antiques?

A small part of the answer came sooner than expected. Mitsy's friend Kate rang for a chat. Kate lived upstairs and she was as bored as everyone else with the imposed lockdown, although of course she hoped that Judy would recover soon.

During their conversation, Kate mentioned Mrs Podsiadlo. "Did you know that Mrs P has been quite ill?" she asked Mitsy.

"Oh dear no. Is it the dementia or something else?"

"Well apparently, she had a minor stroke. She has been in hospital but is back in her care home now. Mr Longhope has had to deal with some of the legal implications."

"I didn't know there were any legal implications, Kate. How do you know all this?"

"A friend of mine is in the same care home as Mrs P. so she tells me things, on the days when she's not confused. She said that Mrs P still owns Appledore House."

"I don't think that can be right Kate," said Mitsy.

"Well Mr Longhope bought the business in exchange for giving Mrs P lifetime accommodation in one of his care homes that specialises in dementia care."

"Hmm. I see. I did know that. But I just thought the house was included in it."

"It seems not. So, they are trying to sort out what would happen to the house if/ when she dies. A new will is being drawn up."

"Well, I jolly well hope they get it all sorted. It makes me feel quite vulnerable in case Appledore House has to be sold. Mind you, that probably explains why the antiques are being valued."

Kate was not aware of anything to do with the antiques, but Mitsy just gave her the barest outline as she wanted to think it all through herself. She trusted Kate absolutely, but Mitsy was also aware how easily gossip can spread like wildfire.

They finished their conversation with Mitsy promising Kate that they would go for a walk together as soon as they were allowed outside again.

Not surprisingly, much of this was mulled over all evening and Mitsy would have found it quite difficult to go off to sleep, were it not for the gentle purr of Puss who seemed to know when she was troubled. Curled up by Mitsy's feet, she was a warm and comforting presence.

When Mitsy did wake, it was pitch dark and she rightly guessed it was the middle of the night. However, over by the window was a white glow which soon revealed itself to be the White Lady or Violet, as Mitsy was happy to call her.

"Oh. Hello Violet. You haven't visited me for such a long time that I assumed you had gone away"

She never heard any response from Violet but she was quite happy to speak softly to her. Mitsy was probably correct in observing previously that Violet seemed to appear when she was worried about something.

From a quick glance at her alarm Mitsy could see that it was after one o'clock. She rarely used the alarm to wake up but as it had a phosphorescent dial this was handy in the night. She noticed that the air was quite cold. 'That's probably because of the rain' she said to herself. Then she noticed something else, or to be more precise she noticed its absence. Where was Puss? The door was locked and the window closed so she could not have got out. How curious!

Looking over at Violet again, she could see that the ghostly figure was busy. It was almost as if she was bending down at regular intervals to look at something as she walked around the room. Mitsy suddenly realised that it was as if she was back during the war carrying out her hospital duties, calling at every bed to check on the patients. When the ghostly figure reached the door, she nodded as if to say 'that's all OK' then she bent down low. Mitsy watched, spellbound. In front of her eyes, Violet faded into the dark and at the exact same time, Puss leapt up on Mitsy's bed purring loudly.

Mitsy reached down towards Puss and gave her a gentle stroke. Puss was happy and she curled up in her usual place to go to sleep. Mitsy felt quite calm and before her busy mind could question what she had seen, she fell into a calm and deep sleep.

14

Live Long, Live Well

Eventually, all the residents of Appledore House were given a clean bill of health. Judy's covid tests were clear and the care home where Judy, Meena and Charlotte came from was dried out, dehumidified, aired, and redecorated so that the three of them could return. Everyone breathed a sigh of relief that they could go back to normal.

It seemed that while the latest local lockdown was in place, the staff had carried out a thorough Spring clean in all the common rooms. There was a strong smell of lavender polish and all the wood surfaces gleamed. Mitsy noticed that all of the oil paintings and antique ceramics had been removed and so she assumed that was all part of the clean-up.

She and Arthur were planning to resume their weekly trip to the Standsfield Arms; they had missed their lunchtime outings, chatting to the staff and making a fuss of Mickey. They also hoped to book a table for four for the coming Saturday as, at last, it seemed they could conclude their wedding celebrations with Jackie and Pete.

She was just opening her wardrobe and sighing that she had nothing new to wear when there was a firm but gentle knock on the door. Mitsy, ever polite, walked to the door to see who was there.

"Oh, hello Maggie. Do come in," she said to the kind and hard working head of Appledore House. Some people called her Matron but she did not really like the title and Mitsy was careful to address her by name, unless Mr Longhope was around and, in that case, she referred to her as Mrs Baxter.

“Good morning Mitsy,” she said as she sat down opposite her favourite resident. Of course, they were not supposed to have favourites, but it happened anyway.

“I’ve got some good news and some sad news, Mitsy,” she said. Without pausing for a reaction, she launched straight away into the news she had to share. Maggie had to call in to speak to each resident and she was starting with Mitsy, knowing that this would offer a rehearsal for a difficult conversation with some people.

“First, the sad news. I’m sorry to say that Mrs Podsiadlo passed away last night. I’m sure you were aware that she had not been well for quite a while. Mr Longhope’s staff were very fond of her and supported her right to the end. Mrs P was very well thought of when she and her husband ran Appledore House and we will be thinking about how we can honour her memory.”

Maggie paused for breath, just long enough for Mitsy to offer her condolences and reminisce how kind she and Antoni had been to her when she first moved into Appledore House.

“Now, I know that some rumours have been flying around about our home here so I just wanted to reassure you all that the ownership of the building is being sorted out and there is nothing to worry about.”

Again, Mitsy was given just long enough to say that she was reassured to hear this news and was not concerned about the future.

At this point, Maggie stood up to leave when she suddenly turned round and sat down again.

“I almost forgot! I have some good news, I think, just for you.”

Mitsy looked puzzled.

“Do you remember a young girl called Beth Mackenzie?”

“The name is a little familiar but I cannot think where from. Did she work here?”

“No. If I remember rightly,” said Maggie, “when she was at school, she wrote to you about ***Violet’s Story*** because she thought she could be distantly related to the Doughty family and she wanted to know more about the research you had done about Appledore House and the Doughty family during the war."

"Oh yes. I remember now. Someone had shown her the article that dreadful journalist had written about me and she got in touch. We wrote to each other for a while but I've since lost touch."

"Well, she's written to me on behalf of her employer and I received a formal request from her to ask if she could contact you. It seems she is working for a charity and they have plans to write a guide for older people, to help them think through the implications of moving into a care home. The charity is a national one, called Live Long, Live Well."

"Oh. That sounds interesting and I'd be happy to help her. She was at school in the Highlands when we were in touch before. We could talk on the phone or maybe she would be willing to travel down here."

"Fine. Leave it with me Mitsy and I will see what I can organise." Maggie headed once more for the door, aware that these conversations would take all morning.

Outside stood Val, with a mug of coffee made just how Mitsy liked it.

Mitsy sipped her hot drink and reflected on the conversation. It would be lovely to meet Beth if that were possible and if not, a conversation on the phone would be enjoyable. It was good to think that Beth had started work with a charity for older people. Mitsy thought of several national charities relating to older people but she had not heard of Live Long, Live Well.

She was quite keen to help with the task of writing a guide for people in a similar position to herself, although she realised that probably nothing would come of it for weeks or months.

Mitsy remembered that when she and Pete discussed whether she should move into a care home, they had written a big list of pro's and con's. 'I wonder if I kept that list?' she asked herself before delving into the desk drawer in the hope that she would find it.

It was there, and Mitsy was quite amused to see what helped to sway her decision in the end was the fact that her cat had just died. She remembered saying to Pete that she was lonely now she was all alone in the house. She put the crumpled notes back in the desk drawer so that she could find them easily when, or if, Beth visited.

After lunch, Mitsy and Kate sat outside on one of the garden benches. It had not rained that morning so the bench was dry and the air was warm.

Kate wordlessly offered Mitsy an extra strong mint.

"Thank you, Kate. I haven't had any sweets for ages."

Kate smiled. "Do you remember going to the sweet shop when you were little?" she asked.

"I do. I wasn't allowed to go very often because mum thought we would lose our teeth if we had too many sweeties!"

"My mum used to say to me 'now, Caitlin, you can only spend tuppence today'."

"Hehe. I'd forgotten about those old pennies. They were so big compared to today's tiny decimal coins. You could get four black jacks for a penny."

"And four fruit salads for a penny too. Mind you, I preferred the sherbet fountain with the liquorish straw to suck through; I invariably coughed and choked on it even thought I loved it."

"My favourites were 'shrimps' and 'flying saucers'," said Mitsy.

"Hmm. It's so different for young people today. Ours was such an innocent time, in some ways. I know we had just got through the war and anything sweet, after rationing, was truly a treat. These days, children are terrified they are going to put on weight, stressed that they are not wearing or doing what the latest influencer suggests and frightened that something horrible will happen to them."

"I suppose so," said Mitsy "they certainly don't have the freedom to wander the streets playing these days."

"My niece's kids seem to spend all their time on their phones, rather than talking to each other."

"My Pete was into all sorts of things as a teenager. He was obsessive about skateboarding and had to wear all the 'accepted' brands of tee-shirts, sweatshirts, and footwear, none of which was cheap. Still, he was outdoors with his mates so I suppose that was good."

"Well, every generation has its craze or fashion. I believe the term 'teenage' was coined in our era."

Kate and Mitsy smiled at these reminiscences and would probably have continued if Raymond had not been spotted strolling across the grass to them.

"How are you two ladies?" he asked. Then he smiled, "is that OK to say these days or will you be offended? I don't want to be cancelled by my favourite neighbours!"

They smiled and assured Raymond that the term ladies would be fine.

"In fact, Raymond, we were just saying how hard it is for young people these days. We've been reminiscing about being allowed to buy sweeties."

"Have you ever been to Beamish? It's an open-air museum with original buildings from the past including a sweet shop and a Victorian classroom and the people who run it dress up in the costume of the time."

"Oh, that sounds interesting Raymond, perhaps we could ask for an outing there?"

"That's an idea," said Kate and Raymond together. They laughed. "Well, next time I'm talking to Maggie I will ask, if you like?" said Mitsy.

15

Not As Easy As You Think

Mitsy was quietly enjoying her toast and marmalade when she became aware of an uncomfortable atmosphere at the far end of the breakfast table. There wasn't anything she could put her finger on, just an awareness that the easy, gentle chatter had come to an abrupt halt.

After the residents had all finished, Billy came in to clear the table and Mitsy waited until Eva stood up to leave. "Eva, may I have a word?" said Mitsy and the pair wandered off slowly together towards Mitsy's room.

"Is everything OK?" she asked

"Well, sort of," said Eva. Mitsy waited until her friend was ready to say more. Eva was still quite new at Appledore House and maybe there had been a minor misunderstanding.

Inside room six, Mitsy discreetly brushed off the chair in case there was evidence that Puss had been sleeping there overnight and gestured to Eva.

"Well, its funny Mitsy. I thought everyone here was kind and friendly but I'm beginning to have my doubts about Mariam."

Mitsy frowned and nodded, to encourage Eva to say more.

"Someone said they liked my cardigan and I said thank you and then mentioned that it was one of my 'colours'. Mariam asked what I meant and so I explained about the colours session we went to. Mariam got angry because she had wanted to go to that but no one had told her when it was, so she missed it. I thought it would be helpful to say that there would be another one soon as Julie said she would come back for a session on style. Unfortunately, that seemed to annoy Mariam even more and she started to go on about not needing anyone to tell her what clothes suited her. I thought it best to change the subject so I mentioned the weather forecast which is looking quite good for today. Mariam then said 'oh do shut up Eva, we are trying to eat our breakfast.' So, I stopped talking and so did everyone else."

"Ahh. I wondered why it suddenly went quiet," said Mitsy.

"I'm really not sure why I seemed to annoy her," said Eva, verging on tears.

"Now, don't you worry about her. I've noticed that Mariam can be quite rude. To be honest, she reminds me a bit of my sister. Sky can pick a fight with anyone about anything and she is always convinced that she is in the right. Perhaps Mariam got out of the wrong side of the bed!"

Once Eva seemed calmer, Mitsy suggested she was thinking of going to the post office, if Eva wanted to accompany her on a short walk. Eva said she had other things to do, so they went their separate ways.

On her way out of Appledore House en route to the post office, Mitsy heard raised voices and was shocked to see Mariam red-faced and appearing to stamp her foot in conversation with Tessa, who had recently started work as a cleaner.

Mitsy was unsure whether to intervene but concluded that would be interfering.

The post office was busy when she got there so she joined the queue which was moving quite slowly. At least there were plenty of things to look at on the displays of cards, packets of sweets and even – heaven forbid – some Christmas decorations.

The queue moved up slowly and when the door opened Mitsy realised that Mariam had just come in. She smiled and decided it might be best not to engage her in conversation.

Mariam was definitely not in a good mood and it appeared that she had decided to involve Mitsy in whatever was troubling her.

"That Eva drives me round the bend," she said, raising her voice so that everyone in the queue could hear, as well as the two post office staff who were clearly working as fast as they could to deal with the queue waiting at the counters.

"Oh, that is a shame. I think she is just starting to settle in. I remember how uncomfortable I was in my first few weeks at Appledore House," said Mitsy, hoping to calm things down.

"Well, that's her problem. She shouldn't annoy other people just because of that."

Mitsy concluded that any further conversation with Mariam was not going to be pleasant today, so she turned towards the post office counter and hoped sincerely that she would be served soon.

Fortunately, the queue moved up quite quickly and so Mitsy spent the next couple of minutes appearing to rummage in her handbag to look for something until she was served.

Once her postage stamps were purchased, she headed straight for the door and walked back home as quickly as she could go, without actually breaking into a run.

Indoors, there were two letters addressed to herself on the sideboard which she scooped into her handbag to read later.

At that moment Tessa came out of Maggie's room, apparently in tears. Mitsy, always kind and thoughtful, asked if she was alright.

"Not really," said Tessa, wiping her eyes.

"Come and sit here for a minute," suggested Mitsy, pointing to a bench seat. "What's happened?"

"Well, I seem to have really annoyed one of the residents and she has complained about me to Mrs Baxter. I was just starting to enjoy working here but I'm afraid I will get the sack."

"Oh, I don't know. Maggie is generally very reasonable and I'm sure you did not mean to upset anyone. We older people can get a bit crotchety, you know."

Tessa sniffed, wiped her eyes, and smiled at Mitsy. "Thank you very much. I'd better get on with dusting the dining room."

Mitsy had guessed it was Mariam who was involved and as she didn't want to cross her path once she got in from the post office, she immediately headed for her own room.

It was good to receive a letter from Sky, which was – for once – not too grumpy. It seemed that Jim was feeling better and was recovering from covid and Sky was also happy to congratulate Pete and Jackie on their marriage, without sounding as if she wished she had been invited.

The other letter was from Jackie. It was a pretty notelet and the contents added to Mitsy's good opinion of her. Jackie had realised that today was the anniversary of Mitsy's husband Peter's death. Probably Pete had told her. She had just sent a few words saying that she was thinking of Mitsy today. What a thoughtful young woman her son's new wife was!

Mitsy was rather troubled to think that she had not remembered the date herself but then she was much more likely to think of Peter on their wedding anniversary and his birthday.

Just as Mitsy was wondering how she might fill her morning after her trip to the post office, there was a knock at the door.

"Come in, Kate."

Kate had a strange expression of her face that Mitsy was not able to fathom.

"Hello Mitsy. How are you?"

"I'm fine thank you," she replied. "I must tell you what has just happened to me," she said, barely pausing for breath.

"I was going to the sideboard in the hall, you know, the one by the front door, to see if there was any mail. There was just one letter from an old school friend that I keep in touch with. I opened it to start reading it, when that Mariam came in the door. Do you know, Mitsy, she pushed past me – shoving me to one side with her hands – and shouted at me."

"Fortunately, I didn't fall over but I was very wobbly. She said: 'for goodness sake get out of my way woman!!' I was so shocked I couldn't say anything. It was really unpleasant."

Mitsy hugged her friend. "Wow, that's horrible Kate."

"I don't think I was in her way, she just wanted to be nasty."

"Well, she seems to have been very upset with several people today. I don't know what's wrong with her. I think we'd all better keep a low profile until she's got over it."

Kate and Mitsy chatted for a few minutes and when Kate returned to her room Mitsy said, "Take care!"

It wasn't until nearly lunchtime that Mitsy had an idea. She decided to go a few minutes early for lunch and tapped gently on Maggie's door, which was next to the dining room.

"Excuse me, Maggie. May I have a quick word?"

"Of course, Mitsy, what can I do for you?"

Maggie was used to residents calling into her room for a chat or to complain about something. Thankfully the latter was not common but she saw it as a key part of her role in managing Appledore House to keep abreast of anything the residents were concerned about.

"You may, perhaps, be aware that one of the residents seems to be rather 'fractious' today."

Mitsy wasn't quite sure if that was the correct word but as Maggie didn't question it, she carried on.

"She has shouted at other residents and a member of staff and she also tried to start a row with me in the post office." Mitsy took a deep breath.

"I am not complaining. I just remember many years ago that one of my neighbours, when I lived in Harrogate, went through a phase of being angry for no obvious reason. Eventually they discovered that she had undiagnosed diabetes. Apparently, it's a known phenomenon."

Maggie nodded and smiled. "I know who you are referring to Mitsy and that thought had already briefly crossed my mind. Thank you for drawing my attention to it. I had thought it was just a one-off but if she has been bad tempered with several people, we need to do something about it, especially if a pattern is emerging. Leave it with me and I will see what we can do."

Maggie smiled again at Mitsy. She really wasn't nosey; it was just that she had a lively mind that was always seeking to make sense of things. Maggie made a note on some paper on her desk, to remind herself to talk to the GP practice and see if they could do a fasting blood test for Mariam, if she was willing. That last part would be difficult. Everyone thought that running care home was a simple matter of keeping a group of kindly old women and men warm, safe, clean and fed. She often said to her friends 'ah, its not as easy as you think' but they didn't believe her.

16

The Plot Thickens

Appledore House returned to its somewhat more relaxed way of life after the departure of Judy, Meena and Charlotte; this was helped by everyone, including the staff, becoming reasonably relaxed that covid had again been excluded from their midst.

Mitsy and Arthur resumed their Wednesday lunchtimes at the Standsfield Arms. Finally, Jackie and Pete were able to visit their parents and a pleasant celebratory lunch was also held in the pub, even though their wedding had been a few months earlier.

Kate and Mitsy enjoyed a few gentle walks when the weather was suitable. It had been inordinately wet and often the dinner table discussion centred around climate change, its impact and what the government really ought to do about it.

Elaine and Mitsy enjoyed their weekly coffee and chats too. Thankfully, Elaine's insurance payout had enabled her to buy a modest second-hand car to replace the one that went up in smoke. It was small and rather flimsy by comparison but at least she had the sense not to resort to pressure from Martin who was initially keen to move in with her. Elaine had heard little from her son Grant but her approach was to assume that 'no news is good news'.

Mitsy was happy that daily life had returned to normal, but she could not help wondering what had happened to the oil painting by the Polish artist, especially now the news of Mrs Podsiadlo's death was public knowledge.

The ceramic pieces she had admired also seemed to have disappeared and she was saddened that she did not have them to look at any more in the public rooms, just as she was learning about antiques from her study of the internet and TV programmes.

Joyce, who usually did the evening medication round, was on holiday so Anna took on this task. One evening Anna found that she had forgotten to bring one of Mitsy's night-time tablets and promised to call back once she had seen everyone else.

Around nine o'clock there was a gentle tap on the door. Anna was carrying a hot chocolate drink for Mitsy by way of an apology for missing her out earlier. She was about to end her shift but for once was not really in a hurry to get home so when Mitsy asked if she wanted to give her feet a rest for a few minutes she was happy to do so.

"Is there any news about the ownership of Appledore House?" she asked. Mitsy was of the view that if there was something worrying her it was always best to address the problem head on.

"Well, I think it is all sorted and Mr Longhope has bought the freehold of the property. You know how it is Mitsy, the solicitors always seem to find things to quibble over so I don't think it is official yet. I'm sure Maggie will tell us all once the paperwork is signed."

"Oh, that will be a relief," sighed Mitsy. "I suppose they will have to sort out the furniture and fixtures, not to mention the things that were valued by the antiques specialists."

"Hmm. I don't know anything about that?"

"Well, there's a valuable oil painting that used to hang by the front door and that has gone to be cleaned. Also, all sorts of other valuable china like Clarice Cliff and Moorcroft. I think they were moved somewhere else when you all did the Spring clean, as none of them are here now."

Anna looked puzzled. "I'm not aware of things being moved. I can't even picture what you mean."

At this, Mitsy fetched her notebook and phone so she could show Anna the list of items that were originally in the house including those she had taken photos of.

They agreed that it was all rather a conundrum and Anna said that she would ask Maggie where the painting and other things had gone. With that, she left as she did need to go home now even though she liked chatting to Mitsy.

Puss had been waiting patiently outside Mitsy's window and as soon as Anna left, Mitsy could see the cat's face peering in expectantly. After a few minutes sitting on Mitsy's lap for a stroke and rather exuberant purring, she stepped down gently and arranged herself at the end of Mity's bed, ready for a good night's sleep.

Mitsy smiled. There wasn't anything that she wanted to see on the TV tonight so she gave in to Puss's unspoken request and turned in for the night too.

17

Beth

Mitsy had almost forgotten her conversation with Maggie about the request for help from Beth Mackenzie. It turned out that Maggie, with Mitsy's agreement, had passed on Mitsy's email address to Beth.

Beth wrote:

Dear Mrs Howard (may I call you Mitsy?)

You may remember that I got in touch with you a while ago for my school homework as I wanted to find out if the Doughty family, who originally owned Appledore House, were related to me. Thank you for your help then; with your support I was able to discover that Violet Doughty and her brother were in fact distantly related to our family and cousins to my great-grandfather.

I have since left school and I am working for Live Long, Live Well; this is a charitable organisation which provides services for older people. I have explained to your Matron that I am writing a guide which will help people as they think through the implications of moving into residential care.

I remembered you and your helpful common sense, as well as your achievement in writing the novel ***Violet's Story*** *and I wondered if you would be willing to answer a few questions to assist me in writing this guide?*

If you agree, I will send you the questions by email so that you can have time to think about them. Then I will phone you at your convenience and we can discuss. Please let me know by email, if this would be possible.

Kind regards
Beth Mackenzie
Editor

Of course, Mitsy had already understood much of this from Maggie so she wrote back immediately, confirming her willingness to help.

In due course she received the questions which were quite straightforward. She printed them off and made notes in the margin, in preparation for their phone call.

Later the same day, as she and Arthur strolled up to the Standsfield Arms for lunch, Mitsy mentioned her renewed contact with Beth as well as the reason for the planned phone call.

"Well, Mitsy. It's an interesting topic. For my own part I had never given any thought to moving into residential care while Ivy was alive. Even afterwards, although it was a massive adjustment, I was managing just fine living on my own – or so I thought. As you know, one day I tripped very badly on the pavement outside my house and ended up in hospital with cuts, bruises, and a broken arm. My daughters came to see me in hospital and both Jackie and Marie tried to convince me to move down to London to be nearer to them. But I didn't really think I'd fit in to London life at my age. Their main argument was 'what if it happens again?' I suppose for most people the decision to give up one's independence happens when there is a crisis."

Mitsy nodded silently. She found Arthur's comments useful and mentally tucked them away for her conversation with Beth.

"Yes. I suppose that's true. I didn't have a crisis but to be honest I just found I was exhausted all the time. It had become a juggling act trying to keep the house cleaned, the garden tidy and the shopping, washing and ironing etc. under control. When Pete suggested it to me, we thought about the benefits and I had to agree that no housework, no cooking and freedom from all those things I had to do for myself was appealing."

They smiled as they arrived at the pub and Mickey the new puppy, who had already grown quite big, came to greet them.

After lunch, they returned to the topic of conversation from earlier.

"What concerned you most about moving to Appledore House, Arthur?"

"I think I was worried about being closeted with a load of older people who were boring and infirm! Then I met you and I realised that the move gave me a chance to get to know different people that I wouldn't have been able to otherwise."

"Thank you! I shall take that as a compliment then," smiled Mitsy to her friend. "It was different for me," she said. "I was worried that we could not afford the fees. Then I was worried about communal living; maybe that was a bit like you. Most of all I didn't want to lose my independence."

"On the other hand, I was so tired all the time that I looked forward to someone else cleaning, cooking, washing and ironing, not to mention the relief I felt when I realised that I would not be stuck indoors because Appledore House has a lovely garden."

"Did you used to feel safe when you lived on your own?" asked Arthur.

"Yes. I did, most of the time. But every time there was an escaped prisoner or a horrible break-in or murder, I started to feel insecure. By contrast, I feel safe here, the carers are lovely and always kind and there's not much to worry about any more."

Arthur nodded and commented: "although some of those TV adverts drive me mad, I think there's something to be said for their oft-quoted 'peace of mind'!"

"You're so right, Arthur. We know that someone will look after us no matter what."

"Well, I'm not so sure about those of us who go wandering off into derelict buildings in the dead of night, or get themselves locked in unoccupied air-raid shelters!"

Mitsy laughed. She didn't mind Arthur teasing her because he meant well.

In fact, the next morning she began sharing some of this conversation with others over the breakfast table. It was interesting to discover what constituted peace of mind when they had each considered the potential benefits of moving into residential care. Family complications were often mentioned, such as not wanting to be a burden to others. Probably the most important factor in many people's choice was the fact that Appledore House felt "right" from the outset.

All this was very useful, as Mitsy was expecting a phone call from Beth later this morning.

Beth rang Mitsy on the dot of eleven o'clock, as proposed in her email. Mitsy was delighted to find that Beth was very much as she had imagined, sounding bright and cheerful with a soft Scottish accent.

"Now, I'd like to begin with a few thoughts from me, then we can go through your questions and my answers. Is that OK, Beth?" Mitsy was always one to take control; sometimes that was irritating to other people but it was well intended.

"That's great thank you, Mrs Howard."

"Oh, do call me Mitsy, everyone does. Right. These are my top ideas:

- find out the fees of your local residential care home and work out what is included and how you will pay. This needs to be funded for several years.

- research the local homes and check reviews, opinions, and recent reports by the CQC (Care Quality Commission).

- discuss with family or friends the pro's and con's of moving to a care home versus staying where you are.

- find out which homes have vacancies and arrange to visit, preferably with a friend or family member, taking with you a note of any questions you want to ask. Notice which home feels "right".

"That all sounds sensible," said Beth.

"Of course, this applies only to people who are reading your guide and thinking through whether they want to make the move. What I have discovered, from talking to my friends here, which of course is not a representative sample, is that most people go into residential care as a result of a crisis. So, I would suggest that you need to design your guide for those people too."

At this point Mitsy shared several examples about the many and varied fears that her friends had, before moving into a care home.

"My assumption is that you are not 'selling' care homes in your publication but trying to help people come to informed decisions."

"That's right Mitsy. I knew you would understand! I really wish that you were working for Live Long, Live Well; I'm afraid some of my colleagues are all too ready to believe everything that care home companies tell them."

"Well, I have lots of other ideas but I think we have to be careful not to frighten your readers."

Beth was quiet for a moment, then asked, "can you give me an example?"

Mitsy took a deep breath: " I did not do this myself, but I probably would now. People might want to check with Companies House, to make sure that the owners of a care home are financially viable. You can do this, for free, on line. It's because you don't want to move in and then the business goes bankrupt."

"Hmm. That makes sense, but it's rather sad," observed Beth.

"True. Let's go through your questions systematically now Beth, if you wish."

By the time they had completed this and Beth had carefully written down in long hand all the useful suggestions made by Mitsy, she was feeling exhausted.

"Wow. That's amazing, Mitsy. I think you have virtually written my guide for me. Can I suggest that we both have a rest now? I would like to get on with writing this up while it is all still fresh in my mind. When I've done that, may I send you the first draft?"

"Of course, Beth. I would very much like to see how it turns out."

"I will, of course, credit you as my professional adviser!"

Mitsy laughed. "I don't know about that Beth, but do let me know how you get on."

Mitsy was tired after her phone call with Beth. In fact, she may have dropped off to sleep for a while. She liked Beth and she was pleased to be able to help her.

18

Tête-à-tête with Gerald Longhope

One morning, Mitsy was relaxing in her rocking chair before going to breakfast, when there was a knock at her door. This was unusual, as she invariably knew in advance if a fellow resident was calling at this time.

She glanced across at the office chair in front of her desk, where Puss was sitting. She was fast asleep and it seemed a shame to move her, so Mitsy answered the door in the hope that the visitor was not planning to stay.

It was Maggie. "Hello Mitsy! I was just checking that you were up and dressed. I know you are usually an early riser but as Mr Longhope wanted to talk to you, I thought it best to be sure you were ready to receive an unexpected guest."

Mitsy felt like asking what Mr Longhope wanted at this time of the morning, but it seemed rather rude, so she smiled and indicated that she was ready for anyone.

"I will just go and fetch him," said Maggie.

This gave Mitsy just enough time to open her window, scoop up Puss and encourage her to sit on the boxes outside the window. Puss managed a rather feeble miaow of displeasure; she got away with staying in Mitsy's room enough to know that she would not have been ejected unless it was necessary.

Mitsy wondered where Puss really lived as she spent a great deal of her time lurking around in the garden at Appledore House during the day and with Mitsy at night. She did not seem to be feral as she was always clean and appeared well-fed.

Mitsy glanced in the bathroom mirror. She had recently been to the hairdressers so her hair was neat and, she noticed, quite shiny.

A gentle knock at her door announced Gerald Longhope and Mitsy opened the door. Before she could say hello or react in any way a very large bouquet of colourful summer flowers was thrust towards her.

"Oh. Oh. It's not my birthday, you know," she said. "Do come in, Mr Longhope. Sit down," she gestured to the spare chair.

"Good morning, Mitsy. I'm sure you know me well enough to call me Gerald," he said. "I know it's not your birthday yet. This is to say thank you."

Mitsy looked puzzled. "Whatever for?" she replied, thinking as she said it that she sounded impolite. "But thank you very much!"

She took the flowers into her bathroom, placed them in the wash basin and ran some cold water over the stems.

As she sat down on her rocking chair, facing Mr Longhope, he began to explain.

"Do you remember asking Maggie if she knew what had happened to the oil painting that was hanging in the hall?"

"Yes, I do."

"And you very helpfully kept a note, and photos, of many of the valuable items that subsequently went missing?"

"Yes."

"Well, at last the mystery has been uncovered. It seems that the man and woman who came to the house under the pretext of carrying out a valuation of our antiques were, in fact, running a fraudulent scheme. Maggie thought that I had booked them, and I thought she had booked them. When you first saw these people, they were 'casing the joint' – I think that is what it is called."

Mitsy looked shocked and shook her head in disbelief that everyone had been so easily fooled.

"Once you had pointed out to Anna that things were going missing, as well as giving her your notes and photos, she told Maggie and we immediately involved the police. To give them their due, the police were highly efficient and they were able to check with all the local auction houses to see if anyone could recognise these stolen goods. The Four Winds Auction House came up trumps and were able to stop the items from being sold."

"Oh, my goodness. Fancy that!" grinned Mitsy, rather enjoying the story.

"Now, we have not got the Polish artist's oil painting or any of the china pieces back yet, but we have every hope of doing so. The police think it unlikely that they will track the couple down, although I suppose if they move on to carry out this scam in other homes around the area, the police will be on the alert."

Gerald smiled at Mitsy. "It does mean that we shall have to set up some new arrangements for all visitors to the building. I guess we have got a bit lax over opening the door to anyone who says they are family or friends of our residents, especially after the covid regulations were relaxed."

He paused for breath while Mitsy nodded in agreement. "Of course, it's not just Appledore House, but all our homes will need to tighten up their systems."

At last, Mitsy was able to get a word in edgeways: "I am pleased I was able to help but I do hope you don't think I'm being nosey, Gerald. It's just that I notice things and I get pleasure from learning something new. Once I had noticed how many antiques we had here, I wanted to know more about them. So I've been watching all those antique programmes on the TV as well as making good use of the internet."

"Far from it, Mitsy. You are an asset to Appledore House and I am very grateful that you noticed that something out of the ordinary was taking place. Your research was critical and it provided exactly the evidence that was needed. You know, maybe we have teased you a little in the past for allowing your curiosity full rein but I for one think that it is an admirable trait, especially in an older person who could be forgiven for losing interest in the world around them."

He took a deep breath after this speech, and smiled broadly. "So, the flowers are just our way of saying thank you for being you!"

He stood up and was heading for the door when Misty asked, "Is this public information or shall I keep it to myself for now?"

"I think it would be wise to keep this under wraps. I suppose there is a possibility that the thieves have a connection to either residents or a member of staff, so we should wait until the police tell us that the case is closed."

Misty closed the door quietly behind Mr Longhope and started to arrange the flowers. There were so many in the bouquet that they would easily fill two vases. She checked her watch and realised that it was still over fifteen minutes until breakfast time.

Standing at the window, she could see the garden that Greg and Alan tended so carefully, Puss wandering around in the damp grass and the sky just turning blue to greet the day. Shortly, she would be sitting next to her special friends Kate and Arthur, enjoying breakfast. Later she would go for coffee to Elaine's house where, no doubt, Elaine will have news of Martin the chef and maybe even her son, the elusive Grant.

She was happy to feel appreciated and to live in a safe, caring, and friendly environment. We shall leave Mitsy here, and wish her good health and many more happy and interesting years at Appledore House.

Note From The Author

If you enjoyed reading ***The Complete Mitsy Howard***, I would be delighted if you would consider writing a short review for me. You can do this on https://www.amazon.co.uk. Reviews are very important for authors, as well as for anyone wondering whether to order a book, so any way in which you can help is much appreciated!

All my books are available via Amazon or to order through any good bookseller. They are also held in the British Library and in some local libraries. They are available in paperback and e-book editions. Further information can be found on the following pages.

You can also checkout my Facebook author page www.facebook.com/carolesusansmith which provides news, updates and information about current activities.

If you would like to send me any comments, feedback or criticism you can message me on the Facebook page as I love to hear from readers!

MEMOIRS BY THIS AUTHOR

TravelWorks
HomeWorks
Oh, and another thing...

NOVELS BY THIS AUTHOR

14 Viney Hill
The Enduring Curiosity of Mitsy Howard: A Walk in the Mill
Mitsy Howard: In the Dark
What Mitsy Did Next